A MOST
Peculiar
CIRCUMSTANCE

A MOST *Peculiar* CIRCUMSTANCE

JEN TURANO

BETHANYHOUSE
a division of Baker Publishing Group
Minneapolis, Minnesota

© 2013 by Jennifer L. Turano

Published by Bethany House Publishers
11400 Hampshire Avenue South
Bloomington, Minnesota 55438
www.bethanyhouse.com

Bethany House Publishers is a division of
Baker Publishing Group, Grand Rapids, Michigan

Printed in the United States of America

Library of Congress Cataloging-in-Publication Data
Turano, Jen.
    A most peculiar circumstance / Jen Turano.
      pages cm
    Summary: "Private Investigator Theodore Wilder is on a mission to find Arabella Beckett. But this feisty suffragette may be more trouble than he bargained for!"—Provided by publisher.
    ISBN 978-0-7642-1019-8 (pbk.)
    I. Title.
PS3620.U7455M67 2013
813'.6—dc23   2013002249

Cover design by John Hamilton Design

Author is represented by The Seymour Agency

13 14 15 16 17 18 19   7 6 5 4 3 2 1

In Memory of
W. Calvin Turner

*This certainly would have given you something
to chat about with the gents at the mall, Dad,
instead of old football stats. Wish you were still
around to share this adventure with me.
Miss you more than I can say.
All my love,
Jennifer*

1

*M*iss Arabella Beckett had always been proud of the fact she'd never ended up in jail.

She could no longer make that claim.

Her gaze traveled over the roughhewn walls of the cell and then dropped to the floor, lingering on rusty stains that appeared to be splatters of blood. She frowned as she noticed a trail of muddy water flowing toward and then over the stains. She looked down and realized the mud was coming from the soaking and filthy hem of her gown.

Hitching up her skirt, she stepped over the water and hobbled over to a stone bench. She plopped down and released a huff when a glob of something undoubtedly vile dribbled down her back. She ignored the dribble as irritation began to simmer.

Once again, her propensity for involving herself in matters that were none of her concern had managed to land her in a slight bit of trouble.

She should have stuck to her original plan of traveling

directly from Chicago to her home in New York instead of agreeing to help one Mrs. James—a woman she had just happened upon at the train station—track down her errant daughter.

She shot a glance to the young lady sleeping soundly on the only cot the cell offered and blew out a breath. There was no sense dwelling on what might have been. The reality was she *had* gotten off the train in Gilman, and she was simply going to have to live with that decision. At least she could take solace in the knowledge that Miss James was now somewhat safe rather than enduring what would have certainly been a fate worse than death.

She leaned her head back against the cold wall, ignored the sodden fabric of the skirt that was now sticking to her legs, and forced her weary mind to think.

She was being charged with four counts of assault, which was completely ludicrous considering she hadn't assaulted anyone, let alone four officers of the law.

If those officers would have given her the courtesy of an explanation before trying to apprehend her, she would not have felt compelled to make a run for it. She also wouldn't have chosen an escape route that led through a remarkably foul pigpen.

There was no possible way she could have known a deranged pig lurked on the other side of that completely innocent-looking fence. She'd only taken a few steps after she'd bolted over the top before the beast had charged directly toward her. That disturbing circumstance had caused her to spin around as best she could through the muck and make a beeline for the fence, pushing past the dumbfounded officers who'd followed her. In hindsight, it might have been prudent to have given them fair warning as to what was coming their way, but she'd been distracted by a troublesome piece of splintered fence that had snagged her hair.

As she'd struggled to get free, the pig had set its attention on the officers.

It had not been a pretty sight.

Bodies had scrambled around in a blur, squeals were emitted—and not just from the pig—and the foul substance that littered the pen had drenched everyone.

That unfortunate result had not endeared Arabella to the officers in the least, especially Sheriff Dawson, who'd made short shrift of getting her released from the fence with one deliberate slice of a wicked-looking knife.

She lifted her hand and patted the left side of her head, encountering a mess of ragged, blond curls that had been a good eight inches longer when she'd started the day but now appeared to be no longer than the bottom of her chin. She gave her hair one last pat, dropped her hand to her lap, and noticed the grime clinging to her fingers. She rubbed them against the fabric of her gown and, realizing she was only making them muddier, decided that contemplating her current lack of hygiene and missing hair would have to wait. There were more important matters to ponder.

She turned her head and studied Miss James, wondering what had possessed the young lady to attempt to procure a husband through the mail. Had the young lady resorted to such drastic measures because of pressure from family members, or had the advertisement Miss James answered been written in such an enticing fashion that the lady simply couldn't help herself?

It truly was unfortunate, whatever the lady's reasoning, that Miss James apparently felt one was not complete unless one had the attention of a gentleman, even if said gentleman was one she'd never met.

Deciding her time would be better spent figuring a way out of jail instead of contemplating the workings of a young lady's mind, Arabella closed her eyes and turned to God.

Dear Lord, thank you for lending me your guidance and support in the matter of rescuing Miss James. Please continue to keep her safe, and if you could, would it be possible to send me some assistance?

She opened her eyes and nodded. That should do the trick. God would show her a way out, but until that time, she needed to keep a clear head and mull through her options.

She had rights. Granted, they were slim to none since she was a woman, but she could not be held indefinitely, could she?

Knowing far too well that the rights of women were cast aside on the whims of gentlemen on a daily basis, Arabella felt her jaw clench. The reality was that, yes, she might be held behind bars for a very long time.

She should have been more diligent in her attempts at getting the laws changed.

It certainly lent a different perspective to the inequalities facing women when she was the one behind bars, yet now was hardly the time to think about that.

As she smoothed down the wrinkled mess of her skirt, her attention settled on the good six inches of mud attached to her hem, and she suddenly remembered the money she'd stashed in that hem. She could offer the sheriff the money and secure her release.

No, that would never do. She blew out a breath. The sheriff would surely look at that as a bribe, and then she would never escape the confines of the small cell.

The sound of footsteps caused her to blink out of her thoughts and lean forward on the bench, her attention focused on the narrow hallway in the dank and dreary basement jail that led to her cell.

The footsteps stopped and a gentleman came into view. It was rather odd, but she got the distinct impression he was annoyed, probably because he was glaring at her through the bars.

She swallowed a sigh. As a woman who was known for having strong opinions, dealing with annoyed gentlemen seemed to be a common occurrence in her life. She leaned farther forward on the bench, intent on addressing the gentleman, but suddenly found she was at a complete loss for words when she got a good look at his face.

The gentleman was possessed of features that could have been sculpted by a master.

Sharp cheekbones complemented a straight blade of a nose, and his eyes were as dark as his brows, which were currently drawn together as if the man were contemplating a weighty matter. Her gaze drifted to his hair, which was liberally streaked with gold and looked quite untidy at the moment, as though the gentleman had been running his hands through it out of sheer aggravation.

She had the sneaking suspicion she might be the cause of that aggravation.

Her gaze drifted downward, lingering on shoulders encased in an overcoat of exceptionally fine wool.

An attorney would wear such a coat.

Perhaps God was already answering her prayer regarding assistance, and perhaps the man was only annoyed with her because he'd been roused from his house in the middle of the night to bail her out of jail.

Feeling a bit more charitable toward the gentleman, she allowed herself a moment to finish her perusal. He was very brawny, but no, that wasn't quite right. She tilted her head. He was tall, certainly, well over six feet from what she could tell, but his overcoat was tailored at the waist, lending the impression of trimness, while his shoulders . . . a frisson of something unexpected raced down her spine.

That was peculiar. She'd never felt a frisson of anything quite like that before, but maybe it had only been another one of those pesky globs of mud that was still attached to her person. She nodded in relief over that particular reasoning, and regarded his shoulders once again, unable to help being somewhat impressed. They were so broad, and they gave testimony to the fact that here was a gentleman who could handle himself well in disturbing situations.

Her eyes widened as she realized he was a gentleman who commanded attention, and he was also one who would have no trouble getting her and Miss James released from jail.

She shifted her gaze back to his face, frowning when she realized the gentleman's mouth was moving.

Funny, in her consideration of the man, she'd neglected to realize he was speaking to her.

She'd apparently been struck deaf as well as mute.

"I beg your pardon, sir," she began, finally finding her voice. "Were you speaking to me?"

The gentleman's mouth stopped moving as he sent her a look of what could only be described as disbelief before he nodded.

"Would you be so kind as to repeat what you said?"

"I was inquiring whether or not you are Miss Arabella Beckett."

His voice was deep and slightly raspy, and it held a distinct note of exasperation. She summoned up a smile even as she ignored the irritation that had begun to hum through her. "I readily admit that I am, indeed, Miss Beckett. May I dare hope you've come to secure my release?"

"I don't see that I have any other option."

Temper began to bubble up inside of her, but before she could formulate a suitable retort to his surly response, he ran a hand through his untidy hair and took a step forward, shaking his finger at her through the bars.

She felt as if she were suddenly back in primary school, being taken to task for some silly prank.

Her temper boiled hotter.

"You have led me on a merry chase, Miss Beckett," the gentleman growled. "You were supposed to be in Chicago, and before that, Kansas. Imagine my surprise when I tracked you to Gilman, only to discover you'd somehow managed to get arrested."

She slowly rose from the bench. "You've been searching for me?"

The gentleman stopped wagging his finger, withdrew it from between the bars, and then gave a short jerk of his head. "For well over a month. Your family sent me after you when they became aware of the fact you'd gone missing."

Arabella plucked the wet material of her dress away from her legs and took a step forward, pausing when she realized she seemed to be missing a shoe. She lifted her skirt, glanced down, and felt a grin tug her lips as bare toes peeking through tattered and torn stockings came into focus.

That certainly explained all the hobbling she'd been doing. With the chaos surrounding her arrest and subsequent transport to jail, she'd neglected to realize she'd lost her shoe somewhere along the way.

A loud clearing of a throat had her lifting her head, even as the grin slid off her face. The gentleman was staring at her with clear annoyance stamped on his all-too-handsome face, and that had her gritting her teeth even as she took a teetering step forward.

"Who are you?" she asked as she reached the front of the cell, grabbing onto the cold bars separating them and wobbling on her one heel.

The gentleman's lips thinned. "I already told you, I'm Mr. Theodore Wilder. Were you not listening to a word I said?"

Even though she was in desperate need of assistance, she was tempted to demand that the gentleman take his leave. She tightened her grip on the bars, took a deep breath, released it in one huff, and then sucked in another. "You're the famous private investigator."

"I see my reputation precedes me."

"Why would my family go to the bother of hiring you? I assure you, I was not missing. I was perfectly aware of where I was at all times, and, truth be told, I was actually on my way home before I took this detour."

Mr. Wilder cocked a brow. "You might not have gone 'missing,' Miss Beckett, but any fool can see you need assistance. I would think you would find it a fortuitous circumstance that I came after you, unless of course you would prefer I pretend I *didn't* find you and leave you here to rot."

Although she knew more than her share of unpleasant gentlemen, given that she was an adamant supporter of the suffrage movement, she was quite certain she'd never met one this unpleasant before. She felt tempted once again to demand he leave, but practicality intervened, so instead she lifted her chin. "If you were to abandon me here to rot, you wouldn't be able to collect the hefty fee you're most likely charging my family for your services."

"I'm not charging them a fee."

She blinked. "Why not?"

"Your brother Zayne is a good friend of mine. When your family needed someone to find you, I offered my services, never realizing you would be so difficult to run to ground."

Arabella reached through the bars and grabbed Mr. Wilder's arm. "What happened?"

The gentleman barely glanced at the mud now staining his sleeve from her filthy hand before his attention shifted to her face. "I do beg your pardon, Miss Beckett. It was inexcusable of me to lend you the impression something horrible has occurred. I was sent after you because your presence was desired at your brother's wedding."

Relief surged over her, but was quickly replaced with confusion. "My brother is getting married?"

Mr. Wilder patted her hand, which was still clutching his

14

arm, watched her as she snatched it back through the bars, and then shook his head. "I'm afraid I must now be the bearer of some distressing news. Unfortunately, given the fact I was not able to locate you in a timely fashion, you missed the wedding."

"My brother got married without me?"

"He did."

Arabella spun on her heel and tried to pace around the room, finally giving up when she realized pacing was not practical when one was missing a shoe. She came to a stop and caught Mr. Wilder's eye. "Zayne's been contemplating marriage for years. I find it difficult to believe he was suddenly overcome with emotion and simply had to marry Helena before I was able to return home."

"Zayne didn't marry Helena."

"Oh, thank goodness." She limped back across the cell and sagged against the bars.

"You don't care for Miss Helena Collins?"

"I'm sure she's a perfectly lovely woman when she's not bemoaning her many ailments," Arabella said. "Tell me, who did Zayne marry?"

"Zayne didn't get married. Your brother Hamilton did."

"Hamilton? He hasn't shown interest in a lady since his wife died."

"He's shown a great deal of interest in Lady Eliza Sumner."

"How did he become acquainted with an aristocrat?"

Mr. Wilder looked at her for a moment and then . . . he rolled his eyes.

He really was an unlikable sort.

"Miss Beckett," Mr. Wilder began before she could tell him exactly what she thought of him, "while I certainly understand your curiosity regarding your brother's new wife, I must point out to you that you are in a somewhat dire predicament. Let us dispense with the gossip and devote ourselves to the pressing matter of getting you out of jail."

While he was quite correct, she did not care for his snippy tone in the least. She plopped her hands on her hips and regarded him with narrowed eyes as an uncomfortable silence settled over them.

A full minute later, Mr. Wilder rolled his eyes again, put *his* hands on *his* hips, and sent her another glare. "Very well, since you seem to be possessed of a stubborn nature—one, by the way, no one in your family made me aware of—I'll tell you a condensed version of what transpired in New York."

"You are too kind."

As Mr. Wilder's dark eyes turned glacial, he ran a hand once again through his hair and finally opened his mouth, speaking so rapidly she barely caught his words. "Hamilton met Lady Eliza at a dinner party held at the Watsons'. He then bailed her out of jail, and when she was dismissed from her position as the Watsons' governess, he took her home with him where they promptly fell in love."

"That's your condensed version?"

"I thought it fairly sufficient."

It was just like a gentleman to leave out all the pertinent details. "You told me absolutely nothing of consequence, such as why the lady ended up in jail, and why an aristocrat was working as a governess."

If anything, his words came out even faster. "She was working as a governess because her fortune was stolen, and she was arrested because she was mistaken for a lady of the night." He smiled. "I think you and Lady Eliza will get along famously, since both of you seem to have a propensity for attracting trouble."

"I do not have a propensity for attracting trouble."

Mr. Wilder's smile widened as he gestured to the cell.

Arabella forced a smile of her own. "This is the first time I've been arrested."

"Really?"

"I do not make a habit of breaking the law, Mr. Wilder. I may occasionally attract unfavorable attention as I work to secure women the right to vote, but the suffrage movement is a peaceful movement, not one that lands me in jail on a frequent basis."

"The suffrage movement can hardly be considered peaceful, Miss Beckett," Theodore countered. "Women are being encouraged to rebel, and that certainly does not lend itself to a peaceful home."

It was fortunate for him that there were bars separating them.

Arabella began tapping her one shoe against the hard floor, immediately stilling when she teetered from the motion. "I *encourage* women to stand up for their rights, Mr. Wilder. We are held accountable to the same laws as men, and yet we have no say regarding the passage of these laws."

"You think all women wish for the same rights as men?"

"Not all of them, but that stems from a lack of education, which is a direct result of unequal rights."

"Most ladies of my acquaintance desire marriage above all else."

"You must not have a large group of female acquaintances."

A laugh burst out of his mouth, causing her teeth to clench. "How in the world do you expect me to address that statement? Why, if I contradict you, you'll think I'm a braggart, and if I agree with you, I'll be a liar."

"A braggart would actually be an improvement over the impression I've already formed of you."

Mr. Wilder let out another laugh and then waved a dismissive hand in the air. "While this is certainly a riveting conversation, I do believe it is past time we addressed your reason for being behind bars, instead of our differing opinions regarding my personality and views on the preposterous suffrage movement."

Arabella opened her mouth, found she once again had no words at her disposal, so instead snapped it shut and simply watched him as he began to stalk back and forth in front of the cell. He stopped and crossed his arms over his chest.

"You're going to have to afford me some explanations."

"There really is not much to explain. My arrest was a simple misunderstanding."

Mr. Wilder let out a grunt. "That's what all criminals say. Explain the assault and theft charges."

"I didn't steal anything."

"Are you inferring that you *did* assault four officers?"

There was just something about the gentleman's tone that annoyed her from the top of her head to the tips of her toes. She forced another smile. "Mr. Wilder, forgive me, but are these questions really necessary? Given your reputation, I would assume you are more than capable of securing my release with relative ease."

Mr. Wilder took a step closer and, for some strange reason, waved a hand toward the floor.

She looked at the floor and then back to him. "Surely you're not suggesting I take a seat?"

"Miss Beckett, your gown is beyond filthy and the floor will cause it no additional harm. Since you seem to be a difficult sort, and I'm somewhat weary from chasing you around the country, I would like to get comfortable before you begin explaining what happened, and just so we're clear, explain it you will."

She opened her mouth, but before she could get a single word out, the annoying gentleman continued. "Even though you are a most unusual lady, you are still a lady, and it's been my experience that ladies are notoriously wordy when they begin to explain something, so we should take the weight off our feet and sit down."

Realizing that if she responded to that bit of nonsense,

he would probably take her response as proof about wordy ladies, she kept her lips tightly shut and plopped down on the cold floor. She folded her mud-encrusted hands demurely in her lap and swore she would not speak a single word until Mr. Wilder apologized for his all-too-pompous attitude.

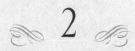

2

The seconds ticked away as Mr. Wilder lowered his large frame to the ground and sent Arabella an expectant look.

Keeping her lips pressed tightly together, she lifted her gaze to the ceiling, where she began contemplating the mold that resided there. A shiver suddenly caught her by surprise, and then another as the cold from the floor seeped through her sodden gown.

Her gaze dropped from the ceiling when Mr. Wilder began to mutter something under his breath, even as he pushed himself to his feet, shrugged out of his overcoat, and thrust it through the bars.

"Put this on."

She remained perfectly still. She'd never been one who followed orders well and wasn't about to start now.

He dropped the coat, and it settled to the ground beside her. "Don't be ridiculous, put it on. It's apparent you're freezing. I certainly don't want to have to explain to your brother why I couldn't bring you back because you died from exposure.

You've caused me quite enough trouble as it is, and I'm beginning to lose patience with you."

Her eyes narrowed, but another shiver stole over her, causing her to snatch the overcoat as she struggled to her feet. She slipped her arms through the sleeves and stifled the urge to sigh in delight as wonderful warmth stole over her.

The coat was huge and smelled of sandalwood and something that was all male. She snuggled it around her, breathed in deeply, lifted her head, and found Mr. Wilder frowning at her.

"I need that back."

Chivalry, apparently, was definitely dead.

Her vow to remain silent disappeared in a split second. "You can't have it back."

"I don't need it for long. I just need something from the front pocket."

Arabella reached into the pocket and pulled out a gun.

"Be careful with that, Miss Beckett. It's loaded, and I have no wish for you to shoot yourself."

"I wasn't planning on shooting *myself*."

His eyes widened just a touch before they turned hard. "A gun is not a toy. I'll thank you to hand it to me gently through the bars. It will not help my attempt to get you released if the sheriff discovers you're armed."

He might have a point.

She moved forward, held out the gun, and couldn't seem to resist allowing her gaze to wander over him again. Without the overcoat, he really did possess a trim figure and . . . somewhat impressive muscles.

She jumped when his fingers drifted over hers and quickly pulled her hand back through the bars as soon as he took possession of the gun. He shoved it into the waistband of his trousers and then casually stepped away from her, apparently unaware his touch had left her fingers feeling slightly scorched.

She sank back to the floor and arranged the coat around her, hoping he wouldn't notice her cheeks were probably flaming.

What was it about this particular gentleman? He made her uneasy, and it was not a feeling she enjoyed.

Maybe the events of the day really had affected her nerves.

Her cheeks cooled immediately and she lifted her head, finding Mr. Wilder once again on the floor, staring at her with an unreadable expression on his face.

She felt the unusual urge to fidget under his regard.

"May we finally return to why you're behind bars?" he asked.

Her urge to fidget ceased.

"By all means, Mr. Wilder, let us move this conversation forward. What would you care to know?"

"I need you to explain the assault charges. Assaulting officers of the law is a very serious offense, one that usually results in a stiff punishment."

"I didn't assault anyone. A pig did."

"I see," Mr. Wilder said slowly. "Very well, let us move on to the theft. From what I've been told, a Mr. Brown is insisting you made off with his horse without his permission."

"I paid *Mrs.* Brown five dollars for the use of that nag, which I might add was exorbitant, given the fact I only needed the animal for a brief period of time while I checked on Miss James."

"Who is Miss James?"

Arabella waved toward the cot. "That's Miss James."

Mr. Wilder craned his neck. "May I suggest you wake her so I can get a clear picture of what occurred?"

It would be exactly what the gentleman deserved if she took his advice and woke Miss James, but she would also be affected by the chaos that would take over the cell if the lady awoke. "That would not be wise, Mr. Wilder. From what I've

22

discovered of Miss James, she's the dramatic sort and prone to hysterics. You'll get no worthy explanations out of her. It's best if we allow her to remain sleeping."

"May I assume she's a friend of yours?"

"I've never seen her before today, and quite frankly I've been rethinking the whole rushing-to-her-rescue business," Arabella muttered.

"I'm afraid I don't understand."

Since it was rapidly becoming clear that Mr. Wilder was not going to negotiate her release until she gave him some type of explanation, Arabella decided she might as well give in and tell him her story. "I was minding my own business at the train station in Chicago when a lady by the name of Mrs. James sat down next to me and burst into tears. She told me that her daughter, Miss Alice James, had run away from home to answer an advertisement for a mail-order bride. Mrs. James was desperate to get some news of her daughter, so I agreed to stop in Gilman, the place the advertisement originated from, and see if I could find the young lady and give her a message from her mother. From what I gathered from Mrs. James, she shares a tumultuous relationship with Alice and was afraid her daughter would refuse to meet with her if she made the trip herself."

"Are you in jail because you tried to intercede between Miss James and this groom?"

"There was no groom to be had. Miss James managed to land herself smack in the middle of what I've come to believe is a prostitution ring."

Mr. Wilder closed his eyes and began muttering under his breath. When the muttering continued for a full thirty seconds, she felt it was time to move the conversation along. "I believe Miss James was lured here for the express purpose of selling her off to the highest bidder."

Mr. Wilder's eyes flashed open. "Why do you believe that?"

Arabella shrugged. "From what little I've been able to get out of her, she was met at the station by a gentleman who told her he was escorting her to her future husband. When she arrived at a farmhouse about a mile out of town, instead of encountering an eager groom, she was tied to a chair and left there to await her fate."

"How do you know she was tied to a chair?"

Arabella felt the unusual urge to scoot to the opposite side of the cell, even though she was separated from Mr. Wilder by bars. "That's how I found her."

Mr. Wilder leaned forward, and Arabella couldn't help but notice that a vein was now throbbing on his forehead.

"You went out to the farmhouse?"

"How else would I have given Miss James that message from her mother? Unfortunately," she continued as Mr. Wilder began to sputter, "I did not find Miss James in a happy state, and the situation deteriorated rather quickly."

"Should I ask what happened next?" he asked between gritted teeth.

"Well, not if it's going to upset you."

"I do not get *upset*."

Feeling it would be unproductive to point out the obvious, Arabella curled her legs underneath her. "I've come to the conclusion that the gentleman who gave me directions as to where I could find Miss James was most likely in on the dastardly plot. I think he might be the same gentleman who escorted Miss James from the train station, but I can't swear to that, as I've not been able to get much out of Miss James as of yet. I've also come to the conclusion that he sent me out to the farmhouse with the same fate in mind for me as was intended for Miss James. I believe it was only due to the fact that God was watching out for me that I was not taken and forced into a life of prostitution." A shudder caught her by surprise. "I've never had a reason to think about such a degrading life, but now, considering what almost happened to me, I shall definitely have to explore options to help women in such appalling circumstances when I get home."

"When you get home, you should explore ways to stay out of trouble," Theodore returned. "But enough about that. Tell me, where did you come into contact with this man who just happened to have the whereabouts of Miss James on hand?"

"He was lurking around the train station."

"And it never crossed your mind that a man who was 'lurking' might not be the best source of information?"

"I didn't actually think of him as lurking at that particular moment. If you must know, the gentleman was perfectly pleasant and only too willing to assist me. He helped me stow my luggage at the station and told me where I could rent a horse. He then gave me detailed instructions on how to locate the farmhouse and bid me a cheerful farewell."

"But things went wrong once you reached the farmhouse?"

"I must admit that they did, although at first it didn't appear to me as if anyone was around. I pounded on the door for a good few minutes, and no one ever opened it."

"Did it never occur to you to leave when no one answered the door?"

"I was about to leave when I heard the distinct sound of someone crying from inside the house." She arched a brow at him. "You cannot tell me you would have left under those circumstances."

"I wouldn't have, but I'm a man."

"*Anyway,* I found the door locked, but the crying soon intensified, so I made my way to the back of the house and peered into a window."

"Why didn't you peer into a front window?"

"They were boarded up."

"That didn't alarm you?"

She'd be lucky to have any teeth left considering she was

quite certain she was grinding them down to mere stubs. "Of course it did, but again, someone was *crying*, and that someone turned out to be Miss James." She dropped her head and focused on her mud-splattered gown, knowing perfectly well Mr. Wilder would not react favorably to what she was going to say next. "After I broke the glass in the window to gain entrance, I'd just started untying Miss James when that man burst into the room."

"The man who gave you directions?"

"No, a different man."

"Miss Beckett, you are not very adept at explaining, are you?"

She felt the strangest urge to throttle Mr. Wilder, which was odd considering she wasn't normally the violent type. She cleared her throat and opened her mouth to deliver a scathing retort, but before a single word could pass her lips, Mr. Wilder pushed himself to his feet, stalked closer to the bars, and let out a shrill whistle.

"Miss James, wake up," he called.

Had he not listened to what she'd said regarding Miss James?

She scrambled to her feet and turned just as Miss James shot upright on the cot, her face already screwed up in an expression that seemed, based on the short time Arabella had been acquainted with the young lady, to foreshadow a hysterical episode.

At least Mr. Wilder could not claim she hadn't warned him.

Miss James let out a ragged sob, but then the lady's eyes widened as she glanced past Arabella. The sob turned to a sigh, and Miss James smiled and released a giggle. The young lady rose to her feet, shook out her gown, and glided across the room, her goal obviously to get to Mr. Wilder as soon as her dainty feet would allow.

Arabella spun on her one heel, expecting to see Mr. Wilder's ever-present scowl, but instead the gentleman was smiling a charming smile and . . . bowing in Miss James's direction.

He'd certainly never bowed to her.

"Miss James, I do beg your pardon for waking you in such an abrupt manner," Mr. Wilder said, "but I fear Miss Beckett's thoughts have been addled by her experience. I'm hopeful you'll be able to give me the answers I so desperately need. I'm Mr. Wilder, at your service."

"My thoughts are not addled," Arabella snapped.

Mr. Wilder ignored her and took the hand Miss James thrust through the bars, bringing it to his lips in a move that was all too practiced. Miss James giggled again and began batting her lashes.

"I will be more than happy to answer any questions you might have, Mr. Wilder," Miss James purred. "I have suffered a truly horrendous day, but I must say that my fears have simply melted away, knowing a big, strong gentleman has come to my rescue."

"How do you know he's here to rescue us?" Arabella couldn't resist asking.

"Why, one only has to look at the gentleman to know he's a knight in shining armor come to life," Miss James simpered.

Miss James was obviously the easily impressed sort.

"You may rest assured that I *am* here to rescue you, Miss James," Mr. Wilder said, "but first, I do need to ask you some questions."

Miss James looked mildly disappointed when Mr. Wilder released her hand and took a step back, but she rallied quickly and sent him an adorable smile as she pressed herself against the iron bars. "What do you need to know?"

"Miss Beckett told me that there was a man who entered the farmhouse while she was attempting to untie you. Have you ever seen that man or seen the man who escorted you there before, and do you happen to know their names?"

Miss James nibbled on her lip. "I'm afraid I'd never seen either man before, Mr. Wilder, and neither one of them bothered to give me their names." She gave a small sniff. "I first met the larger of the two men at the train station, and he told me he'd been charged with delivering me to my intended. Once we reached the farmhouse, he handed me over to that gentleman you just asked me about, who was short in stature and possessed little hair on his head. That gentleman proceeded to tie me to a chair and told me they would be back shortly. It was my understanding they were off to fetch my groom." She batted her eyes again. "I still have no idea why they felt the need to tie me up. I can assure you, I was only too willing to get married. I recently turned eighteen and have no desire to obtain the title of spinster."

That explained the reasoning behind answering the advertisement.

Arabella swung her head and watched as Mr. Wilder's smile faded.

"Miss James," he said, "surely you must realize that there was never any groom?"

Miss James giggled. "Of course there was." She sobered and sent Arabella a scowl. "Miss Beckett must have scared him off when she shot that man."

"You conveniently forgot to mention anything about shooting a man, Miss Beckett," Mr. Wilder snapped.

Arabella lifted her chin. "I was about to tell you, but you decided to wake Miss James, and with all the pleasantries being exchanged, I haven't had a chance to finish my tale."

"She was quite ferocious when she fired that pistol," Miss James said. "Why, I'm surprised she didn't hit me in the process, since the man she shot was rather close to me at the time."

"He was across the room from you, and his intention was clear. He did not want me to free you," Arabella muttered.

"He only wanted to keep me safe for my soon-to-be husband," Miss James argued.

This was what happened when ladies were not given the benefit of a suitable education.

"Where did you get a gun?" Mr. Wilder asked, drawing her attention.

"I always have a pistol at my disposal."

"Did you kill him?"

"Good heavens, I should think not. I aimed for his shoulder."

Mr. Wilder cocked a brow.

"I'm an expert markswoman. I don't fire a pistol unless I'm completely certain of what I'm about to hit."

Mr. Wilder's other brow joined the first one.

He didn't believe her.

He was the most obnoxious, chauvinistic, old-fashioned gentleman she'd ever had the misfortune to meet.

"There was blood everywhere," Miss James said, "and some of it even got on my favorite dress." She pointed to a small smudge on her skirt and then gestured to Arabella. "I still do not understand what happened to Miss Beckett. She was not covered in filth when I first met her, but then, after we were thrown into a wagon, she had taken a turn for the worse. I readily admit the scent of her made me quite nauseous."

"How *did* you come to be in such disrepair?" Mr. Wilder asked.

"Perhaps you should ask Miss James," Arabella said sweetly. "That is why you woke her."

"Miss James just stated she doesn't know."

Arabella blew out a breath. There was nothing to do but finish her story. She was tired of being in jail, longed to take a bath, and longed to part ways with Mr. Wilder. She plopped back down on the cold floor and looked up. "After I shot the man—he was the balding one, in case you're wondering—I finished untying Miss James, and then we were just about to make our escape when the sheriff showed up. Unfortunately, he took one look at the man bleeding on the floor and immediately placed me under arrest."

"And that's the entire story?" Mr. Wilder asked.

"You're forgetting the pig."

"Miss Beckett started to act all funny when the large man who'd graciously given me a ride out to the farmhouse showed up. For some reason, she didn't appear to like the fact that the gentleman was known to the sheriff. Before I could stop her, she darted away," Miss James said. "As I said before, the next time I saw her, she was filthy and missing a large chunk of her hair."

Mr. Wilder's gaze sharpened as he peered down at her. "Your odd hairstyle is not intentional?"

"Hardly, nor is this circumstance of only sporting one shoe. The blame for both situations can be laid at Sheriff Dawson's feet."

"Can they now?"

Right before her eyes, Mr. Theodore Wilder went from annoying to lethal.

"I'll be back," he rasped as he spun on his heel and strode away.

"Where are you going?"

"Sheriff Dawson and I need to have a little chat," he called over his shoulder before he disappeared down the hallway.

Arabella struggled to her feet and looked through the bars, turning when Miss James let out another giggle.

"Oh, he is divine," the young lady breathed.

Divine was not the word Arabella would have used to describe Mr. Wilder. Arrogant, annoying, and infuriating fit him better, but . . . something about finding out the sheriff had cut off her hair had changed his attitude toward her, and she knew without a shadow of a doubt they would soon be free.

She limped over to the stone bench, sat down, and couldn't hold back a smile.

Mr. Wilder was certainly not who she'd thought God would send her, but he was what she'd gotten, and she couldn't help but be thankful for the assistance.

She raised her eyes to the ceiling.

Thank you, Lord.

3

Miss Arabella Beckett was opinionated, bossy, and not at all what Theodore had expected when he'd agreed to fetch her home.

Her brother Zayne was a likable sort, but Miss Beckett was one of those odd ladies who wanted to turn the world upside down and take over roles that gentlemen had held forever.

She was not his cup of tea in the least, but she was a member of the fairer sex, and as such he was honor-bound to assist her.

It didn't sit well with him that she'd been sorely mistreated. Granted, he now knew firsthand she was exasperating, but someone—Sheriff Dawson it seemed—had divested Miss Beckett of her hair.

That simply was never done.

The good sheriff had also tossed her into a gloomy cell without allowing her the benefit of a good washing, and besides being forced to wallow in her own filth, Miss Beckett had most likely been terrified as she'd waited to learn her fate.

He paused when he reached the top of the steps. Funny, she hadn't seemed terrified. Although he had detected a slight trembling in her voice when she'd talked about almost being forced into a life of prostitution. His attitude toward her had softened in that moment, until she'd rallied a mere second later and proclaimed the disturbing idea that she was now determined to assist women down on their luck.

Proper ladies were supposed to leave nasty business like that to gentlemen.

They were also expected to be charming, not hoydens who were all too annoying and who, for some unfathomable reason, seemed to believe they were entitled to equal rights.

He'd always been of the belief that ladies should appreciate their delicate status and the fact that they were not required to provide a living or train for a profession. No, all they were truly required to do was produce children and ease a gentleman's life.

Why any lady would balk at that was beyond him. It was also beyond him why a lady wouldn't prefer to act docile and sweet and look to a man for guidance.

He highly doubted Miss Beckett looked to a man for anything, let alone guidance. It was clear she was quite lovely—at least the bit of her he'd managed to see beneath the grime—but she was obviously strong-willed, and she seemed more intelligent than most gentlemen he knew.

It gave a man pause.

It should have been an easy matter to retrieve Miss Beckett and escort her back to New York. Unfortunately, the lady appeared to possess a restless spirit, which her mother, Mrs. Gloria Beckett, had conveniently neglected to mention when she'd convinced him to go after her daughter. He'd spent weeks traveling from city to city, always one step behind the elusive Miss Beckett. He was about to give up in Kansas, but a lucky circumstance had him making the acquaintance of Mrs. Ellen Wallaby. After that woman forced him to listen to a rambling lecture on her dismal views of men in general, she finally informed him that Miss Beckett was on her way to Chicago to attend a rally.

He'd immediately boarded a train for Chicago, but once there, discovered the rally over and Miss Beckett gone. It was only due to the fact that Miss Beckett was a beautiful woman, when she wasn't covered in pig slop, that he'd been able to learn she'd traveled to Gilman. Most people he'd spoken with had taken note of her presence, each and every one of them more than willing to describe her in minute detail. It seemed her strikingly dramatic face, large blue eyes, delicately arched brows, and rosy soft lips were obviously difficult to forget. More than one person had waxed on about her honey-blond hair, and now some of that hair had apparently gone missing from her head.

She didn't seem overly distressed about that.

It was disconcerting, this lack of expected feminine dramatics.

His sister would have dissolved into a fit of the vapors if her hair suddenly went flying off her head.

A shout of laughter pulled him abruptly back to reality. His feet set to motion, and a few seconds later he was standing in front of a closed door, the sound of laughter still drifting through it. He twisted the knob and stalked into the room.

Sheriff Dawson was sitting behind a desk, a cigar clamped between his teeth. Three deputies were sprawled around him in wooden chairs, glasses of whiskey clenched in their hands. His temper changed to amusement when he noted the dismal state of their clothing. Liberal streaks of something foul coated every man, and a glimmer of satisfaction flowed through him. At least Miss Beckett was not the only one who'd suffered from the encounter with the pig.

"Gentlemen," he exclaimed as he strolled across the floor and stopped in front of the sheriff's desk, "we have matters to discuss."

"Is she the lady you sought?" Sheriff Dawson asked.

"She is."

The sheriff took a puff of his cigar. "Did she tell you she shot a man and caused me and my deputies no small amount of distress?"

Theodore eased down into a chair and crossed his ankle over his leg. "I find it difficult to believe one refined lady was capable of causing too much distress. As for the shooting incident, we'll need to discuss that in private."

Sheriff Dawson frowned. "That woman is no 'refined lady,' and I see no need for privacy, since my men were the victims of her crime spree."

"Rescuing a woman from a prostitution ring hardly constitutes a crime spree."

"We don't have a prostitution ring here in Gilman," one of the deputies said as he ambled to his feet and moved to a table where he proceeded to pour himself another drink.

"Prostitution may be nonexistent in your small town, but I can assure you, something of a disturbing nature is happening on the outskirts." Theodore looked to Sheriff Dawson. "As for Miss Beckett, you and your men arrested the only daughter of Mr. Douglas Beckett, owner of Beckett Railroads."

An uneasy silence filled the room.

"She's a railroad Beckett?" Sheriff Dawson asked as a bead of sweat dribbled off his nose.

"She is, and that's why I'm going to suggest you immediately release her and Miss James into my custody."

Sheriff Dawson settled back in his chair. "I'm afraid I can't do that. Railroad royalty or not, she did shoot a man and then tried to evade arrest."

"Which I find perfectly understandable, considering Miss Beckett was confronted by a man of the criminal persuasion who tried to stop her from saving Miss James. I would have shot the man too, and I certainly would have tried to evade arrest if the authorities didn't seem very interested in apprehending the true criminal."

Sheriff Dawson released a boisterous laugh. "Don't tell me you believe all that nonsense, boy? These are women you're dealing with, and everyone knows you can't trust a woman to tell the truth. Don't let Miss Beckett and Miss James hoodwink you into believing they're innocent just because they are pretty ladies."

"Don't call me boy, and don't presume that I'm an idiot." He reached into his pocket, drew out his billfold, extracted a card, and tossed it across the desk toward Sheriff Dawson.

"You already told me you're a private investigator."

"Read the card."

Sheriff Dawson plucked the card off the table, scanned it, and turned a little pale. He gestured to his men. "I need to speak with this gentleman, alone."

"I don't think that's wise, boss," the deputy who'd spoken earlier said before he tipped his glass back and took a noisy swig. "I don't trust him."

Sheriff Dawson pulled open a drawer on his desk, extracted a pistol, and sent the deputy a wink. "I'll be fine, Cunningham."

Even though the three deputies began to mutter under their breaths, they did finally meander from the room. Theodore waited until the door closed behind the last deputy before he turned back to the sheriff and arched a brow.

"What's going on in your town?"

"You work for the government?" Sheriff Dawson asked, ignoring Theodore's question.

Two could play that game. "Who are the men at the farmhouse?"

Sheriff Dawson narrowed his eyes. "You tell me about the government and I'll tell you about the men."

"I work for the government."

"And?"

"That's all you need to know," Theodore said. "And maybe the fact that if you don't cooperate, I won't leave your town as soon as I get the ladies released. I can assure you, that won't be something you'll enjoy."

More sweat popped out on the sheriff's forehead. "The only names I have for those men are Carl and Wallie. They moved here a few months ago, and I don't know much more about them."

"What about the prostitution ring?"

"I'm not at liberty to discuss that."

Every muscle in Theodore's body tensed. "Why not?"

"It's somewhat of an internal affair."

Understanding was immediate, as was trepidation. Theodore pushed out of his chair, snatched up the pistol Sheriff Dawson had laid on the desk, and directed it toward the sheriff. "I'm going to need the keys to the cell."

"Have you lost your mind?"

"Not at all. If I understand you correctly, you suspect someone on your staff of participating in whatever shady business is going on in your town, and that someone could even now be prowling the halls of this building. You've left the ladies at that man's mercy."

Sheriff Dawson eyed him for a second, brushed away the river of sweat that was now covering his face, and got to his feet, hurrying over to a peg on the wall where he grabbed a ring of keys. He gestured to the door.

"You first," Theodore said as he casually pointed to the door with the pistol.

"There's no need for that," Sheriff Dawson muttered as he strode out of the room, Theodore dodging his steps.

Theodore tightened his grip on the pistol. "Oh, I'm afraid there's every need."

He followed the sheriff down the hallway, but then brushed past the man and broke into a run when he suddenly heard a high-pitched squeal. He took the steps two at a time, but skidded to a stop at the unusual sight that met his eyes.

Miss James was pressed against the bars, holding hands with one of the deputies and giggling as if she were in the midst of a party.

Perhaps Miss Beckett had been right and he should *not* have woken the lady.

"Step away from the cell," he ordered, drawing the deputy's attention as he directed his pistol at the man.

"Mr. Wilder," Arabella exclaimed as she pressed her face against the bars and stared at him with wide eyes. "Whatever in the world are you doing?"

"Getting you released," he said before he returned his attention to the deputy, who still retained possession of Miss James's hand.

"I would have thought your diplomatic skills would have allowed you to secure our release without actually shooting our way out of jail."

Annoyance snaked through him. "I'm not busting you out of jail. I'm simply trying to get this deputy to release Miss James's hand."

"Oh, well, that's somewhat disappointing."

He felt his jaw clench. "Did you want me to shoot someone?"

"While that idea is vastly appealing, I suppose we should do this the normal way and just pay bail." Arabella bent over, fiddled with the hem of her skirt, and then straightened, thrusting what looked to be slimy bills in his direction. "This should cover it."

He edged forward and took the bills. "Do you always carry money in that unusual place?"

"I must admit that I do. I also must admit that I'm a bit bewildered as to why I wasn't given an opportunity to pay bail before this." Arabella sent a glare to the sheriff, who'd come to stand beside him. "You have been quite negligent in your treatment of me, Sheriff, and . . ." Her voice trailed off as she frowned and shifted her attention back to Theodore. "May I suggest you lower your weapon, Mr. Wilder? If it has escaped your notice, there are two deputies right behind you, and both of them have guns currently pointed in your direction."

He looked over his shoulder, discovered the deputy Sheriff Dawson had called Cunningham, and another deputy standing five feet away from him with their weapons drawn. "I'm afraid I won't lower my gun until that deputy steps away from Miss James."

Miss James suddenly let out a shrill laugh. He blinked when she batted her lashes at him and wiggled the fingers of her free hand through the bars. "Mr. Wilder, there is no need to become distraught because I'm showing Deputy Jud Hansen some attention." She beamed at the deputy. "He's just been a dear, holding my hand and soothing away my fears."

"Miss James, forgive me, but if he doesn't let go of your hand soon, I'm afraid I really am going to have to shoot him, and then that lovely gown of yours will sport more than just a smidgen of blood."

Miss James withdrew her hand from Deputy Hansen's grasp so fast that Theodore felt the distinct urge to laugh.

"You, sir, are despicable," Deputy Hansen spat as he stepped away from the cell and glared at Theodore. "My mother brought me up to respect ladies and to cater to their delicate sensibilities. Poor Miss James, from what I've learned, is completely innocent of all the wrongdoings that transpired today. I was simply trying to reassure her that all will be well in the end."

"Oh, that was lovely," Miss James cooed.

Theodore resisted the urge to roll his eyes. "Lovely or not, Miss James, I'm afraid you're going to have to bid Deputy Hansen goodbye now. Sheriff Dawson has agreed to release you and Miss Beckett into my custody, and we really do need to take our leave."

Deputy Hansen took a step forward and jerked his head toward Arabella. "But she shot a man."

Sheriff Dawson cleared his throat. "That's enough, Deputy Hansen. Mr. Wilder is now responsible for these ladies, and I say good riddance." He turned and nodded to the two deputies who were still standing with their pistols at the ready. "All of you may go. I'll meet up with you in my office momentarily."

"But . . . you can't just let Miss Beckett go," Deputy Hansen argued. "Justice has not been served."

"We'll discuss it later," Sheriff Dawson snapped.

Deputy Hansen spun around and, without speaking another word, stalked down the narrow hallway and disappeared from sight, the other two deputies following him a moment later.

"Well, that was interesting," Arabella said before she waved the sheriff forward. "If I'm to assume that we really are going to be freed, don't you think it might be prudent to unlock this cell?"

Sheriff Dawson eyed the slimy money Theodore still held in his hand. "I really should demand you give me that for all the aggravation this lady has caused."

"But since you and I both know she didn't do anything to warrant arrest, I think I'll give it back to her," Theodore said as he handed Miss Beckett her money through the bars and watched as she stuffed it down her bodice.

Was she opposed to carrying the always-present female accessory of a reticule, or did she simply find it more convenient to keep her money close at hand at all times?

"Come, Miss James," Arabella said as Sheriff Dawson stepped to the cell door, pushed the key into the lock, and pulled the door open. "We must get you home." She took hold of Miss James's arm, but then dropped it a second later when the young lady refused to budge.

"You didn't say anything about returning me to Chicago," Miss James said with a sniff.

"Chicago is your home," Miss Beckett pointed out.

"But . . . what about my husband?" Miss James wailed.

Miss Beckett muttered something under her breath before she took hold of Miss James's arm once again and tugged the lady out of the cell and into the hallway. She let out a grunt when Miss James dug in her heels and stopped moving.

"I'm not going back to Chicago without a husband by my side."

To Theodore's surprise, Miss Beckett gave Miss James an awkward pat on the shoulder.

"I don't mean to distress you, but that advertisement you answered was simply a ploy to get you down here. Those two men from the farmhouse had nefarious plans for you, and I'm afraid there was *never* a husband to be had." She gave Miss James another pat. "You're a lovely young lady, one I'm certain any gentleman would be proud to call his own. I'm quite certain if you put your mind to it, you'll be able to secure the attention of some nice gentleman back in Chicago. Then you won't need to worry about becoming a spinster." She looked at him. "Wouldn't you agree, Mr. Wilder?"

He blinked. "Ah, of course. Why, I would be astonished if Miss James wasn't happily married within the year."

Miss James's gaze suddenly sharpened. "Are you married, Mr. Wilder?"

Before he could address that piece of nonsense, Miss Beckett grabbed Miss James's arm and began pulling her down the hallway, and something that sounded very much like "Set your sights a little higher dear," drifted back to his ears.

Honestly, Miss Beckett was a nuisance. There was no other way to describe her.

41

"We should probably follow them," Sheriff Dawson said, prompting Theodore to grimace even as he began to trudge up the steps after the ladies.

He reached the top and moved to where Miss Beckett was whispering something to Miss James, stopping when she caught sight of him. She straightened, sent Miss James a look that clearly stated she was beginning to lose patience with the lady, and then opened her mouth. "You've neglected to mention what our plans are from here, so Miss James and I were uncertain how to proceed." She let out a breath. "Miss James believes we should scurry over to the hotel and get a restful night's sleep, but I was hoping you have a carriage at your disposal, which would allow us to depart from this pleasant town immediately."

"I'm afraid I have no carriage at my disposal, I learned this afternoon that the hotel has no vacancies, and I'm quite certain we'll have to spend the night at the train station, since no trains run through Gilman this time of night."

"My mother would never approve of me spending the night in a train station with a gentleman," Miss James proclaimed.

Miss Beckett narrowed her eyes. "Miss James, forgive me, but you ran away from home to rendezvous with some unknown man whom you apparently were convinced you would marry. I don't believe your mother will care if you accompany Mr. Wilder and me to the train station because, again, it's a train station. Mr. Wilder is a well-respected private investigator, and I'm certain he's spent more than a few nights guarding his clients in unusual places."

"Oh, private investigators are so . . . compelling," Miss James breathed.

Here was a reminder of why he was not getting married anytime in the near future. Ladies were trouble wrapped up in pretty packages, or in Miss Beckett's case, wrapped up in clothing that could most likely walk on its own.

"Tell me, Sheriff," Arabella said, causing Theodore to blink back to the conversation at hand, "what happened to the two men who were back at the farmhouse?"

With all the intrigue swirling around, he'd completely neglected to ask that pertinent question, which certainly didn't say much about his investigating skills at the moment.

Sheriff Dawson turned rather red. "I'm afraid those men have disappeared."

Miss Beckett's expression turned formidable. "Surely you're not suggesting they escaped, are you?"

Sheriff Dawson's color increased. "They took off on Mr. Brown's horse, and no one has seen them since."

Miss Beckett crossed her arms over her chest. "If those men took Mr. Brown's horse, explain to me why I'm being charged with its theft?"

"Someone had to be held accountable."

It really was somewhat impressive how the lady could make everyone aware of her displeasure without speaking a single word. Sparks were literally spewing from her eyes, her lips were pinched, and annoyance radiated from her every pore.

"I'll need your gun," Miss Beckett said as she held out her hand to Theodore.

"My gun?"

"Yes, that object you have clenched in your hand."

"I don't think that would be wise, and besides, this isn't actually my gun. I took it from Sheriff Dawson's desk."

Miss Beckett's gaze locked on the gun in his hand, and she suddenly released a snort. "That's my gun, and I'll have it back, if you please."

Sheriff Dawson stepped forward and shook his head. "I'm afraid that won't be possible, Miss Beckett. You did use that weapon to shoot a man, so I'm going to need to enter it into evidence."

"Since the man I shot is nowhere to be found, you have no witness to the shooting," Miss Beckett snapped.

"I saw you shoot that man," Miss James said.

Miss Beckett turned ever so slowly and cocked a brow at Miss James, who flinched and retreated rapidly back into silence.

Theodore tucked the gun into the waistband of his trousers, believing it would be the safest place for it, before he extended his arm to Miss Beckett. "I'll return your gun once we get on a train and once the temptation of shooting Sheriff Dawson is removed."

"Thank you for that," Sheriff Dawson muttered.

"You're welcome," he replied before he looked at his arm and then to Miss Beckett. "Shall we go?"

She refused the offer of his arm and stuck her nose in the air. "What about my hair?"

Of course she would turn difficult. He blew out a breath. "While I would adore nothing more than to return your hair to your head, I do believe you are going to have to accept the fact that it's gone for good."

"I don't want it back. I want the sheriff to apologize."

For a split second, Theodore thought Sheriff Dawson was going to refuse, but then the sheriff sent Miss Beckett a glare even as he inclined his head. "My apologies, ma'am."

Her nose went further up in the air. "Come, Miss James, it is past time we took our leave of this horrible place." She grabbed Miss James's hand and towed her toward the door.

"I can't say I'll be upset to see the last of her, and you for that matter," Sheriff Dawson mumbled.

"Who said you've seen the last of me?" Theodore asked as he pulled his gaze away from the ladies and settled it on the sheriff.

"I gave you what you wanted."

"Did you?"

"I'm letting you take Miss Beckett."

"Only because she's annoying and you don't want to deal with her any longer."

The sheriff opened his mouth, and then snapped it shut before a sliver of a grin crossed his face. "Speaking of annoying, she just left the building without you."

She was going to be the death of him.

"Until we meet again," he said to the sheriff before he turned and strode out of the jail. Temper stole over him when he caught sight of Miss Beckett limping down the road, apparently oblivious to the danger that stalked her every uneven step.

"Miss Beckett, stop right there, if you please," he called, somewhat amazed when she actually tottered to a stop and turned.

"Mr. Wilder, we cannot dawdle in the middle of the street. If you've forgotten, there are real criminals on the loose."

He broke into a slow run, caught up to them, took a firm grip on her arm, and hustled her back into motion, their rapid pace causing Miss James to begin to whine.

"I'm perfectly aware of the danger, Miss Beckett, although I cannot say the same for you," he said, steering her toward the train station while ignoring the overly dramatic breaths Miss James was now expelling.

He was forced to stop when Miss Beckett ceased moving. He assumed what he hoped was a somewhat pleasant expression. "Yes?"

"If your attitude is going to continue to be disagreeable, Mr. Wilder, we should part ways right now."

"If only that were a viable choice."

Miss Beckett assumed an expression that was downright alarming. She shook off his arm and pulled Miss James into motion. "Come, Miss James. The train station is just in sight, and I for one am desperate to use their washroom." She didn't bother to see if he was following her but began to stomp away on her one remaining shoe.

She was beyond aggravating, a nightmare of a lady with a pushy attitude that was certain to haunt him for quite some time.

Why then did he feel compelled to go after her?

4

*I*t had been one of the strangest weeks of Arabella's life.

Not only had she almost been forced into a life of ill repute and been arrested, she'd also been forced to spend five days with the most unpleasant Mr. Wilder. If that wasn't bad enough, she'd been left to deal with a disheartened Miss James after the young lady had fallen head over heels in infatuation with Mr. Wilder on their long train ride to Chicago.

To give Mr. Wilder his due, he had not actually encouraged Miss James, but there just seemed to be something about him that made him irresistible to most ladies.

She did not see his appeal.

He was very set in his way of thinking, especially in regard to women, and although he'd been completely charming, in a rather distant way, to Miss James, he'd been abrupt and downright cantankerous with her.

He'd also expected her to deal with Miss James once they'd returned the lady to her parents. She'd been required to listen as the lady bemoaned the sad state of affairs resulting from Mr. Wilder *not* returning her affections. She'd tried to be sympathetic, but after an hour of sobbing, pleading, and downright silliness, she'd finally lost patience. She'd told Miss James in no uncertain terms that she needed to reevaluate her priorities, bid a very appreciative Mrs. James goodbye, and then made a mad dash for the door. She'd been less than amused when she'd found Mr. Wilder sleeping in the carriage as if he didn't have a care in the world.

Once she'd shaken him awake, the irritating gentleman had not even given her a thank-you for extracting him from Miss James's misplaced affections. He seemed to take it for granted that she'd deal with what he'd called "lady business" and had even had the audacity to suggest that Miss James's infatuation had been Arabella's fault in the first place.

The quality of their time together since then had rapidly gone downhill.

They couldn't seem to spend five minutes in each other's company without trading barbs, and quite frankly she was relieved they were almost to New York. She knew it was only a matter of time until the gentleman said something that would send her over the edge, and she was rather afraid that when he did, she might be tempted to do something to him that would put her back behind bars.

Arabella lowered the newspaper she'd been attempting to read and rolled her eyes at the sight of Theodore sleeping soundly once again, his head lolling against the window of the train car as his mouth gaped open.

She hated to admit it, but he was actually somewhat appealing when he was asleep . . . mostly because he wasn't speaking.

That thought had a grin teasing her lips.

It really was rather unfortunate that he was a gentleman who held such archaic views. He did seem to be intelligent, if misguided, and it would be interesting, if he would engage in conversation with her, to see if she could change some of his less-than-acceptable ideas.

She glanced at the small watch she'd attached to her reticule, saw that they still had at least an hour until they reached New York, and felt her grin widen. There was still time to change him, but she would need him to wake up.

She rattled the newspaper, and then rattled it again when he didn't budge, reluctantly admitting defeat after the third rattle. One would think, given his profession, that he would be a gentleman who slept lightly.

She raised the newspaper and scanned the articles, her attention soon caught by an announcement pertaining to a suffrage rally that was to be held in Central Park the following week. Deciding that would be the perfect opportunity to return to something normal, she set the newspaper aside and pulled her reticule into her lap. She rooted around in the bag, pulled out the pistol Theodore had finally returned to her, pushed aside a few forgotten sweets, and finally located a small pad of paper.

"You do realize it's not exactly honorable to shoot a man while he's sleeping, don't you?"

She lifted her head and found him watching her warily. "Since it would seem you are no longer asleep, it wouldn't be exactly dishonorable." She patted her gun, stuffed it back into the reticule, and narrowed her eyes when he surprised her with a laugh.

He normally woke up surly.

"May I dare hope we're almost to New York?"

Before she could answer, he stretched his arms over his head, the motion causing her to notice the muscles she'd been trying to ignore for days strain against his shirt.

It was beyond irritating, the fact that the gentleman was so intriguingly put together. Not once had he failed to attract the attention of every lady in his vicinity, and now *she* was gawking at him just like everyone else.

The effects of the past week's events must finally be catching up with her.

She jerked her gaze away from his chest and looked out the window, trying to hide the fact her cheeks had taken to heating.

What had he asked her again?

Oh yes, something about New York.

"It looks as if nasty weather is preceding our arrival into the city, but yes, we shouldn't have much longer until we arrive."

"Ah, lovely, nasty weather. Just what I was hoping for, and quite a safe topic for us to discuss, I might add."

Annoyance slid over her. "Would you prefer I discuss something besides the weather?"

"No, the weather is a fine topic of conversation, much more preferable than the suffrage movement." He shuddered. "I must say I've heard enough about that to last me a lifetime."

He really was insufferable.

"Do you think it will begin to snow before we reach our respective homes?" he asked.

He really was going to continue discussing the weather.

"Ah, well . . . perhaps" was all she could think to reply.

"Well, that topic didn't occupy us for long, did it?" Theodore gestured to her dress. "May I remark that the gown you're wearing today is quite lovely? I must admit that purple certainly does seem to bring out the blue of your eyes, and your matching hat does wonders in hiding the deplorable state of your hair."

She blinked. Not once in the entire time they'd spent together had he ever given her a compliment. Granted, he hadn't seemed able to resist pointing out the condition of her hair, but still . . .

Maybe he was coming down with something.

"I wore this gown two days ago."

"Did you? Then I must apologize for not speaking up then and telling you how delightful it looks on you."

50

"Two days ago, you barely spoke a word to me, except to tell me I was taking too long with the newspaper."

"I escorted you to that general store when the train made a stop."

"True, but you didn't actually speak while you escorted me."

Theodore looked at her for a long moment and then leaned forward. "Miss Beckett, I do beg your pardon if you found me a less-than-pleasant traveling companion. I readily admit my mind has been occupied with other matters, namely what is transpiring in Gilman. Throw in the nasty business of fending off Miss James's advances, and I probably have not been at my best. Allow me to make up for my disgraceful lack of attention toward you. I promise to discuss anything within reason that you care to discuss during the time we have left together."

He really must be coming down with something.

She felt her lips twitch. "You would discuss the suffrage movement with me?"

"I would much rather discuss ladies' fashions, the ingredients for assembling a cake, or even the many ailments that plague people, but since you do *not* seem to like conversing on subjects the majority of ladies enjoy, then yes, I will discuss, or at least listen to, your views on the suffrage movement once again."

His words stung.

She enjoyed the latest fashions as much as the next lady, and while she was not overly proficient in the kitchen, she did know how to bake a cake.

Yet he did have a point. Every single time they'd attempted to converse, she'd brought up her cause and . . . good heavens, she'd somehow managed to become a bore.

It was little wonder he hadn't wanted to engage in conversation with her during the past few days. He'd probably been lulled almost to the point of slumber, which certainly would explain all the naps he'd taken.

She needed to bring up a topic for conversation they both would enjoy, but her mind was a complete blank.

"Tell me, Miss Beckett," Theodore began, breaking the silence that had settled over them. "I noticed you carry a yellow parasol with you quite often, and that parasol, interestingly enough, is trimmed in pink. May I assume it was a gift, and that you hold it dear to your heart?"

For some reason, she got the impression he found it odd that she would own anything with pink on it.

She reached down and plucked up the parasol in question. "I purchased this adorable parasol in a small shop while I was staying in California. The reason I carry it so often is because I absolutely adore the color pink." She twirled the closed parasol around for a second and frowned. "I had a gown made up to complement this parasol, but alas it was destroyed by my encounter with that dastardly pig."

"Very good, Miss Beckett, that was a subject of conversation that any normal young lady would have brought up, except for the 'dastardly pig' part, that is."

She eyed the parasol and couldn't help but wonder if it would survive intact if she used it to give Mr. Wilder a good wallop.

"I must admit that you've taken me by surprise with your admission that you enjoy pink," Theodore continued, completely oblivious to the fact she was longing to do him bodily harm. "Pink is not a color I would normally associate with you."

She laid the parasol back on the floor, just far enough away from her that it wouldn't be a temptation. "And exactly what colors do you associate with me?"

"I think bold colors suit you, like red or . . . black."

She tilted her chin. "Black is not a color."

"But it suits you."

"I've never worn black in your presence, something you would know if you'd actually been paying attention to me. What color did I wear yesterday?"

"Yellow."

She bit her lip. He was right, she had worn yellow yesterday. She tilted her chin. "What about the day we met?"

He laughed. "Miss Beckett, surely you realize that given the fact you were covered in mud, I can't really say what color you were wearing." He grinned. "But since it appears we have descended into bickering over what I thought would be a safe subject, may I suggest we move on to discuss anything of note you read in the paper?"

She lifted her chin. "I did read about a rally that is to be held in Central Park, but I wouldn't want to bore you with the pesky details." She gritted her teeth when he had the audacity to send her a charming and all-too-attractive grin. "However," she said, reaching for the newspaper and shaking it open to page three, "I must admit I found this article on the clothing mills extremely well-written. It's by a Mr. Alfred Wallenstate, and he has a wonderful way with words."

Theodore's grin disappeared in a split second. "May I see that?"

Arabella handed him the paper and watched as he disappeared behind it, reappearing a moment later with a frown on his face.

"Did you not appreciate the story?" she asked.

"It is well-written."

"And that disappoints you?"

"It does," Theodore admitted. "If you must know, Mr. Wallenstate is actually Miss Agatha Watson, and I readily admit I did not realize she possessed so much talent."

"May I assume you are known to this Miss Watson?"

"She is a dear friend of your new sister-in-law, Eliza, and

I must tell you now, she is trouble. I encouraged her to abandon her quest to become a journalist, but as you can see, she didn't heed my advice. I wonder what her father makes of the fact his daughter is behaving in a manner hardly suitable to her social status."

"I would hope her father is proud of her. She has a true gift."

"She is taking a job away from a man who could have penned just that article. Miss Watson has no need to earn funds. She has a wealthy father to provide for her, and besides that, she is an attractive woman and holds an enviable position in society. She would have no difficulty finding a husband if she would only put aside her strange notions regarding a profession and behave in a more ladylike manner."

"You believe she should abandon her talent and settle for marriage?"

"You say that as if it's a horrible fate."

Arabella straightened in her seat. "Did you ever consider the fact that God blessed Miss Watson with a talent for the written word, and perhaps He expects her to put that talent to use? If you ask me, Miss Watson, through insightful writing, has brought to attention a condition in the clothing mills that most people know nothing about."

"I think God created man in His image and expects men to lead, while He created women to remain in the background and raise children while being a source of comfort to men."

She eyed the window and wondered if she'd suffer a horrible death if she flung herself out it.

Theodore chuckled. "I see I've finally rendered you speechless."

She drew in a breath. "I cannot believe my brother thought it was a good idea to have you come after me."

"Your brother isn't the one who approached me; your mother did."

Horror was swift. "My mother—as in Gloria Beckett—asked you to come fetch me home?"

He nodded. "She thought you might want to be present at your brother's wedding."

"Which is certainly understandable, and yet . . ." Arabella squared her shoulders. "May I inquire how she was acting when she made her request?"

"What do you mean?"

"Was she perhaps a little . . . giddy?"

"Ah, well, no, I wouldn't say she was giddy," Theodore said slowly. "She was extremely grateful, but not giddy."

"Of course she was," Arabella said before she let out an unladylike snort. "I love her dearly, but honestly I'd thought she'd gotten past her unfortunate habit of meddling, at least in regard to me."

"I'm afraid I'm not following you."

Arabella bit her lip. "What did she tell you about me?"

"She told me you were possessed of a pleasant disposition and that you were absolutely delightful."

"And you didn't find that odd?"

"Not at the time. Most mothers do proclaim their daughters to be delightful."

"But now?"

His lips twitched. "I think Gloria might have slightly exaggerated how well-behaved you are, and she certainly neglected to tell me about your propensity for getting into trouble."

"Why do you think she did that?"

Theodore's eyes widened. "Surely you're not suggesting she was trying her hand at matchmaking, are you?"

"I'm afraid there is no other explanation."

"But your mother knows me fairly well."

"Hmm . . . then this is peculiar, because, forgive me, Mr. Wilder, but you are the last gentleman on earth I would ever consider as a potential spouse. If my mother truly does know you, she would realize that."

"I am considered one of the most eligible bachelors in New York."

She stifled a grin at his surly tone of voice. "Of course you are, Mr. Wilder. You're from a prominent family, attractive in a manly sort of way, and you enjoy an exciting career. I'm certain there are ladies flocking to your side at each and every society event you attend." She frowned. "Speaking of society events, why do you suppose, given the fact you're friends with Zayne, we have never met?"

"I try to avoid society events whenever possible," he admitted slowly. "Matchmaking mothers always seem to have me in their sights, and since I have no desire to marry anytime in the near future, it's better for my digestion if I simply avoid those particular situations. Quite honestly, I prefer to spend my time working or relaxing at my club."

"May I presume no ladies are allowed at your club?"

"I knew it would be difficult for you to go more than ten minutes without bringing up something that pertains to your cause."

And here she'd almost been enjoying his company.

"Ah, feel that?" Theodore asked before she could think of a clever retort. "The train is slowing. We're almost home." He picked up the newspaper still lying on his lap and held it up. "Would you like me to dispose of this for you?"

A thread of annoyance slid through her at his now-jovial tone. Apparently, he was thrilled to soon part ways with her. She held out her hand. "I actually need that back. I didn't jot down the specific date and time of that suffrage rally I mentioned."

He handed the paper to her. "Don't you ever get tired of going to those?"

"Not when there's so much work still left to be done to get women the right to vote."

"When is the rally?"

"I believe it's sometime next week in Central Park."

"I might be able to go."

She suddenly felt a little warm. "I beg your pardon?"

"I'll have to look at my schedule, and hopefully I'll be in town, but if you'd like, I could escort you there."

"You want to go to a suffrage rally?"

"Of course not," he said with a smile before he sobered. "But I still have grave concerns over what happened in Gilman, and I'm not certain you're out of danger quite yet. You shot a man, and it's been my experience that men who've been shot have a desire to seek revenge. A rally is a perfect spot for someone to ambush you, and since I went through so much trouble to bring you back, I'd hate for someone to harm you. That would make my efforts all for naught."

Temper replaced the warm, fuzzy feeling of a moment before. Good heavens, what could she have been thinking?

It was not as if he'd shown any interest in her, so why in the world was she feeling a touch disappointed that he only wanted to attend the rally with her to keep her safe, not because he longed to be in her company?

Before she could contemplate that to satisfaction, the train shuddered to a complete stop. Theodore stood, extended her his arm, and then hustled her out into Grand Central Depot.

5

"Arabella, darling, I'm over here."

Arabella stood on her tiptoes and craned her neck, scanning the throngs of people that bustled around Grand Central Depot. A grin teased the corners of her mouth when the sight of her mother came into view. Her grin widened as she realized Gloria had climbed on top of someone's luggage and was waving madly in her direction, completely oblivious to the owner of said luggage's less-than-pleased look.

Arabella dropped her hold on Theodore's arm and took off into the crowd, her pace increasing with every step. Muttering an apology after stumbling against a burly gentleman, she squeezed through a group of ladies, who sent her exasperated looks and barely glanced at another gentleman tipping his hat to her, until she finally found herself snatched into her mother's embrace. She breathed in the familiar scent of Gloria Beckett's perfume and felt tears sting her eyes.

"Thank the good Lord you're safe," Gloria exclaimed as she took a step back and swiped at her own face with a lace handkerchief. "I didn't know what to think when I received that telegram from Mr. Wilder. Jail, Arabella?"

"It was completely unintentional."

"Of course it was, darling," Gloria said before she pulled her close for another hug. "You can tell me all about it once we get home. I have a feeling you'll only be able to do justice to the story over a bracing cup of tea." Gloria released her, stepped back, and looked over Arabella's shoulder. "Where is that charming scamp I sent after you?"

Her mother really did have her heart set on matchmaking, so much so that she was seemingly willing to cut their tender reunion short.

"I lost that 'charming scamp' in the crowd, but he's certain to turn up soon. Bad pennies always do. But before he gets here, Mother, you and I need to come to an understanding. Mr. Theodore Wilder is not for me. You need to stop, immediately, with whatever scheming you've got rattling around that diabolical mind of yours."

Gloria blinked innocent eyes back at her. "I'm sure I have no idea what you're talking about, dear. Of course you and Mr. Wilder would never suit. The mere idea is preposterous." She reached out and rubbed Arabella's arm. "I do believe you must be suffering a great deal of fatigue from your stint in jail."

"At least *I* can still make the claim, as can Hamilton, of never being incarcerated."

Arabella turned and found herself swept off her feet, her brother Zayne crushing her in a bone-jarring hug.

"Zayne, you're squeezing me too hard," she mumbled.

Zayne set her on her feet and released his hold on her, brushing a lock of burnished brown hair out of his eyes and shaking his head. "You, my independent yet exasperating sister, have worried everyone endlessly. Would it have killed you to have sent us word regarding where you were heading or when you expected to return to town? We were stunned to receive that telegram from Theodore telling us you'd been arrested."

"But . . . didn't he explain that he'd gotten me released?"

"Would we be waiting for you here if he hadn't?" He switched his attention to something behind her and grinned. "Ah, there's the gentleman of the hour. Now we'll finally be able to get all of our questions answered to satisfaction."

Arabella wrinkled her nose, even as her gaze settled on Theodore, who was striding toward them. She couldn't help but notice how the crowd simply disappeared around him, making it possible for him to walk at a rapid clip without interruption.

She tore her attention away from him. "Just so you know, Zayne, I'm perfectly capable of explaining my adventure to satisfaction. There's no reason to badger Mr. Wilder, and . . ." Her voice trailed off as Zayne, apparently unaware she'd been speaking, moved forward and then laughed as he and Theodore shook hands and even hugged, as if Theodore were the returning hero no one had seen for ages.

She certainly hadn't been greeted quite so enthusiastically. Admittedly, her mother had clearly been thrilled to see her, but . . . she had the sneaking suspicion Gloria was just as thrilled to see Theodore, especially given the fact her mother was currently bustling over to the gentleman, her face wreathed in a wide smile.

Arabella trudged after everyone, coming to a stop beside Zayne just as her mother let out a tinkling laugh when Theodore picked up her hand and placed a kiss on her knuckles.

"My dear, dear boy," Gloria exclaimed as Theodore released her hand. "Douglas and I can't thank you enough for returning our sweet Arabella to us." She reached up and patted him on the cheek. "We were hoping of course you'd get her back in time for the wedding, but alas it's hardly your fault she uncharacteristically became embroiled in a concerning matter."

Her mother, bless her heart, had not listened to a word she'd said. She was still intent on a bit of romantic maneuvering in regard to Mr. Wilder. Why else would she attempt to give the gentleman the impression it was uncharacteristic for her daughter to get into trouble?

Arabella cleared her throat, gaining only her mother's attention as Zayne and Theodore continued to catch up. "I do so hate to interrupt this touching yet disturbing scene, but we have been traveling for days, and I, for one, would like to go home."

Gloria shook her head. "We have to wait for Hamilton."

"Hamilton's here?" Arabella asked.

"Of course he's here, dear. He's been very anxious to introduce you to his Eliza, and I must say, he's had to wait entirely too long. Far be it from me to tell you what to do, but in the future, it might be wise if you'd check in with us every once in a while. That would alleviate the need to send a private investigator after you and would ensure you don't miss any weddings in the future."

A stab of remorse ran through her. "I am sorry, Mother, for being so negligent. I'm afraid I sometimes get so consumed with my cause that I occasionally forget to keep you and Father abreast of my whereabouts. I didn't realize I would be so late in returning to New York, but I kept getting requests to speak at rallies, and I just couldn't seem to pass up such wonderful opportunities." She smiled. "As for missing future weddings, I highly doubt anyone else will decide to marry on the spur of the moment."

Gloria's eyes began to twinkle, right before she sent an all-too-telling wink in Theodore's direction. Arabella decided it would be prudent to change the topic from weddings to something a little safer. "Speaking of waiting around, are we also waiting for Father?"

Gloria's eyes went from twinkling to shifty. "He really wanted to come, dear, but since it's such a lovely day, I wanted to bring the phaeton, and for some odd reason, your father suddenly remembered a bit of pressing business. He told me to extend to you his deepest apologies for not meeting you here, but he said you'd understand."

Her mother really was incorrigible, and her father, to give him credit, completely adored his wife and put up with many of her antics. The one thing Douglas Beckett did balk at was willingly riding in a phaeton with Gloria at the reins.

He'd frequently told Arabella that sitting there, waiting for disaster to happen, played havoc with his nerves.

It took everything she had not to grin. "I completely understand Father's reasoning, although I really do have to point out that it is *not* a lovely day. From my view on the train, the wind looked to be growing fiercer by the second, and you and I will be frozen solid by the time we reach the house."

Gloria waved her comments away with an airy flick of her hand. "A brisk wind does wonders for a lady's complexion, and you are looking a bit peaked." She stepped closer and tilted her head. "I was going to ask you this over tea, but since Hamilton seems to be dawdling and this particular question has been plaguing me constantly, tell me what possessed you to travel across the country without your paid companion?"

She should have known that would come up eventually.

"How do you know I traveled without her?"

Gloria gestured to the crowd swarming around them. "Miss Hunt is obviously not with you, and Theodore mentioned absolutely nothing about her in his telegram, and your father told me he ran into Miss Hunt back in California, *after* you'd made your departure."

Theodore suddenly stopped talking in mid-conversation with Zayne and turned his head. "You have a paid companion?"

"I *had* a paid companion, up until about two months ago, but then she met a gentleman she claimed she couldn't live without. Since I had no intention of traveling the country with two people who are madly in love, I allowed her to get out of our agreement."

"You could have hired a new companion," Theodore said.

Arabella shrugged. "I'm perfectly capable of traveling on my own, Mr. Wilder. I'm no girl fresh out of the schoolroom, but a lady who is almost twenty-five. Those years should afford me a certain amount of freedom."

"You wouldn't have ended up in trouble if you'd been accompanied by a companion."

"I doubt even having a companion along with me would have stopped me from assisting Miss James."

"It might have slowed you down."

"Or it might have gotten another lady arrested."

"There is that," Theodore muttered.

"Time for me to check on the luggage," Zayne said before he spun on his heel and disappeared into the crowd.

Gloria shook her head. "He never has been comfortable being in the midst of squabbles."

"Who was squabbling?" Arabella and Theodore asked at the same time.

Gloria's eyes turned cunning in a split second. Her lips spread into a smile, and she began whistling a jaunty tune under her breath.

Arabella was surprised it wasn't the wedding march.

Theodore cleared his throat. "Ah, perhaps I should go look for Hamilton."

Gloria stopped whistling. "He'll be along shortly, dear. Piper and Ben noticed a vendor selling cakes, and Eliza couldn't resist indulging them." She smiled. "I must say, she's a wonderful mother to the children, very affectionate, and they adore her."

"Speaking of affectionate, may I hope that Hamilton and Eliza have ceased with their somewhat disturbing propensity of mooning over each other?" Theodore asked.

Gloria laughed. "I'm pleased to say their mooning has gotten worse. Zayne claims they're an embarrassment to the entire family, but I find them delightful."

Theodore let out a sigh. "I'm going to have to leave town again soon."

Gloria swatted him on the arm. "Now, that's no way to think, dear. Love is a glorious thing, and I'm hopeful you'll be in Hamilton's shoes someday." She sent him one of her disturbing winks and then nodded toward Arabella.

Arabella wished a huge hole would suddenly open up right in front of her so that she could leap into it and escape from her mother's embarrassing maneuvers. To her relief, Theodore ignored her mother's comment and began to whistle his own tune under his breath, thankfully not one of a romantic nature.

Needing a distraction, Arabella began to adjust her hat, but her hand stilled when a man off in the distance caught her attention. There was something familiar about him. He lifted his head, and all the breath rushed out of her in a split second as recognition set in.

He was one of the men from the farmhouse.

She hitched up her skirt and broke into a run, dodging an elderly gentleman who brandished his cane at her before she increased her pace. "Stop right there," she yelled as she jumped over a piece of black luggage, tripped on the hem of her gown, lifted her skirts higher, and plowed forward.

The man she was chasing turned for a brief moment, but then plunged into the crowd in a desperate manner, proving she was after the right man.

She developed a stitch in her side, but ignored it and the voice yelling behind her.

She raced down a small flight of stairs, satisfaction flowing through her as she realized she was gaining on the man. She pushed herself harder, leaped up on an empty bench, then launched herself into the air. As she landed on the man with a thud, the impact sent both of them tumbling to the ground, even as the breath left her in one harsh *oof*.

"Get off me," the man snarled as he sucked in a ragged breath right before putting his hands over his head when she smacked him with her reticule.

A dull thud caused her to remember that her gun was inside her bag. She stilled for just a second, but remembered the horror the man had put her and Miss James through, and hit him again.

Strong hands suddenly seized her from behind, and she felt herself being lifted into the air. Her teeth clinked together when Theodore dropped her to the ground, and she winced when she saw the barely concealed fury in his eyes.

"Have you taken leave of your senses?"

She raised her chin. "I don't believe so. Why do you ask?"

"You just attacked that man."

"Indeed I did, and for good reason. You were right about those men following me back here." She pointed to the man cowering on the ground, his hands still covering his head. "That, Mr. Wilder, is one of the men from the farmhouse. I'm hopeful you have some gadget at your disposal we can use to secure him, because I certainly don't want the man to slip away, not after the effort it took on my part to capture him."

"It wouldn't have taken any effort on your part if you'd behaved as a lady ought to behave and told me who this was in the first place. *I* would have then taken measures to apprehend him."

"It's very unattractive when you sulk."

Theodore opened his mouth, and his face turned a vivid shade of purple, but before he could get a single, scathing word out, the man on the ground suddenly rolled over and released a groan, even as he peered up at her through a small space between the fingers he had pressed over his eyes. "You're crazy."

She leaned over, peeled his hand away, and was about to give him a piece of her mind, but froze when she got a good look at the man's face.

She'd never seen this gentleman before in her life.

She'd assaulted the wrong man. Not only had she knocked him to the ground, she'd also hit him with her reticle.

She could have caused the gentleman serious injury.

Her gaze traveled over him and lingered on a large rip in the man's trousers.

She straightened, felt her cheeks heat despite the cold, and cleared her throat. "I must beg your pardon, sir." A nervous laugh slipped from her lips. "It is somewhat amusing, in a strange sort of way, but I mistook you for someone else, a dastardly criminal if you must know, but . . ."

"This is not the man from the farmhouse?" Theodore snapped, interrupting her in mid-sentence.

"I'm afraid not."

Right before her eyes, Theodore appeared to get larger. "Why, pray tell, did you not make certain he was the right man before you attacked him?"

"That would have been a little difficult to do since his back was toward me as I chased him." She nibbled on her lip. "Besides, he was acting in a very suspicious manner. He did run from me, and if that doesn't suggest guilt, I don't know what does."

The man on the ground suddenly sat up and sent her a glare. "The only thing I'm guilty of is being late for my mother's dinner. She specifically told me she's cooking a roast, and she does so hate to serve a dry roast. That's why I was moving briskly. Well, until I realized I had a crazy lady chasing after me. Then I started to run."

"I really am sorry" was all she could think to say.

"'Sorry' isn't going to stop my mother from ranting at me for being late, nor is it going to take away the pain in my head. I think we should call the authorities and allow them to straighten this matter out to my satisfaction."

Being sent back to jail would be no more than she deserved.

Before she could apologize again, Theodore stepped forward and pulled the man to his feet, dusting off the dirt that stained the man's jacket.

"I do understand your desire to see this lady held accountable for her ruthless assault on you, sir," Theodore said. "However, I must point out the fact that this lady, unfortunately, appears to suffer from a severe mental ailment, which I believe is what provoked her attack in the first place." He reached into his pocket, pulled out his billfold, and pressed a wad of bills into the man's hand. "I hope this will alleviate some of your suffering, and I would appreciate it if we could keep this little matter strictly between us."

The man looked at the bills, sent her another glare, and then nodded to Theodore before he turned and limped away without speaking another word.

"I am not unbalanced."

"Oh? Do you know of any other proper young lady who would accost an innocent gentleman, especially when said lady had a private investigator at her disposal to deal with such matters?"

She opened her mouth, but found there was absolutely nothing to say to that somewhat insightful statement, so she pursed her lips and took the arm he shoved at her. She soon found herself being nudged through a crowd of curious onlookers and felt a flicker of indignation steal over her.

"None of this would have happened if you hadn't put the thought of those men in my mind."

Theodore stopped in his tracks, leaving her no choice but to stop as well. "You cannot truly believe any of this is my fault."

She shrugged, the action causing a lock of hair to fall in her eyes. She pushed it out of her face with her free hand, noticing she seemed to have lost her hat. She glanced over her shoulder, saw that people were still regarding her curiously, and decided that hatless was how she was going to have to travel home.

". . . and granted, I did bring up the idea that those men might follow you back to New York, but they certainly weren't on the train with us, and it's not as if I expected them to be waiting for you at the train station."

She drew in a breath, let it out slowly, and prodded him into motion. "If you would have explained that more thoroughly, I wouldn't have reacted as I did. How was I to know you didn't believe the men would have time to meet me here, and come to think of it . . . how would they even know where to find me?"

For some odd reason, Theodore's hand tightened on her arm, but then he relaxed and continued moving forward without bothering to respond to her question.

"Is there something you haven't told me?"

"What possessed you to hit that poor man over the head with your reticule?"

Arabella blinked. "I think we've already discussed that incident to satisfaction. I thought he was the criminal who'd tried to abduct me, so hitting him about the head with the only object I had on hand seemed the logical thing to do."

"It wasn't logical in the least. Ladies do not beat innocent gentlemen with their dainty reticules, and why in the world was your reticule actually causing the man serious pain?"

"Don't you remember? My pistol's inside."

"Well, I suppose we can give thanks to God that you didn't decide to use that pistol, or we might have had a dead man on our hands instead of a slightly bruised one."

"I wouldn't have killed him," she muttered before she stumbled when Theodore came to another abrupt stop. She glanced in the direction he was currently staring and resisted the urge to sigh.

Gloria, Zayne, her brother, Hamilton, and a beautiful lady with red hair and sparkling blue eyes were standing before them, all with different expressions on their faces.

Gloria looked disheartened. Zayne looked amused. Hamilton, well, he might just be smiling because he was happy to see her, and the beautiful lady she assumed was Eliza was looking exasperated.

"Honestly, Theodore, you're probably scaring old ladies and children with that scowl on your face," the beautiful lady said as she stepped forward. "I told everyone it was not a good idea for you to run off and fetch Arabella, but did anyone listen to me? Of course not," she finished before anyone had a chance to respond. She grinned, and a delightful dimple popped out on her cheek as she moved to Arabella's side. She sent Theodore an arch look, which had him dropping his hold on Arabella, and then she pulled her into a hug.

"I've been so looking forward to meeting you, my dear sister. I'm Eliza."

Arabella caught a scent of violets mixed with berries before Eliza gave her one last squeeze and stepped back. "I hope we'll be the best of friends, and I also hope you're not too put out that your brother and I got married without you in town." She grinned. "I just couldn't seem to wait."

Eliza was completely delightful, and Arabella couldn't help but fall immediately in love with her new sister.

"I'm certainly not put out with you for marrying my brother, Eliza. Hamilton was in desperate need of someone to keep him in line, and from what I've heard so far, you're perfect for that job."

Eliza beamed back at her. "Why, thank you, Arabella. I think you and I are destined to get along famously." She turned and gestured Hamilton forward.

Hamilton smiled and obliged his wife, reaching Arabella's side and lifting her off her feet. He gave her an enthusiastic hug and then set her back down even as his smile widened. "You missed my wedding."

"I could respond that you should have waited, but after meeting your lovely wife, I can understand why you didn't."

"We ordered you a dress from B. Altman's *and* a special hat, but you never showed up, Aunt Arabella."

She looked down and found Piper, her five-year-old niece scowling up at her. She glanced to Piper's right and saw Ben, Piper's younger brother, watching her with an almost identical scowl on his face.

That was rather odd. Normally she got along famously with her niece and nephew. She was about to ask them to explain their less-than-pleasant greeting when Theodore suddenly stepped forward, bent down, and opened up his arms.

Childish squeals of delight rent the air, and she could only watch in dumbfounded amazement as Piper and Ben threw themselves into Theodore's arms.

The infuriating gentleman of only a few minutes before was nowhere to be found as he tickled and laughed with Piper and Ben. He finally released his hold on them and straightened, but still reached out and patted Ben on the head and pulled Piper's pigtail.

It was not something she'd ever expected to see him do. Who would have thought he'd have a way with children?

It was disconcerting, that's what it was, and it made him seem almost . . . likable.

"What took you so long to find Aunt Arabella, Mr. Wilder?"

Piper asked. "Ben and I thought you'd be back in plenty of time for the wedding."

"Your aunt seems to have the unfortunate habit of being hard to find."

"I heard Daddy tell Mama that Aunt Arabella got arrested," Piper said before she turned and sent Arabella another scowl. "Did you murder someone?"

Arabella released a snort. "What a thing to ask, and no, I didn't murder anyone, although I have recently been tempted."

If anything, Piper's scowl intensified. "You were glaring at poor Mr. Wilder, and he helped save me and Ben from a horrible, horrible death."

Theodore hadn't mentioned anything at all about saving Piper's and Ben's lives. She opened her mouth to lecture Theodore on his insufficient storytelling abilities, but before she could speak, a whistle rent the air and the sound of a lady's voice followed.

"Mrs. Beckett, yoo-hoo, Mrs. Beckett."

Arabella turned and found Mrs. Murdock, one of New York's most colorful society matrons, rapidly approaching and tugging her daughter Felicia by the arm as she set her sights on them.

"I cannot believe what a lucky circumstance this is, running into all of you here," Mrs. Murdock exclaimed. "Felicia and I just saw my dear aunt off on a train bound for Ohio." She beamed at Arabella. "It's so lovely to see you've returned home, Miss Beckett, but . . . good heavens, what have you done with your hair? Your pins are falling out and . . . dear me, is your hair lopsided?"

How to explain?

To her relief, Zayne stepped forward and grinned at Mrs. Murdock. "My sister has always been one to embrace the latest fashions, and I assumed her unusual look was a new rage she'd picked up in California."

"Or jail," she heard Theodore mutter behind her.

She stepped back slowly and brought the heel of her shoe down right on top of his toes.

A soft *umph* was his only response, but it was enough . . . for now.

"How . . . interesting," Mrs. Murdock said slowly. "I'm not certain that particular rage will catch on here, Miss Beckett, so you might consider letting your hair grow out again, only that might take some time."

"Well, it was delightful seeing everyone," Felicia said, suddenly speaking up. "I fear the weather is beginning to turn, so Mother and I should be on our way."

"But I haven't seen Gloria in forever," Mrs. Murdock said. "Or Arabella, for that matter. And Eliza and I haven't had a proper talk since that disaster at my ball."

Gloria stepped forward. "Then you simply must agree to come to the small dinner party I'm holding tonight in honor of Arabella's return. We'll catch up then."

"I would adore that," Mrs. Murdock said.

"Do bring Felicia and your husband, and if any of those charming sons of yours aren't busy tonight, by all means bring them as well," Gloria said with another telling wink.

It would seem her mother wasn't exactly particular anymore about which gentlemen she shoved into Arabella's path.

"I'm afraid my sons have already made plans to attend the opera this evening," Mrs. Murdock said. "I'll be certain to tell Jeffrey, though, that your daughter has returned to town. He's always spoken very highly of her." She sent Arabella a smile, but then her eyes widened as she glanced to Arabella's right. "Mr. Wilder, I didn't see you there. Is something the matter, dear? You've got a most peculiar look on your face."

Arabella shot a glance at Theodore, and once again the man was scowling. But then he blinked, the look disappeared, and a charming smile spread over his face. "I was just contemplating why all of us are standing around when we'll soon be together again at the dinner party I had no idea Gloria was hosting but am certainly looking forward to attending." He nodded to Felicia. "Miss Murdock, you're looking lovely today."

Felicia turned red, grabbed her mother's arm, and began pulling her away.

"Felicia, what has gotten into you?" Arabella heard Mrs. Murdock mutter before her voice drifted to nothing and they disappeared from view.

Gloria waited until Mrs. Murdock's hat was out of sight before she moved to Arabella's side and frowned. "Dear, you have yet to explain why you went running off into the crowd in that surprising fashion. By Theodore's less-than-pleased expression when you returned, I'm afraid you've once again become embroiled in something uncharacteristically disturbing."

Arabella blew out a breath. "Mother, in case you've forgotten, I've just arrived here. While I would love nothing more than to explain my recent behavior, may I suggest we wait to do so until we're driving home? If you're hosting a dinner party tonight, I, for one, will need time to freshen up."

"That's a stellar idea, Arabella" Zayne said. "I took the liberty of having your luggage delivered to Hamilton's carriage, while Theodore's has been taken to mine."

"Were three carriages really necessary?" Arabella asked.

"I don't consider Mother's phaeton a real carriage, and besides, there is the pesky little matter of her driving abilities to consider." Zayne smiled at Gloria when she let out a huff and then turned back to Arabella. "It's true that I could have traveled with Hamilton and Eliza, but, well, just look at them, exchanging those nauseating looks all the time, and well . . . it was best I brought my own conveyance."

"Why can't I ride with you?" Arabella asked.

"Because you and Theodore seem just about ready to strangle each other. I'm going to allow my friend a respite from your company, and hopefully, by the time he rejoins us this evening, he'll not completely regret agreeing to fetch you home."

Before she could formulate a witty response to that piece of nonsense, Zayne turned on his heel, as did Theodore, and the two gentlemen walked rapidly away from them. Hamilton, Eliza, and the children followed a moment later.

"Well, that turned out better than I expected," Gloria said before she took Arabella's hand and tugged her forward. "I was certain as I watched you and Theodore bicker that there really was no hope, but . . . my goodness, Theodore looked quite fierce when Mrs. Murdock mentioned Jeffrey." She squeezed Arabella's hand. "And speaking of Jeffrey Murdock, if Theodore doesn't come up to scratch, Jeffrey would be a fine catch." She paused and caught Arabella's eye. "It is so lovely that you've finally come home. I've decided, seeing that Hamilton's so happy, my new mission in life is to find you and your brother suitable mates."

Arabella suddenly felt the most pressing urge to go back to jail.

6

Theodore smiled as Piper stole up beside him and took his hand. She began chatting about anything and everything under the sun as they left the train station. She tugged him over to where Zayne was standing beside a shiny buggy. "That sure is a nice buggy, Uncle Zayne."

"Thank you, Piper. I got it just last week. It's called a Corning Buggy, and even though it's not as fast as my phaeton, it does allow me more room." Zayne gestured under the seat. "The porter went ahead and stowed your luggage, Theodore, so we can get on our way." He nodded to Hamilton. "You'll be going to Mother's house?"

"Since my carriage is stuffed with Arabella's trunks, yes, I'll be making an extra stop," Hamilton said. "We'll be lucky to have enough room to sit."

"But . . . I wanted Mr. Wilder to ride with us," Piper said as her pretty blue eyes suddenly got a little misty, and she dropped Theodore's hand to take a swipe at her nose.

Theodore squatted down beside her. "I'm not going to your grandmother's house, darling. I have to go to my house, but I'll see you later. I told your grandmother I'd come for dinner, remember?"

"But that's forever away from now, and . . . I have a lot of questions to ask you."

"What kind of questions?"

Piper opened her mouth and, before he could even blink, began launching questions at him with rapid speed. "Why did Aunt Arabella get sent to jail, and why won't anyone in my family explain it properly to me? Did she really murder someone and everyone's trying to keep it hushed up, or . . . maybe she got really angry at some of those men who protest at her rallies, and she got into a tussle with them." She drew in a breath of air and arched a tiny brow at him. "Well?"

So much for believing the little darling had wanted him to ride in her carriage because she'd missed him.

"Well, hmm . . . that's a lot of questions, Piper, and all I'm going to tell you is that your aunt didn't murder anyone, nor did she get into a 'tussle' with protesters, although . . ." His voice trailed off as he shook his head. Piper was only five and certainly didn't need to know anything about her aunt assaulting an innocent gentleman at the train station.

Piper's lower lip began to tremble. "But you haven't explained anything properly either, Mr. Theodore. Are you sure you can't ride with us?"

His heart gave a little lurch at the extremely pathetic look she was sending him. "I suppose I could sit on top of Arabella's luggage . . ."

"Piper, really," Eliza said as she moved to stand by her stepdaughter and chucked her under the chin as Theodore straightened. "Stop trying to manipulate Theodore with your crocodile tears in order to get answers we've recently told you were none of your business." She let out a snort. "Besides, one of the reasons Theodore was so keen to leave town was because he's very uncomfortable around affectionate people.

I'm quite certain the last thing he wants to do at the moment is ride in a carriage with your daddy and me. I swear he breaks into a sweat every time I even hold your father's hand."

Piper's lip stopped trembling. "You do more than hold Daddy's hand, Mama. You kiss him, all the time."

"Eww," Ben proclaimed as he sidled up next to Theodore and plopped his thumb in his mouth.

Theodore laughed and scooped Ben up in his arms. "Someday you'll appreciate a fine-looking woman and will most likely try to kiss her."

"Nope."

"I'll remind you of this conversation in around fifteen years."

"He's only three," Piper said.

Theodore handed Ben to Eliza and hefted Piper up, the sounds of her shrieks warming him down to his toes. He hugged her close for a moment and then held her away from him. "Just so we're clear, Miss Beckett, you will not even consider kissing until you're at least thirty."

"Twenty."

"Fair enough, so long as you promise to have whatever young gentleman you set your sights on speak with me before you allow him a kiss."

Piper narrowed her eyes. "Why?"

"I think that's a wonderful idea," Hamilton said as he held out his hands and Theodore passed Piper over to him. "I'll be sure to remind Mr. Wilder of his offer when you get older."

"Nobody will ever want to kiss me then," Piper said. "I'll be one of those, those . . . spider ladies."

Theodore grinned. "Do you mean spinster ladies?"

Piper nodded. "That's what I'll be, a spinster."

Theodore tilted his head. "You, my dear girl, will have the men falling at your feet, begging for your favor."

Piper looked positively delighted even as Hamilton released

a growl and set Piper on the ground. "She doesn't need encouragement, Theodore. Eliza and I are perfectly aware of the fact we'll have our hands full when she's older."

Eliza laughed. "We'll just return the favor once Theodore has children of his own."

"I wouldn't count on that anytime soon," Theodore said. "I have yet to find a suitable wife."

Zayne cleared his throat. "Perhaps if you stopped annoying all the ladies on a frequent basis, you wouldn't have that problem."

"I rarely annoy all the ladies, Zayne, only a select few, and I wouldn't annoy those few if they'd start behaving," Theodore said before Eliza began to sputter.

"Perhaps we should get on the road before you say something that will really get you into trouble," Zayne muttered.

"But Mr. Theodore still hasn't told us why Aunt Arabella ended up arrested." Piper plopped her hands on her thin hips. "And even though Daddy keeps saying it's none of my business, I know he's curious." She nodded. "I still believe it was something dastardly, like a shooting, even if nobody ended up dead."

"Well, there *might* have been a shooting, but you are too young to hear the particulars," Theodore said, not surprised in the least when Piper's lower lip suddenly jutted out. He ignored it and smiled. "Now then, Zayne and I really must get on the road, but I will see everyone later." He sent Piper a wink. "I might even feel compelled to bring you a treat if you promise to behave for the rest of the afternoon."

"Would that work with all those other ladies you think need to behave?" Piper asked.

"You know, you might just be on to something, Piper." He tousled her hair, tweaked Ben's nose, and quickly climbed into the buggy when he heard Eliza sputtering once again behind him. He sent her a jaunty wave as he watched Hamilton tug her over to their carriage and turned when Zayne landed on the seat beside him. "I certainly appreciate you seeing me home, Zayne, even if this buggy of yours is not exactly appropriate for the weather."

"I think I must have some of my mother in me," Zayne said before he flicked the reins lightly over the horses and the buggy rolled into the street. "And no need to thank me for seeing you home. I more than owe you for bringing Arabella back."

"You never told me she was a little . . . difficult."

Zayne winced. "Can you forgive me?"

He waved the comment away. "It wasn't all horrible, Zayne. Your sister is actually incredibly intelligent, which did allow us to have some interesting debates."

"She's also beautiful."

Theodore frowned. "That goes without saying, but I got the distinct impression she prefers her intelligence over her beauty. Not once did I ever see her pull out a hand mirror to check her appearance."

Zayne released a dramatic sigh. "She's never been normal."

"On that we can both agree."

Zayne grinned, but then sobered. "I must warn you that my parents are going to be throwing questions at you this evening even faster than Piper did. They're incredibly concerned about Arabella's arrest and even more concerned about the two of you spending so much time alone together."

"That wouldn't have happened if she'd had her companion with her."

Zayne steered the horses around a slow-moving delivery wagon and then shrugged. "It was only a matter of time until Arabella found a way to get rid of Miss Hunt, but there's nothing to do about that now. Perhaps you should explain everything to me. That way, if my parents get any strange ideas, I'll be better equipped to lend you my assistance."

"Strange ideas?"

"Shotgun weddings spring to mind."

Theodore swallowed and immediately launched into an explanation of what had transpired over the course of the last few weeks. Zayne's expression went from amused to slightly horrified by the time Theodore had finished his tale.

"So Arabella shot a man, tumbled into something you believe involves the law, and . . . might still be in danger?"

"That about sums it up. May I suggest, before we continue, that you pull the horses over?" Theodore said as he gripped his seat with one hand and waved apologetically with his other to a gentleman who was sprinting out of their way. "You seem somewhat distracted, and we'll never make your mother's dinner if you maim someone."

"Good thinking," Zayne said, pulling the horses to the side of the road and bringing them to a halt. "I'm afraid I'm still bemused regarding the danger Arabella might be in."

"I readily admit I'm a touch bemused as well." He let out a breath. "All I can say is that I believe those men who were holding Miss James, and then lured Arabella to that farmhouse, most likely are, or were, operating a very lucrative venture. Your sister, as you said before, is remarkably beautiful, and I'm afraid she might be too tempting for them to ignore."

"I said beautiful, not 'remarkably' beautiful."

Hmm, so he had. Theodore cleared his throat. "I do have to check in at my office tomorrow, make sure there's nothing pressing waiting for me, but then I'm heading back to Gilman. I don't like leaving matters unresolved, and there was just something about that town that had my instincts humming."

"Would you like me to accompany you?"

"While I truly appreciate your offer, Zayne, your time might be better spent keeping an eye on your sister. I can certainly put some of my men on guard duty, but I have the strangest feeling Arabella would balk at that. Knowing your sister, she might show her displeasure by shooting one of them or bashing them over the head with her reticule."

Zayne winced. "I still cannot believe she attacked that man at the station. You must allow me to reimburse you the amount you gave that gentleman for his troubles."

"There's no need for that. Truth be told, I was a little responsible for what happened. I did make the mistake of telling Arabella someone might be following her." He shook his head. "Even though your sister claims to be a progressive lady, she is *still* a lady, and as such, her reasoning can be easily swayed by a man's suggestions."

"It's no wonder she was staring daggers at you when you first came back to us."

"I didn't actually tell her that, mostly because I hadn't thought of it, but it will be interesting to see her reaction once I do get around to sharing that thought."

Zayne narrowed his eyes. "Why in the world would you put yourself through that, unless . . . you enjoy arguing with her?"

Theodore blinked. "Of course I don't enjoy arguing with your sister, Zayne, but that's neither here nor there. May I count on you to keep an eye on Arabella while I'm away?"

"It's my job to look after my sister," Zayne said. "Your responsibility ended when you handed her over to my mother back at the station."

"You know that's not true," Theodore said. "My responsibility won't end until I settle matters back in Gilman, but I was under the impression you were leaving soon to join your Miss Collins. It will be difficult for you to watch Arabella if you're in a different state."

"I'm sure Helena will understand if I delay joining her for a week or so to help Arabella."

"I got the feeling Arabella and Helena weren't the best of friends."

"Yes, well, no need to go into that at the moment. You

have more than enough troubles to occupy your thoughts." Zayne flicked the reins and set the buggy back on the road, silence settling over them as they traversed the busy street. They turned on Park Avenue, and Theodore realized that although they only had a few blocks to go to reach his home, they were almost to his parents' house. The warm reunion he'd witnessed between Arabella and her family sprang to mind and he felt a trickle of remorse run over him. He'd mentioned to his mother over a month ago that he was traveling out of town, but the thought never entered his head to send her a telegram explaining he'd been delayed.

"Would it be too much of a bother to ask you to set me down at my parents' house?" he asked.

"Not at all, and you must extend your mother an invitation to dinner this evening from me if she and your father don't already have plans."

Theodore barely suppressed a shudder. "That wouldn't be a good idea. Mother's been extremely vocal of late regarding the fact that I'm getting ever closer to thirty and haven't settled on a wife. If I need remind you, there will be at least three eligible ladies at your parents' house tonight."

"Theodore, I know your mother, and I hardly believe she would find Arabella or Agatha suitable for you."

"True, but Miss Murdock will also be in attendance, and she's completely respectable."

"You don't like Felicia?" Zayne asked as he pulled the buggy to a halt in front of the Park Avenue mansion Theodore had grown up in.

"Felicia's a lovely lady, but I seem to make her incredibly nervous."

"You're probably right," Zayne said. "Felicia is a very retiring sort, and you're . . . not."

"I think I've just been insulted."

Zayne laughed. "You need someone with spirit, someone

who will stand up to you and not allow you to run roughshod over them."

"I don't run roughshod over ladies."

"You do, but that's a conversation for another day."

Theodore jumped from the buggy, fetched his bags, and turned back to Zayne. "You weren't bringing up that lady-with-spirit business because you're subtly trying to push your sister at me, were you?"

"Don't be an idiot. I'd never encourage you to pursue Arabella. The two of you are not well suited in the least. You'd kill each other within a month if you spent much time together."

"All right then, as long as we're in agreement," Theodore said as Zayne sent him a little salute, flicked the reins, and took off down the street.

It was good to have friends who understood him more than he realized.

Theodore strode up the sidewalk, pausing to set his bags down before knocking on the door. It was opened immediately by Mr. Stewart, the Wilders' butler. The man's weathered face split into a smile as he ushered Theodore into the house before grabbing the bags from the porch.

"I am certainly glad to see you, Mr. Wilder," Mr. Stewart said, closing the door behind them. He lowered his voice. "Your mother was just speaking about you this morning, and I'm hopeful your arrival will improve her spirits."

"She's in ill spirits?"

"She is, as is your sister, who is also here. If I may be so bold, sir, she's in an even worse frame of mind than your mother."

"Maybe we should just pretend I never stopped by to visit."

"There's no cause to be a coward," Mr. Stewart said as he pointed him down the hall. "They're in the blue room. I'll send fresh tea."

"Is my father at home?"

"He sent a note an hour ago stating he'd be late. I understand your sister's husband, Mr. Gibson, is with your father, and I fear that is the reason for the dismal mood which has settled over the house."

Something that felt very much like worry hit him out of the blue, which was peculiar. He'd never worried about his mother and sister before, believing they'd been successful in achieving what every woman longed to achieve: securing husbands who provided a more-than-substantial living.

"You said they're in the blue room?" he asked.

"They are, and I will meet you there shortly with your tea." Mr. Stewart bowed and made his exit, leaving Theodore to make his way to the blue room. He hesitated outside the open door as his gaze traveled across the room. His mother was sitting on a beautiful brocade chair, her needlepoint lying in her lap, while his sister sat on the edge of a chaise covered in green silk, staring morosely into the fire. He forced his feet into motion.

"This looks like a cheery atmosphere," he said, making his way to his mother's side.

Louise Wilder looked up. "Theodore, this is a surprise."

Theodore leaned over, kissed his mother's cheek, and then straightened, wincing when she blinked somewhat owlishly back at him. When was the last time he'd felt compelled to kiss his own mother? He turned to his sister. "Hello, Kate."

Katherine Gibson sent him a glare. "You know I don't care to be called Kate."

"I suppose I could call you Mrs. Gibson, but that seems overly formal."

"Would you care for tea?" Louise asked when Katherine began to sputter. "I'm afraid it might be tepid by this time."

"Mr. Stewart is fetching a fresh pot," Theodore returned.

"He always did cater to you," Katherine muttered.

Theodore sat down beside his sister, taking hold of her hand and refusing to let go when she tried to pull it out of his grasp. "Are you put out with me for some reason?"

Katherine tugged harder. "Don't be silly."

"Your sister is never put out with you, darling," Louise said. "The two of you have always gotten along quite well."

Did he get along with Katherine? The truth of the matter was he barely knew her anymore. She was always at family functions, but they never talked, not about anything important, and yet . . . he distinctly remembered, during one of his slightly combative conversations with Arabella, making the claim his sister was happy.

If this was what happy looked like, he hated to think how she would appear if she was miserable.

"How's Harold?" he asked.

"Harold?" Katherine repeated.

"Your husband?"

Katherine narrowed her eyes. "Why do you want to know how Harold is?"

Theodore narrowed his eyes right back at her. "Shouldn't I want to know how my brother-in-law is?"

A rather bland expression suddenly drifted over her face. "Oh, you're trying to make polite conversation."

"No," Theodore corrected, "I'm trying to figure out what's wrong with your husband."

"My goodness, Theodore, there is nothing wrong with Harold," Louise said. "He and your father are currently out having a late lunch, and then they'll be attending a charity event."

"Father and Harold are going to a charity event?"

"That is what his note stated," Louise said, her voice dropping off when Mr. Stewart, followed by a maid, entered the room. Theodore watched as the maid put the tea on the table, curtsied, and left.

"Will you be staying long, Mr. Wilder?" Mr. Stewart asked.

"I'm afraid not, Mr. Stewart. I've been away for a month and I do need to check on my house. Make sure it's still standing and all that."

"Very good, sir," Mr. Stewart said with a bow. "Will you need transportation home?"

"Why would he need transportation?" Katherine asked. "Didn't he get here on a horse?"

"Zayne Beckett dropped me off."

For some reason, Mr. Stewart turned sharply on his heel and, although a gentleman of a rather advanced age, practically sprinted from the room.

He arched a brow at his sister. "What was that all about?"

Katherine's face turned a delightful shade of pink. "I'm sure I have no idea."

"Your sister used to have a rather small infatuation with Mr. Beckett, and I'm afraid she used to coerce Mr. Stewart into accompanying her as she forced our driver to take the carriage again, and again, and again, past Zayne's residence," Louise said.

Theodore felt his mouth drop open. "You never told me you liked Zayne."

Katherine's pink face turned to red. "I didn't want you to mock me, and besides, it was a worthless infatuation. Zayne's been more than open about his association with Helena, and everyone has always known they'd eventually get married."

"Which I have always felt is a true shame," Louise said as she rose to her feet and began pouring out the tea. "Zayne Beckett is far too nice of a gentleman to be burdened with Helena forever, but to each his own."

Theodore stood up, walked to his mother's side, and accepted the two cups she handed him. He handed a cup of tea to Katherine, and then settled back down next to her on the chaise with his own cup. He took a sip, swallowed, and shook his head.

"I wonder if he ever knew."

"If you say anything to him . . ." Katherine said before she gulped down some tea and promptly choked on it.

Theodore set his cup aside and pounded her soundly on the back. "Are you all right?"

"She'll be fine," Louise said, "especially if you stop teasing her. Honestly, I don't know what's gotten into you." She edged down on her chair. "Perhaps it would be wise to change the subject. Tell me, dear, how was your business trip?"

"It wasn't exactly business, Mother, and I'll explain further in just a bit, but first tell me about this charity event Father and Harold are attending. Why aren't the two of you with them?"

Louise smiled a smile that was less than amused. "Apparently this event is being held in a church in a rather rough section of town, thus the reason Katherine and I have been excluded."

"Since when has Father shown an interest in church charities?" Theodore asked.

"Are you questioning your father's faith?"

"I wasn't aware Father had a faith to question."

"As if you do," Katherine muttered under her breath.

He couldn't ever remember a time his family had discussed faith, and after being with Arabella, a lady who brought God into conversations as easily as she breathed, it now struck him as somewhat sad.

"I believe in God," he began slowly, "not that I enjoy a close relationship with Him as I know others do, but I know He guides my life, even if I believe His guidance is slightly distant. I cannot claim I'm an overly devout gentleman, but I try to live my life according to God's rules. I'm hopeful that someday I'll be able to say my spiritual journey has experienced growth."

Katherine looked at him for a long minute and then began to fidget.

He'd made her uncomfortable, probably because *he* wasn't comfortable discussing God, and he certainly couldn't compare to Arabella's comfort with the subject.

How would it feel to have such an abiding faith?

Before he could think of anything to say to ease the tension that had settled over the room, his mother set her teacup on the table with an uncharacteristic thud and smiled brightly in his direction.

"Getting back to why your sister and I are not in the most pleasant frames of mind," Louise said. "We had made plans to go to dinner with your father and Harold, but they canceled our plans without even allowing us the courtesy of a chance to respond."

Even though his mother was smiling, there was fury pouring out of her eyes. He'd never once seen his mother display anything other than slight disapproval.

"You could always join me for dinner," Theodore heard come out of his mouth, even as his heart began to ache when his mother and sister sent him looks of obvious astonishment.

"I fear I must have misheard, Katherine, but I swear Theodore just invited us out to dinner with him," Louise said slowly.

Theodore summoned up a smile. "I've been invited to dine at Douglas and Gloria Beckett's house, and Zayne made a point of telling me to extend you an invitation. The dinner begins at six."

Louise frowned. "You've never asked us to accompany you to dinner."

"Then I've been very remiss in my duties as a son."

Louise stood up and moved to stand in front of Theodore,

leaning over to touch his forehead. "Are you feeling well, dear?"

Another pang settled in his heart. "I'm fine."

"He looks fine to me," Katherine said, "although he is acting unusual."

"He must be tired from his trip. That would explain his odd mood," Louise said, surprising Theodore when she scooted next to him on the chaise. "What were you doing while you were out of town?"

"I was fetching Miss Arabella Beckett home."

"Why?"

"My objective was to get her back in time for Hamilton Beckett's wedding, but unfortunately, Miss Beckett was rather difficult to find."

"She was lost?" Katherine asked.

"*Misplaced* is a better word."

"How does one get misplaced?" Louise asked.

"If you knew Miss Beckett, you'd understand."

Louise bit her lip. "Now that I think about it, I don't know if we should come with you tonight. Your father does not approve of progressive women, and Miss Beckett is one of the most progressive women in the country."

"Harold would definitely not approve of me associating with such an independent, and need I say, vocal lady," Katherine said.

Alarm shot over Theodore when his mother and Katherine exchanged some type of odd look that he didn't comprehend before both ladies jumped to their feet and headed for the door.

His mother suddenly paused and looked over her shoulder at him. "You may return for us at exactly thirty minutes before six and not a moment sooner. Katherine and I need to make ourselves presentable for the dinner party." With that, she hitched up her skirt and raced out of the room behind Katherine.

He simply sat there for a moment, at a complete loss as to what had just occurred, until the thought came to him that he'd somehow managed, unintentionally of course, to open up a rather large can of worms.

He had a sneaking suspicion his father and brother-in-law were not going to be amused.

7

"I do so hate to say this, Mother, but it seems that while I've been away, your abilities with the reins have taken a turn for the worse," Arabella said as she leapt off the phaeton before the groom could assist her, resisted the urge to kiss the ground, and then looked up to discover her mother scowling down at her.

"My driving is perfectly acceptable," Gloria said before she accepted the hand of another groom and stepped onto the sidewalk in front of their Fifth Avenue mansion. "It was hardly my fault that gentleman dashed in front of me and almost caused me to run him over. Why, if I wasn't so proficient with the reins, he would have suffered a horrible fate."

"The only reason we were able to miss him was because another gentleman, one, I might add, who seemed quite elderly, hobbled to his aid and pushed him out of the way."

Gloria ignored that statement as she looked past Arabella and grinned. "Oh, lovely, my dear friend has come to call."

Arabella turned. A lady about her mother's age was striding their way, with a beautiful younger lady by her side. The younger lady was gowned in the first state of fashion and had an air about her that sizzled with barely suppressed energy.

"Cora, what a delightful surprise," Gloria said as she gave the woman a hug, then did the same to the younger lady. "Agatha, you're looking as lovely as ever. Come, I've been dying to introduce you to my daughter." She pulled the two ladies over to Arabella. "Arabella, this is my very good friend, Cora Watson, and her daughter, Agatha."

Cora beamed at Arabella. "We're not here for long, since everyone does need to get ready for the dinner party, but I just had to make certain you returned home safely."

"That was very kind of you, Mrs. Watson," Arabella said.

Mrs. Watson's eyes twinkled as she lowered her voice. "If you must know, I had planned on going with your mother to greet you at the station, but then . . ." She gestured with her head toward the phaeton and shuddered.

Arabella swallowed a laugh. "I do believe that might have been the reasoning behind my own father not making the journey to welcome me home."

"I am standing right here," Gloria muttered before she turned to Agatha. "Tell me, dear, is that why you accompanied your mother? Were you afraid I'd done Arabella in with my driving?"

"Not at all," Agatha said. "I simply came to make certain Arabella had not suffered overly much from her forced time in Theodore's company."

She and Agatha Watson were destined to become great friends.

"Theodore is a charming gentleman, Agatha," Cora said, "and eligible."

"Theodore is only charming with ladies who do not challenge him, Mother, and you of all people should know Theodore is the last man I'd ever consider as a future mate." Agatha reached out, grabbed hold of Arabella's hand, and gave it a good pat. "I said from the very beginning that it was madness to send Theodore after you. You're known for your independent ways, and putting you and Theodore in direct contact with each other was a certain recipe for disaster."

"He can be difficult at times," Arabella agreed with a smile, "and I did, upon occasion, long to throttle the gentleman." Her smile widened. "I must say I'm delighted to finally make your acquaintance, Miss Watson. Theodore mentioned you frequently, and any lady who has the ability to confound that gentleman with her progressive ways is a lady after my own heart."

Agatha's smile dimmed. "Miss Beckett, we've met before at a rally."

"Have we really?"

Agatha heaved a dramatic sigh. "Why is it that no one in your family ever remembers me? Zayne thought I was fresh out of the schoolroom when we ran into each other a few months back, and then I encountered your mother in Central Park and she didn't recall meeting me, and now . . . you."

"I can assure you that Arabella will never forget you again, dear. As for Zayne, well . . ." Gloria glanced at Cora. They exchanged a strange look and then, without speaking another word, spun on their heels and marched up to and into the house, closing the door behind them with a resounding thud.

"What was that about?" Arabella asked.

"They're plotting," Agatha replied. "They're always plotting these days." She took Arabella's arm and began to stroll toward the house. "One would think that since Hamilton and Eliza only just got married, our mothers would be satisfied for a while, but instead they seem to have come to the conclusion that everyone needs to enter into the state of wedded bliss. Quite frankly, they've turned scary." Agatha stopped walking and grinned. "I have high hopes they'll settle their attention on you now that you've returned home. You are older than I, after all, and I'm sure they'll take that into consideration."

"I'm not *that* much older," Arabella said, "but I must admit my mother has already informed me that she's determined to see me married. Knowing she's joined forces with your mother sends chills down my spine."

"There's the prodigal daughter at last."

Arabella turned from a chuckling Agatha and laughed in delight. She let go of Agatha's arm and raced up the steps, launching herself into her father's embrace.

Douglas Beckett gave her a hard squeeze before he set her away from him, his eyes twinkling down at her. "I hope you're not too upset with me for not meeting you at the station, dear." His glance slid over to the phaeton that the groom was beginning to drive away, and just like Mrs. Watson, he shuddered.

Arabella laughed again. "I knew exactly why you didn't accompany Mother, and besides, you and I saw each other not so long ago, so it's not as if we've been parted forever."

"Speaking of being parted, though, when you left California ahead of me, I was under the impression you were simply leaving early to catch a rally or two. From the telegrams Mr. Wilder sent back, it seems as if you attended a good dozen, and what were you thinking by leaving Miss Hunt behind?"

"I was hoping you wouldn't find out about Miss Hunt."

"I ran into the lady at the fish market, three days after you departed."

"Rotten luck there," Arabella muttered before she brightened. "But as you can see, I made it back perfectly unscathed and with a barrel of stories to share with you."

"Stories which will have to wait, since your mother is determined to throw this dinner party to welcome you home," Douglas said before he looked over her head. "Ah, Miss Watson, I didn't know you were here."

"Hello, Mr. Beckett," Agatha said as she climbed the steps to join them. "I didn't want to interrupt your reunion."

"Very kind of you," Douglas said. "Did you come with your mother, or did Zayne bring you?"

Agatha turned a lovely shade of pink.

Arabella blinked and then blinked again. Could it be that the delightful lady blushing right in front of her carried a bit of affection for Zayne? If that was the case, well, she'd certainly have to push things along. Agatha was a definite improvement over Helena, and—

"I came with my mother," Agatha said, abruptly pulling Arabella out of her daydream. "But look, there's Hamilton's carriage. What's he doing here?"

"Hamilton and Eliza took my luggage because Mother didn't think it would fit in the phaeton," Arabella answered.

"I'm surprised you didn't make the claim *you* wouldn't fit in the phaeton," Douglas said.

"Believe me, it did cross my mind, but then Zayne told me Hamilton and Eliza have a tendency to, well, display affection for each other at times, and I decided braving Mother's driving was the more pleasant option."

"Their 'affection' will ensure I'll have another grandbaby before too long," Gloria said, stepping outside as she settled her attention on Arabella and Agatha. "Our next order of business will be finding suitable gentlemen for the two of you." She sent them a nod, then disappeared once again through the door.

"Maybe I should consider another extended trip," Arabella said.

Douglas laughed. "You'll do no such thing. The holidays are right around the corner, and we expect you to remain in town to enjoy the festivities. Besides, haven't you had enough adventures for a while?"

"I enjoy adventures," Arabella said, "and everything about my latest one turned out fine in the end."

"Thanks to the efforts of Mr. Wilder, whom I don't seem to see at the moment," Douglas said.

"Zayne's taking him home," Arabella said before she narrowed her eyes. "Why?"

"I need to have a chat with him."

"Why?"

Douglas shrugged. "You spent quite a lot of time alone with the gentleman, and while your mother and I do encourage you to live your life to the fullest, there are still rules, and you've unfortunately broken quite a few of them."

Arabella sighed. "Father, I understand your concern, but nothing untoward happened between Theodore and me. We barely tolerated each other's company. I'll be completely mortified if you do something unexpected, such as pulling out your rifle and demanding that Theodore make an honest woman of me."

"He is considered quite the catch," Douglas pointed out. "He's handsome too, from what I've heard ladies say."

"He's also chauvinistic, arrogant, and believes women are best kept in the kitchen or at parties. And while this is certainly a fascinating and disturbing conversation, we're going to have to push it aside since I see your grandchildren sprinting your way."

"This 'disturbing conversation' is not at an end," Douglas warned before he moved down the steps with his arms opened wide. He swept Piper and Ben into an embrace even as he planted loud kisses on their cheeks.

He really was an exceptional gentleman and wonderful with children. For some odd reason, an image of Theodore hugging Piper and Ben at the train station suddenly flashed to her mind.

She blinked. Now, that wouldn't do. She'd been anxiously waiting for the moment when they'd part ways, and she certainly didn't need him popping into her thoughts when she least expected it.

It was rather peculiar.

"Why, pray tell, is everyone standing around outside?" Eliza asked as she scurried up the walk and hurried past Arabella to stride through the door before she turned. "It's freezing outside."

"She does have a point," Agatha said as she followed Eliza, with Arabella following a second later.

"Hamilton told me we don't have much time," Eliza said before she shrugged out of her coat and handed it to a waiting maid, sending the maid a smile. "He's afraid we'll get immersed in lady talk, and then I'll fret about not having enough time to dress for dinner."

Arabella had the strangest feeling "lady talk" was actually a subtle way of saying "Theodore talk," and since she really didn't want to talk about him, especially since she'd just been contemplating the gentleman, she needed to come up with something a little less troubling.

She'd recently read a riveting article about poisons.

"Ladies, there is no time to dawdle," Gloria said as she strode into the room. "The dinner is still hours away, but Arabella is a disaster, at least in regard to her hair. I've just now summoned Mrs. Cook. That dear lady, after hearing we are facing an emergency, has agreed to drop everything and come to our aid, which means Arabella needs to go immediately to her room and prepare herself."

"You allowed Mrs. Cook to believe my hair constitutes an emergency?" Arabella asked.

"Obviously you have not looked in a mirror lately, darling, because your hair *is* an emergency. Why, poor Mrs. Murdock was having quite the time of it not gawking in your direction, but no worries now. Mrs. Cook is a genius when it comes to wielding a pair of shears, and she'll have you looking shipshape in no time." Gloria pointed to the steps, and since Arabella knew a lost cause when she saw one, she took Eliza and Agatha by the hand and pulled them with her up the stairs.

"Am I imagining things or is Gloria acting odder than usual?" Eliza asked once they reached the top of the steps and Arabella gestured to a hallway to the right.

"Agatha and I believe she's plotting."

Eliza smiled. "Ah, that explains it. I was recently the recipient of one of her plots, but I must say, everything turned out rather well for me in the end." She released a satisfied sigh.

"Oh, here we go again," Agatha said as they came to a stop in front of a closed door. "Just wait, Arabella. You're in for a rough time of it because your brother and Eliza can be quite nauseating to be around at times." She let out a grunt. "It's beyond embarrassing when they ogle each other. They try to be discreet, but I catch them at it all the time. You'll soon be like me, finding any reason to stare at ceilings, watch the dust float by, or one time I was forced to pretend I was picking a scab."

Eliza's mouth dropped open. "That's revolting."

"Not when compared to your behavior with Hamilton."

"When you have a husband, dear, you'll behave exactly the same way."

"Yes, I'm so looking forward to that," Agatha said. "You do realize you called me *dear*, exactly like my mother."

"I did, didn't I?" Eliza said. She shrugged. "Marriage has obviously matured me."

"It's turned you a bit nutty," Agatha countered.

"Yes, well, enough about me," Eliza said as she turned to Arabella. "I'm dying to know what happened between you and Theodore."

Arabella reached out and turned the knob on the door to her private suite of rooms, stepping aside as she ushered Eliza and Agatha in. To her relief, Eliza seemed to forget all about Theodore when she stepped into the room.

"It's pink," Eliza proclaimed.

"Shockingly pink," Agatha added as she strode across the floor and headed for a large bookcase that spanned the opposite wall. "Are these all romance novels?" she asked as she ran her finger along some of their spines.

Arabella smiled. "I do enjoy a good romance, but . . . don't let that information be known to just anyone. I have a reputation to uphold."

"What did Theodore say when he learned you read romance?" Eliza asked.

Arabella moved to a comfortable chaise upholstered in soft pink and rose, took a seat, and patted the cushion beside her, waiting until Eliza took a seat before she spoke. "I don't think he's aware of my reading preferences, except for the newspaper. I keep telling everyone that Theodore and I did not spend an exorbitant amount of time chatting, yet no one seems to believe me."

"I've never known Theodore to be less than chatty," Agatha said as she set down the book she'd been skimming and moved to the window. "I think Mrs. Cook must have arrived, which is unfortunate since the conversation was just starting to get interesting."

"There is nothing of interest to tell you about Theodore," Arabella said.

"I'm quite certain that isn't exactly true," Gloria said, stepping into the room with Cora right behind her. "But Agatha's right. Mrs. Cook has arrived. I'm certain she's going to have a fit of the vapors when she sees your hair, so talk of Theodore and how interesting he is will simply have to wait." She tilted her head. "How are we going to explain what happened to you?"

"We could tell her the hair just fell off my head," Arabella said.

"Because that happens every day," Gloria muttered.

"Having a crazed sheriff slice off my hair with a knife isn't exactly something that happens every day either."

Gloria plopped down on a bright pink chair with pink tassels hanging from its skirt. "You will start at the beginning, my dear, and do not even consider withholding a single detail."

Thirty minutes later, Arabella found herself winding up her story as Mrs. Cook clucked and tittered with every snip of her scissors. There had been no point in using Mrs. Cook as an excuse to delay telling her tale, not after the woman had bustled into the room and Gloria blithely announced the reason for Arabella's missing hair. Mrs. Cook insisted on hearing all the details, and Arabella hadn't been able to come up with a sufficient reason to refuse.

"So then, Theodore left me alone in the cell, and not long after that he came back with Sheriff Dawson in tow, and I was released."

"That is so romantic," Mrs. Cook gushed.

"There was nothing romantic about it," Arabella argued.

Gloria cleared her throat. "Oh, I don't know about that, Arabella. There certainly is something romantic about a dashing gentleman such as Theodore racing to a damsel-in-distress's rescue and saving said damsel—which is you, by the way—from a most unpleasant fate."

"Do you know, the first time I saw Mr. Wilder, I got a bit weak at the knees," Cora said.

What did that have to do with anything?

"Perhaps I shouldn't have extended an invitation to Mrs. and Miss Murdock," Gloria said slowly. "Felicia is a charming young lady, and I'd certainly hate for Theodore to become distracted from the plot, or, ah . . . well, you know."

Perhaps she had not been clear regarding her interest, or lack thereof, in Theodore.

She cleared her throat. "Mother, you know I hate to disappoint you, but I'm an independent woman, more independent than most because of Grandmother's inheritance. I'm not opposed to marriage . . . eventually. However, Theodore Wilder is not meant for me. You must realize his idea of the ideal wife is a demure lady who will not be opposed to catering to his every whim."

"If you love someone, dear," Cora said, "you want to do special little things for them."

"Yes, but it should be a choice," Arabella argued. "I have the distinct feeling Theodore was brought up in an environment where those 'special little things' are expected of women. There's a difference between wanting to do for a man and having it expected of you."

"She does have a point," Agatha said. "And everyone in this room—well, besides you, Mrs. Cook—is aware of the fact that Theodore is beyond old-fashioned."

"Even I know that Mr. Theodore Wilder is a fine figure of a man," Mrs. Cook said with a chuckle as she made a final cut and tousled Arabella's hair. "There, it's the best I can do."

Arabella smiled her thanks and pulled off the piece of linen Mrs. Cook had set around her shoulders to catch any falling hair. She rose to her feet. "I suppose I should change my dress."

"Aren't you going to look in the mirror?" Eliza asked.

"Arabella's never been overly concerned with her appearance," Gloria said.

"If I looked like Miss Beckett, I would find it difficult to pull myself away from my reflection," Mrs. Cook declared. "If I do say so myself, dear, I did a lovely job layering your locks so your shorter hair blends in. With the amount of curl you possess, and your reputation for being fashionable, I doubt anyone will even realize your style was not intentional. You look absolutely charming."

Arabella glanced around and found all the ladies nodding in agreement. Feeling a bit self-conscious but not wanting to hurt Mrs. Cook's feelings, she moved to her mirror and couldn't quite stifle the gasp that escaped her lips. She leaned closer. Her hair was a shiny mass of loose curls that tumbled to her shoulders. The area of her head where her hair had been cut off was layered quite adeptly, but . . . Arabella narrowed her eyes. She didn't look like herself anymore.

"You remind me of an imp," Agatha said.

"An imp?"

"Yes, you know, those mischievous creatures that frolic in children's books."

"I thought an imp was like an urchin," Eliza said.

"She certainly doesn't look like an urchin," Cora exclaimed. "In fact, she looks, hmm . . ."

"Approachable," Gloria finished for Cora. "Oh, this is so exciting."

"Why would you find this exciting?" Arabella asked as alarm began sliding through her.

"You've always shown such little regard for your appearance, darling, but now you will no longer be able to secure your hair back in that stern chignon you've been wearing for years. You look five years younger, and need I say a bit frivolous?"

"I look frivolous?" Arabella asked, spinning back to look in the mirror. She *did* look frivolous. The riot of curls framing her face seemed to accent her eyes, and for some reason it appeared as if her eyes were now larger.

"I look as if I've lost my intelligence," she muttered.

"A girl should never have too much intelligence," Mrs. Cook proclaimed. "You are going to have the gentlemen of New York falling at your feet."

"I certainly hope not," Arabella said, although . . . it would be interesting to see if Theodore would feel compelled to fall at her feet.

She blinked at her reflection even as the thought came to her that perhaps she really had lost a little of her intelligence with each inch of hair Mrs. Cook had cut away.

She turned and forced a smile. "Since I have now been sufficiently groomed to attend Mother's dinner party, may I suggest we continue our conversation at a later date? I'm sure everyone would love an opportunity to freshen up a bit before the festivities begin."

She bid Eliza and Agatha goodbye, ignored the smug looks she saw her mother and Cora exchange, thanked Mrs. Cook once again, and finally plopped into a chair once everyone had left her room.

She permitted herself a moment to simply sit, but then a restless urge swept over her. She pushed to her feet and strode to the wardrobe. As she rummaged around the contents of her closet, the thought kept springing to mind that, for some unknown reason, it was imperative she find the perfect outfit to wear to dinner.

8

Theodore stretched his legs and regarded his mother and sister, who were sitting on the opposite side of the carriage. Both of them were fidgeting, a circumstance that was slightly alarming.

He'd always thought of them as practically motionless, except when they were moving of course.

He muffled a snort at that ridiculous reasoning and was suddenly thankful when the carriage began to slow. He needed a diversion from the strange notions that kept plaguing his every thought.

"What was I thinking?" Louise asked as the carriage came to a stop.

"Harold is going to be so disappointed with me," Katherine said, although her cheeks sported a rosy hue and her dark eyes sparkled.

Theodore could not remember the last time Katherine's eyes had held anything but aloofness. She almost seemed a bit mischievous at the moment, her attitude most likely brought on by the fact she was doing something her staid and formal husband would not approve of in the least.

It gave Theodore pause.

Was he like Harold and his own father, Samuel? Did he believe a woman should be expected to wait at home while a gentleman was free to cavort around as he pleased?

His collar suddenly felt rather tight. He tugged on it, but stilled when Louise sent him a frown.

"Are you not feeling well, dear?" she asked, and before he could respond, continued, "I have to imagine you're beginning to experience a trickle of unease regarding our plans for this evening. Have you come to the same conclusion I have, that this is not a good idea?"

He pushed his troubling thoughts away and summoned up a smile. "Of course not, Mother. Having dinner with the Beckett family is a fine way to pass the evening. I'm sure you'll have a wonderful time. If nothing else, it will certainly be more pleasant for you than spending the evening moping at home."

"I don't mope," Louise said.

"Nor do I," Katherine added.

Theodore grinned. "You have no reason to mope now, Kate. Zayne will be here tonight, and that's certain to improve your spirits."

"If you even so much as hint to him about my old infatuation, I promise I will hunt you down after the dinner party and inflict bodily harm upon you."

"I'd forgotten what a bloodthirsty wench you can be when you put your mind to it."

"It is hardly appropriate to call me a 'wench,' and you must know, if word gets back to Harold regarding my past, er, infatuation, he'll be furious with me."

Theodore's amusement died a rapid death. "Surely you know I would never intentionally embarrass you. As for Harold, he has little reason to be furious with you about anything. He should have made himself available to escort you to dinner tonight."

Louise's brow furrowed as she regarded him warily. "What has gotten into you? You are not behaving in your normal fashion."

"What is my normal fashion?"

"Well . . . normal," Louise said before she leaned forward and peered out the window. "Oh, look, there's another carriage pulling up."

Theodore glanced out the window. "It's Mr. and Mrs. Murdock, and I do believe that's Miss Murdock climbing down now."

Louise leaned back and patted her hair. "Well then, this is all right. The Murdock family is completely respectable." She smiled. "I have always enjoyed Miss Felicia Murdock. She is very proper and would make any gentleman an excellent wife."

"I'm not planning on getting married in the foreseeable future."

"You're rapidly on your way to becoming thirty. Your father and I married when he was only twenty-four."

"Which goes far in explaining why the two of you barely speak anymore," Theodore uttered under his breath.

"What's that?" Louise asked.

"Nothing," Theodore said. "Do not, and I repeat, do not attempt your hand at matchmaking this evening, Mother. We've come to celebrate Miss Beckett's return home, and that's all we're going to do."

"Do you know, I don't believe Miss Murdock's ever missed a church service? A lady like that doesn't come around often. You would be lucky to attract her interest."

Katherine released a grunt. "Theodore doesn't have a problem attracting interest from the ladies. Honestly, it's annoying to have ladies seek out my company when I know perfectly well they're only doing so in order to get closer to Theodore."

Theodore shifted in his seat. "I didn't know ladies bothered you in the hopes of becoming known to me."

"I'm certain there's a lot you don't know."

"Katherine, stop baiting your brother," Louise said before she glanced at Theodore. "Now then, returning to Miss Murdock. She is a very devout woman and would suit you admirably."

"I doubt even Miss Murdock would be up for the task of saving Theodore's soul," Katherine muttered, softening the words when she sent him a grin.

He returned the grin. "As we discussed not that long ago, sister dear, my soul is perfectly fine."

"I doubt that, but I suppose you can always hope," Katherine said. "Perhaps you should seek out Miss Murdock and her devout ways after all."

Theodore shook his head but was spared a response when his mother pressed her face up against the window and made a *tsk*ing sound under her breath.

"I do wish Mrs. Murdock would not encourage her daughter to gown herself in such unexpected colors. Why, a lady possessed of Miss Murdock's fair complexion should never wear that particular shade of green. She looks peaked even from this distance."

"While Miss Murdock's unfortunate choice of a gown is indeed riveting, may I suggest we get out of the carriage and greet the Murdock family? I think they may be waiting for us," Theodore said.

Louise let out a sniff. "No need to get testy. I was simply pointing out the obvious." She smoothed down her gown as Theodore opened the carriage door.

He stepped out and took his mother's hand, helping her to the ground. "You look lovely."

Louise began blinking rather rapidly. "That is quite the nicest thing you've said to me in years."

A stab of regret pierced Theodore. He told women on a daily basis how lovely they looked. How could he have neglected to pay the same compliment to his own mother?

"I'll try to be more diligent in the future," he said quietly.

"You really are ill, aren't you?" Katherine asked as she paused in the door of the carriage.

"I'm fine," Theodore said, helping her down.

Katherine lowered her voice. "Have you been drinking?"

Theodore arched a brow.

Katherine arched a brow right back at him. "Pity . . . that was the only explanation I could come up with to explain your odd behavior."

"Mr. Wilder," Mrs. Murdock called, drawing his attention, "we meet again."

Theodore took his mother's arm and extended his other one to Katherine before strolling up the cobblestone pathway to stop in front of Mrs. Murdock. He inclined his head to her and Felicia and smiled at Mr. Murdock, who was struggling to carry a large box.

"Allow me to assist you with that, Mr. Murdock," he said, taking a step forward as his mother and sister dropped their hold on him.

"Thank you," Mr. Murdock said, then handed the box to Theodore. "It was heavier than I was led to believe. I thought it only held a quilt."

Louise bit her lip. "I didn't realize gifts were expected."

"Oh, don't concern yourself, Mrs. Wilder," Mrs. Murdock said. "That isn't a present for Miss Beckett. It's for Hamilton and Eliza. We gave them a gift at their wedding, of course, but Felicia and I have been working day and night on a special quilt for the new couple. They married so quickly that we didn't have time to complete it before the ceremony."

"You know how to quilt, Miss Murdock?" Louise asked before sending a telling smile in Theodore's direction.

"I do, Mrs. Wilder, but I can't claim to be overly proficient at the art," Felicia said.

"Nonsense," Mrs. Murdock said with a wave of her hand. "Felicia is highly competent with all the feminine pursuits. Why, she even knows how to cook."

Two bright spots of color appeared on Felicia's cheeks. Theodore was about to intervene, being all too familiar with the antics of parents— especially mothers who were prone to push their daughters' attributes in front of every available gentleman—but before he had an opportunity, his sister stepped forward, took Felicia by the arm, and began strolling toward the house.

"I love to cook," Katherine said. "Isn't it amusing that you and I have been acquainted with each other for years and yet I didn't know that about you?"

"It is not as if we speak on a regular basis, Mrs. Gibson," Felicia said while Theodore dropped into place beside her. "You have moved on to the married set, whereas I'm still lurking on the outskirts of society, trying to avoid the maneuverings of my mother."

Katherine leaned closer to her and whispered, "I can certainly sympathize with your plight. My mother's maneuverings used to drive me mad."

Felicia stopped walking, glanced over her shoulder, then turned back to Katherine and Theodore. "Even though my mother makes the claim I'm adept in the kitchen, I'm really not. Our cook has forbidden me to step foot into her domain ever since I set the stove on fire. Funny thing, it turns out that grease really *will* explode if you allow it to get too hot."

Theodore juggled the box in his arms and smiled. When Felicia wasn't suffering from embarrassment over her mother's attention, she was quite lovely and seemed to possess a wonderful sense of humor. He tilted his head and considered

109

her. With her blond hair, fair complexion, and eyes gleaming with mischief, Miss Murdock was actually incredibly lovely.

Why then did he not feel one single bit of attraction for her?

"Oh no," Felicia moaned.

Theodore glanced where Felicia was staring and realized another carriage had pulled up. A gentleman was climbing out of it, and in his arms he carried a small dark-haired girl.

"This is marvelous," Mrs. Murdock exclaimed as she hurried up to join them, Louise and Mr. Murdock following more sedately after her. "I was unaware Lord Sefton would be here." She waved cheerfully and let out what sounded like a giggle when Grayson Sumner, Lord of Sefton, lifted his head, smiled, and began to stride toward them.

"Mrs. Murdock, how lovely to see you," Grayson said as he rearranged his small daughter, Ming, against his shoulder, and then grinned at Felicia. "Miss Murdock, you're looking well this fine evening."

Theodore couldn't help but notice that Felicia turned a deeper shade of pink. It was obvious by the way Mrs. Murdock was beaming at Grayson that she wasn't at all opposed to Felicia attracting notice from this particular gentleman.

"Mr. Wilder," Grayson said as he sent Theodore a nod, "it's good to find you back in town. I understand congratulations are in order this evening. You were finally able to locate Miss Beckett and return her to the folds of her appreciative family."

"Lord Sefton," Theodore replied as he inclined his head. "I suppose congratulations are in order, considering it turned into a rather large ordeal to locate and return Miss Beckett to New York."

"She sounds like a delightful minx," Grayson said with a charming smile, which for some peculiar reason made Theodore long to hit him. "And please, call me Grayson. I've recently abandoned my title and truly do prefer being addressed like everyone else."

"How does one abandon a title?" Katherine asked.

"It's easy," Grayson said with another smile, "especially when one no longer resides in England."

"I do beg your pardon, Grayson," Theodore said. "I've forgotten my manners. This is my mother, Mrs. Samuel Wilder, and this is my sister, Mrs. Harold Gibson."

"It is an honor to make your acquaintance," Grayson said, gesturing to the little girl now burying her head in his neck. "This is my daughter, Ming."

Ming lifted her head before she plopped her thumb in her mouth.

"Hello, Ming," Felicia said.

Ming stretched out her little arms, and Felicia stepped closer, scooping the child into her embrace. She nuzzled Ming with her nose, causing the girl to giggle.

"I wasn't aware you knew Ming," Mrs. Murdock said, her eyes brimming with delight.

"She's been at the church a few times," Felicia said.

"My Felicia has a special way with children," Mrs. Murdock declared.

Theodore wasn't certain, but he thought he heard Felicia release an exasperated sigh. He cleared his throat. "Perhaps it would be best if we made our way inside? I must admit that this box isn't getting any lighter."

"Oh, forgive me, Mr. Wilder," Mrs. Murdock exclaimed. "I forgot I added a few books for Hamilton and Eliza to enjoy. You know, the ones regarding childhood ailments and baby names?" She released a loud sigh. "The good Lord alone knows none of my children will need them anytime in the near future."

Louise smiled. "Why, Mrs. Murdock, your daughter is a lovely young lady who is certain to form an alliance soon." She winked. "Perhaps you should take back those books."

Mrs. Murdock beamed as she exchanged a look with Louise

before both ladies looked at him and then switched their attention to Grayson.

He felt slightly like a cow being brought to auction.

"I do hope you're right, Mrs. Wilder," Mrs. Murdock said. "You are fortunate to have your daughter so well-married."

"Yes, fortunate," Katherine muttered, which caused him to frown and wonder yet again why he'd failed to realize his sister was unhappy.

He searched his mind for a delicate way to question her about her marriage, realized it was hardly the appropriate time to enter into such a private conversation, so instead turned toward the door, pausing when it suddenly sprang open and Piper skipped out.

"I've been waiting for you forever," she squealed as she ran up to him, stopped by his side and grinned. "Why is everyone standing around outside in the freezing cold when the house is toasty warm?"

"That is an excellent question, Piper," Grayson said. He took Ming from Felicia and strode inside, the others following behind him.

Theodore moved to join them, but found his way blocked by Piper, who was staring at the box in his arms, a look of glee on her tiny face.

"Is that my surprise?"

"I'm afraid it's not."

Piper's face fell, and her lips began to tremble.

"Piper, you've forgotten your manners," Hamilton said as he appeared on the stoop beside them. "Theodore only just returned to town after chasing your aunt around the country for weeks. He's barely had a moment to settle in and certainly hasn't had time to pick you up a surprise."

Piper's blue eyes filled with tears, causing Theodore's heart to lurch.

"Here," he said, thrusting the box into Hamilton's arms. "Make yourself useful."

He squatted down in front of Piper and wiped a tear from her cheek. "You don't actually believe I would have forgotten my promise to you, do you, darling? For your information, I made a special stop at the toy store before I went to fetch my mother and sister. Perhaps you would care to walk with me back to the carriage so we can retrieve your present?"

Piper's tears miraculously disappeared. She grabbed his hand and tugged, causing him to laugh as he straightened and nodded to Hamilton. "We'll be right back."

Piper chatted incessantly as they hurried down the sidewalk and to the back of the house where the grooms had parked the carriages. He opened the door to his carriage, reached inside, and extracted three packages. He stepped back and rolled his eyes at Piper's expectant expression.

"Now, don't get your hopes up. Only one of these is for you; the others are for Ben and Ming." He handed the box wrapped in red paper to Piper, who let out an excited giggle. He tucked the other two boxes under his arms and began walking back to the front of the house, Piper beside him, shaking the box again and again with every step she took. She suddenly stopped and sent him a bright smile.

"Thank you so much for getting me whatever is in this box, Mr. Theodore. I don't care what everyone else says, you're a very nice gentleman."

He smiled at her comment, but then the rest of her words registered and he couldn't quite hold back a grunt. "What does everyone else say about me?"

Piper shook her head. "God doesn't like us to gossip about what we've heard, but it isn't completely horrible what everyone says." Her eyes crinkled at the corners. "Grandmother adores you."

"What about Eliza and Agatha?"

113

"Hmm . . . I suppose they adore you as well, especially since you saved Ben and me from a terrible, painful death."

He really did love this precocious child.

They rounded the corner of the house and walked briskly up the steps, the butler holding the door open for them before they even reached it. Theodore sent him a nod of thanks and entered the house, not surprised in the least when Ben barreled straight for him, Ming scampering at his side.

Theodore bent down and gave Ben his package and smiled when Ben set it on the floor and took the package from him that was meant for Ming.

"She's shy," Ben said. He handed the present to Ming and then scooped his off the floor. He bolted out of the room, shouting a "thank you!" over his shoulder, with Ming and Piper running after him.

"It was very kind of you to remember Ming," Hamilton said, stepping into the foyer.

Theodore shrugged. "Kind is my middle name. Zayne mentioned that Grayson was bringing Ming with him tonight, so it wouldn't have been acceptable to exclude her."

"You really are nicer than people give you credit for, aren't you?"

He was going to have to reevaluate how he projected himself to the world.

"I keep telling all the ladies that you are . . ."

Hamilton's words faded to nothing when an enticing laugh drifted from the next room, causing Theodore to move into motion, hardly aware of leaving Hamilton still speaking behind him. He reached the large receiving room and froze.

Arabella was standing a few feet from him and she looked absolutely . . . enchanting.

He felt his mouth drop open as his gaze traveled over her.

Her hair, which he'd become accustomed to seeing pulled ruthlessly from her face and secured at the nape of her neck, was now a flirty mop of shining curls that seemed to accentuate her high cheekbones. His gaze dropped and settled on her gown even as his mouth snapped shut. She was dressed in a delightful scrap of froth that drew attention to her curves.

His mouth ran dry as his mind went numb. Why had he never noticed how exquisite she was?

Granted, he'd known she was beautiful, but in all the time they'd spent together, he'd never once felt as if he'd been punched in the stomach.

He was finding it difficult to breathe.

It was most peculiar.

He tilted his head and allowed himself the luxury of studying her for another moment, his mind trying to discern why feelings he'd never felt before were coursing through his body.

Finally what was so different about her came to him. In shedding her long locks and abandoning the functional gowns she'd always worn around him, she'd gained something in the process.

Allure.

No longer was she a woman simply possessed of uncommon beauty. No, now she was . . . approachable.

That thought caused him to blink out of his stupor.

He was being fanciful. Arabella was still the same woman he'd first met in Gilman—the same woman who held radical ideas—and he would do well to remember that.

He gulped in a breath of air, gulped in another when the first one didn't seem to settle his emotions, and blew out a grunt when Arabella laughed again, his blood beginning to race through his veins.

What was the matter with him?

It wasn't as if he'd never heard the lady laugh before, but her laugh had certainly never caused his pulse to quicken.

Perhaps he was coming down with something.

His mother and sister had both remarked on his unusual behavior, and illness would explain his strange feelings.

He began to move forward but stopped in his tracks when Arabella laughed again, and he discovered the reason behind her amusement.

He narrowed his eyes as he watched Grayson pluck Arabella's hand into his, bring it to his lips, and place a lingering kiss on her knuckles.

The room turned red as an odd buzzing noise suddenly sounded in his head.

"Theodore, I say, whatever is the matter?"

Theodore forced his attention away from Arabella and turned, finding Zayne standing right beside him, a look of concern in his eyes.

He cleared his throat, shook his head to clear it of the last vestiges of red, and tried to smile, realizing he'd failed miserably when Zayne looked downright alarmed.

"I'm fine," he finally managed to mutter.

"You look ill."

Ah, there it was, the confirmation he'd been hoping to receive. He really must be coming down with some dastardly illness.

Feeling better, his smile became genuine. "You know, I do feel a little off." He chanced a glance at Arabella, noticed Grayson was still holding her hand, and felt his hands clench into fists.

"Well, that explains it," Zayne said with a laugh even as he shook his head. "I must say, I never saw this coming."

"Saw what coming?" Theodore asked, hearing what sounded like a thread of panic in his voice.

Zayne nodded toward Arabella and Grayson.

"You've lost your mind if you're insinuating I'm interested in your sister."

"Explain then, if you please, why you keep watching Grayson as if you intend to throttle him."

"I'm not jealous."

Zayne quirked a brow. "He's very handsome, at least that is what the ladies tell me, and he's reportedly extremely wealthy."

"I'm considered handsome, and you of all people are perfectly aware of the fact I'm wealthy in my own right." Theodore winced as soon as the words left his mouth.

"Grayson's foreign," Zayne remarked.

Theodore snorted. "He's from England."

"Again, a foreign land."

"I've always found English gentlemen to be rather cold."

"He doesn't look cold to me."

No, Grayson certainly didn't look cold as he retained possession of Arabella's hand. In fact, the man seemed overly warm and entirely too friendly. Another stab of something unexpected shot through him.

"He also has a title," Zayne said.

"He doesn't use it."

"I think he's ruthless."

Theodore turned his full attention to Zayne. "What do you mean, ruthless?"

Zayne shrugged. "I think Grayson is a man who lets nothing stand in the way of what he desires."

"Do you think he's a threat to Arabella?"

"I think he's a threat to you."

"I'm not in a competition with him."

Zayne arched another brow.

"I'm not," Theodore insisted.

"I find the fact that you protest so vehemently interesting."

"What do you protest so vehemently?"

Somehow, while he'd been conversing with Zayne, Arabella had managed to steal up beside him. The sight of her caused his mouth to run dry again, and as he drew in a breath, her perfume teased all of his senses and caused his stomach to clench.

A disturbing thought struck him out of the blue.

He was behaving in the exact same manner he'd observed numerous women behaving around him too many times to recount. He knew without a shadow of a doubt he most likely sported a dazed and anxious expression, and that idea didn't sit well with him. He was not the sort to become tongue-tied when a pretty lady spoke to him. He was a man, a man who prided himself on his strict code of self-control.

"It's nice to discover you've managed to recapture the use of your hand," he heard come out of his mouth.

That was certainly not what he'd intended to say.

Arabella's eyes turned cloudy with obvious confusion. "The use of my hand?"

"I thought for certain Mr. Sumner was about to make off with it."

Zayne began whistling under his breath as Arabella started sputtering, her eyes going from cloudy to stormy.

"Are you suggesting I was behaving in an untoward manner with Grayson?"

"You call him Grayson?"

"He gave me leave to use his given name, seeing as how his sister is married to my brother. That makes us practically family."

"I don't believe Grayson's thoughts were platonic as he was assaulting your hand."

Arabella crossed her arms over her chest, drawing attention to her curves, but he didn't have much time to appreciate them, because she began tapping her fashionably shod foot against the floor.

"He was not assaulting my hand. He was merely showing me a common courtesy as he made my acquaintance."

"It didn't look like a common courtesy to me."

Arabella's foot stopped tapping as she sent him a glare. "What did it look like to you?"

"You were flirting."

Arabella drew herself up and lifted her chin. "I never flirt."

Theodore opened his mouth, intent on arguing that ludicrous point, but then closed it a split second later when a disturbing thought flashed to mind.

He was not acting like his normal self. He was behaving and speaking rashly, and that shook him to his core.

What was it about this woman that caused his normal good sense and level thinking to fly out the window?

She was dangerous.

The second the thought entered his head, he knew it was nothing less than the truth. Miss Arabella Beckett was a danger to everything he believed. He took a deep breath and forced a smile. "If you'll excuse me, I need to go find Piper."

"You're just going to walk away from me after provoking an argument?" Arabella demanded.

"I didn't provoke an argument. You're allowing your emotions to cloud your judgment."

"What?"

"You were flirting, and you know it, but you hate the fact that a man pointed it out to you."

"You've lost your mind."

Theodore shook his head. "I think I've finally found it. Now, if you'll excuse me, I really must find Piper."

He extended her a bow and strode away as quickly as he could without actually breaking into a run.

He refused to contemplate why he suddenly felt truly ill.

9

In the two weeks since the ill-fated dinner party, Arabella had tried her best to keep the annoying Mr. Wilder out of her thoughts. She'd spent the days in the company of her family and friends, catching up on everything that had transpired while she'd been away. Keeping so busy had distracted her from dwelling on Mr. Wilder and his abysmal behavior toward her.

Now, however, as she strolled down Broadway with Agatha on one side of her and Eliza on the other, thoughts of the gentleman she'd sworn not to think about kept flitting to mind.

He'd had the audacity to take her to task for conversing with Grayson.

He'd accused her of flirting.

As if flirting was some type of criminal activity. She didn't know a single lady who didn't flirt upon occasion. Granted, she'd blithely claimed to Theodore that she never flirted, but that really wasn't the case.

She was a lady, and ladies were prone to flirting every now and again. It was not as if she'd been behaving in an untoward manner, and she certainly hadn't deserved to be treated as if she'd suddenly sprouted two heads and taken to breathing fire.

He'd ruined her enjoyment of the evening by his rude observations.

He hadn't even commented on her new appearance.

"I don't believe Arabella's listening to us," Agatha said, pulling Arabella rather abruptly from her thoughts.

"I think you're right," Eliza agreed with a bob of her head, the motion causing the charming hat she was wearing to bounce up and down. "Did you notice the way her lips were moving, but no sounds escaped?"

"I wasn't talking to myself," Arabella said.

Agatha stopped walking and patted Arabella's arm. "Of course you weren't, dear. Only crazy people talk to themselves."

Arabella grinned. In the few weeks she'd spent with Agatha Watson, she'd discovered a kindred spirit and enjoyed the lady's company immensely, as well as the company of Eliza.

"She's thinking about Theodore again," Eliza said.

The grin slid off her face. "No, I'm not."

Agatha sent her a commiserating smile. "You have every right to be irritated with the gentleman. Why, I get annoyed with Theodore on a regular basis, and I'm not even attracted to the man."

"I'm not attracted to him," Arabella said between gritted teeth.

Agatha raised a delicate brow. "So, you've simply been in a horrible mood for no good reason at all?"

"I've been in a perfectly fine mood."

"You barely touched your meal during the Thanksgiving feast," Eliza pointed out. "I stuffed myself to the gills and felt somewhat guilty in the process, since you were obviously not enjoying yours."

"I ate two pieces of turkey."

"You pushed your turkey around on your plate," Eliza corrected. "That does not constitute eating and proves the point that you've been out of sorts."

"Perhaps I don't care for turkey."

Agatha rolled her eyes, ignored Arabella's remark, and patted her arm yet again. "You weren't even excited about the rally we attended last week. I was certain your attitude would improve when you were pressed into service at the last minute to introduce Elizabeth Cady Stanton, but alas, that didn't happen. You were obviously in a dismal frame of mind the entire day."

Arabella pushed a strand of hair that the blustery breeze had stirred up out of her face and frowned. "Could you tell I was in a dismal mood while I was performing Mrs. Stanton's introduction?"

Agatha's lips twitched. "Truthfully, yes, but I doubt anyone else except Eliza, your mother, my mother, and Mrs. Murdock noticed."

Arabella began walking again as temper slithered through her.

What was wrong with her?

She'd been given the extreme honor of introducing Elizabeth Cady Stanton. Instead of relishing the moment, she'd retreated into a bit of a sulk because Theodore had not shown up as promised.

Agatha and Eliza caught up to her, both of them slightly out of breath.

"While I'm all for a brisk stroll to get the blood flowing," Eliza said with a pant, "don't you believe it would be advisable to slow down just a touch? These sidewalks still have ice on them from the nasty weather we received yesterday, and I for one don't care to break a limb."

Arabella slowed, even as a reluctant grin teased her mouth.

"I do beg your pardon, ladies. I don't know what's come over me lately."

"*I* happen to believe Theodore is what has 'come over' you lately, even if you disagree," Agatha said. "You might actually feel better if you talked it over with us, and then we, being experts in affairs of the heart, can advise you."

Arabella came to an immediate stop, forcing her friends to do the same. "You are hardly an expert on affairs of the heart, Agatha. From what I've overheard from my mother *and* yours, you gave up on Zayne all too quickly."

"Need I remind you that Zayne's engaged to Miss Collins?"

"He's practically engaged," Arabella corrected, "and I would, forgive me, prefer you as a sister-in-law over Miss Collins any day."

Agatha turned an interesting shade of red, and Arabella was quite certain it wasn't because of the cold wind.

"While it is very sweet to learn you'd enjoy having me as your sister, I fear I cannot indulge you and replace Miss Collins," Agatha said. "Your brother is determined to marry the lady, and besides, he annoys me."

Eliza laughed, causing Arabella and Agatha to turn to her. She shrugged. "It's very interesting to me how both of you claim to be annoyed by certain gentlemen, yet can't seem to stop talking about them."

Arabella exchanged a rolling of the eyes with Agatha. "The only reason I talk about Theodore is because he disappointed me and my plans for him."

"You have plans for Theodore?" Eliza asked as her eyes went wide.

"Not *those* types of plans," Arabella said with a sniff. "If you must know why I was less than pleased at the rally, it was because Mr. Wilder had promised to attend it with me. I was looking forward to using that occasion to perhaps . . . change some of his ridiculous views. To my disappointment, he didn't come, nor did he so much as send me a note of regret. He simply didn't acknowledge the occasion at all."

"Oh, dear, she's back to calling him Mr. Wilder," Eliza said before she shook her head, causing her hat to bobble again. "I'm not certain if you know this or not, but Hamilton told me Theodore is out of town on business. I imagine something of a pressing nature, given his profession, came up, and he didn't have time to pen you a note."

"He could have sent me a telegram," Arabella muttered.

"Like you did so often with your parents while you were out of town?" Agatha asked.

She did have a point.

Arabella saw Eliza shiver and realized it was incredibly silly to stand around chatting as the wind chafed their faces and stole through their coats.

"We should save this conversation for later," she said. "It is freezing, and my mother told me B. Altman's is having a wonderful sale on parasols. I think Piper would enjoy a nice pink parasol for Christmas." She looked at Eliza. "Unless of course there is something else you think she would care for more."

Eliza took her arm, grabbed Agatha's hand, and laughed as she tugged them down the sidewalk. "Christmas is still a month away, Arabella, but I'm sure Piper would love a pink parasol. Pink is one of her favorite colors, which is why I believe she's declared the doll Theodore gave her at your dinner party her most treasured possession. It's clothed in the most exquisite pink gown I've ever seen."

"*Theodore* gave Piper that doll?" Arabella asked as a large dose of disgruntlement settled over her. She did not care to hear about Theodore being considerate. That attribute was not one she wanted to associate with the gentleman who'd been horrible to her.

Eliza quickened her pace while a blast of wind swept over

them and snow began falling. "Didn't he tell you that at the party?"

"Mr. Wilder did not speak to me during dinner. If you will recall, he spent the majority of his time with Felicia. I readily admit *she* would be a wonderful companion to the man. *She* is possessed of a sweet disposition and an apparent willingness to overlook the man's many faults."

"I got the impression Felicia was terrified throughout dinner, and I assumed it was because she was Theodore's dinner partner," Agatha said.

Eliza dropped her hold on Arabella as a gust of wind tore the hat from her head. She charged after it, used her foot to catch it as it rolled along the snowy sidewalk, and then released a grunt of disgust when she picked up what only moments before had been a charming hat but now resembled something squashed.

She moved back to rejoin Arabella and Agatha, even as she plopped the misshapen hat back on her head. "Getting back to Felicia," she said as if she hadn't just ruined her accessory, "I don't think she was terrified of Theodore, only the fact he was paying attention to her. Surely you noticed how delighted her mother was by that turn of events? I'm quite certain Mrs. Murdock has already procured the services of a dressmaker to begin fitting Felicia for a wedding gown."

That idea, for some strange reason, caused Arabella's spirits to sink rapidly.

"I well remember the horror of having my mother thrust me in front of every available gentleman," Agatha said with a delicate shudder. "It was dreadful."

"She was still doing that only a few months ago," Eliza pointed out.

"And that is why I can sympathize with Felicia," Agatha said before she raised her eyes to the cloudy sky and smiled. "I can only thank the good Lord above for blessing me with a talent for the written word. That talent has allowed me to escape the normal expectations placed on ladies, namely being paraded about town with the hopes of obtaining a husband." She dropped her gaze. "Unfortunately, I don't believe Felicia has any interest in pursuing a profession. She seems rather shy, and I fear she will simply accept the path her mother chooses for her."

"I disagree," Eliza said. "I've spent numerous hours with Felicia as she's helped me with the new orphanage, and I think, underneath her unfortunate gowns, she is a lady who possesses a strong will. I also believe that Felicia has already set her sights on a specific gentleman, but for some reason she has yet to share his name."

"Her mother will be sorely disappointed that she won't get Theodore as a son-in-law," Arabella said even as she felt a grin tease her lips, which she quickly hid behind a gloved hand when Agatha sent her a telling look.

"*Psst*, Miss Watson, over here."

Arabella turned along with Agatha and peered through the blanket of snow now falling steadily from the sky. She squinted and could just make out the form of a lady standing in a small alleyway.

Agatha took a hesitant step forward. "Who's there?"

The woman slipped out of the alley and hurried toward them. She was dressed in a garish blue gown with a coat of shabby red velvet thrown over it. Her cheeks were caked with rouge, her eyes wary. "It's me, Violet, remember? We shared a jail cell a few months back."

Agatha took another step toward the woman. "Violet, of course, how have you been?"

"Oh, you know, trying to make a living."

Agatha let out a sigh. "Forgive me, but I seem to recall, as we languished behind bars, a conversation we shared regarding you and the rest of your friends seeking out a different line of work. Given your choice of attire, may I assume that didn't come to fruition?"

"We tried to take your suggestion, Miss Watson, really we did, but quite frankly, no one wanted to hire old harlots," Violet said. "But *that* has nothing to do with why I sought you out. I have a pressing matter of grave importance to discuss with you, yet due to the madness that is sweeping through the city, I'm afraid to discuss it with you out here in the open."

"We were just on our way to B. Altman's," Agatha said. "Would you care to join us for a cup of tea in their tea-room?"

"B. Altman's doesn't allow ladies like me to enter their fine establishment," Violet said with a smile, the action revealing missing teeth. "I was hoping you'd agree to come back to my house."

Eliza bit her lip. "We promised Zayne we would go directly to B. Altman's and nowhere else."

It had not escaped Arabella's notice that her brother had found reasons to be constantly in her presence the past two weeks. She had the sneaking suspicion Theodore had told him to keep an eye on her, but since absolutely nothing of a disturbing nature had occurred, Zayne's dogging of her every step had become a little ridiculous. She'd finally gotten terse with him that morning, resulting in Zayne going off to work and leaving her to her own devices after he'd lectured her about keeping to well-traveled places and not getting into mischief.

She'd never particularly cared for anyone telling her what to do, and she'd never given Zayne her promise.

"I say we go to Violet's house and listen to what the lady has to say," she heard come out of her mouth.

Agatha sent her a grin before she moved with Violet into the alley, leaving Arabella standing with Eliza.

"I don't think this is a good idea," Eliza muttered as she grabbed onto Arabella's hand and they hurried after Agatha.

As they traveled farther down the alley, Arabella began to suspect that Eliza was right. Gone were the polished facades of buildings and swept-clean sidewalks. They were replaced with crumbling brick walls, rubbish-strewn walkways, and rats that scurried around in plain sight. There was an unsettling sense of danger about the place. She shivered, sent up a prayer to ask God to watch over them, and then stumbled a few minutes later when she ran smack into Agatha, who'd come to an abrupt stop.

"We're here," Violet said, gesturing to a sagging flight of steps that led to a battered door. "Watch yourself when you get to the top; there's a hole."

Arabella tightened her grip on Eliza's hand and followed Violet into the house, soon finding herself in a dimly lit parlor where three women, obviously of the same occupation as Violet, stood watching them.

"I met with success," Violet exclaimed as she took their coats. Arabella passed hers over rather reluctantly, shivering when the cold of the room seeped through her gown.

It was almost colder in here than it was outside, and her heart suddenly ached when she realized this hovel was actually these ladies' home.

"Miss Watson, Mrs. Beckett, and Miss Beckett kindly agreed to listen to us," Violet said as she took the coats and spread them over a chair that was near a barely lit fire.

"Excuse me," Arabella said, stepping forward, "but how do you know all of our names?"

"Oh, that's easy," Violet said. She motioned for them to join her by the feeble fire, even as she picked up one of the few logs that rested by it, gave it a look of regret, and then tossed it onto the grate. "We met Mrs. Beckett and Miss Watson in jail, and every lady knows who you are, Miss Beckett, even us harlots."

"We've been watching you," one of the other ladies with greasy black hair said.

"That's somewhat disturbing," Agatha said before she took a seat on a three-legged chair that promptly listed to the left. "Why doesn't someone start at the beginning, but first, I do think it might be pleasant if everyone introduced themselves. All of you seem to know our names, but we only know Violet's."

Violet stopped rubbing her hands in front of a now-sputtering fireplace. "I've forgotten my manners. I'm Violet, of course, and that is Lottie in the green dress and red hair, Hannah with the black hair, and Sarah with the yellow hair and brown coat."

"Did you convince Miss Watson to help us?" Hannah asked as she moved up beside Violet and scooted as close to the fire as she could without causing her gown to catch fire.

Violet shook her head. "I haven't had a chance. I didn't want anyone to see me talking to these ladies."

"Good thinking," Hannah said. "These are dangerous times."

"Indeed they are," Violet agreed. She lowered her voice, even as she glanced around the room, almost as if she was afraid someone was listening to them. "We fear there's a madman loose in New York."

"What kind of a madman?" Agatha asked.

"The kind that snatches ladies like us from the street," the woman named Lottie said from her position across the room.

"We keep disappearing," Violet added. "I mean, granted, in our line of work it does happen upon occasion, but this is different. Evil seems to be dodging our footsteps, and nobody wants to help us."

"Could you explain how it's different this time?" Arabella

asked, sitting forward in the seat she'd chosen, not because she wanted to hear better but because something of a sharp nature kept piercing her skin through the skirt of her gown.

"We've had ten girls disappear in a little over a week."

"Ten?" Agatha sputtered.

Violet nodded. "That's why we need your help."

A wave of horror swept over Arabella. "Have you taken this information to the police?"

Lottie made a sound like an angry cat. "They said they'd look into the matter, but we know they won't."

Agatha stood up, the action causing her chair to topple over and the sound to echo loudly throughout the room. Two of the ladies jumped before nervous laughs rang out. "Sorry about that," Agatha said. She righted the chair and began to pace back and forth. Then she stopped and looked to Violet. "When you said 'disappear,' does that mean no bodies have been discovered?"

"Not a one," Violet said. "We've searched down by the docks during the day. That's where we think everyone has gone missing, but there's nothing to find. We're scared to work, but if we don't, well, we don't have much now as it is."

Arabella's gaze traveled over the room, taking in the peeling paint, the mismatched and broken furniture, the meager supply of wood, and the condition of the ladies.

All of them were thin, painfully so, and it suddenly struck her how much she took for granted in her life. She was always warm, usually safe, and never hungry. She truly needed to be more appreciative of the life God had given her, and . . . she needed to find a way she could help these ladies who were living such dismal existences.

Eliza cleared her throat. "Why did you seek *us* out?"

Violet began wringing her hands. "We're hoping Miss Watson will agree to write an article about what's been happening on the streets. Maybe someone would come forward and offer us some help. It could be a story that might garner you attention as a journalist, Miss Watson."

Agatha narrowed her eyes. "How do you know I work for the newspaper?"

"I told you, we've been keeping an eye on you," Violet said. "Me and the girls thought it was the least we could do after you got us released from jail a few months back." She smiled. "We've never seen society ladies get into so much mischief."

Lottie flicked her red, straggly hair out of her face and walked across the room, stopping in front of Eliza. She looked down at her as a cheeky grin flashed across her face. "I like watching you the best, especially when that delicious husband of yours is about." She gave a throaty laugh. "It's even better when his brother comes around. I must say, that Zayne Beckett is a mouth-watering feast for any woman's eyes."

Dead silence settled over the room at that proclamation. Arabella swallowed a laugh and decided it would probably be best to get the conversation back on track. "So, if I understand correctly, ladies of the night are disappearing at an alarming rate?"

"At the rate we're going, New York will soon be without women walking the streets," Hannah said.

"And you think you will get the assistance you need if Agatha writes a story concerning your plight?" Arabella pressed.

"It's all we've been able to come up with," Violet admitted. "Women like us don't have many options, Miss Beckett, as you know for yourself. Why, I have to admit that out of all the ladies here, you're in just as much danger as ladies of my kind."

Arabella frowned. "I'm not in any danger. Granted, I do occasionally run into a few disgruntled gentlemen who don't like what I speak about, but they're hardly dangerous."

"It's not the *gentlemen* you should be concerned about, it's the *men*," Hannah said with a snort. "The men we've heard talking about you don't possess fancy manners, and they have no trouble turning their fists on ladies."

"Men talk about me?"

"I'm afraid they do," Violet said.

Arabella settled back in her chair, but then yelped when another sharp something stabbed her behind. She got to her feet. "I must admit that it's disturbing to discover I'm a source of gossip among men, but I suppose it comes with the territory." She walked over to the fireplace, held out her hands to enjoy the warmth for a minute, and then turned. "But enough about me. We've more pressing matters to discuss. What would you have Agatha write in her article?"

"She needs to write that we're going missing," Lottie said.

"True, but she needs to make the article riveting," Arabella said. "It would add interest if the story pointed out the injustices of your life. I've recently found myself wondering why women in your chosen profession end up in jail on such a frequent basis, while the men who solicit your services seem to get away free and clear."

"Pardon me for asking, Miss Beckett, but why would you be wondering something like that?" Violet asked.

"I recently had reason to believe I was heading for a life much like yours, but was fortunately able to extract myself from that situation. I regret to admit I'd never actually considered the plight of women forced into procuring a living by walking the streets, but now, well, my eyes have certainly been opened."

"Arabella, you never mentioned anything about that," Agatha said.

"It must have slipped my mind. Now, getting back to your article, what else should be added?"

Agatha plopped down in an empty chair, yanked up the

skirt of her dress, and pulled out a pad of paper and a pen. She looked expectantly at Violet. "Tell me in explicit detail what you know about these disappearances."

Violet winced. "We don't know anything more than what we've already told you."

Agatha's hand paused over the paper. "No one has seen anyone suspicious?"

"Everyone who walks the streets late at night is suspicious," Lottie said.

Eliza got to her feet and shook out her skirt. "It's clear to me what must be done at this point. Even if Agatha does get an article printed, it won't be for at least a few days. More of you could go missing in the meantime, so we'll have to get you off the streets."

Arabella watched as Violet's rouged cheeks darkened and her eyes narrowed. "We're barely surviving as it is, Mrs. Beckett. If we don't get back on the streets, we won't have food or any firewood. If you haven't noticed, the weather has turned foul."

"True," Eliza agreed. "I'm more than happy to give you money to see you through until the culprit behind the disappearances is apprehended."

Lottie stepped beside Violet, her eyes blazing. "We don't take charity."

Eliza lifted her chin. "It's not charity. It's a means to keep you safe, but instead of splitting hairs over this, you may think of it as a loan and pay me back at your earliest convenience."

Four sets of eyes glared at her.

Agatha strode to the fireplace and turned. "Ladies, it's your decision whether or not to return to the streets, and we'll respect whatever you decide." She sent a look of warning to Eliza, who'd taken to sputtering. "However, in order for me to help you, I need more information or else my publisher will not approve the article."

"But we don't have any more information," Violet said slowly. "And I don't know how to get you more."

Agatha smiled and waved a hand in the air. "Not to worry. I've just come up with the perfect plan. We're going to go undercover."

10

The following afternoon, Arabella glanced at herself in the dressing room mirror, wincing at the unusual reflection staring back at her. An intricate white wig sat high on her head, the paste gems woven throughout the hair sparkling in the room's bright lights. Her eyes looked rather mysterious with their coating of blue paint on the eyelids, and the kohl she'd used to outline them gave her a slightly naughty appearance. Not that she'd purposefully tried to obtain that particular look. She was less than proficient applying paint to her face, and even though she'd been aiming for simply disguising her features, she'd ended up with an enticing look. She plucked up an old-fashioned beauty patch and brought it to her face, pausing when the silk curtain to her right rustled and Agatha flounced out.

She laughed. "Well, well, don't you look . . . lovely?"

Agatha spun around, the motion causing the huge swath of fabric that made up the skirt of her garish green gown to puff up around her. She teetered to a stop on ridiculously high heels, even as she twirled a strand of her brash red wig around her fingers. "Do you think the color of my hair goes well with my pale complexion?"

"Ah . . . well, no, but by the time we reach our destination, it'll be dark."

Agatha tottered over to the mirror and peered into it. "Good heavens, I look sallow." She straightened, turned, and narrowed her eyes. "Your wig makes you look luminescent."

"I'd be more than happy to exchange wigs with you, but again, it'll be dark."

Agatha went to where Eliza was sitting on a chaise of purple velvet and plopped down beside her, only to spring back up a second later. "Maybe I just need more rouge."

Arabella was fairly certain that if Agatha applied another layer of color, the makeup would begin to crack, but one look at Eliza, who was shaking her head, had her swallowing her words. She turned back to the mirror, deftly stuck the beauty patch right beside her upper lip, and then got to her feet, shaking out the folds of her gown before she moved to join Eliza. She sat down ever so gingerly on the chaise, pushed her billowing skirts down with a slap of her hand, and grinned. "This dress is beyond ridiculous."

Eliza returned the grin. "I still cannot believe how fortunate it was that you were able to procure costumes on such short notice. Mrs. Davis must owe you a huge favor."

Arabella looked toward the back of the large dressing room where Mrs. Davis was puttering around, apparently organizing outfits for the performance later that night. "If you must know, Mrs. Davis found herself in a very precarious situation a few years back. I was able to direct her to a reputable attorney she found to her satisfaction."

"Should I assume *his* name is Mr. Davis?"

"Funny enough, it is indeed."

Eliza laughed and then sobered. "I wish I could go with you."

"We've been over this, more than once. It would hardly do to become fodder for the gossips at this stage in your life. Besides, you said Hamilton is working late this evening, and you told Piper and Ben you would be home to have dinner with them. You wouldn't want to disappoint them, would you?"

"Of course not, but I have to admit I feel as if I'm the girl left on the edge of the dance floor while everyone else is dancing."

"*I* certainly appreciate the fact you ladies decided to include me."

Arabella swung her attention around and watched as Katherine Gibson breezed through another silk curtain, gowned in a hideous creation of putrid pink, a towering black wig perched on her head. "*We* didn't decide to include you, Mrs. Gibson. If you will recall, you blackmailed us into agreeing to let you tag along."

"*Blackmail* is such a nasty little word, and please, under the circumstances, don't you think you should call me Katherine?"

Agatha took a step forward, wobbled on her shoes, kicked them off in disgust, then stalked over to stand in front of Katherine. "Fine, we'll address you as Katherine, but you still resorted to blackmail."

"Honestly, Agatha, I would think you would be more sympathetic to my plight," Katherine said. "If you've neglected to remember, I was facing an evening spent with parents."

"You were the one who accepted an invitation to dine with them," Arabella pointed out.

"True, and I admit I was perfectly content to enjoy their company until I discovered the adventure planned for the evening."

"You were eavesdropping outside my bedroom door," Arabella said.

"I stand guilty as charged, but I have no remorse over my underhanded method. If I hadn't followed you after I saw the three of you skulking past the parlor, I'd still be socializing with the old people." Katherine gave a delicate shudder, the act causing her wig to lean to one side.

Arabella crossed her arms over her chest. "Don't you think your mother is going to become concerned after a few hours when you don't reappear from using the powder room?"

"Did I forget to mention that I went back to the parlor and told everyone that you had graciously included me in your plans for the evening?"

"Yes, you did forget to mention that," Arabella muttered. "I must admit I'm a little astonished your mother agreed to your change of plans. I was under the distinct impression she doesn't approve of me."

"She's had a change of heart, dear. Truth be told, she's been a little rebellious of late, and I do think her change can be laid squarely at your feet, and those of your mother."

Alarm trickled down Arabella's spine. "But . . . your mother and I barely exchanged a word between us at the dinner party."

Katherine waved a gloved hand in the air. "I know, but there you have it."

Arabella frowned. "Where *did* you tell your mother you were going tonight?"

"I was ingeniously vague, not that I had a choice in the matter considering none of you extended to me all the particulars about the evening." Her eyes began to twinkle. "Where did you tell *your* parents you were going?"

Arabella smiled. "I was ingeniously vague as well, although . . . I didn't lie when I told my mother we were going to the theater." She gestured around the room. "We *are* at the theater."

Katherine rolled her eyes. "We're in the dressing room, and it's not as if we're planning on seeing the show."

Eliza stood up and moved to stand beside Katherine. "Have you considered how you're going to explain tonight to your husband? I hate to bring this up, but there is always the chance something will go wrong, as has happened all too frequently with some of our plans, and then what will you do?"

Katherine shrugged. "I'll worry about that if and when something goes awry. I readily admit that Harold and I are not on good terms at the moment, so, quite frankly, I don't care if my actions cause him distress." She blew out a breath. "He's been very difficult of late, accusing me of becoming 'bothersome' simply because I pressed him to explain some of his recent activities." She nodded to Arabella. "I believe he holds you responsible because I spent an evening in your presence."

How in the world was she supposed to respond to that?

"If you ask me," Katherine continued, "he's simply throwing nasty accusations my way to muddy up the waters regarding his recent carousing."

"Carousing?" Agatha asked.

"Oh, not with women, mind you, but I do believe quite a few pubs have been involved. He was very put out regarding my questions. It would seem he only wants me to speak of mundane things and nothing of any substance."

Arabella swallowed as she realized Katherine's blasé attitude hid a world of hurt. She couldn't imagine being married to a gentleman who refused to engage in heated conversations, and her attitude toward the lady changed immediately. She rose to her feet, walked to Katherine's side, and reached out to touch her arm. "Have the two of you ever spoken of anything other than the mundane?"

Katherine's eyes turned a little misty. "He was more attentive while we were courting. That went away almost the moment the vows were exchanged. Now we're simply strangers sharing the same roof, and all he expects from me is demure behavior and no trouble."

"You certainly look like trouble now," Arabella said.

Katherine's lips twitched. "My entire family would be appalled if they knew what I was up to. Well, maybe not my mother. She's apparently as annoyed with my father as I am with Harold. I believe that might have been why she accepted the invitation to dinner this evening. She knew full well that socializing with Mrs. Beckett and Mrs. Watson would cause my father a bit of aggravation."

Arabella tilted her head. "Your brother will be beyond aggravated if he discovers you went with us tonight."

"I don't care what Theodore thinks."

"You're only saying that because he's not in town at the moment."

"Oh, he's in town. He got back last night and stopped by for a visit."

A thread of temper began to stir. Even though Arabella had tried not to think about Theodore, he'd occasionally invaded her thoughts, and with those thoughts had come worry. The man did have a dangerous job after all, and the least he could have done was allow her the common courtesy of letting her know he'd returned safely.

Honestly, what was she thinking? It was not as if they'd parted on friendly terms, and he certainly didn't owe her a nicely penned note telling her he'd—

"He was in a foul frame of mind," Katherine said.

Arabella's temper cooled considerably. "Oh?"

"I think you had something to do with his dismal mood." Katherine frowned. "He kept badgering me about whether I'd seen you while he'd been away, and what you'd been doing."

Arabella tilted her head. "Why would he expect you to know what I'd been doing?"

Katherine shrugged. "I have no idea, nor do I really understand why he showed up at my house. It's not as if my brother visits often." She tapped a finger on her chin. "It was most peculiar, especially when he turned downright surly after I mentioned that I'd heard you'd been shopping."

"He was surly because I'd been shopping?"

"That is what I came to believe, unless you did something other than shopping that might have annoyed Theodore?"

Arabella paused for a moment even as her lips twitched. "I might have breathed."

Katherine's eyes crinkled at the corners. "Yes, breathing has been known to send Theodore over the edge, but I have no wish to dwell on my dear brother at the moment. He is cut from the very same cloth as Harold and my father, and I'm tired of contemplating men and their irritating ways. They are much more trouble than they're worth."

"Excuse me, Miss Beckett, but it's almost time for Madame Antoinette to arrive, and she will not react well to finding all of you taking up space in her domain," Mrs. Davis said, bustling up beside them.

Arabella smiled. "Then we shall be on our way, Mrs. Davis, because I for one certainly don't want to incur the wrath of Madame Antoinette. Thank you again for lending us such lovely costumes."

"I don't know if I'd go so far as to make the claim my costume is lovely," Katherine muttered.

Arabella ignored her, watched as Agatha shoved her feet into her high shoes, and couldn't help but roll her eyes. "You do remember that it snowed yesterday, don't you?"

"I need to look authentic," Agatha said before she smiled at Mrs. Davis, grabbed her reticule off a table, and pranced somewhat gingerly out of the room, Eliza laughing by her side.

"Are you certain you want to go through with this?" Arabella asked as she and Katherine strolled toward the door.

"This is the most fun I've had in quite some time."

"Fun has a way of turning into trouble," Arabella said. She took Katherine's arm, hurried through the theater and out the door, sucking in a breath as cold air smacked her in the face. She bent her head and hurried to the carriage, gave the driver instructions on where to take them, but then told him to wait a minute when she noticed Eliza sitting there on the seat.

"Did you forget that you brought your carriage?" she asked as she scrambled to take her seat, scooting over to make room for Katherine.

"I only wanted to give all of you some last minute encouragement and to remind you to not do anything dangerous."

Agatha pulled a blanket from under the carriage seat, threw it on top of herself, and smiled. "There's no need to worry about us. We're only going to ask some questions and perhaps do a bit of snooping."

Eliza narrowed her eyes. "You never said anything about snooping."

"If I'm going to write an award-winning article, snooping will be required."

"Now I'll never relax until I get word you're safe," Eliza said.

Arabella reached over and took Eliza's hand. "I know not being able to accompany us is difficult, but . . . if you need a distraction, you could think of ways to get the ladies off the streets for good. It was an ingenious move on Agatha's part to insist they not solicit customers this evening so they could help us, but that only gets them away from their job for a single evening."

"I'm surprised they agreed to my suggestion," Agatha said. "They were so adamant about not accepting charity."

Arabella released Eliza's hand and settled back in the seat. "That's why I was rather ambiguous when I was discussing their payment for assisting us tonight. I admit I might have led them to believe the wages they're earning are coming from the *New-York Tribune*. We'll need to be careful and not mention that I'm the one paying them."

"I'm still not comfortable with you absorbing the full amount," Eliza said.

"I have more than enough money at my disposal, Eliza, and besides, I've decided that helping women get off the streets is going to be my newest cause."

"I thought your cause was to secure the right to vote," Katherine said slowly.

"It's not as if I'm going to abandon the suffrage movement, but I've come to realize that while I've been campaigning around the country, true atrocities are occurring to women right here in New York. I believe God has had His hand in recent events and is pushing me to lend these ladies my assistance."

Eliza frowned. "I don't want to discourage you, Arabella, but I don't know if these ladies will be receptive to any assistance from you. They were quite adamant about not appreciating charity."

"It wouldn't be charity if we found them another way to procure a living," Arabella argued.

"I have no idea what manner of employment they would be willing to accept," Eliza said. "From what we've seen, they're relatively uneducated, and you and I both know New York society is incredibly particular regarding what type of servants they allow in their grand houses."

Katherine blew out a breath. "Perhaps we should simply ask them what they'd like to do with their lives."

"Now, there's an idea," Arabella said. "Simple yet brilliant. I should have thought of it."

Katherine rolled her eyes. "I don't believe you're the type of lady who likes to settle for 'simple.'"

Eliza laughed. "On that note, I'm going to take my leave before events turn violent." She shoved open the carriage door, the act causing a frigid burst of air to whip over them. She jumped to the ground and turned. "You will be careful, won't you?"

Agatha rooted around on the carriage seat, located her reticule, and pulled a pistol from it.

"Why am I not surprised you're armed?" Eliza said.

"I have one too," Arabella said, lifting up her skirt to display the pistol securely attached to her leg with a frilly garter.

Eliza shifted her gaze to Katherine. "Just make certain you stick next to these two."

Katherine whipped up her skirt and pointed to two pistols, one attached to each leg. She dropped her skirt and grinned. "I am Theodore's sister after all."

"God help you," Eliza said before she closed the door and hurried away.

Arabella watched out the frosty window until she saw Eliza disappear into her own carriage, then rapped on the roof and leaned back in her seat when the carriage set to moving.

"So, Arabella," Katherine began, drawing her attention, "I'm still curious as to what you did to my brother to make him so disagreeable to me."

Arabella opened her mouth, shutting it when absolutely nothing came to her, but was saved the bother of a response when Katherine continued on as if she hadn't just asked a question.

"There I was, sitting in my parlor with Theodore, fielding question after question about you, but then I told him your mother mentioned you'd been spending a bit of time shopping, and he got testy. It was rather odd, especially since Theodore has been known to escort more than his fair share of ladies through the shops."

Arabella wouldn't allow herself the luxury of contemplating why that statement rankled her. "I have no idea why the idea of shopping would have made Theodore testy. I can assure you, I've never once enjoyed a turn through the shops with your brother by my side."

Agatha made a *tsk*ing sound under her breath. "Theodore's surliness had nothing to do with shopping. I think it results from his finding you fascinating, Arabella, but being too stubborn to admit it. I think he realized he wasn't behaving in his normal fashion and turned surly to distract from his behavior."

"Theodore does not find me fascinating. Irritating perhaps, but not fascinating."

Agatha smiled. "Why else would he have accused you of flirting with Grayson?"

"Because he enjoys annoying me?"

"Well, there is that," Agatha mumbled.

Arabella turned back to the window and allowed her gaze to drift over the people scurrying around the streets, their heads bent and their shoulders hunched against the cold. She caught a glimpse of ships in the distance and turned from the window. "We're almost to the docks."

Katherine's eyes widened. "I didn't know we were going to hawk our wares at the docks."

"We're not hawking our wares. We're just asking questions. There will be no need for any *hawking*."

"But . . . the docks are exceedingly dangerous. What should I do if some man approaches me?"

"I doubt we'll encounter that," Arabella said. "I'm more than certain our appearance will be a deterrent rather than an enticement. Just stay by me and you'll be fine, or you could always remain in the carriage."

Katherine lifted her chin. "Although I admit I did not realize what our final destination was going to be, I'm not a coward. I'm going with you just as I promised, and I'm determined to be useful."

"Look, there's Violet," Agatha said as the carriage rolled to a stop. She opened the door and jumped to the ground, the long skirts of her gown trailing behind her.

Arabella struggled through the door, followed immediately by Katherine, and took a moment to collect her bearings as a strong gust of wind smacked into her, causing her wig to wobble and her dress to lift up around her. She pushed the gown down, straightened her wig, and took hold of Katherine's arm before they hurried over to Violet.

Violet's mouth dropped open as her gaze went from Arabella to Agatha and then lingered on Katherine. "Good heavens, would you look at the three of you."

"You ladies look like a bunch of traveling actors," Lottie said as she strode up to join them, with Sarah and Hannah following a few steps behind.

Katherine shook out her skirts. "We're wearing opera gowns."

Lottie frowned. "You're not Mrs. Beckett."

"I'm Mrs. Gibson, but you may call me Katherine, or maybe Kate would be more appropriate for this evening."

Lottie's frown deepened. "Are you married to Mr. Harold Gibson?"

Katherine narrowed her eyes. "You are familiar with Harold?"

"Not personally," Lottie said, taking a step back as Katherine advanced.

"How do you know him?"

"He's one of the richest men in New York," Violet said.

"We know all the rich folks. It can come in handy at times if you catch one of them doing something shady."

"Yes, well," Arabella said quickly when Katherine began to sputter, "we should get into our places. Where do you suggest we start, Violet?"

"As we discussed yesterday, we'll go to the far end of the docks where most of the girls have gone missing. We'll stroll around and see if anyone suspicious turns up." Violet drew in a breath and slowly released it. "There's always the chance that we might run into the madman who's been stealing our friends, so if any of you feel uneasy about someone, don't hesitate to yell. Remember, even though we're going to split up into smaller groups, everyone needs to be with another lady at all times. It would be a cruel ending to this evening if someone else was snatched."

A shiver ran down Arabella's spine at those ominous words. She fell into step with the other ladies and tried to ignore the vulgar comments that began coming their way from the men lining the docks. She straightened her shoulders, stifled the urge to address the rude comments, and continued forward, the moisture from the sea stealing through her clothing and causing her to shiver. She couldn't help the sadness that seeped into her very soul as the thought came to her that Violet and her friends were out on these docks nightly, forced to ignore the elements in order to earn a living.

She was more determined than ever to help them into a better life because *this* was no way to live.

"Here's where we split up," Violet said, coming to a halt. "Kate, stick with Hannah and Sarah. Agatha, I thought it would be best for you to come with me."

"I'll stay with Lottie," Arabella said as she caught Katherine's eye. "Keep your pistol handy, and if you run into trouble, scream."

"If I run into trouble, I plan on shooting first and then

screaming," Katherine said. She followed Hannah to stand a few yards away.

Arabella and Agatha exchanged nods and took off in opposite directions, and Arabella and Lottie finally came to a stop under a gas lamp. "What now?"

"We wait for the men."

Five minutes later, Arabella released a sigh. "I don't think anyone is going to come up to us, Lottie."

"It's your dress. It's a bit off-putting."

"Perhaps we should take matters into our own hands."

Lottie arched a brow. "You want to do the approaching?"

Arabella arched a brow right back. "I was thinking more that we forget about the men and question some of the other ladies down here. Someone must have seen something."

"You can go talk to that group," Lottie said with a nod toward five women who were huddled together and looked as if they were scared to death. "I'll see if any of those fine gents standing over there by that light have seen anything tonight."

Arabella shook her head. "We should stay together."

"I won't get anything out of them if you're with me," Lottie said. "Your speech is too refined and your gown too hideous." She patted her hair. "I've been dealing with men for more years than I care to admit, and besides, it's not as if there's just a single man. I don't think they're going to grab me and bolt from the docks."

"I don't know, Lottie. I still think we should stick together."

"I'm only going to be a few feet from you. You can keep an eye on me, and if I think something's wrong, I'll give you a yell."

Before Arabella had a chance to protest further, Lottie sauntered away from her, let out a boisterous laugh when she reached the men, and was soon deep in conversation with a man who was thin and shorter than Lottie by at least a head.

Knowing full well that Lottie was right and that the man

chatting with her wasn't exactly a threat, Arabella squared her shoulders and marched her way over to the huddled group of ladies. Once they got over their initial hysterics regarding her appearance, they warmed up to her and told her everything they knew, which wasn't much. After ten minutes of useless questioning, she finally gave up and was just stepping in the direction of Lottie and her crowd of men when Agatha suddenly appeared by her side, causing her to jump.

"You scared me half to death."

Agatha smiled. "Sorry about that. Have you had any luck?"

"I'm afraid to say I haven't."

"Should we finish here?" Katherine asked as she sidled up next to them. "I don't recall a time I have been so thoroughly insulted. Do you know, a gentleman came up to me and offered me twenty cents? *Twenty cents*."

"You should count yourself fortunate. I haven't been offered anything," Agatha said. "And no, we can't leave quite yet. I haven't discovered anything relating to the disappearances."

"The man who offered me twenty cents told me there've been some new faces down here tonight," Katherine said. "I tried to learn more, but he wasn't interested in *talking* to me, and I had to graciously refuse his offer."

"You pulled out your gun, didn't you?" Agatha asked.

"I did," Katherine admitted. "That, unfortunately, brought any attempt at conversation to an abrupt end."

"Would you recognize the man again?" Agatha asked.

"I don't think I'll ever be able to forget him."

"We should go look for him," Agatha said. She turned toward Arabella. "Do you want to come with us?"

Arabella shook her head and gestured to where Lottie was still laughing with the men. "I don't want to leave her alone, and . . . why are the two of you not with Violet and Hannah?"

"They said we were putting a damper on their investigation," Katherine said with a grin. "Agatha and I didn't want to be shuffled off to stand beneath a streetlight, so we decided to investigate together."

"We won't be long," Agatha said. "It looks like it's going to snow again, and these ridiculous shoes I decided to wear will not allow me to remain standing if that happens."

Arabella smiled. "I told you they were a little too much, but you're right, it does feel like it's about to snow. Go check on Katherine's man, and then we should probably be on our way."

Arabella watched them stride away and took one step toward Lottie, but then froze in place as a shiver swept down her spine. She squinted into the darkness off to her right.

No one was there.

She rubbed her hands down her arms and forced herself to take a deep breath. It was clear her imagination was getting away from her, but . . . why then did she have the distinct feeling someone was watching her?

A trickle of sweat rolled down her neck despite the cold, and she could hear the harsh intake of her breathing. Her breathing increased when a figure of a man, cloaked in a flowing cape, stepped into the feeble light of a gas lamp, his features hidden beneath a cap he'd pulled down almost to his eyes.

A feeling of abject terror swept over Arabella as she realized the man had settled his attention on her. He took a step toward her, and she opened her mouth to scream.

Horror filled her when she realized she was incapable of speech, not even a whisper. She glanced around, searching for help, and saw that everyone had drifted away from her.

She was completely alone.

She yanked up her skirt and pulled her pistol from her leg, but stilled when a rough hand grabbed her arm, causing a high-pitched squeak to spill from her lips.

"Give me that."

Arabella raised her gaze and sagged in relief when she recognized an officer of the law. She swallowed. "There's a man," she finally managed to get out.

"Isn't there always?" the officer said, grabbing the gun out of her hand before he began pulling Arabella up the street.

Arabella tried again. "No, you misunderstood me. There was a man . . . a sinister man."

The officer didn't slow his pace as he hauled her to a waiting police wagon. He shoved her into the dark space without speaking another word and slammed the door.

She landed on a bench and sat there for a moment, her pulse racing. The door opened seconds later and more ladies sailed through it, the last one being Agatha, who plopped down on the bench right beside her.

"Rotten luck, getting arrested," Agatha said. Looking around, she asked, "Where's Katherine?"

"I'm here," Katherine said from the very back of the wagon, peering around Lottie. "I must say, I've never been in a police wagon before, and this isn't exactly what I imagined." She blew out a breath. "Tell me, what should we do now?"

Agatha sat forward. "I think Violet managed to slip away. Hopefully she'll think to contact Eliza."

"What if Violet didn't slip away?" Katherine asked.

"We'll probably have to send for your brother," Agatha said. "He's the one with the most experience in these matters."

Arabella could not shake her head fast enough, the motion sending her wig into her lap. She ignored it. "There is absolutely no way we can send for Theodore. In case you've forgotten, he bailed me out of jail only a few weeks ago, and he won't be keen to do it again. Besides, Katherine's involved as well, and you can't tell me she wants Theodore at the jail either."

"You do make an excellent point," Katherine said with a bob of her head.

"But . . . if we don't summon someone, how are we going to get out of jail?" Agatha asked. "I have a few dollars on me, but I didn't bring much since I didn't want it stolen down at the docks."

Arabella leaned over her wig and whistled to get Lottie's attention. "What normally happens after you get arrested?"

"Well, first we get taken to jail," Lottie said, "and then we'll get thrown in a cell where we'll probably stay until morning. Once the judge arrives, we get to stand before him, where all of us will solemnly tell him we'll never walk the streets again." She grinned and stuck her hand down her bodice, rooted around for a moment, and retrieved some crumpled bills. "He'll take this from us, and then it's back to the streets we go."

It was somewhat amusing to discover other ladies stashed their funds down their bodices. Arabella shoved her amusement aside, ignored Katherine's incredibly wide eyes, and tilted her head. "Is there any possibility of getting released tonight?"

"Only if someone important shows up to bail you out," Lottie said. "That's your only hope."

Katherine leaned around Lottie. "Agatha, don't you have any credentials from the paper?"

"Excellent thinking, Katherine," Agatha said. "Unfortunately, those credentials have the name Alfred Wallenstate on them. And I don't think anyone's going to believe me when I make the claim I'm the gentleman in question." She suddenly brightened. "But since we're off to jail, we might as well make the most of it. We'll be able to question some of the inmates, so maybe the night won't be a total loss."

A small shiver ran through Arabella at the reminder of why they'd been out in the first place. She sat up straight.

"We'll need to be diligent in questioning those other inmates, because unfortunately I encountered something of a grave nature down at the docks tonight."

"What was it?" Katherine asked.

"Evil."

11

Theodore rubbed a hand across his face and squinted at the document he was attempting to read. He loathed paperwork, preferring to spend his time on the streets working a case, but he procured the majority of his clients through written requests, so he had little choice but to sort through the petitions hopeful clients had sent him while he'd been away.

He sighed and leaned back in his chair, knowing full well that the reason the paperwork seemed so daunting was his dismal mood.

He'd spent two weeks trying to discover what was transpiring in Gilman to no avail, mostly because every single officer of the law seemed to have disappeared.

The few people he'd managed to coerce into talking with him told a very strange tale indeed. Apparently, Sheriff Dawson and his men were involved in a secret case, which had forced them to leave town in order to pursue leads and keep the good people of Gilman safe.

Leaving a town completely devoid of protection certainly wasn't what he considered keeping the people safe.

It was beyond odd.

What was also odd was that all his investigating efforts had turned up absolutely nothing.

He'd been forced to finally admit defeat, something that didn't sit well with him, and return to New York. He'd spent the entire train ride brooding about the mysteries plaguing Gilman. Unfortunately, once he'd reached the comforts of his home, his brooding had turned to the annoying Miss Arabella Beckett.

Why he was even allowing himself to brood over that particular lady was beyond him. It wasn't as if they shared a common affection for each other. They could barely abide each other's company.

Why then did his thoughts continuously return to her?

Theodore picked up his cup of tea, took a sip, and grimaced as the tepid liquid slid down his throat. He considered ringing for a fresh pot, but thought better of it. There was no sense inflicting his foul mood on the servants.

He probably shouldn't have burdened his sister with his dark company the day before either, but that hadn't stopped him from traveling to her house shortly after he'd gotten back to town.

He hadn't planned on paying Katherine a visit, but when Arabella kept plaguing his every thought, he'd needed a distraction. He'd hopped on his horse, ridden the twenty minutes it took him to get to Katherine's house, and greeted her with the required kiss on the cheek before launching into a full interrogation, all of which revolved around Arabella.

It was little wonder Katherine had been a touch bemused. It wasn't as if he sought out his sister on a regular basis, and he certainly had never bothered to question her about a lady before . . . ever. Katherine had regarded him with wary eyes as he'd ranted on and on, until finally, after about five minutes, her expression turned speculative instead of wary, which had caused him to turn defensive.

It had not been one of his finest moments.

He took another sip of tea and consoled himself with the knowledge that he most likely questioned Katherine in such a direct manner because his deepest fear, as he'd traveled back to New York, was that Sheriff Dawson and his men had followed Arabella home. His fear made absolutely no sense whatsoever, but had stayed in the back of his mind from the moment he'd discovered the sheriff and his deputies missing.

It didn't explain why he'd gotten so angry when Katherine informed him Arabella was perfectly fine and that she'd been spending her time shopping.

Shopping was such a perfectly normal and expected activity for a lady.

A sliver of relief shot through him. Shopping explained everything. He set down his cup and folded his hands over his stomach.

It was no wonder he'd been surly and short-tempered with Katherine. She'd brought to his attention the fact that Arabella was just a normal everyday lady, and that wasn't a notion he wanted tickling his brain.

It made her approachable, in the same way her new appearance did.

An image of Arabella at the dinner party—looking entirely too delightful with her flirty little hairstyle and her eyes sparkling with mischief as Grayson lingered over her hand—flashed to mind.

"You're becoming obsessed," Theodore muttered, pushing Arabella out of his thoughts as best he could as he reached for his paperwork.

She pushed her way right back in.

Honestly, the amount of time Arabella spent in his head was enough to drive him mad. It was also making him short-tempered. He was never unpleasant with his sister, but he'd certainly been unpleasant the day before, and he knew he needed to make amends.

He began sifting through the papers, hoping to find something that would occupy his thoughts and allow him to discontinue pondering the all-too-annoying Arabella. He finally found a few interesting requests, one for help in locating a missing relative and another for assistance with a delicate matter concerning the disappearance of a priceless painting. Either one would provide a welcome distraction.

He picked up a fountain pen and began scribbling notes, his hand pausing over the paper when the door to his study opened and his father, Samuel, followed by his brother-in-law, Harold Gibson, strode into the room.

"It's about time you got home," Samuel Wilder said, stopping in front of Theodore's desk. "Your grandfather has been pestering me endlessly the past few days, demanding to know when you were expected to return. I believe he wishes to speak with you."

"Is he all right?" Theodore asked, getting to his feet to shake his father's hand before gesturing Samuel into a chair. He lifted his head and nodded at Harold, who for some strange reason ignored the nod and moved directly to the window, immediately presenting Theodore with his back.

Theodore frowned. He and Harold did not enjoy what anyone would call a close relationship, but the gentleman had never been downright rude to him.

"I'm sure your grandfather is perfectly fine," Samuel said, pulling Theodore back into the conversation. "He'll outlive us all."

"He must have a new business proposition for me," Theodore said as he settled back in his chair. "He most likely sent a note over, but since I've been away so long, I'm somewhat behind on my correspondence."

Samuel leaned forward, his dark eyes flashing. "I wish he

would cease and desist with his business propositions. It's bad enough you've abandoned the family business, but to operate an investigation agency? You're wasting your talent."

"My agency is incredibly lucrative, Father. You know that, and you also know I use my agency as a front for the jobs I do for the government. It's not as if I'm a criminal."

"You have the brains for finance."

Theodore nodded to his brother-in-law, who was still turned away from him. "So does Harold, which is why it was so fortunate for you when he married Katherine. He's perfectly capable of taking over the family business if you ever decide to slow down. I would not be satisfied sitting behind a desk all day poring over figures."

"*Hmph*," Samuel muttered as he leaned back in his chair. "I didn't come here specifically as a messenger for your grandfather. I came to speak with you on another matter. You've caused quite a bit of trouble lately."

"Indeed," Harold Gibson said as he finally spun around and glared at Theodore. "Katherine is no longer the sweet and compliant woman I married, and it's entirely your fault."

Theodore's mood improved dramatically. It was refreshing to discover he wasn't the only one plagued with difficulties of the feminine type. "I hate to tell you this, Harold, but I don't recall ever thinking Katherine was exceptionally sweet."

"That's preposterous," Harold said. "I mean, granted, at the moment she does seem to have a slight edge to her demeanor, but before you went and introduced her to that horrid Miss Beckett and Miss Beckett's mother, she was completely delightful. Now my entire world has gone topsy-turvy."

Theodore arched a brow. "Katherine's temperament changed because I introduced her to Mrs. and Miss Beckett?"

"Katherine's not the only one who has acquired a change in personality," Samuel added. "Your mother has obtained some very peculiar ideas of late, and I must tell you, I am not amused. She had the audacity to lock me out of the house three nights ago when I arrived home past midnight." He drew in a shuddering breath. "I was forced to climb through a window on the second floor. I could have lost my life."

"You obviously didn't."

"That is completely beside the point, and I'll have you know I'm covered in bruises from missing the window and sliding halfway down the gutter."

Theodore choked back a laugh. "How did you manage to get back to the window?"

Samuel puffed himself up, rose from the chair, and began to pace about the room. "I certainly didn't get back to the window with any help from our servants." He paused in mid-pace. "I have no idea why not a single one of them came to my aid. They must have heard me. I was yelling rather loudly." Samuel shook his head. "I finally managed to inch my way up the gutters, then used the vines to swing my way back to the window. To add insult to injury, your mother was calmly standing right before the window, and she didn't even bother to ask about my welfare."

"At least you got into the house," Harold said, moving to Samuel's side and giving him a commiserating pat on the back. "Katherine locked me out last week. She claims it was an accident, but I was forced to spend the night at my parents' house."

"It's a conspiracy, I tell you," Samuel said. He stalked back to Theodore's desk and banged his fist on it, causing papers to drift to the floor. "It's your fault, Theodore, and Harold and I are here to demand you set matters right."

"You're sadly mistaken if you believe I know anything about women these days." He crossed his arms over his chest. "I will say this, though. The two of you created your situations, not I. Did you truly think Mother and Katherine would believe that ridiculous story you made up about spending an evening participating in a charity event and at a church no less?"

"Are you suggesting I lied to your mother?" Samuel asked.

"I'm not *suggesting* anything, Father. I know you lied to her. You and Harold were most likely off at a pub."

Harold lowered himself into a chair. "There's nothing wrong with pubs."

"Then why didn't you tell Katherine that's where you were going?"

Harold ignored Theodore's question. "None of this would have ever happened if you hadn't introduced them to those two Beckett women. They've been a horrible influence on Louise and Katherine. Katherine's never questioned my actions before, and I don't appreciate the fact that she's doing it now. I want my adorable little wife back, not the hoyden who has somehow taken her place."

"Mrs. Beckett and Miss Beckett are wonderful ladies," Theodore said, unwilling to contemplate why Harold's disparaging statement rankled so much when he'd been lecturing Katherine along the same lines, at least in regard to Arabella. "Mrs. Beckett is a prominent member of society, and Miss Beckett is a woman who has devoted her life to helping others."

Samuel's face turned red. "Miss Beckett has devoted her life to convincing other women they need to throw off their feminine manners and behave like men."

"Exactly how is Mother behaving like a man?" Theodore asked.

"She questions me, and it's not a woman's place to know what her husband is up to every single minute."

Theodore considered his father for a moment. "This is going to sound odd, coming from me, but don't you think you and Mother might be happier if you actually attempted to share more of your lives together? You might discover you enjoy spending time in her company."

"Miss Beckett's gotten to him," Harold said.

"Miss Beckett has nothing to do with any of this," Theodore said, even though he feared that was slightly less than the truth. "The only reason I invited Mother and Katherine to attend the dinner party in the first place was because you two left them alone that night. I found them upset and unhappy, so I took it upon myself to improve their situation by getting them out of the house. My plan worked because Mother and Katherine had a lovely time. You two should be thanking me."

Samuel's face went from red to purple. "You think I should thank you? Are you aware that your mother and sister are spending the evening dining with the Beckett family instead of being home where they belong? Add to that the pesky little fact that Mr. and Mrs. Watson have also been included, and I shudder to think what nonsense Louise will be spouting once she does come home."

"Mr. and Mrs. Watson are very nice," Theodore said. "In fact, I'm surprised you haven't socialized with them before. Mr. Watson adores everything to do with the financial markets, and he would welcome an opportunity to seek your advice."

"I'm very aware of the fact that Roger Watson is a capital gentleman, Theodore," Samuel said. "But his wife, on the other hand . . ." He shuddered and took a deep breath. "I have no idea why Roger would permit his wife to associate on a regular basis with Gloria Beckett."

"I would have to believe that Mrs. Watson never bothered to ask her husband if she could become friends with Mrs. Beckett," Theodore said. "But Mr. Watson was wise enough to know he needed to accept Gloria if he wished to remain in accord with his wife. Besides, I've come to know the woman quite well, and I find her enchanting."

Samuel wiped his brow with the back of his hand and,

glaring at Theodore, lowered himself into a chair. "You think I should simply go along with your mother's madness?"

"If you don't want to continue getting locked out of your own house, yes."

The sound of running feet caused Theodore to shove his chair back and get to his feet just as Eliza rushed into the room, accompanied by a woman who looked slightly familiar. He narrowed his eyes as Eliza skidded to a halt in front of him and placed one hand on his desk while she used the other to press against what must be a stitch in her side.

She tilted her head and peered at him through hair that had somehow managed to escape its pins. "I need your help."

He lifted a brow. "That's obvious."

She dropped her gaze, brushed the hair out of her face, and turned her head ever so slightly before he heard her suck in a loud gulp of air. She suddenly straightened, her hands clenched, and then she lifted her chin, batted almost-innocent eyes at him, and let out a giggle.

Eliza never giggled.

She laughed, snorted, grunted, and raged in a temper from time to time, but not once since he'd made her acquaintance had he ever heard her giggle.

Something dire was obviously afoot.

"I do beg your pardon," she practically purred, which was also something Eliza never did. "I was somewhat distracted and didn't realize you have company. Violet and I will just be on our way."

Violet, that's who the other lady was, and . . . he knew her from the streets.

Something definitely was afoot.

He walked around his desk and took Eliza's arm, staring down into her now-perspiring face. "What happened?"

"It's not terribly important, and there's no need to involve you in it. If you'll excuse us, we'll just be on our way."

He tightened his grip. "You're not going anywhere until you explain exactly what you're doing here and why you're here with that lady."

Eliza's expression turned stubborn. "It's a bit of a tricky situation, but Violet is a friend of mine and sought out my help when a slightly disturbing incident took place. Since you have guests, I'm not comfortable going into all the troubling details."

"These gentlemen aren't exactly guests. That's my father, Mr. Samuel Wilder, and that's my brother-in-law, Mr. Harold Gibson."

He wasn't certain, but he thought he heard her mutter something that sounded very much like "This is awkward" before she glanced at Harold, turned rather pale, and then squared her shoulders. "Gentlemen, it was lovely to see everyone this evening, but I truly do believe the best option at this point would be for me to go find Hamilton."

"Hamilton's missing?" Theodore asked.

"Not at all. He's working late with Zayne, but they're away from the office. That's actually why I came here, but apparently, given the fact you have company, I'm going to have to see if I can run him to ground."

"I say, am I to understand you're Mrs. Hamilton Beckett?" Harold asked.

Eliza nodded, bit her lip, and dipped into a curtsy as Harold bowed in her direction. "It's a pleasure to make your acquaintance, Mr. Gibson."

"The pleasure is mine, Mrs. Beckett. I've been meaning to pay you and your husband a visit. I have quite a few investment strategies to share with you."

Theodore felt his teeth clink together. "Harold, this is hardly the appropriate moment to sell your services."

"Where are you manners, Theodore?" Samuel said as he rose to his feet and sent Theodore a look of disgust. "Honestly,

I assumed this was a mere client, but . . . to find out she's Mrs. Beckett, the newly arrived aristocrat from London, well, I must beg your pardon for not getting to my feet sooner, my dear."

What was wrong with everyone tonight? It was clear from Eliza's attitude that something was dreadfully amiss, and here his father and brother-in-law were acting as if they should be sitting down to tea with the lady.

He pushed aside his aggravation. "I am sorry, Father, for not paying proper attention to the social necessities. This is, indeed, Mrs. Hamilton Beckett, and I believe Eliza said the woman with her is Violet."

Violet sent him a cheeky grin from her position by the door, and he felt his lips twitch when he realized she'd been edging her way back to the door ever since Eliza had acknowledged his guests.

"It is an honor to meet you, Mr. Wilder," Eliza said. "Your son was of great assistance to me when I first entered the country, and that is why I've sought out his counsel this evening. Having said that, I do believe I may have overreacted to the situation, and now, if you'll excuse me, Violet and I will be on our way. Good evening." She shook off Theodore's hold, strode to Violet's side, and began pulling the woman closer to the door.

"Has Agatha gotten herself into trouble again?" Theodore called, causing Eliza to pause on the threshold and turn.

"Why would you assume that?"

"Process of elimination."

"Maybe I'm here concerning Zayne."

"You said he was working late with Hamilton."

"It really is unfortunate you're so bright."

"What was that?" Theodore asked.

"Nothing," Eliza replied as she began moving once again. "We'll just see ourselves out. Have a good night."

"Is she in jail?"

Eliza stopped, turned, and released a dramatic sigh. "Why would you assume someone's in jail?"

"Because it's late, you've opted to seek me out, and you're in the company of a rather questionable character," Theodore said before he smiled at Violet. "No offense meant, of course, Violet."

"None taken, Mr. Wilder," Violet said.

Theodore returned his attention to Eliza, who, much to his amusement, appeared to be slowly scooting back through the door. "So, Agatha's landed herself in jail again. Is she alone?"

"You're very annoying," Eliza said, pausing in mid-scoot.

He arched a brow.

Eliza threw up her hands. "Fine, you're right, Agatha's in jail."

"And?" Theodore prompted.

"And what?"

"Is she alone?"

Eliza shot a look to Harold, and then for some odd reason turned her attention to the ceiling as if she found it incredibly interesting. "Of course she's not completely alone, Theodore. I'm sure there are other people in jail with her."

Why were women such difficult creatures, and why did it seem as if he was constantly engaged in a battle of wits with them lately?

"Would one of these other people just happen to be Arabella Beckett?"

Eliza's perusal of the ceiling ended as she winced. "Arabella might be with Agatha."

"Are you suggesting Miss Arabella Beckett is currently residing in the city jail?" Harold blustered.

"I wish it was only a suggestion," Eliza said before she lifted her chin and glanced at Violet. "We really should go."

"Just how are you planning on getting Agatha and Arabella out of jail without my help?" Theodore asked.

"It can't be that difficult," Eliza said. "I did bring money. I'm certain the officials at the jail will be more than happy to divest me of it."

"Why don't you want me to go?" Theodore asked.

Eliza glanced once again to Harold, winced, and turned back to Theodore. "You have guests. It would be rude for you to abandon them."

"My father-in-law and I will come with you," Harold proclaimed.

"Why would you want to do that?" Eliza asked, panic now clearly visible in her voice. "It will hardly be a pleasant outing."

"Pleasant outing or not," Harold began, "observing Miss Beckett behind bars will give me the ammunition I need to encourage my wife to discontinue her association with the Beckett family."

Eliza narrowed her eyes. "Mr. Gibson, I am now a member of the Beckett family, and I take great offense at your insinuation that they are somehow undesirable. They are a prominent New York family with abundant wealth at their disposal, and someone in your profession should certainly not throw aspersions on their good name. It would not serve you well to insult a family who has more than sufficient funds tied up in the stock market and in stocks I'm certain you represent."

Harold's lips thinned. "Your sister-in-law has been a bad influence on my wife. Katherine has not been herself ever since she made Miss Beckett's acquaintance."

"Your wife has spent relatively little time with Arabella," Eliza said. "If she's not been herself lately, I would have to believe the fault for that lies with you. Maybe you shouldn't spend so much time carousing."

Harold blinked. "Where did you hear that?"

Eliza shrugged. "Katherine mentioned it to me."

"When did you have a conversation with my wife?"

Eliza turned to Violet. "Ready?"

Violet nodded.

Theodore strode forward and stepped in front of Eliza, effectively blocking her from the door.

"You really must step aside," she hissed.

"I'm afraid I can't do that just yet. When did you talk to Katherine?"

"I really shouldn't say."

Alarm began to snake through him. "Why not?"

"It wouldn't be appropriate given your . . . guests."

"Who else is with Agatha and Arabella in jail?"

Violet stepped forward. "I think Lottie and Hannah got snatched."

Theodore could feel the vein begin to throb on his forehead and drew in a deep breath, trying to control the anger now coursing through him. "Forgive me, Violet, but you know your friends were not who I meant."

"You're not very attractive when you snarl like that, Mr. Wilder," Violet said with a sniff before she looked at Eliza. "We should be on our way."

"No one is going anywhere," Theodore said, "until I learn exactly who is behind bars with Arabella and Agatha."

"I demand someone explain what is going on," Harold said, joining Theodore and looking from Eliza to Violet. "What does it matter who is with Miss Beckett and Miss Watson, unless . . ." Confusion clouded his eyes. "You're not suggesting that Katherine and Louise are involved in this madness, are you?"

Before Theodore had a chance to reply, his father strode up to them and let out a chuckle. "Of course no one is suggesting our wives are involved, Harold. Why, you and I both know that Louise and Katherine are dining at the Beckett house this evening."

Theodore watched as Eliza exchanged a horrified glance

with Violet before she batted innocent eyes once again, still not speaking a single word.

Ladies were much more trouble than they were worth, and he needed to remember that.

He drew in another deep breath and slowly released it. "Are my mother and sister enjoying a lovely dinner at the moment?"

"I'm sure your mother is."

Theodore felt as if his head were about to explode. "And Katherine?"

"I don't appreciate your tone, Mr. Wilder."

"I don't like that you're hiding something, Mrs. Beckett."

Eliza's eyes spewed sparks as she considered him for a long moment, and then she smiled. "Fine, have it your way." She turned to Harold, her smile widening. "I do hate to be the one to tell you this, Mr. Gibson, but your wife is not having dinner. She's in jail."

Harold began to sputter, abruptly stopping when Eliza stepped closer to him and added, "And just to be clear, the reason Katherine's in jail? She blackmailed Agatha and Arabella into allowing her to tag along this evening. So if you think you're going to blame Arabella for your wife's foray into criminal activity, you're sadly mistaken."

Eliza curtsied, took Violet's arm, sent Theodore a glare that had him moving out of the way, and stalked from the room, her head held high.

12

Arabella hunched her shoulders, hoping to appear as small as possible as she huddled against the cold iron bars of yet another cell.

She chanced a glance at the eight ladies of the night who were lounging on the opposite side of their shared space, and could only thank God this particular cell was not as small as the one she'd been stuck in back in Gilman.

From the angry looks some of the ladies kept sending her way, as well as the looks they were sending Agatha and Katherine, she wasn't exactly certain a larger cell was going to help them survive the night.

Honestly, she was a bit befuddled by the looks. It certainly wasn't as if she'd done anything that had caused them to get arrested, and neither had Agatha or Katherine. If anything, the ladies should be grateful they'd been arrested with her in tow. She had more than enough money to see them all released, once someone showed up to bail them out, and—

"Listen, Alfred, or whoever you're claiming to be, I'm not going to tell you again," a police officer growled, causing

Arabella to direct her attention to the heated conversation taking place a foot away from her. The officer stabbed a stubby finger toward Agatha through the bars. "None of us believe you're actually a journalist for the *New-York Tribune*, so you might as well save your breath. Besides, I think your screeching is beginning to antagonize your cell mates, and quite frankly, that's not something I'd recommend."

Agatha began to sputter. "But, but . . . you have to listen to . . ."

"Not another word," the police officer snapped before he withdrew his finger, spun on his heel, and stalked away.

Agatha threw up her hands. "He doesn't believe me."

"Of course he doesn't believe you," Arabella retorted. "You're completely overwrought, and I don't think you've noticed that your wig is barely attached to your head, lending you a somewhat deranged appearance."

"I'm never overwrought."

Arabella threw up her own hands. "Fine, you're not over-wrought, but you certainly don't look like a journalist, which is why the officer doesn't believe you."

Agatha narrowed her eyes. "I certainly don't look like a lady of the night either. If you'll recall, we're wearing opera dresses, and"—she hiked up her skirt and lifted her foot—"as I only just realized tonight, would any self-respecting lady of the night go out to work in shoes like these?" She dropped her skirt and continued before Arabella could respond. "I think not, proving that I am, in fact, a journalist."

"You've lost your mind," Arabella muttered before she grabbed Agatha's hand and pulled her rapidly across the cell until she reached a stone bench. She gestured to Katherine, who was sitting stiff as a poker on the bench, to scoot over, pushed Agatha down, and then plopped next to her. "There now, this is cozy."

Agatha's only response was a growl.

Katherine leaned forward. "Do you think we'll have to stay here all night?"

"Unless Violet really did get away and thinks to go to Eliza for help," Arabella replied.

"Why do you think she'd go to Eliza?" Katherine asked.

Arabella shrugged. "Violet's a smart lady, and since she and her friends admitted to keeping an eye on all of us, she must know where Eliza lives. But we have no way of knowing if Violet will seek out Eliza, so we'll just have to wait and see what happens."

Katherine's eyes began to gleam with satisfaction. "Harold is going to be beside himself with worry when I don't come home. Maybe he'll begin to appreciate me more."

"Or maybe he'll send you packing off to the country," Agatha said. "That's what my father threatened to do the first time I landed in jail."

"Harold's not my father, but . . . I bet he will try to pack me off to our country home. Truth be told, I adore languishing in the country. It's so very restoring to my spirit." She surprised Arabella when she laughed and then laughed again. "The two of you simply must agree to join me. We'll have a splendid time."

Perhaps Agatha wasn't the only one who'd lost her mind.

Arabella got to her feet, moved around Agatha's skirt, and came to a stop in front of Katherine. She reached out and patted Katherine's shoulder. "Dear, I hate to point out the obvious, but I don't believe Harold will be too keen on allowing you to be in our company again after what happened tonight."

"Harold won't be given a choice any longer regarding whom I associate with, and I take full responsibility for my being behind bars. You and Agatha are certainly not to blame, and I intend to tell Harold exactly that."

"You're enjoying this, aren't you?" Arabella asked.

Katherine grinned. "I readily admit that I am. I feel as if I've seen a completely new side of the world." Her grin faded. "You would not believe some of the stories I heard from those women tonight. They tore at my heart and made me realize what a pampered existence I live."

Agatha sat forward on the bench. "Perhaps the night isn't a complete loss after all." She bent over, fought with the fabric of her skirt, and raised it above her knees as her head disappeared into the folds of silk. She reappeared a moment later with a small pad of paper and pen in her hand.

"How in the world did you manage to retain that when the officers divested us of our weapons?" Katherine asked.

"I always try to keep my tools of the trade, so to speak, up high on my thigh." Agatha's eyes sparkled. "The officer who was given the job of frisking me was a shy sort, and he didn't bother to go much past my knee. Besides, I think they thought they'd confiscated all the good stuff when they took away my reticule." She plopped the pad of paper on top of her skirt and nodded to Katherine. "So, tell me about those wrenching stories you heard."

Katherine opened her mouth, but didn't speak as her gaze suddenly settled on something beyond Arabella's shoulder. She snapped her mouth shut, her eyes widened, and she pressed herself back against the wall.

Arabella turned as a hard-looking lady with brassy hair and an attitude to match stepped up in front of the bench and glared down at Agatha. "What are you doing?"

Agatha barely batted an eye. "I'm going to jot down some notes for my story. What does it look like I'm doing?"

The lady's mouth thinned. "Judging by your constant complaining during the entire ride here, me and the other ladies came to believe you and your little friends hadn't discovered anything of importance tonight. If that's not true, you need to tell us what you found out. If it is true, you don't have anything to write about."

Agatha tapped her pen on the paper. "We did *not* find out anything about who is behind the missing ladies, but Katherine was just about to tell me some of the heart-wrenching stories she heard tonight. I could write a wonderful feature story with those."

"We don't need any bleeding-heart story," the lady said. "The last thing we want is for all those do-gooders—women like the three of you, I might add—to read a sad tale and take to the streets to try to save us all."

Lottie, with Hannah following a step behind, pushed her way through the group of ladies and stomped across the cell, her expression determined.

"That's enough, Dot," Lottie snapped as she stopped in front of Arabella and turned to face Dot. "These ladies braved much tonight to try and help us, and there is no reason to be rude to them."

Dot's eyes glittered. "I'm being rude?" She released a laugh that was more angry than amused. "I'm not the one who decided to play dress-up tonight and take to the streets. It's no wonder we were raided with those three dressed in such ridiculous gowns."

Arabella cleared her throat. "I hardly believe the blame for getting arrested can be laid at our feet. From what I understand, raids are a common occurrence in your line of work."

"You understand nothing with your fancy manners and condescending air," Dot hissed. "I heard you questioning some of the girls, asking them how you could assist them into a better life." Another scary laugh erupted out of her mouth. "You, a woman who has never known a day of hardship in her life, think you know what's best for us?"

An uncomfortable silence settled over the cell.

Arabella lifted her chin. "You don't know me."

Dot rolled her eyes. "You're the great and mighty Arabella Beckett, champion of women across the country. How smug you must feel every day when you wake up and realize you're so much better than every other woman out there."

Hannah moved past Dot and, to Arabella's surprise, stood in front of her, as if trying to block her from Dot's harsh words.

"You go too far, Dot," Hannah said. "Arabella didn't have to help us."

"But of course she did. A lady like Arabella Beckett loves nothing more than catering to those she feels are beneath her. It makes her feel important."

Arabella felt every muscle in her body tense. She slipped around Hannah and caught Dot's gaze. "You're wrong about me. I don't feel anyone is beneath me, and besides, everyone is equal in God's eyes. If you must know, the reason I've devoted my life to assisting women in need is because I've always believed it was God's will."

"Ah, so this is a divine intervention, then, and has nothing to do with the fact that ladies like you always seem to act so much superior to all of us sinners." Dot began tapping her foot against the floor. "If I understand you correctly, God, our heavenly Father, has specifically chosen *you* to carry out His will, and that's why you work tirelessly for the cause, saving souls as you travel from city to city."

Arabella stepped closer to Dot, facing her directly. "I realize your life has probably been extremely difficult, Dot, but I'm afraid I don't understand why you're targeting me with your anger. I've done nothing to deserve your disdain."

"You're incredibly judgmental."

"I am not."

"Then why do you assume your life is so much better than ours?"

Arabella blinked as something unpleasant settled in her

stomach. Could Dot's accusation have merit? Did she assume her life was better?

The unpleasantness in her stomach increased even as the truth swirled around in her mind.

Of course her life was better, no question about it, but did that make her judgmental?

She paused for a moment, choosing her words carefully. "I have been blessed with a comfortable existence, so yes, I do believe my life is better. I don't face the dangers you face every time you walk the streets, and I certainly can't understand how anyone in your position could be content with such a life."

Dot shrugged. "You might have a comfortable existence, Miss Beckett, but I have true freedom."

Agatha stood, pushed down her skirt, and dropped her paper and pen to the bench. "Freedom you might have, but at what cost? Your life is frequently at risk. My friends and I never meant to insult any of you, but we are in a position to assist you. We can get you off the streets and into better positions."

Dot's eyes turned icy as she lifted her chin. "If you're about to whip out a Bible from under that skirt of yours and start reading us Scripture, I might just feel compelled to smack you."

"I didn't actually have enough room to strap my Bible to my leg," Agatha returned with a lift of her own chin.

"Well, we can thank the good Lord for that small favor."

Lottie held up a hand. "I think that will do, Dot. It's clear there are differences of opinion here, and nothing productive is going to come of spending our time bickering. Shall we agree to a truce and try to spend the rest of the night as pleasantly as possible?"

Dot looked as if she wanted to argue, but then without another word, she turned and flounced over to the front of the cell, presenting them with her back as she gripped the bars and began to converse with the ladies locked up in a cell across the hall.

Arabella breathed a silent sigh of relief when all the other ladies, except Lottie and Hannah, went to join Dot. She moved to the bench, sat down next to Katherine, and saw that her hands had taken to trembling. Lottie sat down beside her and rubbed her arm. "Don't let Dot upset you, Arabella. She's a bitter woman, and she doesn't like anyone who is more fortunate than she is trying to tell her how to lead her life."

Arabella blinked as unexpected tears stung her eyes. She swiped her eyes with her sleeve and drew in a shaky breath. "I didn't mean to offend her."

"I'm sure you didn't," Hannah said, moving to stand in front of her. "She was very harsh with you, and it was completely undeserved. There is no way you could really understand our lives. You live in a different world, one that I couldn't possibly understand."

"Maybe I really am judgmental," Arabella whispered as she ducked her head to hide the fact her eyes had taken to tearing up again.

"Good heavens, Arabella, everyone is judgmental to a certain extent," Katherine said, rubbing Arabella's back. "Why, I freely admit I was judgmental in regard to you until I really got to know you."

Arabella raised her head. "What do you mean?"

Katherine pursed her lips. "I thought you were certain to be an unpleasant and masculine type, but instead I've discovered you're delightful."

Arabella's eyes misted over again and she let out a small hiccup, but before she could thank Katherine for that rather odd compliment, Agatha interrupted.

"Shh, someone's coming."

The sound of a male voice drifted into the cell, becoming more audible as Dot and her friends went quiet.

Agatha's mouth dropped open. "I think that's Theodore."

For just a moment, a glimmer of relief flowed through her, until she rapidly came to her senses. She turned to Lottie. "You're going to have to hide us."

"What do you mean, hide you?"

"You know, stand in front of us. If that's really Theodore, we can't let him know we're here."

Katherine scooted forward on the bench. "I'm afraid you're not making much sense, Arabella. The only reason my brother would be here would be because he's come to fetch us, and . . ." Katherine's voice trailed off, her mouth went slack, and the red rouge on her face stood out vividly against her now pale face. She suddenly began shoving Lottie off the seat. "Don't just sit there, Lottie, hide us. That's my brother, my completely unreasonable brother, out there, and we can't let him know I'm here. Why, just look at the way I'm dressed, and this wig I'm wearing, and . . ."

Arabella couldn't help but grin as Katherine's words came out faster and faster, until Arabella couldn't even decipher what Katherine was saying.

"She's rather pushy," Lottie said with a sniff. She gestured to Hannah after she got to her feet. The two ladies presented Arabella with a nice view of their backs as they spread out their skirts.

"I need to be on that bench too," Agatha said, then slipped past Lottie and Hannah and sat down between Arabella and Katherine. "We need to make ourselves as small as possible."

"Good luck with that," Lottie tossed over her shoulder. Then she turned her head and began to whistle an unrecognizable tune.

Theodore's voice suddenly sounded incredibly close, and Arabella winced as Katherine dug her fingers into her arm.

"You're hurting me," she whispered.

Katherine sent her an apologetic look but didn't remove her fingers. Arabella began to pry them off, then stilled when Dot let out a loud, remarkably shrill laugh.

"Mr. Wilder. What a delicious surprise."

"Dot, how lovely to see you, although not under these conditions," Theodore said, his raspy voice causing a trail of goose bumps to travel down Arabella's arm.

"I cannot believe he is personally acquainted with these ladies," Arabella whispered.

"He's a private investigator," Katherine said, keeping her voice low. "He knows all sorts of people, ladies included."

"We've missed your charming company," Dot purred.

Arabella's mouth dropped open. "Private investigator or not, Dot seems a bit . . . familiar with him."

"For a lady who claims to hold no interest in my brother, you sound almost jealous."

"Don't be ridiculous," Arabella hissed before she leaned to the right in order to peer cautiously around Lottie.

She tried to ignore the way her pulse quickened when she got her first good look at Theodore. He was standing in front of their cell, completely at his ease as he conversed with Dot, his hair attractively rumpled, and his mouth curved into an amused smile. She blew out a breath. Who looked that handsome when it was the middle of the night and after most likely having been pulled from sleep? For some strange reason, her temper began to simmer when she realized, by the way Dot and all the other ladies were cooing and batting their lashes at Theodore, that they'd obviously taken note of Theodore's all-too-handsome face and masculine appeal as well. Her temper moved from simmering to boiling.

Why, he was being charming, deliberately so. Her jaw clenched. He was never charming in her company, only annoying. Why did he reserve his charm for ladies who . . . She blinked and wouldn't allow her mind to finish the thought as shame shot through her.

Good heavens, Dot was right. She did believe she was better than the ladies now pressed against the bars of the cell, and that certainly didn't speak well of her character. She sagged against the cold wall and pretended not to notice the concerned looks Katherine and Agatha were sending her way. Her dark thoughts were distracted when one of the ladies standing at the front of the cell suddenly let out a giggle.

"Do tell us what you're doing here tonight, Mr. Wilder. Have you just taken into custody a horrible criminal and brought him to jail to await justice?"

Theodore released a booming laugh, the sound setting Arabella's teeth on edge, which, strange as it seemed, caused her to feel a little better. Anger was always much easier to deal with than self-reflection.

"No criminals for me tonight, darling. I'm actually looking for three ladies."

Dot's throaty gurgle bounced around the cell. "I'd say you've found about thirty."

Theodore's laugh joined Dot's, which had Arabella wishing she had something to throw at the man. He was too suave and debonair for his own good. Of course, if she did throw something at him, it would completely defeat the purpose of hiding.

"While it does seem as if I've been fortunate to stumble upon a bevy of beauties," Theodore began, "I'm looking for two lovely blondes and one black-haired lady."

"I'm a blonde," Dot said.

"And a very attractive one at that," Theodore said. "But I have three specific ladies in mind. From what I understand, they decided to go undercover to obtain a story, so they might be disguised."

"Oh, those ladies." Dot let out a grunt of obvious disgust.

"I don't know why you'd want to seek out those do-gooders, Mr. Wilder. We've been forced to spend the entire evening listening to them preach on and on about our derelict lives. I readily admit they've gotten on my nerves. They're a dreary lot, whereas me and the girls here, well . . ." Another throaty laugh sounded around the room, causing Arabella's hackles to rise.

"Where are they?" Theodore asked.

"Oh, very well. If you must know, they're hiding behind those two women at the back there."

"There is no honor amongst thieves," Katherine whispered and then shook her head. "But that was a silly thing for me to say. We're not thieves."

"You lot, hush," Lottie hissed without turning her head. "I think Mr. Wilder knows you're behind us."

"He doesn't know for certain," Katherine hissed back. "Keep standing there, and for heaven's sake look innocent."

"That might be a stretch," Lottie muttered.

"Arabella, I know you're there. You might as well stop hiding," Theodore called.

"Why is he singling me out? Surely he can't believe this was my idea, can he? I mean, we distinctly heard him tell the ladies that he knew we were running down a story. You're the journalist, Agatha, not me. He should be yelling for you right about now."

"This just proves the point I made hours ago regarding Theodore's fascination with you. He's calling for you because he's desperate to see you again."

"That wig is squeezing your head too tight."

"Arabella, I'm waiting," Theodore snapped.

"Does he ever sound this impatient with anyone other than me?" Arabella asked.

"He's normally fairly composed," Katherine said. "Bit unusual, to tell you the truth, but I guess it just proves Agatha's statement. You've garnered his attention."

"Of course I've garnered his attention," Arabella said. "He's currently yelling my name."

She considered the backs of Hannah and Lottie, wondering what in the world she was supposed to do now. It was obvious Theodore wasn't leaving anytime soon.

"I'm going to start counting to five."

She blinked and couldn't help but shake her head. What would he do once he reached five? There were bars separating them, and she was fairly certain he wasn't quite strong enough to break through them.

"One."

"You'd better get it over with," Agatha said. "He's beginning to sound really upset."

"Don't tell him I'm with you," Katherine added before she tugged on Arabella's arm as if to prod her forward faster.

"Two."

Arabella refused to budge. "He asked about three ladies. I'm pretty certain he knows you're here."

"Oh, right," Katherine said glumly and then brightened. "Maybe he thinks the other lady is Eliza."

"Three."

Arabella winced when she noticed the pesky little fact that Theodore's voice was becoming slightly menacing.

"You don't think he'll recognize you?" Arabella asked, still refusing to budge.

"I can always hope," Katherine said with a wink as she patted her wig back into place and smoothed the flounces of her gown.

"Four, and my patience is beginning to wane."

Arabella blew out a breath, stood up and looked at her friends. "How do I look?"

Agatha quirked a brow. "You're not serious?"

Arabella swallowed a laugh. Agatha did have a point. She was dressed in a garish gown, wearing an outdated wig, and beauty patches were attached to her face along with a thick layer of hideous blue color smeared around her eyes.

She was not at her best.

"Five. So help me, Arabella, if I have to go fetch those keys and drag you out of there, as God is my witness, I will."

Now really, there was no cause for threats.

Lifting her skirt, she strode around Hannah and Lottie. She paused, squared her shoulders, and moved as gracefully as she could to the front of the cell, feeling every eye upon her, including Theodore's. She swore right there and then that she would not allow him to see her so much as flinch.

"You called?" she asked as she stopped in front of him, meeting his gaze and rethinking her flinching vow when she took note of the barely controlled fury pouring out of his eyes. She swallowed when his gaze left hers and traveled down her figure.

"I cannot believe you had the nerve to leave your house dressed like that. Have you lost all sense of propriety?"

He truly was the most disagreeable gentleman she'd ever met, and she certainly shouldn't have spent hours thinking about him or worrying about his welfare while he'd been out of town.

She lifted her chin. "I think I look quite fetching, and I've done nothing to cause you to question my sense of propriety."

A vein began to throb on Theodore's forehead. "I have half a mind to leave you here."

Her chin lifted even higher. "By your attitude at the moment, I have to believe you're only possessed of half a mind."

Theodore moved closer, grabbed the bars with both hands, and Arabella couldn't help but notice how his knuckles had gone white.

"I would walk away right now, even though I told Eliza I'd get you released, if only my sister weren't involved."

182

"I didn't pull your sister into any scheme. It just sort of happened."

A low groan sounded from behind Arabella, causing her to grimace. She'd forgotten Katherine was still trying to remain undetected.

"Why are you dressed in that ridiculous gown, and why have you painted your face in that disturbing fashion?" Theodore shot at her, pulling her abruptly back to the realization she was in the midst of an unpleasant conversation.

She patted her wig. "I needed to be inconspicuous."

"You don't honestly believe you achieved that, do you?"

His incredulous tone of voice was beginning to wear on her nerves. "Anyone would be hard-pressed to recognize me at the moment."

"You look like a deranged actress," Theodore said. "I'm certain you attracted more attention than any of the ladies you were trying to emulate."

"Not one single gentleman even approached me."

"Is that a note of disappointment I hear in your voice?" Theodore asked.

Her patience was now at an end. "You are a horrible man, and I don't care to speak with you any longer." She spun on her heel, but stopped when Dot suddenly blocked her way.

"Mr. Wilder has done you a kindness by tracking you down," Dot said. "You will grant him the courtesy of listening to him yell at you." She grabbed Arabella's arm and turned her back around until they were both facing Theodore. "Continue, Mr. Wilder," Dot said, even as she pushed Arabella closer to the bars.

Theodore blinked and seemed, for the moment, to be at a loss for words.

"Don't fail me now, Mr. Wilder," Dot added. "Seeing this snooty lady being given what she's due is the most enjoyment I've had all evening." She batted her lashes. "You would not believe the nerve she had toward me and the other ladies. She wanted to change us, she did."

"I never said I wanted to change you, only help you," Arabella countered.

Dot waved a hand into the air. "You're a meddler."

Before Arabella could respond to Dot's latest insult, she glanced to Theodore and found the gentleman nodding his head.

Heat began to bubble through her entire body until she felt as if she might explode.

"She does make an excellent point," Theodore said.

"I don't meddle."

"Oh, you're discreet about it, I'll give you that, but you do like to change people."

She had the uncanny suspicion they'd suddenly stopped talking about her trying to change Dot. "I never tried to change you."

Theodore arched a brow. "You didn't hope that by relentlessly bringing your suffrage movement into the conversation every time we spoke, I would change my mind about it?"

How to respond? She opened her mouth, but Theodore didn't allow her the luxury of a response.

"You didn't set out to change my sister by pulling her into this ridiculous scheme tonight? She was happy and content being a wife to Harold until you got involved."

His words hurt, as did his tone.

She dashed a hand across her face to brush away the angry tears that leaked from her eyes. "If you believe Katherine was happy and content, you're delusional."

Theodore shrugged. "Perhaps, but you can't deny your goal was to change her, make her long for more, and . . . are you crying?"

She brushed away another tear and ignored the small bit

of concern she saw in his eyes. "Don't let that discourage you from your rant, Mr. Wilder. Please continue."

Theodore leaned closer and peered through the bars. "Did I hurt your feelings?"

She drew in a shuddering breath and then another as it suddenly dawned on her exactly why she'd been dwelling on Theodore over the past few weeks.

She was attracted to him, or had been until he'd shown up at the jail.

She was a fool.

They were complete opposites, and to even consider them together was absurd, and . . . she *had* thought she might be able to change him.

That thought caused a fresh bout of tears to dribble out of her eyes. They were right, Theodore and Dot. She did expect people to change to her way of thinking.

She was a horrible, horrible person.

She'd been using the excuse of working on God's behalf, when in actuality she was simply trying to make everyone do what she felt was best for them.

Her life was a sham.

That idea forced her to draw in a shaky breath, but before she could think of something to say, Agatha slipped up beside her and put an arm around her waist, sending Theodore a glare through the bars.

"What did you do to Arabella?" Agatha hissed. "Why is she crying?"

Theodore didn't answer right away, but took a moment to fish in one of his pockets, drawing out a pristine handkerchief, which he then thrust through the bars at Arabella. She turned and settled her attention on Agatha's wig that was tilted back on her head, wisps of black hair now mingling with the red.

For some reason, the sight caused her lips to twitch, until

Theodore pushed the handkerchief at Agatha, who took it and began dabbing at the tears that seemed to still be streaming down Arabella's face.

Theodore cleared his throat. "I'm not certain, but I think I might have hurt her feelings."

"Of course you hurt her feelings," Katherine said as she stepped between Arabella and Agatha and then shook a finger at her brother. "I am deeply ashamed to even admit we're related. Really, Theodore, it is not well done of you in the least to blame Arabella for this situation. I readily admit to dabbling in a bit of blackmail to force them to allow me to come with them." She smiled. "I told them I'd inform their mothers what they were really up to this evening, and they simply had no choice but to let me tag along."

"Harold is going to have a fit when he sees you dressed like that," Theodore said.

"You're right," Katherine said as she fluffed out the skirt of her gown. "I was quite distressed when I first laid eyes on this hideous monstrosity of a dress, knowing perfectly well Arabella chose it for me out of a sense of revenge. But now, well, I think it makes a statement, and that is exactly what I hoped would come of this evening."

Theodore eyed Katherine for a long moment before switching his gaze to Agatha. "Eliza mentioned something about a story you're working on. She was annoyingly closemouthed regarding the more pertinent details, so you'll need to fill me in."

Agatha planted her hands on her hips. "I hope you didn't make Eliza cry."

"I don't make a habit of bringing ladies to tears."

Agatha reached out, dabbed at fresh tears trailing down Arabella's cheeks, and then waved the handkerchief at Theodore.

Theodore muttered something under his breath and caught Arabella's gaze with his own. "I didn't realize you had such tender feelings, Arabella. I never meant to cause you this level of distress."

His statement sent more hurt through her.

She was a lady, much as he didn't seem to realize it. Most ladies did possess "tender feelings," but his words gave testimony to the fact he didn't see her as a normal lady.

She pushed aside the hurt, straightened her spine, accepted the handkerchief Agatha offered, and blew her nose loudly. She lifted her head and forced a smile. "I'm not distressed in the least. In fact, I'm perfectly fine."

"You're not perfectly fine," Katherine argued. "Even though we've embarked on a thrilling adventure this evening down at the docks, we've still landed in jail, and you've been forced to bear the brunt of my brother's anger. It's no wonder you're a bit distressed."

Silence suddenly fell over everyone when Theodore took one step forward, crossed his arms over his chest, and settled what could only be described as a smoldering glare on his sister. "You were down at the docks?"

Katherine turned a shade lighter, but her voice didn't waver when she spoke. "That is where all those poor women went missing."

Theodore's color turned the exact opposite shade of his sister's. "What missing women?"

Katherine reached out a hand, snagged Agatha's arm, and pulled her front and center. "You tell him."

Agatha winced, but then drew in a breath, released it, drew in another, and then another, and . . .

Theodore was now an interesting shade of purple. "You're stalling. Tell me now, and do not even think about leaving out any details. What missing women?"

Agatha blew out one last breath. "Fine. If you must know, women have been disappearing in rapid succession from the streets, and nobody, specifically the police, seems to want to help them. We, or rather Arabella and I—Katherine was not involved at first—agreed to assist them. In order to help them, we had to travel to the docks, where the majority of women have gone missing. Unfortunately, we were not very successful gathering information, so our investigation tonight seems to have failed."

Dead silence settled over the cell as everyone waited with bated breath for Theodore's reaction to that startling bit of news.

They didn't have long to wait.

13

$\mathcal{T}$heodore couldn't seem to stem the flow of words that kept spewing out of his mouth. Things like "completely ridiculous" and "what were you thinking?" and "you've obviously lost your mind" continued to pour from his lips as he stalked back and forth in front of the cell. It was only when "all of you need a good spanking" burst out that he suddenly realized he might have gone too far. He came to an abrupt halt and winced when all the ladies—not just Katherine, Agatha, and Arabella—began making rather loud hissing noises.

He braced himself when Katherine, surprisingly haughty in her outlandish outfit, stepped up to the bars, pressed her face as far as she could through them, and sent him a glare he hadn't received from her since childhood.

"While that was certainly uncalled-for, brother dear, I'm going to excuse your behavior just this once because it's apparent that *you* have lost your mind, not the other way around."

Before he could reply, she drew back and let out a huff. "Now then, you may feel free to continue your rant, but may

I suggest you do so at a later time? I for one am weary of this place. I'm sure your time would be better spent securing our release, so run along and do whatever it is you need to do. We'll wait for you here."

A flash of something he hadn't felt in a very long time crashed over him. It almost felt like remorse, or perhaps it was embarrassment, or . . .

A snapping of a finger had him narrowing his eyes at his sister. "Don't ever . . . do that . . . again," he bit out.

Katherine lifted her hand, snapped her fingers, not once but twice, and then turned her back on him. She pushed her way past Dot, moved to the opposite side of the cell, and sat down on a bench without speaking another word as she began to inspect her fingernails.

A glimmer of reluctant admiration ran through him.

A loud clearing of a throat from behind forced him to drag his attention away from his sister and turn. He discovered a police officer standing a few feet from him, watching him warily.

"Is, ah, everything all right, Mr. Wilder?"

Theodore summoned up a smile. "Of course, everything is fine."

"I thought I heard you yelling and, well, I must state most emphatically that we really don't condone spanking prisoners."

He really shouldn't have allowed his temper free rein.

It wasn't how he normally reacted to disturbing news, but the thought of the ladies blithely traveling around the docks had unfortunately sent him over the edge.

How to explain?

No explanation came to him, so he gave the officer a nod, hoped the man would take that as a sign he wasn't going to spank anyone, and decided his only option was to change the subject. "What have you heard about women disappearing from the streets?"

The officer shook his head. "I'm afraid I don't know what you're talking about."

Theodore heard Dot mutter something less than ladylike under her breath. He turned back to the cell and watched as she strode up to the bars and glared at the officer through them. "I knew no one would believe me and file a report." She caught Theodore's eye. "That's why some of the ladies got it into their heads to seek out Miss Watson and have her help us. She was their last hope, or at least that's what they thought until she failed miserably tonight."

"I didn't completely fail, at least not yet," Agatha said as she moved to Dot's side. "I'm sure if I continue questioning people, something will turn up eventually."

These ladies were going to be the death of him.

Theodore glanced over his shoulder at the officer. "Are you certain that spanking isn't allowed?"

The officer laughed, but then smothered another one with his hand when the ladies began grumbling.

Theodore's lips twitched, yet he sobered when he glanced at Agatha and found her nodding at him, as if she believed he should be in full agreement with her plan. "Let me be perfectly clear, Agatha. Your involvement in this matter is now at an end, and just to refresh your memory, I don't need any assistance, not from you or any of your friends."

"I don't remember offering you my assistance," Agatha snapped.

Theodore blew out a breath. How had it come to this?

The world had once been a relatively pleasant place to live, back in the days when men and women knew and kept to their respective roles.

Now everything was upside down, and he didn't care for it at all, not one little bit.

He wanted things to go back to the way they'd been before,

when life was easy and women weren't running amok, when men were taking care of business.

His gaze traveled over the collection of ladies, taking in Katherine's outlandish pink gown and black wig, and then moved over the ladies of the night, all of whom were dressed in shabby outfits. He narrowed his eyes as he noticed each outfit seemed to be individualized, as if each lady had taken pains to retain a certain amount of self. He shifted his attention to Arabella and felt something strange settle in his stomach. She was only standing a few feet away from him, but for some reason—perhaps because she wasn't looking at him—she seemed unapproachable, and that . . . disturbed him. He took a step forward, unable to help but notice that even though her gown dwarfed her curves and her white wig was askew, she was beautiful. He tore his gaze away from her, unwilling to dwell on her beauty, wanting instead to dwell on how furious he still was with her.

He conjured up a smile as he returned his attention to Agatha, who was now tapping her foot against the floor and appeared to be grinding her teeth. "Perhaps you and I could agree to compromise?"

Agatha stopped grinding her teeth. "I'm listening."

"From what I can surmise, there's probably a killer or, at the very least, a kidnapper on the loose. You cannot argue the point that it's safe for you to continue investigating this matter, so here's what I'm going to suggest. I will pick up where you left off and I'll share everything I discover with you."

"You won't let me go with you?"

"No, you can't go with me, and if you don't agree to my terms, I'm going to tell your mother what you've been up to, and both of us know how that will work out for you."

"You're being completely unreasonable," Agatha snapped.

"I'm never unreasonable."

Katherine let out a loud snort, rose from the bench, and glided up to the front of the cell, shaking her head as she came to a stop. "What about the time I chopped off all the heads of your toy soldiers?"

"What?"

"Come now, surely you remember? You'd made me angry, and to get back at you, I took a knife and lopped off all their heads."

"You're bringing that up now?"

Katherine sent him a beautiful smile. "You stated you're never unreasonable, and yet you were completely unreasonable when you discovered your soldiers had taken leave of their heads. I can still remember your fit of hysterics."

"I was not hysterical, and just to clarify, not only did you chop off their heads, you stomped on them and broke their bodies into little pieces."

"Ah, so you do remember."

"This is a ridiculous conversation and certainly does not prove your point. I was a child when that happened, and I can assure you, I would not be the slightest bit concerned if you were to chop the heads off of toy soldiers now."

"You don't have any toy soldiers left for me to chop," Katherine said with a smug nod of her head. "Otherwise they would be in danger."

"Kate, enough," Theodore said, although his anger had cooled to next to nothing. He'd forgotten how well-equipped she was to divert his temper. He'd also forgotten she used to be mischievous and fun. He released a breath and forced himself to concentrate on the situation at hand.

"I need to know how many women have gone missing."

Dot began ticking them off on her fingers, every tick causing him to realize the situation was dire indeed.

"Ten," she finally proclaimed, "and all ten of them within the past week and a half."

Theodore turned and set his sights on the police officer still standing in the same spot. "I'll need for you to arrange an appointment for me to see the chief. If ten women have disappeared, we have a problem on our hands."

"But . . . no bodies have shown up, at least not that many," the officer said.

"Which makes it even more concerning," Theodore said. He began to pace again, trying to collect his thoughts, and stopped to address the ladies of the night. "I need all of you to think. Someone has to have seen something unusual, no matter how small it might be. Ladies don't just disappear without a trace."

Agatha drew his attention when she suddenly hit her forehead with her hand. "I completely forgot about that man Arabella saw tonight."

Trepidation flowed over him. He gripped the bar with one hand and gestured with his other to Arabella, who was watching him with something indescribable in her eyes, something he almost believed was hurt.

He was responsible for that look.

He pushed that thought to the back of his mind, knowing full well it would push front and center again soon enough, and tried to smile at Arabella, realizing he failed miserably when her eyes turned from hurt to stormy. He winced. "What can you tell me about that man you saw?"

For a second, he thought she was going to refuse to answer, but then she shrugged, pushed her wig further back on her head, and opened her mouth. "I didn't get a good look at him because he'd pulled his cap low over his face. I don't believe he was as tall as you are, nor as broad, but he was . . . scary."

"Scary, how?"

She shivered and then wrapped her arms around her middle. "He had this air about him, it was . . . evil, and he watched me for a long moment, and then . . . he started walking toward me. I felt the distinct urge to run." She shivered again. "Before he reached me, though, a police officer grabbed me, and when I looked over my shoulder for him, he'd disappeared."

A feeling he'd never before felt in his life swept over him, stealing the breath from his body. She was in mortal danger. He knew it as well as he knew she'd been just feet away from the killer.

He swore then and there he'd do everything to protect her, because . . . well, he couldn't think about that now. Her life was at risk, and that's what he needed to concentrate on from this moment forward.

He began striding back and forth as his thoughts whirled. Arabella was an uncommonly beautiful woman, so uncommon that people tended to never forget her face, as he'd learned while he'd traveled the country looking for her.

A killer of women would remember her face and would go to great lengths to find her again.

That idea shook him to his very core.

He strode over to the officer and stopped. "I need to get these ladies out of jail as soon as possible."

"Their bail has already been paid, Mr. Wilder," the officer said. "It's one of the reasons I came down to find you. They're free to go."

"Well, what are we waiting for?" Katherine exclaimed. "We've been dawdling down here for no reason at all." She smiled. "I just might be able to beat Harold home, and that will save me some uncomfortable questions."

As a distraction to get his emotions under control, dealing with Katherine worked wonders. "I hate to be the one to tell you this, Kate, but Harold's waiting for you upstairs."

Katherine blinked. "He is not."

"I assure you, he is. The last time I saw him, he was attempting to post your bail."

"Why didn't you post my bail?" Katherine snapped. "I know you have more than enough money at your disposal. Why did you have to involve Harold in this? I cannot believe you sought him out and tattled on me."

A slice of sadness stole over him. Did his sister really believe he would choose Harold over her? Didn't she realize that he loved her, or . . . maybe she didn't. It wasn't as if he told her on a regular basis, or ever, now that he thought about it. "I didn't seek out Harold, Katherine. He sought me."

Katherine let out a breath. "Let me guess, he wanted to complain to you about my abysmal behavior of late."

"Well, yes, that is about the gist of what his complaints centered around, but enough of that for now. We really do need to get all of you out of here." He gestured to the officer, who stepped forward and placed the key in the lock.

"What about us?" Dot asked, causing the officer to pause. "Are you going to let us go, or do we have to wait until morning?"

"You're all free to go. Bail has been paid for everyone," the officer said.

"Thank you, Mr. Wilder," Dot simpered.

"Don't thank me, Dot. Mrs. Hamilton Beckett insisted on traveling here with me, and she took it upon herself to pay bail for all of you ladies."

Dot smiled. "That was very kind of Mrs. Beckett. You will thank her for us, won't you?"

"So much for not accepting help from do-gooders," Theodore heard Arabella mutter.

Dot drew herself up, but before she could say a word, the officer opened the door and Theodore had to step quickly out of the way as the ladies rushed past him, Dot leading the way. The officer moved to the other cells filled with women, and they rapidly filed out, nodding their thanks as they scurried after their friends. Before he knew it, he was standing with only Arabella, Katherine, Agatha, and three ladies of the night.

"Sarah, there you are," a woman he thought was named Lottie said. "Hannah and I were hoping you were in one of the other cells, but with all the commotion, we couldn't find you."

"I was trying to stay unnoticed," Sarah said softly. "You know I don't like crowds much."

A piece of his hardened heart suddenly softened. He worked with the dregs of society on a daily basis, but he'd never truly considered their feelings.

The woman Lottie had called Hannah stepped to Sarah's side and gave her a hug, then released her and smiled. "Not to worry now, dear. The crowds are gone, and we'll have you home soon."

His heart gave a lurch at the mere thought of these women traveling back through the streets, probably to a house that was less than a home. His feet suddenly began to move, and he found himself standing right beside Sarah, who regarded him nervously. "You won't be safe until this culprit is caught. I'm going to suggest you and your friends travel home with me, spend the night there where you can get some sleep without worrying about your safety, and then tomorrow we'll speak about a better plan."

He heard Arabella draw in a sharp breath and turned to look at her. She was watching him as if she'd never seen him before, and the look in her eyes was . . . different. Before he could figure out what the look meant, she smiled, and every single thought in his head disappeared.

How long he stood there staring at her, he couldn't say, but Katherine suddenly laughed, grabbed his arm, and began pulling him away from the cell and down a hallway. "Time for me to face the music," she said, although her voice was more amused than troubled.

He shook his head in order to clear it, and when Arabella's smile immediately flashed back to mind, he decided he needed something drastic to chase the image away. "Did I mention that Father is here as well as Harold?"

Katherine came to an immediate stop. "Father's here?"

"He and Harold came to lecture me earlier this evening." He smiled as his thoughts finally came into focus. "Once he learned what had happened, he decided he couldn't miss out on all the excitement."

"Father doesn't like excitement," Katherine said, dropping hold of his arm. To his surprise, she strode back toward the cell, grabbed Agatha's hand and began dragging her along.

"Did you forget something?" he heard Agatha ask.

Katherine stopped and turned to nod at him. "Agatha and I will be staying in jail tonight. She needs an authentic story, and how much more authentic could it get than sleeping the night away behind bars as if we really were ladies of the night?"

Theodore rolled his eyes and stalked back the way he'd just come. He brushed past Arabella, who looked as if she was trying not to grin, then past Sarah and the other ladies before he reached his sister's side, took her arm, and pulled her into motion. She tried to pry herself free, but his patience was wearing thin once again, and before he knew it, they were moving through a heavy door, then standing in another long hallway as Katherine finally succeeded in shaking out of his hold.

She looked up at him and bit her lip. "I'm not certain I'm quite ready to face Harold just yet, Theodore, especially dressed like this." She pushed her wig into place. "I must look like I've just escaped from the asylum."

"I have a wonderful idea," Agatha said, coming up to stand beside them. "We'll tell Harold you've lost your mind and need to seek immediate medical attention. That will allow you to escape this little mess we've gotten into without causing you to have to explain anything to your husband."

"She's not going to claim she lost her mind," Arabella said, walking up to stand in front of Katherine.

Theodore caught a whiff of her perfume when she brushed past him. The scent tickled his nose, and he felt the most unusual urge to lean closer to her. He winced when Agatha elbowed him in the ribs and sent him a wink.

He wasn't certain, but he thought the heat that took over his face just might be a blush. He narrowed his eyes at Agatha and then shifted his attention back to Arabella, who was now holding his sister's hand and smiling.

"You, Katherine Gibson, are a strong, incredibly intelligent woman, who has finally decided to take charge of your life. You didn't do anything illegal or harmful, and you simply need to tell your husband that."

Katherine drew in a breath, squared her shoulders, and nodded. "You're right. I haven't done anything wrong."

Arabella's smile widened, and she dropped Katherine's hand. "That's the attitude. Now, go tell Harold that."

Katherine grabbed Theodore's arm, tightened her fingers into the sleeve of his coat, and smiled a rather wobbly smile. "I'm ready, but just don't leave my side."

He placed his other hand over her arm, squeezed it once, and then they began walking once again, pausing for just a second as he opened the door to where he knew Harold, Samuel, Eliza, and Violet waited.

Dead silence greeted their arrival into the room.

Theodore's gaze went directly to Harold, who was staring back at them, his eyes narrowed as he glanced at Katherine and then back at Theodore.

"Well, where is she?" Harold demanded.

Katherine released his arm and stepped forward. "I'm right here, Harold."

A muffled laugh caught Theodore's attention, and he saw his father spinning around to face the wall, his shoulders shaking with what could only be amusement. Before he could process that peculiar state of affairs, Harold began to rant.

"I assume you've concocted some type of explanation for your deplorable condition?"

Theodore opened his mouth, intent on interceding, but snapped it shut when Arabella moved to Katherine's side and took hold of his sister's hand again.

"I'm certain Eliza has already explained the situation to you fairly well, Mr. Gibson," Arabella said as she nodded to Eliza, who was standing by the window with Violet.

Harold puffed himself up, his face beginning to mottle. "You're Arabella Beckett, aren't you?"

"I readily admit that I am."

"Well, girl, what do you have to say for yourself?"

Theodore's temper flared, and he took a step forward, but then paused when Arabella drew herself up and didn't so much as flinch when Harold stepped closer to her. His respect for her increased immensely, and he felt his lips twitch when Arabella lifted her chin, fixed Harold with an icy look of disdain, and opened her mouth.

"I suppose what I have to say is this: I haven't been called 'girl' in quite some time, and if you wish me to answer your questions, I suggest you use caution in the manner you use to address me."

A tic began to pulse on Harold's cheek. "Your frank demeanor is very unbecoming for a woman."

"As it has already been pointed out to me this evening that I'm judgmental, smug, and act somewhat superior to everyone, your opinion of me barely leaves a mark on my obviously unfeminine skin."

Harold blinked, but then continued on as if Arabella hadn't spoken. "You're to blame for my wife being ruined."

200

Arabella glanced at Katherine. "She doesn't appear ruined to me."

"She's dressed like a tart."

"I'm actually dressed like an opera singer," Katherine said, speaking up.

Harold's face went from mottled to deep red. He glared at Arabella. "Are you proud of yourself? Proud of the fact you've managed to turn my completely respectable wife into a woman of questionable character?"

"I'm afraid you're giving me too much credit."

"Of course I'm giving you too much credit. You're most likely incapable of figuring out the ramifications of your actions."

Arabella's eyes began shooting sparks. "Are you suggesting I'm unintelligent?"

"I'm not suggesting anything," Harold countered. "It is silly women like you who will be the downfall of our great country. Just because you've decided to abandon your God-given position in life does not mean it is remotely acceptable to coerce innocent women to join your side."

Theodore moved then, not coming to a stop until he stood between Harold and Arabella. "That's enough, Harold. Arabella has done nothing to provoke your anger. Katherine admitted she is the one who convinced them to let her go along tonight. Although I certainly don't condone their actions, they believed they were doing something honorable."

Harold looked at him for a long moment and then took a sideways step before shaking a finger at Arabella. "This is all your fault, no matter what anyone else says. You've caused an unfixable rift in my marriage, not that you would understand that as a spinster." He let out a mean laugh. "You'll always be a spinster, what with your radical ideas and masculine behavior."

Theodore's blood began to boil. "You've gone too far, Harold. Apologize to Miss Beckett."

Harold threw him an incredulous look. "I will not apologize, Theodore. Besides, you know everything I've said so far is true. Need I remind you that on our way over here, you mentioned to me you thought Miss Beckett was a menace to men everywhere?"

A soft hiccup of distress drew his attention, and he forced himself to turn from Harold and look at Arabella. Her eyes shone with unshed tears, and he felt a stab of remorse. He'd only spoken those careless words out of anger, but . . . no, that wasn't actually true. He'd meant the words at the time, meant them because finding out Arabella had been taken to jail along with his sister had infuriated him. Gently bred young ladies were not supposed to be hauled off to jail.

It just wasn't done.

He simply didn't know how to deal with a lady like Arabella. She was infuriating, but . . . she also intrigued him.

He blinked and allowed that thought to settle in his mind.

Arabella Beckett intrigued him.

There, that was the reason why she constantly plagued his thoughts. But what was he supposed to do now?

"I do hate to interrupt this lovely conversation everyone is having, but the night is slipping away from us," Eliza said. She walked away from the window and strode briskly across the room. Her expression softened when she reached Arabella's side and took her arm. "You, darling, will ride with me." She sent Theodore a look, which he didn't really understand until he remembered that before he'd gotten lost in his little epiphany, Arabella had learned he'd called her a menace. "You are not invited to follow us home, Mr. Wilder. Arabella has been through enough this evening and certainly doesn't need to suffer your company any longer tonight."

He needed to make amends now, before it was too late and

before Arabella had time to stew about it. "I should not have called you a menace. I'm afraid I allowed my temper to get the best of me, and I spoke out of anger."

Arabella's eyes turned a little misty. "That's when the truth comes out the loudest." She drew in a breath and lifted her chin. "I do want to extend you my gratitude for coming to get us, but your obligation toward me is at an end." She turned to Eliza. "Ready?"

"My carriage is waiting out front."

"That's it?" Harold sputtered, causing everyone to look at him. His face was red and splotchy again, and his eyes were wide and slightly crazed. "Everyone's just going to blithely take their leave with no apologies spoken?"

Katherine was the first to respond. "You want us to apologize?"

"Indeed I do," Harold said. "We were forced out into this blustery night in order to fetch you. An apology is the least you can offer us for that inconvenience."

Katherine tilted her head, the action causing her wig to float to the floor. She ignored it as she considered Harold for a long moment. "I will apologize for inconveniencing you, Harold, but I'm not apologizing for ending up in jail. If anyone should be apologizing, it should be you and Theodore. You've treated Arabella horribly tonight, and she did absolutely nothing to earn your disdain."·

Arabella cleared her throat. "There's no need for them to apologize to me."

"There's every need," Samuel said, speaking up for the first time as he stepped around Harold and stopped in front of Arabella. "You, my dear, have shown a tremendous amount of poise. I must extend to you my deepest regret regarding remarks I made to Theodore and Harold earlier this evening, even though you weren't present to hear those remarks. I was mistakenly under the belief you were the reason my wife has not been herself lately. I see now I was completely off the mark. It is quite clear you are a charming young lady who is not responsible for the recent behavior of my wife *or* my daughter. I hope you will forgive me. I should know better than to form an opinion based on gossip."

"You've heard gossip about me?" Arabella asked.

Samuel sent her a small smile. "Men do talk, and you are often a subject of contemplation." He sighed. "I'm afraid to tell you that I fear gentlemen everywhere blame you for the mischief their wives get into. I think it's easier to blame you than to admit that perhaps we as husbands have not been treating our wives very well."

"I'm sure you treat your wife just fine," Arabella said.

"That's very gracious of you to say, my dear, but I have to admit that I do think I've been a bit neglectful of late, with both my wife and my daughter." Samuel turned from Arabella and nodded to Katherine. "It's very late, and I'm sure you want to get out of here. May I offer you a ride home?"

Harold took a step forward. "If you will recall, Samuel, I brought my carriage. Katherine will ride home with me. We have much left to discuss."

Katherine plucked up her wig, plopped it on her head, and moved to Samuel's side. She sent Harold a look of deepest disdain. "I have nothing to say to you at the moment. I'm riding home with my father, and not to our house, but to his."

"That's ridiculous," Harold snapped. "You're my wife, and you're coming home with me."

"While it's true I'm your wife, you've forgotten what that means." Katherine accepted Samuel's arm, and they strode from the room together.

Harold stood there, apparently at a complete loss as to what to do next, but then he let out a grunt and bolted for the door.

"My goodness, I've never seen Mr. Gibson in such a state,"

Lottie said as she breezed into the room, Hannah and Sarah following a step behind. "We didn't dare come in before for fear we'd make matters worse."

Violet, who'd somehow managed to stay out of sight, hurried over to hug her friend. "I must say, this has been a very interesting evening."

"I can certainly agree with that," Eliza said. She took Arabella's hand in hers. "I am ready to go home."

Theodore summoned up what he hoped was a charming smile and moved to stand in front of them. Unfortunately, Arabella turned her head, and Eliza narrowed her eyes.

He blew out a breath. "I realize you're more than annoyed with me, Eliza, and for good reason, but I'm going to throw myself on your mercy and hope you'll extend me the tiniest little favor."

"You want me to extend you a favor?"

"I have to discuss a matter of grave importance with Arabella, and I cannot wait to discuss it until morning. I need you to take these ladies to my house, where I've offered them refuge for the night. I'll take Arabella home, which will allow us an opportunity to speak."

"I'm not going anywhere with you," Arabella said.

Her snippy response set his teeth to grinding. "Again, I have a matter of grave importance to discuss with you."

"You can send me a note."

"I'm not going to pen you a note. What I have to discuss with you is extremely important, and I certainly couldn't do it justice in a note."

Arabella lifted her chin, and even though he was taller than she was, she somehow managed to appear as if she were looking down her nose at him.

Temper began to simmer through him, which had him inching toward her. Her eyes turned wary and she opened her mouth, but he wasn't in the mood to argue with her anymore.

He crouched down, grabbed her around her middle, hefted her into the air, flung her over his shoulder, and ignored the fists that immediately began pounding against his back. He sent Eliza and Agatha a nod—both ladies staring at him as if he'd grown an extra head—and then he strode out of the room.

14

"You really have lost your mind," Arabella said as she landed on the carriage seat and heard a loud rip. She leaned forward and snatched up the piece of hem that was stuck on the door, wincing when she noticed the damage. "You've ruined my dress, and Mrs. Davis is not going to appreciate that in the least."

Theodore climbed into the carriage, pulled the door shut, and sat down across from her. "You left me no other option, and I'm sure Mrs. Davis, whoever that may be, will be consoled when you tell her I'm more than willing to compensate her for her loss." He rapped on the ceiling with his knuckles, and the carriage lurched forward.

Arabella grabbed onto the hanging strap, steadied herself, and then sent him what she could only hope was a chilly glare. "I told you I didn't have anything to say to you."

"I heard you. Everyone on the entire street heard you. You were quite vocal."

"I don't appreciate being manhandled."

"Quite frankly, Arabella, I don't think you appreciate anything that concerns men."

Normally, words like that didn't bother her, but tonight, after all the insults and truths she'd had to accept about her character, his words stung. Arabella turned her head toward the window, not even bothering to brush away the tears that began running down her cheeks.

"Are you crying again?"

"Can that honestly surprise you, given the circumstances of the night?"

"I'm a little surprised."

She forced her attention from the frosty window. "You didn't think I was capable of tears?"

"You don't really seem the type."

Arabella permitted herself the luxury of a good snort. "Let me guess. Because I support women's rights, I'm not supposed to cry?"

"It seems a little odd, especially since you obviously long to be treated exactly like a gentleman. I've rarely witnessed a gentleman dissolving into tears."

She couldn't help but wonder if she'd suffer an unfortunate fate if she suddenly jumped out of the carriage.

She eyed the door for a long moment, decided plunging to certain death was really not that appealing, and so released another snort instead. "I read romance novels."

"I'm sorry?"

"Was that a question, or are you sorry to discover I enjoy romance novels?"

"It was a question. I never considered the idea you might enjoy cozying up to indulge in a spot of light reading."

"Am I really that unfeminine?"

Theodore frowned. "I would never make the claim that you lack femininity."

"You said I didn't appreciate anything that concerns men."

"What does that have to do with you being feminine?"

Arabella rolled her eyes. "It has everything to do with

being feminine. Feminine women are expected to adore all things concerning men. I've never once proclaimed to have an aversion to men, but it certainly appears to be the general consensus. Who knew so many people spent their time contemplating Arabella Beckett?"

"You're contemplated because you're unusual."

"Don't you mean peculiar?"

"You're not really *that* peculiar."

"That sounded convincing."

Theodore leaned forward. "Arabella, forgive me, I shouldn't make light of your distress."

Arabella blinked. He was apologizing to her, and for some reason that had fresh tears stinging her eyes.

"Oh no, I did hurt your feelings," Theodore said softly.

"You admitted surprise because I'm prone to tears."

"I did, and for that I'm truly sorry."

"I can cry at the drop of a hat."

"You find hat-dropping distressful?"

"If it's a nice hat, and it has dropped in the mud, certainly. I could cry about that for days."

Theodore's eyes began to twinkle. "What about sad stories?"

"I avoid them at all costs, although Hamilton and Zayne used to torment me something awful when I was younger. They'd tell me they were giving me a cheerful book, knowing full well it had a horrible ending, and I would be morose for hours."

"They did that on purpose?"

Arabella smiled. "They were just boys, but they did enjoy tormenting me. Mother used to get so irritated with them for making me cry, until she discovered that I can cry on cue."

"You can make yourself cry at will?"

"It's a talent I've perfected over the years."

"Were you employing that talent tonight?"

"Unfortunately, no."

He looked at her for a long moment. "I didn't mean to insult you tonight."

Arabella arched a brow. "You told your father and Harold I'm a menace."

"As I stated before, I was speaking out of anger. I don't really believe you're a menace, at least not most of the time."

Arabella waved his statement away with a flick of her hand. "Not only do I enjoy having pink trim on my parasols and the trim of my gowns, but my entire room is painted pink. I would bathe in pink if I could."

"I see . . ."

"I don't think you do. You assume things about me, just like everyone else apparently does, and I've come to realize that some of those assumptions are valid. Tonight I learned that I'm judgmental, bossy, and I've spent my entire life believing something that wasn't true." She drew in a shaky breath. "I've been so smug in my belief that God specifically chose me to change the lives of women, when in actuality it seems I'm the one whose life needs to change."

"Don't you think you're being a little hard on yourself? I'm sure you've helped countless women as you've given your speeches over the years."

"No, I haven't. Standing in front of large gatherings of ladies is not actually improving their circumstances. Oh, don't get me wrong. I've told them how to live, but it's not as if I'm an expert on how to lead a productive life. Do you know that I didn't even bother to consider the feelings or wants of those women I was in jail with tonight? I just assumed I knew best how they should live their lives. It was beyond presumptuous of me and condescending to those ladies. It's no wonder Dot reacted the way she did."

"She might have overreacted."

"She didn't. I of all people should understand that. I hate when anyone tries to tell me what to do." She dropped her gaze and began to smooth her gown. "I've become unlikable, and I've become a source of gossip for men all over the country, and not in a complimentary way."

"I would have to imagine that men gossip about you because you're beautiful."

Arabella's breath hitched in her throat as she lifted her head. She narrowed her eyes as Theodore stared calmly back at her, something that almost seemed like compassion in his eyes.

Had it not only been a few minutes ago that the man had been taking her to task?

What in the world had gotten into him? He was being . . . nice, and she wasn't quite sure how to handle a nice Theodore Wilder.

She cleared her throat. "Forgive me, but did you just extend me a compliment?"

Theodore smiled. "I do believe I did."

He was entirely too attractive when he smiled, irresistible even. His smile caused her to want to dissolve into a puddle of mush at his feet, or better yet, throw herself across the seat and allow those strong arms of his to soothe away the disappointments of the night.

She blinked and felt her face heat. Apparently she was more overwrought than she'd believed.

"Ah, yes, well enough about me," she finally managed to say. "Shouldn't we get around to discussing why you threw me over your shoulder and carted me off like a caveman?"

Theodore's mouth twitched before his expression suddenly turned serious. "We need to discuss that man you saw down on the docks."

"There's not much else to discuss."

"Humor me," Theodore said as he stretched his long legs out in front of him. "What were you were doing before you noticed him?"

"I was speaking to Agatha and Katherine."

"They didn't give me the impression they'd actually taken note of the man."

"That's because they went off to investigate a lead."

"And they left you all alone?"

She breathed a silent sigh of relief at the clear disgruntlement now marking Theodore's tone. She knew how to handle a disgruntled Theodore. "Do not presume to lecture me, Theodore. I did have a reason for staying behind. I was keeping an eye on Lottie, and before you ask why I wasn't standing with her, she wouldn't let me." Arabella grinned as she swept her hand over her figure. "She thought I would scare off the men." She glanced at Theodore, expecting him to still be scowling at her, but instead there was a trace of a smile on his lips.

"*I* wouldn't have been scared," he said in voice that flowed like warm honey over her.

These sudden changes in his mood were beyond disconcerting. One minute he was being his normal surly self, and the next he was charming.

He was never charming with her, and since she'd actually admitted, at least to herself, that she was attracted to him, his new and surprisingly odd attitude toward her was making her feel fidgety. . . .

"What happened after Agatha and Katherine left you?"

Arabella blinked, realizing Theodore was still in the midst of a conversation with her, and felt her face heat yet again. "Ah, hmm, of course, something that happened next . . . I, uh, felt something."

"This man was so close to you that you felt him?"

She was rattled. There was no other explanation for why she was being unclear. She drew in a deep breath, looked out the window in hopes that something other than Theodore's face would distract her. When her gaze met nothing but black, she reluctantly turned but kept her attention centered on a spot right over Theodore's head. "Forgive me, but no, I didn't feel the man, not in the physical sense. It was more of an emotional feeling. It made the hair stand up on the nape of my neck. Have you ever had that happen?"

"My hair's standing up right now."

Arabella rolled her eyes even as she smiled. Honestly, he could be adorable, and at the moment she had the feeling he wasn't even trying. She forced her thoughts back to what they'd been talking about. "So there I was, standing there with my hair straight up as this man watched me, and then he stepped out of the shadows and began walking toward me."

"Do you think he got a good look at you?"

"It hardly matters if he did. It's not as if I'm easily recognizable at the moment."

"Someone would recognize you, even dressed as you are, if they'd seen you before tonight."

She frowned. "Surely you don't believe this madman who is snatching women off the streets is known to us, do you?"

"I believe there are currently too many coincidental circumstances for me to not at least entertain that disturbing possibility."

"What?"

"I went back to Gilman."

She narrowed her eyes. "Why?"

"There was unfinished business there that I couldn't ignore."

"You never mentioned anything to me on the long train ride back to New York about 'unfinished business.'"

"You can hardly blame me, considering that all you seemed to want to discuss was the suffrage movement. How was I to know you'd be interested in any other topic of conversation?"

There was the surly gentleman she'd come to know. She swallowed the laugh that was bubbling up in her throat and shook her head. "I think you didn't bring it up because you, mistakenly of course, believe ladies shouldn't be told anything of a distressing nature."

He opened his mouth, snapped it shut, and tilted his head. "You might be right. In hindsight, it would have been prudent to tell you my concerns because then tonight might never have happened. Although I did think that your brother was going to keep an eye on you."

She smiled. "You mustn't blame Zayne. He's been dogging my every footstep up until a day or so ago." Her smile widened. "I knew something was afoot and that you had something to do with my brother's odd behavior. I assumed it concerned those men from the farmhouse, since you had mentioned they might follow me here. But after two weeks went by and nothing dastardly occurred, I decided that having Zayne around all the time was bothersome. I strongly encouraged him to leave me alone."

"Of course you did."

"If *you* would have only explained yourself, I might not have encouraged him so vehemently."

"I was wrong to have kept you in the dark."

Her world suddenly shifted on its axis.

Theodore Wilder had just admitted he'd been wrong.

It was strange, but she didn't feel one little urge to gloat. "Tell me, why did you go back to Gilman?"

He shrugged. "Instinct."

"I'm afraid you're going to have to explain with more than one word."

He smiled. "Oh, very well. If you must know, I realized when we were in Gilman the first time that something disturbing was happening in town. When I went back there the second time, my concerns were proven correct."

"Did you find dead bodies?"

"Why would you think I'd find dead bodies?"

"You did say there was something disturbing happening, and disturbing, in my mind, conjures up dead bodies."

"No, there were no bodies, dead or alive. The sheriff and his men were not in town."

She blinked. "Perhaps their bodies are out there lost somewhere. Perhaps those two men from the farmhouse did away with them in order to avoid arrest."

Theodore laughed even as his eyes began to water. He swiped at them with his hand. "Are you sure you're not reading gothic novels instead of romances?"

He was very appealing when he laughed.

"You explain it then," she said when he finally sobered.

"I wish I could, but it's a mystery. And just so you know, those men from the farmhouse were nowhere to be found either."

"But . . . why do you think I'm in danger?"

"Because I have this feeling some of those men headed to New York."

She frowned. "That doesn't make any sense, especially in regard to Sheriff Dawson and his men. Granted, I did cause them a slight bit of trouble, but I find it hard to believe they'd come after me. It's not as if they could arrest me again."

"I hate to point out the obvious, but you're exceptionally beautiful. Those men from the farmhouse seemed to be dealing in some kind of slavery, and you, my dear, would fetch an exorbitant price. You might just be too tempting for them to ignore."

She couldn't help but feel a little mushy inside.

"I've come to believe that some of Sheriff Dawson's men might be involved in that ugly business, so I'm sure you can understand why I'm concerned about your safety."

The mushiness disappeared in a split second.

"That was the unfinished business you neglected to mention to me, wasn't it?"

Theodore winced. "I'm afraid it was, but in my defense, I really didn't know any particulars, so other than having you try to stay out of trouble, there really wasn't an urgent reason for me to share my thoughts."

She narrowed her eyes. "Why are you so concerned about that man I saw on the docks?"

"I think he has something to do with that nasty business in Gilman."

Her mouth dropped open. "Why do you think that?"

"This is going to sound even crazier, but . . . I get these instincts about things, and my instincts are telling me everything is connected. It seems too much of a coincidence that everyone disappears from Gilman two weeks ago, and then a week and a half ago, ladies start disappearing from the streets of New York."

"Explain the instincts."

"There's not much to explain. They're just feelings I get, but they're normally on target." He smiled. "I know you probably won't believe me, but I think God sends them to me, because there is no other way to explain them."

She looked at him for a long moment. "There really is more substance to you than you let on, isn't there?"

"I'll take that as a compliment," Theodore said. "And just so you know, because I think you may think I'm not a man of faith, I do believe God guides me at times."

Yes, she had doubted whether or not he possessed any faith, but she realized she really didn't know the gentleman sitting across from her at all.

He was becoming more attractive by the second, but that wasn't something she needed to think about right now. There was a mystery to puzzle out, and she was determined he wouldn't leave her out of the puzzling again.

"What do you suggest we do now?" she asked. "Should we set me up as bait in order to capture the criminals?"

"Absolutely not."

"Do you have a better idea?"

"I'm going to take you out of New York."

Her mouth dropped open. "That's a little drastic, and . . . I can't go away with you. It would hardly be proper."

"You travel the country on a regular basis without a chaperone."

"Yes, but I'm alone, certainly not in the company of a man."

"You traveled with me to Chicago, and then to New York."

"True, but it wasn't planned, and it was perfectly innocent."

Theodore grinned. "And traveling with me now wouldn't be innocent?"

"Now we know each other."

"What does that have to do with anything?"

"People would expect things."

"What people?"

Arabella held up her fingers and began counting them off. "My parents, Hamilton, Zayne, and don't even get me started on Eliza and Agatha, let alone your sister. They'd have a complete wedding planned for us before we had an opportunity to blink."

Theodore leaned forward and took her hand from her lap, the action causing a shiver of something unexpected to run up her arm and down her spine. She forced herself not to snatch her hand from his.

"Don't you think you might be overreacting a bit?" Theodore asked. "Your friends and family know we're hardly a suitable match. They've certainly witnessed us arguing enough to realize we'd kill each other within a month of exchanging vows."

Now, that was just . . . probably true, except for Agatha . . . and maybe Katherine.

She lifted her chin. "Agatha thinks I fascinate you."

"She said that?"

"Yes, out loud."

Theodore put her hand back in her lap and frowned. "What do you think about what Agatha said?"

"I don't set much store by it. She was most likely just trying to make me feel better because you'd been so miserable to me at the dinner party."

"I wasn't myself that night."

"You accused me of flirting with Grayson."

"You *were* flirting with Grayson."

Arabella opened her mouth and then closed it. "I might have been flirting."

"See, that's a completely feminine endeavor. There is absolutely no reason for you to doubt your femininity."

"What is wrong with you? You're being nice."

"I'm trying to soften you up so you'll agree to leave the city with me."

"No, you're not. You're just being nice."

"Don't tell anyone. I do have a fierce reputation as a horrid and miserable man to uphold."

Arabella smiled. "I really can't leave town with you."

"You could bring a chaperone."

"I don't have a chaperone waiting in the wings."

"There's always Agatha," Theodore said.

"She would end up killing you before we even got out of New York."

"Agatha likes me; she just pretends to find me repulsive. But she does have that pesky position at the newspaper to consider. They probably wouldn't like it if their new star journalist disappeared from town." He looked out the window for a minute and then turned back to her, a smile creasing his lips. "We could bring Violet and her friends."

Arabella laughed, she couldn't help herself. "They would hardly make respectable chaperones, even though they would most likely be fun. Besides, we would have a hard time remaining unnoticed if we traveled in such a large group and with such a vivid assortment of characters."

"We wouldn't have to travel far," Theodore said. "I can take you to my grandfather's house."

"I'm not certain your grandfather would appreciate hosting such unexpected and unusual guests."

"My grandfather possesses a wonderful sense of humor."

Arabella blinked. "Really?"

"Do you not believe anyone in my family could have a sense of humor?"

"Your sister is amusing."

"My sister and I are very similar."

Arabella arched a brow. "I'll have to take your word for it."

Theodore ignored her statement. "My grandfather will adore you."

"Because . . . ?"

"You're not normal."

"I see we're back to trading insults."

"I meant that as a compliment."

Arabella swallowed a laugh. "I can't go to your grandfather's house in the company of women of the night. He is an older gentleman, most likely set in his ways, and it's just not done."

"My grandfather was responsible for encouraging me to pursue a career as a private investigator."

"And that knowledge is supposed to encourage me to stay at his house?"

"That knowledge is to let you know he's a very progressive man. Also, you should know he supports rights for women."

"You're just saying that to get me to agree to your plan."

"I'm not. He is very modern, and he won't bat an eye if we take Violet and her friends with us."

"I don't know, Theodore. It seems rather . . . well, intimate.

Our families will assume we've formed an attachment to each other."

"No, they won't."

"You do remember that Gloria is my mother, right? If you take me to your grandfather's house, I can guarantee she'll show up with a shotgun slung over her shoulder and demand you marry me."

"You *have* been reading too many romance novels."

Arabella blew out an exasperated breath of air. "This is a bad idea."

"It's a wonderful idea, especially if we bring Violet and her friends with us. You are in need of a distraction, especially since you took a slight beating from Dot tonight. What better way to reaffirm that God does have a purpose for you than to allow you to spend time in the company of women who truly do need your help?"

"I told you, I'm not good at actually helping anyone, and it's obvious I completely misunderstood God's plan for me. Besides, the ladies tonight were more than vocal about my offer to assist them."

"Violet and her friends didn't refuse the offer of a safe haven."

That was an interesting point, but . . . no, she could not continue barging into other people's lives.

"My grandparents would love to help you sort out those ladies," Theodore said, pulling her from her thoughts. "And it would give them a purpose."

"A purpose?"

Theodore shrugged. "My grandfather recently told me he feels a little useless. He's almost eighty years old, and I fear he and my grandmother are not as happy now that they've been forced to slow down due to age. If we were to give them the task of figuring out what to do with the ladies, well, I would have to imagine they'd be forever grateful."

It was amazing how innocent he looked at the moment,

especially since she was fairly certain he'd just spun an incredibly tall tale. For some odd reason, though, she didn't feel like arguing the point with him. Instead, a sense of what felt like anticipation suddenly swept over her.

"We'll have to broach this with my family first, before we begin to make any plans," she heard herself say.

For a brief second, what looked like relief flickered through Theodore's eyes before he blinked and the look disappeared. "Excellent," he said with a grin. "And it's a good thing we've just arrived at your house, because I would hate to allow you an opportunity to change your mind."

The carriage had barely come to a stop before the door wrenched open, Hamilton jumped in, took a seat next to Theodore, and scowled at Arabella.

"You, my dear sister, are a menace."

15

Theodore shifted on the seat to allow Hamilton more room and smiled when Arabella caught his eye, grimaced, then turned her attention to her brother.

"My being a menace does seem to be the general consensus this evening, Hamilton, but I really can't be blamed for all the ills of the world. I'm only responsible for a few of them."

Hamilton narrowed his eyes. "You don't even know why I called you a menace."

"You could never be a menace, Miss Beckett," Grayson exclaimed as he stuck his head in the carriage and then climbed in, taking the seat next to Arabella. He took her hand in his, placed a kiss on it and, to Theodore's annoyance, didn't release his hold. "You look exceedingly lovely this evening."

Theodore's annoyance increased when Arabella grinned—much too flirtatiously, in his opinion—back at Grayson and even seemed to flutter her lashes, drawing attention to her eyes that he just then noticed looked unusually big and . . . intriguing.

He swallowed a sigh. Everything had been much easier when he'd simply thought of her as irritating.

". . . and you must tell me where you've been," Grayson was saying, pulling Theodore rather abruptly back to the conversation at hand. "Your parents, Mr. and Mrs. Watson, and Mrs. Wilder have been in an uproar ever since you neglected to return on time from the theater."

"They got delayed by way of the jail," Theodore muttered.

"Did someone mention jail?" Zayne asked when the door to the carriage swung open again and he climbed in. To Theodore's relief, Zayne squeezed himself in between Grayson and Arabella, forcing Grayson to finally release Arabella's hand.

Zayne let out a grunt when Arabella shoved him, pulled out what looked to be half of her skirt from under him, and then sent her brother a glare as he looked her up and down.

"Nice," Zayne said before he tilted his head. "Tell me, if you please, how it happened that you landed in jail again, especially when you led me to believe you were going to be spending a quiet evening with your friends?"

Arabella went from glaring to pouting, looking somewhat injured as she pouted.

He'd never even considered the fact that she'd have that particular feminine weapon at her disposal, but it was effective.

Hamilton leaned forward. "You're forgetting you're with your brothers, Arabella, so that won't work."

Arabella's pout disappeared in a split second, right before tears filled her lovely eyes.

Hamilton and Zayne rolled their eyes, but Grayson drew in a sharp breath as he got up from the seat, shoved open the carriage door, and extended his hand to Arabella. "My dear, you are becoming distressed. This carriage has turned downright chilly, and I for one believe we should get you immediately into the house."

Theodore, slightly disgruntled he hadn't thought about the chill of the carriage, couldn't help but be impressed at the way Arabella's tears suddenly vanished as she rose to take Grayson's hand and disappeared out into the cold night.

She really could cry on cue.

"*Someone* should have let her rot in jail a little longer," Hamilton said with a pointed look to Theodore.

"She wouldn't have even been in jail if *someone* would have been keeping an eye on her like *someone* said they'd do," Theodore said with a scowl back at Zayne.

Zayne smiled. "At least you can take satisfaction in knowing you've helped me discover I'm not meant to be in the investigation business." He shuddered. "The past two weeks of following my sister around have been a nightmare. I think she might have been on to me almost from the start. She started becoming quite stealthy, as can be seen from what happened tonight."

"She's stealthy, that's for certain," Hamilton said. "She didn't even stick around to tell me what happened to Eliza."

"Oh, she's in the carriage that just arrived," Zayne said.

Hamilton didn't linger. He jumped out the door and neglected to shut it behind him.

A brisk wind whirled around the interior, prompting Theodore to move off his seat and out into the frigid night. To his disappointment, Arabella was nowhere to be seen.

She was probably enjoying the attention of that bounder Grayson, and—

"She doesn't like him in a romantic way," Zayne said, climbing out of the carriage.

"What?"

"Arabella only sees Grayson as a friend."

"I don't think he sees her that way."

"He's just trying to annoy you, and he's doing a bang-up job of it," Zayne said. "Arabella's not even his type, but I think Grayson finds it amusing to bait you. You turn a very interesting shade of red when he dawdles over her hand."

"I do not."

"I'm afraid you do."

"Your sister and I are not well-suited, at least romantically, and I assure you, my feelings for her are strictly those of a friend."

"I don't think that's true."

"You're the one who pointed out that Arabella and I would kill each other if we spent much time together."

"Well, yes, I did, but . . ." Zayne shrugged. "The more I think about it, the more I believe the two of you are well-matched."

"We bicker all the time."

"Again true, but I get the distinct impression both of you enjoy bickering with each other."

Theodore blinked, and then blinked again. He did enjoy his little tussles with Arabella. They were infuriating at times, but also invigorating.

It gave him pause.

"Agatha," Zayne suddenly exclaimed, causing Theodore to turn and grin as Agatha hobbled toward them through the snow on her ridiculously high heels. "I say, you look smashing this evening." Zayne strode over to her, took her arm, and began helping her up the walk. "That is a lovely gown, and what is the color of the hair you're currently sporting?"

Agatha stopped walking, pulled the wig off her head, and thrust it into Zayne's hand. "Revolting red is how I've been thinking of it, and who knew that wigs itched so much? I'm going to have to remember that the next time I go undercover. I imagine dressing as a gentleman would be entirely more comfortable."

"After tonight, you should rethink ever going undercover again," Theodore said.

"Yes, well, no need to talk about that right now," Agatha said with an airy flick of her hand. "It's freezing out here, and I would love a hot cup of tea." She peered toward the house. "Tell me, was that Grayson I saw escorting Arabella into the house?"

Zayne stiffened. "It was."

"What's he doing here?" Agatha frowned. "It's really late, and it's not as if Grayson comes around all that often." She suddenly smiled. "I bet he came to see Arabella."

Theodore felt *his* body stiffen. "Why would he do that, and if he had come to see Arabella, why wouldn't he have left when he learned she wasn't at home?"

Zayne laughed. "Grayson spent the evening with Hamilton and me."

"Why in the world would Grayson Sumner want to spend an evening with you?" Agatha asked.

"There are some who find me an amusing companion," Zayne replied between clenched teeth. "But he was actually tagging along as Hamilton and I worked. Eliza told us he's been at loose ends lately, and we thought he might have an interest in the railroad business."

"Well, no matter," Agatha said briskly. "I've been dying to question him about his time in China, so since he's here, I think I'll go join him."

"Allow me to escort you," Zayne said. He took a firm grip on her arm and, with Theodore falling into step beside them, moved as fast as Agatha's heels would allow up the sidewalk and into the house.

Theodore smiled his thanks to the butler as the man took his hat, but then winced when he looked up and found Mrs. Watson standing not five feet away from them. Normally, Mrs. Watson was a rather pleasant sort, yet now she looked downright ominous. Her arms were folded over her chest, her cheeks were pink, and her lips were not in their customary smiling position.

Agatha, who'd bent over to fiddle with one of her silly

shoes, took that moment to straighten. She froze for just a second, then smiled. "My goodness, Mother, this is a surprise to find you still here."

Cora began tapping her toe against the wooden floor, the sound echoing loudly in the foyer. "Is it? The theater closed hours ago." Her eyes narrowed to mere slits. "Given your appearance, I'm almost of the belief you've abandoned your desire to become a journalist and replaced it with a new occupation in the opera. Unfortunately for you, I've heard you sing."

Agatha opened her mouth, but then quickly closed it when a gentleman's voice bellowed from a room at the opposite end of the hallway.

"Jail again?"

"That sounded like my father. I should go check to see what's keeping Eliza," Agatha said. She lifted up her skirts, spun on her heels, and bolted out the door before the poor butler could even open it for her.

Zayne released a dramatic sigh. "I'll go get her."

"You're leaving me to explain to everyone?" Theodore asked.

Zayne winked at Mrs. Watson, and then, coward that he was, bolted out the door just as Agatha had done seconds before. The butler hurried to shut it, sent Theodore a sympathetic look, and then he too disappeared through a side door without a single word.

"Come, dear," Mrs. Watson said as she held out her arm, waited for him to take it, and strode with him at a rapid clip until they entered a delightful parlor bathed in soft light. He escorted her to the first available chair, helped her into it, and then turned.

Arabella was standing by the fireplace, obviously warming her chilled skin, while Douglas and Gloria Beckett sat on a chaise by the window, looking at their daughter with clear resignation on their faces. His gaze shifted to Mr. Watson, who was not looking resigned in the least, but furious. Grayson, he saw, was standing by the tea cart, calmly sipping a cup of tea, as if he often found himself in contentious situations. Grayson raised his cup to him and quickly brought it to his lips when Mr. Watson began to sputter.

"You will explain to me, if you please, Miss Beckett, exactly why you're dressed in such an outlandish fashion, and why you girls appear to have lied to us regarding plans for this evening."

Arabella blew out a breath. "Forgive me, Mr. Watson, but we didn't actually lie. We were, as you can tell by my dress, at the theater."

"I thought they'd taken to the stage," Mrs. Watson added, "but then I heard you yelling about jail, and all I can think is that they were involved in something shady having nothing at all to do with the theater."

Mr. Watson walked over to his wife and patted her shoulder. "Brace yourself, dear, but once again your daughter was arrested, and Miss Beckett just told me they were down at the docks."

"Oh . . . my," Mrs. Watson whispered before she threw up her hands. "Where did I go wrong?"

"Begging your pardon, ma'am, but you didn't go wrong."

Theodore swiveled around. Violet was standing on the threshold, wringing her hands. He gestured her into the room, but she shook her head. "I'm fine right here, Mr. Wilder. Eliza insisted me and the girls come into the house instead of waiting for you in the carriage, but it wouldn't be proper for me to come into the parlor."

Another piece of his hardened heart melted away. Why had he never noticed the differences in social stations? Why would any lady feel she was not worthy of stepping into a parlor, as if the room would be tainted by her very presence?

Yes, Violet was in a profession that was tawdry and unappealing, but she'd probably never been taught any skills to do anything else, and probably hadn't received any education.

It struck him then, really struck him, exactly what Arabella had been trying to accomplish.

She wasn't some radical lady bent on upsetting the natural order of things. She was a warm, caring woman who wanted to improve the lives of ladies throughout the world.

He'd blithely told her that she could continue on with God's plan for her while at his grandfather's house, but he hadn't really thought about what that meant.

It wasn't a game to her, even if she mistakenly thought she'd been wrong in her pursuits. She was a woman who believed in doing good, doing what God wanted her to do, while he . . . he rarely considered what God wanted from him.

Something freeing swept over him, but before he could truly contemplate the lightness that had settled in his very soul, Gloria drew his attention when she got up from her seat and strode across the room. She stopped in front of Violet. "You shall join us for tea, my dear."

Violet shook her head. "I don't think so."

"Well, I get the feeling you have a story to tell, one that will shed light on what happened tonight, so you will be doing me a service, and in return, you *will* drink tea," Gloria said.

"I told Violet and her friends you would welcome them into your home," Eliza said, her voice slightly breathless as she appeared to be tugging Sarah and Hannah into the room rather forcefully. "Now then, where shall everyone sit?"

"I'll sit with Lottie," Hamilton said, following Eliza into the room, Lottie hanging on his arm and looking completely delighted by it.

"I still don't feel comfortable about this," Violet said, even as she plopped down into the seat Gloria was pointing at and then plucked at the fabric of her shabby coat, trying to rub at a stain that marked the material.

Gloria pulled up a dainty chair next to Violet, sat down, and pulled Violet's hand into her own. Violet looked positively alarmed, but to her credit she didn't snatch her hand back.

"For some reason, my dear . . . ?"

"Violet."

"That's a lovely name, and you may call me Gloria. Now then," Gloria continued even as Violet's mouth dropped open, "you seem to be under the misimpression you're not welcome here or that you don't belong."

"You're high society, and me and the girls are . . . not."

Gloria patted Violet's hand. "I'm of the belief that all of us are God's children, and as such we need to treat each other with respect. I hardly think God would be too pleased with me if I didn't offer you tea, especially since it appears you've been in the company of my daughter and Agatha this evening. You're probably past due for a bracing cup of tea."

"Forgive me, Mrs., er, Gloria, but I don't put much store in God," Violet said softly.

Gloria patted her hand again. "Perfectly understandable, dear, but sometimes God presents us with situations that . . . change our way of thinking."

"Everything all settled?" Agatha asked as she and Zayne strolled into the room. Theodore couldn't help but notice that Zayne was still carrying Agatha's wig, and Agatha had abandoned her shoes somewhere along the way.

Mr. Watson stepped forward. "Nothing has been settled, and . . . what are you wearing, and . . . is that a dog Zayne's carrying?"

"It's my wig, Father, and I'm wearing an opera dress," Agatha said with a nod before she walked across the room, kissed her father's red cheek, and went to stand by Grayson, who passed her a cup of tea before returning to filling the other cups set out on the table.

Theodore's annoyance with the man slowly drifted away as he watched Grayson take cup after cup of tea to Violet and her friends, complimenting each and every one of them. Not once did Theodore see a look of derision cross the gentleman's face.

He was more compassionate than Theodore had given him credit for, and also more of a threat.

What woman could resist a gentleman who was handsome, wealthy, and compassionate?

Arabella suddenly moved from the fireplace and settled down on a comfortable-looking settee. He took one step forward, intent on joining her, but then stopped when Grayson sidled across the room and slid into place beside her. Grayson looked up, sent Theodore a nod, then proceeded to take Arabella's hand as he leaned in closer and whispered something in Arabella's ear that caused her to laugh.

Theodore narrowed his eyes, changed his opinion yet again about the gentleman—and not for the better—and paused as he took another step forward when Zayne caught his eye and winked.

Theodore changed directions, stalked to the fireplace, and stood there for the next fifteen minutes as Arabella and Agatha explained what had happened throughout the night.

"Mrs. Wilder will be so relieved to discover Katherine is safe," Gloria said. "She was quite frazzled when the minutes kept ticking away and none of you showed up back here. I think she only decided to return to her house because, as she barely knows us, she didn't want us to take note of her increasing distress."

"I think my mother is a lot stronger than even I give her credit for," Theodore said. He tried to keep his gaze from returning to Arabella too often, even though Grayson seemed to have moved closer to her and was still holding her hand. "But now that the events of the night have been explained, and the yelling has finally ceased"—he smiled at Mr. Watson, who, to his surprise, grinned in return—"there is something of a pressing nature we need to discuss: Arabella's safety."

Douglas Beckett walked over and joined him by the fire, as did Hamilton and Zayne. Grayson, he couldn't help but notice, remained firmly ensconced on the settee and had moved from holding Arabella's hand to rubbing her shoulder. Theodore stifled the urge to throttle the man, instead turning to look directly at Douglas. He began to explain, telling everyone about his investigation, or lack thereof, in Gilman, and what his concerns were regarding Arabella.

Five minutes later, he stopped, frowned when Grayson whispered something in Arabella's ear yet again, and reluctantly forced his attention back to Hamilton, who was saying something he'd apparently missed.

". . . and we could hire guards like we did when Eliza's life was at stake."

Theodore frowned. "We might be dealing with trained professionals. That is why I have something a little more drastic in mind." He nodded to Violet and her friends. "I know I offered you the use of my house tonight, but—"

"You've rethought that, and I can't say I blame you, Mr. Wilder," Violet said before he could get the rest of his sentence out of his mouth. "You're a fine, upstanding citizen of New York, and it would harm your stellar reputation if word got out you let a bunch of old harlots stay under your roof."

She was so matter-of-fact about her position in society. He glanced at her friends and found all of them nodding in agreement. His heart gave a lurch, and he vowed then and there that, if nothing else, he was going to do his best to save these women, and hopefully help them find a life that didn't bring them constant shame.

"I don't care about my reputation," he said. "All I care about is keeping all of you safe, along with Arabella. My grandparents have a farm not too far from here, a few hours at most, and I would be honored if all of you would consent to travel there with me."

"But . . . what about Arabella?" Violet asked.

"She would be coming with us and—"

"That's a wonderful idea," Grayson interrupted. "I'll come too. We'll make a party of it."

Theodore's vision turned a little red as he watched Grayson smile his too-charming smile at Arabella and then reach up to pull the beauty patch right off her face.

Enough was enough.

His feet went into motion without his even realizing it, and before he knew it, he was standing right in front of Arabella and Grayson. He reached down, pulled her up into his arms, and sent Grayson what he could only hope was a terrifying glare.

"That is kind of you to offer, Mr. Sumner, but I'm afraid your services won't be needed. I'll take care of Arabella from now on." He looked down into Arabella's eyes. "We're leaving . . . immediately."

16

It seemed as though she'd been spending quite a bit of her time lately riding in carriages. Arabella shifted on the seat, but stilled when her elbow made contact with Violet's ribs. "I do beg your pardon, Violet."

"There's no need to apologize. We don't have much room to sneeze, let alone move."

Arabella grinned and looked around the crammed interior of the carriage. Beside Violet, Lottie was dozing with her head against the window, while Hannah and Sarah were sleeping on the other seat, both of their heads pillowed against Theodore's broad shoulders. He was sleeping as well, and in sleep he looked boyish, nothing like the crazed gentleman who had just five hours ago hustled her out of her house with barely any time to pack.

He was a good man—temperamental but good.

Why hadn't she seen that before?

Violet leaned close to her and whispered, "I must say, I envy those two. There's nothing quite like having a strong gentleman to lean against when a lady wants to slumber."

Arabella found she couldn't argue that point, but since her

emotions and her mind hadn't quite reconciled her new feelings for Theodore, she decided it would probably be best to change the subject. "I'm surprised you're not trying to nap, Violet. It was an exhausting evening."

"I've never been out of the city before. I don't want to miss a single thing."

Arabella cast a glance out the window. "It's still dark. There's nothing to miss."

"It'll be light soon, and I've always wanted to watch the sun come up out in the country."

It was such a small thing Violet wanted, and one Arabella had witnessed too many times to count as she'd traveled around the country. Her heart ached ever so slightly, and she closed her eyes for just a moment as thoughts whirled around her mind.

She'd spent years fighting for the right to vote, fighting to improve the lives of women, but she'd never actually gotten to know many of those women. She'd certainly never bothered to see into any of their souls.

Lord, I'm afraid I'm lost at the moment. I've been arrogant and judgmental. I've also been claiming to follow the path you set for me, but I think I've been mistaken. Forgive me for not truly listening and not understanding what you've planned for me. Please hold safe these women surrounding me, and show me how to help them, but only if that is your will.

"Are you all right?"

Her eyes flashed open, and she found Theodore awake and watching her. She smiled. "I'm fine. Just praying."

He returned her smile. "We certainly need all the help we can get."

She shifted carefully on the seat, trying to avoid hitting Violet again, and then winced when she stretched her arm over her head.

"Stiff from the journey?" Theodore asked.

She narrowed her eyes at him and lowered her arm. "If you must know, I'm sore from what happened before you allowed me into the carriage." She shuddered. "Why you felt it was imperative for me to leave my house in a traveling trunk is still beyond me. You did see Zayne and Hamilton drop it, didn't you?"

Violet grinned. "They told me to tell you they were very sorry about that."

"Yes, I could tell they were dreadfully sorry, especially with all the laughter I heard through the one air hole someone considerately remembered to provide." She rolled her eyes. "I think gentlemen in general are deranged."

Theodore laughed. "I didn't stuff you into that trunk because I'm deranged. I did it for your safety. There's a chance you're being followed, and the last thing we needed was for anyone to get a glimpse of you departing with me. If someone was watching your house, all they saw was me leaving with Violet and her friends."

"It was a stroke of genius to have Eliza change into Arabella's costume, Mr. Wilder," Lottie said as she pushed herself off Theodore's shoulder, her eyes remarkably bright for someone who'd just been sleeping. "If anyone *was* watching us leave, they'd have to believe Arabella was still back at her house. Eliza was very convincing when she screeched at you as we made our departure. It's too bad she was born into the aristocracy. She would have made a wonderful actress."

"Yes, she does seem to have missed her calling," Arabella muttered. "But, just to clarify, I don't normally shriek like a fishmonger from the steps of my house, especially in the middle of the night."

Theodore and Lottie exchanged amused glances.

Violet leaned forward. "At least you were not made to stay in the trunk for the entire journey."

Arabella shuddered. "You have no idea how disconcerting it is to know you're tied by flimsy ropes to the top of a swaying carriage. I feared for my life."

"It seems Eliza is not the only one who missed her calling," Theodore said with a grin.

"Have you ever been stuffed into a trunk and made to ride on top of a carriage?"

"I've never been stuffed into a trunk, but there was the time I was put into a coffin in order to escape a gang of smugglers."

"You were involved with smugglers?" Violet breathed.

Arabella released a huff. "He's just teasing."

"Am I?"

Arabella bit her lip as she considered him across the small space. He was gazing innocently back at her, but there was something about his expression, something that made her realize right then and there that Theodore had, indeed, escaped from a gang of smugglers.

Honestly, who came into contact with smugglers on a regular basis?

It made him even more . . . intriguing.

Heat flooded her face, and she was suddenly thankful dawn had not arrived just yet and that their only light came from a small lantern attached to the carriage door. She cleared her throat and struggled for something to say to distract herself from her disturbing thoughts. "I've been wondering why we had to leave New York so abruptly."

Theodore crossed his arms over his chest, his expression somewhat guarded. "I didn't see the need to linger. My main objective is to get you to safety as soon as possible."

"If that's true, why then did we stop off at your house, where you left me lingering on top of the carriage for a good fifteen minutes?"

"I gave you plenty of blankets, so I knew you wouldn't be cold, and you were guarded the entire time by one of my men."

"One of your men just happened to be at your house?" Arabella asked.

"Someone is always at my house. I've made too many enemies to leave my home unprotected."

That certainly wasn't something she'd ever considered.

"I also thought that stopping at my house would be a good diversion tactic, and it allowed me to pack a few personal items for this trip and send word for more of my men to join us."

"More men are going to join us?" Lottie asked, her eyes gleaming.

"Five men already have, and no, you will not get near them," Theodore said firmly.

Lottie slumped back against the seat, but her lips were twitching, and Arabella had the uncanny feeling the lady had been deliberately baiting Theodore.

Here was something else she'd never considered: ladies of the night with mischievous attitudes.

"I realize none of you know where we're going, but I assure you, you'll be safe," Theodore said. "Not only do I have men riding with us, they're also some of the best trackers around. They'll know if we're being followed." He looked directly at Arabella, his expression intense. "I will do everything in my power to make certain nothing, and no one, gets near you."

It was as if all the air had suddenly been sucked right out of the carriage. He was the same gentleman she'd known for a while now, but something had changed between them. What that something was, she really didn't understand, but her world shifted, and she knew it would never be the same again.

The carriage lurched to the right, and Arabella grabbed onto the strap, even as the carriage steadied a moment later. The strange moment with Theodore disappeared.

An hour sped by as light conversation flowed through the carriage, and Arabella couldn't help but notice that Theodore didn't appear at all uneasy being surrounded by five ladies. He told amusing stories every once in a while, but for the most part he spent the time watching her.

It was disconcerting.

She felt his gaze once again and turned toward the window, smiling before she pushed herself up and out of her seat, gestured to Violet to take her place, and then sat down next to her once Violet had moved. "The sun is coming up."

Tears stung her eyes when Violet pressed her nose against the glass, and she couldn't seem to resist looking at Theodore, who was watching her again, only now with something warm in his eyes, something different. She wiped her eyes with the edge of her sleeve and returned her attention to Violet, who began pointing out everything and anything she saw, her excitement contagious.

"Look at that," Violet exclaimed five minutes later. "There's a huge mansion up ahead."

Theodore edged forward and smiled. "That's my grandfather's house."

The carriage turned, and Arabella caught a glimpse of the house out of the small piece of window she could see past Violet's head. She blinked. The house was three stories tall, constructed of red brick, and had at least five pillars bordering the porch that ran the entire length of the building.

"I thought you said your grandparents lived on a farm," she said slowly.

"This is the farm, and that's the farmhouse. My grandfather does like to indulge in the extravagant every once in a while."

"Begging your pardon, Mr. Wilder," Violet said, her eyes huge as she turned from the window, "but that's more than extravagant. You could fit a hundred families in there."

"Probably not that many families, Violet, but there is plenty of space for all of you. You'll be able to relax until we get matters settled back in the city, and you won't have to worry about disturbing anyone."

"We can't stay here," Lottie whispered. "Your grandfather must be one of the richest men in the world to afford such a house. He won't want women like us around."

"Do you honestly believe I would bring you somewhere you weren't welcome?" Theodore asked.

Lottie bit her lip. "We're not considered acceptable."

"You're completely acceptable, and better still, I consider all of you friends." Theodore gestured out the window. "Besides, that's my grandfather standing on the porch, so it's too late now."

Arabella frowned. "What in the world is your grandfather doing up at this time of day?"

"He's always been an early riser, as is my grandmother, and he's probably already been out to the barn to talk to his chickens."

"He talks to chickens?" Hannah asked.

"I thought only crazy people talked to chickens," Sarah said, causing everyone to turn to her. Her face turned pink even as she leaned forward and peered out the window. "He looks scary."

Arabella smiled at Sarah, surprised the lady had actually spoken. She'd only heard her speak once at the jail and couldn't even imagine how nervous the lady must be at the moment. "I'm sure he's not scary, Sarah. He's probably just like Theodore, and you're not scared of Theodore, are you?"

Sarah shook her head, albeit a bit slowly, scooted back in her seat, and lapsed into silence.

"Theodore, is that you?" a voice bellowed as the carriage rolled to a stop.

"Maybe we should be scared," Violet whispered.

"My grandfather is a perfectly amiable soul who will welcome you with open arms." Theodore pushed the door open and jumped down from the carriage. "I heard you were looking for me, Grandfather."

Arabella paused in the process of getting out of the carriage as Theodore's grandfather grabbed Theodore and pulled him into a hug. He stepped back and gestured to the sky. "I told your father I needed to see you, but I never expected you to turn up on my doorstep in the midst of a blizzard."

Arabella glanced at the sky, noticed a few flakes floating lazily to the ground, and looked back to Theodore, who was grinning.

"I don't think this measly little bit of snow can be considered a blizzard."

"The chickens say differently," George said with a hearty laugh. "I just got back from trying to soothe the animals when I saw your carriage driving up. It's a rather unusual time to pay a visit."

Theodore nodded. "I have a bit of a situation on my hands."

Theodore's grandfather squinted at the carriage. "Who do you have in there?"

"A few of my friends."

"Well, get them out of the cold, boy. You've forgotten your manners."

Theodore strode back to the carriage and extended his hand to Arabella. He helped her down and pulled her over to his grandfather. "Grandfather, I'd like you to meet Miss Arabella Beckett. Arabella, this is my grandfather, Mr. George Wilder."

Before Arabella could get a single word out of her mouth, George took her by the arm and nudged her toward the house, leaving Theodore behind. "Good heavens, Miss Beckett, whatever has my grandson done to you? You look as if you've had a rough time of it."

Arabella couldn't help but fall immediately in love with the gentleman. She'd never met him before, but for some strange reason she felt as if she'd known him for years. She sent him a smile as he helped her up the steps to the porch. "I'm afraid I must admit that your grandson made me ride part of the way stuffed into an old trunk on top of the carriage."

George came to a halt. "He stuffed you into a trunk?"

Arabella nodded and was about to embellish, but then Theodore began climbing the steps with the ladies trailing behind him. George was in the midst of shaking his finger at him when he paused in mid-shake and frowned. "Well, who do we have here?"

"I'll tell you as soon as we get the ladies out of the cold," Theodore said before he turned to help Sarah up the steps.

George took her arm again, ushered her quickly into the house, and shut the door once everyone had shuffled inside. He arched a brow in Theodore's direction.

Theodore grinned. "Grandfather, I'd like you to meet my friends. This is Violet, Hannah, Sarah, and Lottie. Ladies, this is my grandfather, Mr. George Wilder."

The ladies muttered hellos and huddled together, all looking terrified.

"Did you stuff them into trunks also?" George asked.

Theodore's grin widened. "There was no need. They aren't as much trouble as Miss Beckett."

Arabella let out a huff. "You did not stuff me into that trunk because I was causing you trouble. Good heavens, Theodore, your grandfather is going to think I'm a complete hoyden."

"My grandfather likes hoydens. My grandmother was famous for landing herself in trouble, much to the dismay of *my* father."

"Indeed I did," a lilting voice said, causing Arabella to spin around to find a lovely older woman with white hair, a fine bone structure, and a regal demeanor walking down the

242

hallway. "Although I readily admit I have not caused much mayhem in recent years. My rheumatism holds me back."

"Hello, Grandmother," Theodore exclaimed. "You're looking more beautiful than ever."

"You did have to inherit your looks from someone," Theodore's grandmother said with a grin, letting out a laugh when Theodore picked her up and squeezed her. He set her back down, and she patted his cheek before she turned and set her sights on Arabella.

"You're Arabella Beckett."

Arabella nodded.

"How lovely it is to finally get to meet you. I'm Ethel Wilder. I had the pleasure of listening to one of your lectures. It was riveting, and you were so eloquent in your speech." Ethel smiled. "May I assume, given the earliness of the hour and your state of slight disrepair, that you've landed yourself into some mischief?"

"I'm afraid I have, but it was completely unintentional."

"It always is," Ethel said, her gaze moving to drift over Violet and her friends. "No sense standing in the foyer with the chill leaking through the door. Shall we move to the parlor where I'll send for some tea and coffee?"

Violet shook her head. "We wouldn't want to put you out, Mrs. Wilder. We can just wait right here until plans can be made for where we'll stay."

Ethel put her hands on her hips. "What is your name, dear?"

"Violet."

"Well, Violet, as I said a moment ago, I'm Ethel Wilder. It's time for breakfast, and in this house I expect everyone to accept my offer of a meal. I suggest you follow Dolly, and she'll take you to wash up. I will expect to find you in the parlor soon, where we will have coffee, tea, and pastries while breakfast is being prepared. Understood?"

"I see it's not only your looks you get from your grandmother," Violet muttered to Theodore before she moved to follow Dolly, who was obviously the downstairs maid. The rest of the ladies followed, Lottie sending Arabella a grin as she passed.

Ethel set her sights on Theodore and arched a brow.

"They're in danger, Gran."

"Should I hide the silver?"

"I don't think you need to worry about that," Theodore said. "I thought they could stay in the room above the barn."

George narrowed his eyes. "They'll be our guests, so they'll stay on the third floor, which will allow them the safety of the house while giving them the space I'm sure they need."

Theodore shook his head. "I'm not certain they'll be comfortable there, Grandfather. It took everything they had just to walk through the door."

"Well, they're not staying in the barn," Ethel said with a snort.

"They might prefer that."

"Will they also prefer the grooms who have their quarters there?" Ethel asked.

Arabella stepped forward. "They won't proposition anyone while they're here, Mrs. Wilder. I've gotten to know these ladies, and they would look on that as dishonorable."

Ethel tilted her head. "Hmm, interesting. I've never met a lady of the night who possessed such strong morals."

"And have you met many ladies of the night?"

"I suppose I haven't," Ethel admitted. She took Arabella by the arm and walked with her down the hall. "The lecture I saw you give was in upstate New York last year. George and I were sufficiently impressed by what was said, and George made a sizable donation to the cause." She lowered her voice. "Don't let that information get out, though. He hates for people to think he's gone soft."

"I heard that," George muttered from behind them. "Now, would someone please explain to me what Miss Beckett was doing locked up in a trunk?"

Ethel stopped walking. "Well, that certainly explains your appearance, Miss Beckett. I have to say, you do look as if you've been put through the ringer." She smiled. "Not that you're anything less than beautiful, as you very well know, but I'm sure you've looked better."

"Grandmother, what a thing to say," Theodore said.

Ethel shrugged. "Miss Beckett is perfectly comfortable with her looks. From one beauty to another, we've learned to live with our burden, haven't we?"

How in the world was she supposed to respond to that? Did she know she possessed a measure of beauty? Certainly, but it wasn't something she ever talked about, and certainly not so frankly. She caught Ethel's gaze and couldn't help but smile at the twinkle she found in the lady's eyes.

"I'm sure you've come to the same conclusion I have, haven't you?" Ethel asked before Arabella could even think of a response to the first question.

"What conclusion is that?" she asked.

"Why, that God gave us our beauty to help us in our chosen path in life. Many years ago, I found my good looks a bit of a burden. Fortunately I realized that they aided me in my work, so I thanked God for them and got on with the plan He'd laid out for me."

Theodore cleared his throat. "You really believe that?"

"Of course, darling, and you should too. There's a reason you've been given your pleasing appearance, and you should take a moment to thank God for your face. You can't tell me you haven't benefited from your charming smile as you've gone about investigating a case. As for Miss Beckett, I know for a fact she uses her smile as a weapon. It certainly worked at the lecture your grandfather and I attended. George practically knocked people over in order to extend her a donation, and then he was most distraught when some elderly lady insisted on taking it from him, instead of allowing him to give it directly to Miss Beckett."

"That's not true," George blustered. "Not that I'm denying you're a beautiful woman, Miss Beckett, but I have only ever had eyes for my Ethel."

"Oh, here we go," Theodore muttered. "If you think Hamilton and Eliza are bad, just wait until you've been made to suffer my grandparents' affection for each other over the next few days. You'll be ready to get back to New York."

"I think it's sweet," Arabella said.

"Ah, you're a romantic," Ethel said. "I thought I detected a kindred spirit."

Theodore rolled his eyes. "Speaking of kindred spirits, you'll have plenty to read while we're here, Arabella. My grandmother keeps a library well-stocked with romance novels." He winked. "I've even caught my grandfather reading them on occasion."

"Theodore, must you divulge all our secrets to this young woman?" George asked, though his tone was more amused than annoyed. "Now then, back to the trunk. You didn't make her ride in it for very long, did you?"

"I let her out a mile past my house. But, just so you know, her appearance was ruffled before she even got into the trunk."

"There is absolutely no need to go into that with your grandparents," Arabella muttered.

"My dear, you must tell us everything," Ethel said as she steered Arabella into a charming parlor decorated in soft pink. "As I said before, I've not been able to indulge in many adventures of late, but I can live vicariously through you."

Arabella stepped farther into the room and smiled in delight. "What an enchanting room. Pink is my favorite color." She took the seat Ethel offered and looked up to find Theodore watching her with something strange in his eyes. "What?"

"I never realized how much in common you have with my grandmother."

Ethel sat down in the chair next to her, a frothy creation covered in pink, and laughed. "That's a high compliment indeed, coming from Theodore. He adores me, and I'm his most favorite female."

"Don't let my mother or sister hear you say that," Theodore said.

Ethel waved his statement away with a dainty flick of her wrist. "Louise most likely knows it's the truth, and Katherine *would* be competition for your affections, if she hadn't turned into such a stick-in-the-mud when she married that Harold."

"I thought you liked Harold," Theodore said.

"I did when he first started courting her, but I'm not pleased with his behavior of late, or your father's for that matter. It is beyond my comprehension why Samuel has taken to abandoning his wife. It's disgraceful, and he's the one who has always been mortified by my behavior," Ethel said with a sniff.

Theodore caught Arabella's eye. "My grandmother had quite the reputation in her youth. "My father was always worried her past indiscretions would reflect poorly on him."

"They weren't actually indiscretions, dear. I don't know if you realize this or not, Theodore, but I used to work with your grandfather, and my work often demanded I place myself in precarious situations."

Arabella winced when Theodore's eyes suddenly turned stormy. "You worked with Grandfather?"

"Indeed," Ethel said with a nod before she lowered her voice. "I was a spy."

17

Arabella opened her eyes and blinked a few times. None of her surroundings looked familiar. Weak light filtered through sheer pink curtains, and the sight of pink brought it all back.

She was at Theodore's grandparents' house, and Ethel had insisted on giving her this particular room because of the pink décor. She'd also insisted Arabella take a short nap after they'd had breakfast, but given the dimness of the light coming through the window, the storm had either taken a turn for the worse or she'd slept the entire day away.

She stretched her arms over her head and wiggled down into the soft mattress, wincing when her body protested the movement. Apparently, being carted around in a traveling trunk was not conducive to a lady's well-being.

Arabella stuffed some pillows behind her back to cushion her aching body and then closed her eyes.

Dear Lord, I feel I have been remiss in praying as often as I should lately. You opened my eyes yesterday and showed me the wrong turns I've been taking. Forgive me for wallowing in self-pity. I'll strive to do better and work harder to help those who wish for my help, while trying not to badger everyone into seeing my point of view. I know you have a path chosen for me, and even though I'm not exactly sure what that path is, I'll try and listen closer to your words. Please give me the strength and the courage to move forward.

She opened her eyes, allowing herself a few minutes to simply be quiet. She'd had a lot to think about since she'd gotten arrested again, and some of her thoughts had been somewhat difficult to accept.

She'd been so angry with Dot, but . . . the lady had been right.

She *was* judgmental and entirely too opinionated.

She'd been walking through life with blinders on, but now they were off. The real horrors of some women's lives had been exposed, and Arabella knew she couldn't simply sit by and do nothing.

All she had to figure out now was how to help without coming across as a condescending, unpleasant know-it-all.

She snuggled down into the covers and closed her eyes again, but an image of Theodore immediately flashed to mind, which had her eyes springing open again.

What was she going to do about him?

She liked him, there was no sense denying it anymore, but she had no idea if he returned the sentiment.

He kept watching her, all the time, with something new and slightly dangerous in his eyes.

What did that mean?

He was a contradiction in every sense of the word. He didn't believe a woman's place was outside the home, but he'd barely batted an eye when his grandmother proclaimed the fact she'd been a spy for the government.

Poor George had turned bright red as he'd advanced on his perfectly calm wife, demanding to know if the woman had just suffered some type of fit. Ethel had simply smiled at her husband and patted his cheek, telling him it was about time the family knew their little secret. Her smile hadn't dimmed when George pointed out that Arabella wasn't exactly family, even though she'd sent Theodore a rather pointed look.

A knock on the door suddenly pulled her from her thoughts. "Yes?"

She peeked over the covers as Ethel stepped into the room, carrying what appeared to be clothing in her arms.

"Good to see you awake, my dear. You must have been exhausted. It's a little past three." Ethel dumped everything she'd been carrying onto the nearest chair and moved closer to the bed. "I'm surprised you were able to sleep so soundly, what with the howling winds battering the house. George was right. We're in the midst of an early blizzard. I'm afraid you'll be stuck with us for quite some time."

That notion didn't seem to bother Arabella in the least.

"Now," Ethel continued, "I hope you don't mind, but I took the liberty of gathering up a few articles of clothing that will be better suited for the weather than those flimsy gowns you brought with you."

"I thought I packed warm gowns."

"Not unless you packed them in a bag Theodore neglected to notice. Upon my word, I would have never believed a woman could travel so lightly. I only found one measly little bag for you, and, good heavens, the three gowns stuffed inside were hardly sufficient for a trip out of town. George is always nagging me endlessly when we travel." Her eyes twinkled. "I tend to bring at least four trunks, even if we're only going away for a few days."

Arabella struggled upright. "Theodore must have dumped out all my clothes in order to fit me in that trunk." She blew out a breath. "It never occurred to me that he'd stuffed me into my own trunk, one, I might add, that I'd packed, somewhat rapidly of course, with all my necessities. He should have just asked my mother for another one."

"He's a man, and men don't often think like we do."

"Now there's a profound statement," Arabella said with a grin. "I guess I will be in need of those clothes, Mrs. Wilder."

"Please, call me Ethel. Mrs. Wilder always brings to mind my mother-in-law."

Amusement began to bubble through her. Ethel was at least in her late seventies, and yet she balked at being called Mrs. Wilder. "Thank you, Ethel. You must call me Arabella."

"How lovely," Ethel exclaimed. "We're already on our way to becoming fast friends. Since we're now friends, I have no remorse whatsoever in asking you some questions."

Arabella laughed, unable to help but adore the woman standing beside her bed. "Ask away."

"You are delightful," Ethel said. "I must admit that I've been thinking about something for hours but knew I wouldn't get a straight answer from Theodore. Since you brought up the traveling trunk, what in the world possessed you to agree to travel in it?"

Arabella shrugged. "I'm not actually certain. I readily admit being tied to the top of the carriage did make me quite queasy, but your grandson has an . . . intuitiveness about him, if you will, and because of that, I realized it was necessary for me to do as he asked."

"Theodore's instincts are usually always right. He takes after his grandfather in that regard."

"From what you said this morning, I would have to believe your grandson got some of his abilities from you."

Ethel grinned and surprised Arabella when she hopped lightly up on the bed and made herself comfortable. "You're probably right. I was quite adept at subterfuge in my younger years, and I do believe Theodore inherited a bit of my talent. George and I were disappointed when it became clear

Samuel was not interested in the family business. Our hopes were restored when Theodore was born. It was clear from an early age he possessed a sense of adventure."

"I thought your family business was finance," Arabella said.

"That was just a front," Ethel replied with an airy wave of her hand. "It was a rather profitable front for us, mind you, but a front all the same."

"Why was there a need for a front?"

"George had to spread something around, dear. He couldn't very well say he'd been rewarded handsomely for tracking down pirates who were plaguing our rivers." Ethel's eyes gleamed. "He was allowed to keep a bit of the booty, you see, but George has always been a cunning man, and he thought it would serve him well to allude to a mysterious circumstance surrounding his newfound wealth. That mystery gave him a daunting reputation that made people wary with their questions. No one ever realized he worked in secret for the government."

"He tracked down river pirates?"

"Indeed, that's how we met."

"You were a pirate?"

"Don't be silly. Although . . . that life would have been exciting when pirates actually traveled the high seas, searching for treasure." She shook her head. "How I do go on. If you must know, one summer I went to spend time with my auntie who lived on the shores of the Ohio River. I was out walking one evening, close to dark if I recall, and spotted what I knew was certainly one of the pirate sloops everyone in the vicinity had been talking about. My curiosity got the better of me, and I'm afraid I couldn't resist investigating. I ended up in a bit of a pickle, and George rescued me." Her lips twitched. "He wasn't exactly thrilled to save me. I was a headstrong lady in those days, and I didn't take to the blistering lecture he felt I deserved after he saved my neck. You see, I'd jeopardized his mission by snooping around, but in my defense, how could anyone be expected to ignore pirates?"

"That *would* have been difficult to ignore. Am I to assume your presence was detected by the pirates as you were snooping around?"

"Indeed, it was. I found myself the captive of a ruthless band of men, and I was certain I was about to be killed."

"What happened?"

Ethel's eyes turned distant. "I remember it as if it were only yesterday. I was locked in a storage room, rats scurrying around me, and I sent up a prayer asking God to send help and then . . . George arrived and saved the day. We've been together ever since."

"You fell in love at first sight?"

"Good heavens, no. We fought almost constantly at first, and I swear I wanted to bash the man over the head almost daily. But then, well, we both began to compromise, just a bit you see. Nothing drastic, except for the fact he stopped demanding I act like a demure lady, and I stopped demanding he act like a more sensitive gentleman. We came to realize we were perfect for each other. We've shared a wonderful life, and I've come to believe it was God's plan all along."

"Why didn't Theodore know you were a spy?"

"That was Samuel's doing. He made me promise to keep my little occupation a secret, even though he finally relented and allowed George to tell Theodore about his position with the government once Theodore got older." She shook her head. "I fear my son thought I would be a bad influence, especially on Katherine, and he was vehemently opposed to his daughter following in my footsteps. Samuel tried to hide it from me, but I always believed he was slightly ashamed to have such unusual parents, or rather, such an unusual mother.

It's what made him the way he is, such a stickler for the proprieties."

"I can't imagine anyone would be ashamed of you."

"That's very sweet of you to say, dear, but after he chose Louise to be his wife, it was quite clear Samuel wanted a wife completely different from his mother. Louise came from a very distinguished family, and I'm certain she's never once dabbled in any mischief."

"She locked Samuel out of the house last week."

"I beg your pardon?"

"It's true, and I have to admit that I do believe your son and Katherine's husband think it's my fault your daughter-in-law and granddaughter are suddenly running amok."

"But that's wonderful. Now they have someone to blame besides me."

"*I* wasn't responsible for Samuel or Harold getting locked out of their houses."

Ethel grinned. "Katherine locked Harold out of the house as well?"

"She did, and from what I understand, Harold was forced to spend the night at his mother's house."

"Oh . . . dear."

"Exactly," Arabella agreed. "I'm still not sure why Samuel blames you for anything, though. You apparently kept your promise and never told Theodore or Katherine about your spying."

"True, but you see, George is the one who was responsible for talking Theodore into opening up his agency. Samuel assumed that once his son graduated from the university, he'd join the *reputable* family business. George understood that Theodore wouldn't be happy doing that. Our grandson has always been extremely active, and sitting behind a desk all day wouldn't have suited him at all. George put Theodore in touch with some of his government contacts, and the rest is history. Samuel didn't speak to us for over a year, and even now our relationship is strained."

Arabella frowned. "What did you mean when you said George put Theodore in touch with his government contacts?"

Ethel's eyes turned crafty. "What do you think I meant?"

"Surely you're not suggesting Theodore works for the government?"

Ethel began whistling under her breath.

"He runs his own private investigating firm," Arabella said.

"Yes, dear, just like George ran a lucrative finance office."

It was no wonder the man was so self-assured and domineering. He was most likely a spy.

"A dangerous man is so attractive, don't you agree?" Ethel asked sweetly.

"I'm sure I don't know what you could be suggesting."

"Don't you?"

Arabella smiled, began whistling in the same manner Ethel had, and turned her attention to the window, noticing in surprise it was growing remarkably dark as snow blew against the pane.

"My grandson is a complicated man."

Arabella stopped watching the snow and turned her head. "I'm beginning to realize that."

"You will need to be patient with him. He's been raised by a father who has tried his best to convince him that women are expected to be pretty, sweet, easily managed, and nothing else."

"Why are you telling me this?"

Ethel looked at her for a long moment. "Theodore has never brought a lady here before today."

Arabella couldn't help but notice that Ethel's eyes were now gleaming in exactly the same way her mother's eyes gleamed when she was dabbling in a bit of matchmaking. She stifled a groan. "Your grandson only brought me here so he could protect me."

"If you say so, dear."

"Ethel, forgive me, but I don't want you to harbor any misconception about your grandson and me. We are not well-suited."

"From what I saw this morning, I think you're very well-suited indeed."

"He's old-fashioned, and I'm . . . not."

"That's why compromise is so lovely."

The conversation was quickly turning dangerous.

"Well, I must be off," Ethel said. She jumped lightly from the bed and headed for the door before Arabella had a chance to think of a proper response to Ethel's compromise statement. Ethel turned when she reached the door. "The bath is just through there, dear, and you'll find everything you need on the shelves." She reached for the doorknob, paused again, and looked over her shoulder. "My grandson seems very possessive of you."

Arabella swallowed. "Does he?"

"Hmm, yes, he does. It's rather peculiar."

"Is it?"

Ethel smiled. "Yes, it is, especially since you're so adamant that the two of you don't suit." Ethel turned on her heel and disappeared through the door.

Having no idea what to make of that, Arabella pushed aside the covers, swung her legs off the bed, and headed for the bath, hoping a good soak in the tub would clear her thoughts.

One hour later, Arabella finished toweling her hair dry and leaned forward to peer into the mirror. She pinched her cheeks, even though they were still rosy from her bath, and fluffed her hair with her fingers, stilling when she realized what she was doing.

She was primping.

She never primped unless she was going out for an evening.

Her eyes widened. Good heavens, she was primping for Theodore.

She bit her lip. Did she want to impress him? Was that even possible?

She released a huff of exasperation at her ridiculous thoughts, got up from the vanity seat, and smoothed down the wool dress Ethel had left for her. Surprisingly enough, it fit rather well.

She couldn't resist giving her reflection one last glance, patting her hair once again, and then rolling her eyes.

Theodore probably wouldn't even notice the extra time she'd taken with her appearance.

Ethel thought he seemed possessive.

Her pulse sped up at that thought, but then she took a deep breath and shook her head. She might be attracted to him, but except for a strange look in his eyes every now and again when he watched her, he'd given her no reason to believe he found her charming instead of annoying.

They were too different, and she would do well to remember that.

Ethel and George had been completely different from each other, and Ethel had admitted they'd fought all the time when they'd first met.

Ethel had longed to bash George over the head on numerous occasions.

They shared a love that was not often seen.

"You're not Ethel, and Theodore's not George," she said to the reflection staring back at her. She turned on her heel and marched from the room, making her way down the stairs and looking in one room after another.

"In here, dear," Ethel's voice called.

Arabella strode down a long hallway, trying to ignore the

butterflies in her stomach. She stepped through the door and her butterflies disappeared.

Theodore was nowhere in sight.

"You look enchanting," Ethel exclaimed, waving her over with a flick of her hand. Her gaze swept over Arabella, and then the gleam returned to her eyes.

"Well-suited or not, my dear, if you continue to look like this, my grandson will have no choice but to fall madly in love with you. Why, I wouldn't be surprised if he proposed before the week is out."

18

Theodore rested his hands on the porch railing, taking a moment to enjoy the way the sunlight glistened off the mounds of snow blanketing the scenery. The snow had stopped falling three days before and the temperature had begun to rise, but they were still relatively buried in, a circumstance that had made it impossible for him and his guests to leave the farm since they'd arrived a week ago.

He lifted his eyes to the sky and drew in a deep breath, a feeling of contentment flowing through him.

He'd never been a man who enjoyed the quiet, but now it almost seemed as if God had sent the storm just for him, to force him to slow down and get to know the real Arabella.

She was completely different from what he'd first imagined.

She was vibrant and caring.

She'd insisted on helping around the farm and had quickly proven she wasn't afraid to get her hands dirty. She'd fed cows, shoveled snow to clear a path to the pasture, and had even shown a strange appreciation for the chicken coop.

She was a most unusual lady.

He turned from the quiet scene in front of him and moved

into the house, taking a moment to shuck off his boots before heading down the hallway. He set his sights on the library and increased his pace, hoping he'd find Arabella in what she'd declared was her favorite room of the house.

He paused in the doorway as his gaze immediately went to Arabella, who was snuggled down in a cozy chair. A thick blanket was tucked around her, and she had abandoned the latest novel she was reading on the floor beside her.

She was sleeping.

She was beautiful when she slept.

He took a step into the room, his eyes never leaving her face. Long, sooty lashes rested against her cheeks, and her curly blond hair was tousled and unbound, tempting him with the sudden urge to smooth it back into place.

He could no longer ignore the fact he was falling a little in love with her. He had spent the past week almost entirely in her company, and being in constant contact with Arabella Beckett was something he'd enjoyed more than anything he'd ever enjoyed in his life.

He'd known she was intelligent but had mistakenly thought that intelligence made her hard.

He couldn't have been more wrong.

She had a razor-sharp wit, one she'd used effectively to promote her cause, but the time he'd spent with her lately had shown him that she could converse quite easily about almost anything.

His grandfather had taken to baiting her on a variety of different subjects, from women's rights to politics in Washington to even the horrible conditions of the immigrants who resided in the slums of New York. Arabella was never without an opinion, but she'd surprised him in that she didn't always insist on being right. She was more interested in what George said than in winning every argument.

His grandparents were completely in love with her. He was

fairly certain he was rapidly going the same way, but . . . he had no idea if she returned his sentiments, nor did he know how to go about the business of allowing her to learn he felt affection for her.

It was a most peculiar circumstance.

He'd never had difficulties with ladies before, but Arabella was different.

A loud snore from the opposite side of the library attracted his attention. He pulled his gaze away from Arabella, walked farther into the room, and grinned when the sight of his grandmother met his eyes.

Ethel was stretched out on the settee in front of the fire, covered in blankets, her head resting on a cushioned pillow, and she was snoring . . . quite loudly. He shook his head. It was little wonder his grandmother was tired; they'd been staying up late every night, laughing and talking and playing games. No one ever seemed to want to seek their beds, and he knew he would cherish forever this time he'd spent with his grandparents.

Not only did it seem to him that God had allowed him an opportunity to relax, God had also given him an opportunity to appreciate the small things that made up his life.

He'd never taken himself for a man of deep faith, but being around Arabella—a lady who seemed to spend a lot of time praying and discussing matters of God with his grandmother—had somehow changed his whole perception of things.

A snuffling sound, and then a snort, erupted behind him, and he glanced away from his grandmother and looked to Arabella again, his heart oddly aching as he noticed her mouth had dropped open and a noise that sounded somewhat like a saw was now escaping her lips.

She was adorable. There was no other way to describe her.

"That's a sound you don't hear all that often," George

said with a chuckle as he strode into the room and stopped by Theodore's side. "Who knew that such awful noise could be produced by such angelic creatures?"

Theodore grinned. "I think their snores are shaking the house."

Ethel stirred on the couch, opened her eyes, sat up, and discreetly wiped her mouth, causing Theodore's grin to widen when he realized she'd been drooling. .

"My goodness but that child can make a lot of noise while she's sleeping," Ethel said with a nod toward Arabella.

George tilted his head. "You've got yourself a special lady there, Theodore."

Arabella's eyes took that moment to flash open. She blinked a few times, pushed the blanket off herself, and stretched. "Why are all of you watching me?"

"You were snoring," Ethel said.

"And you couldn't find something more entertaining to do to pass the time than watch me?"

Theodore moved closer to her. "I was passing my time watching my grandmother snore before she woke up."

The corners of Arabella's lips twitched.

Ethel shifted on the settee. "I don't snore."

"She's been snoring since I met her," George said. He walked across the room and sat down by his wife, taking her hand in his. "I find it one of your most endearing qualities."

"Oh no, here they go again," Theodore muttered.

A look that seemed almost wistful flickered across Arabella's face. "I find them charming."

He found *her* charming.

He opened his mouth to tell her so, uncertain if it was the proper time or if she'd even be receptive to hearing him tell her something so personal, but before he could find the right words, the sound of wheels crunching through the snow met his ears.

He stood there for just a moment, and then his feet began to move as he realized that something had to be wrong. The roads were barely passable, and no one in their right mind would come to pay a social call. He reached the front door and, as an added precaution, pulled his gun from its holster, yanking the door open. He froze.

"I realize you were annoyed with me the last time we saw each other, Theodore, but I don't think that's cause to shoot me," Katherine said as she climbed out of the carriage.

"What are you doing here?" Theodore asked, shoving his pistol back in the holster and heading outside to greet the visitors.

"She insisted we bring her so she could help your grandmother decorate the house for Christmas," Louise said before she jumped lightly to the ground and looked back over her shoulder. "Samuel, darling, be a dear and grab that basket. It's got those cookies I made for your father in it."

Ethel edged up beside Theodore. "Did Louise just call Samuel 'darling'?"

"Just wait," Katherine said, stepping forward to kiss her grandmother's cheek. "Daddy's a new man. Ever since he brought me home from jail, he's taken to wooing Mother."

"He's wooing Mother?" Theodore asked weakly.

"As I said, he's a new man," Katherine said. "I almost returned home to Harold at one point—not that I'm remotely ready to take him back—because our parents have been behaving in a rather interesting fashion. They can't seem to keep their hands off each other, and at times I felt as if I were the parent and they the naughty children. They've been giggling all over the house."

Ethel's eyes sparkled. "How delightful."

"Mother," Samuel called, his head popping out of the carriage, "I hope you don't mind this unexpected visit. Katherine's been longing to see you, and I couldn't refuse her request." He exited the carriage, took Louise's arm, and strolled up the walk. "Here," he said, handing the basket to Theodore. "Your mother made cookies. I helped."

"I didn't realize you still cooked," Theodore said. He took the basket and leaned forward to kiss his mother's cheek.

Louise beamed at him. "Samuel and I went to a special church meeting the other night, once the snow began to melt, and Reverend Fraser made mention of the fact they needed treats for a charity sale. Your father reminded me that everyone always loved my cookies. I volunteered to donate a few batches, and when Katherine told us she was dying to come here, I thought I might as well whip some up for George. I do hope he still has that sweet tooth of his."

Ethel gestured to the carriage. "How long are you planning on staying? That's quite a bit of luggage tied to the top."

"Oh, we shouldn't be here too long," Samuel said. "We have numerous Christmas parties to attend, including Mrs. Murdock's famous Christmas ball." He winked at Theodore. "Mrs. Murdock personally requested your presence, son. I have a feeling she's set her sights on you as a potential son-in-law."

Katherine grinned. "Poor Felicia was mortified when her mother kept going on and on about you, Theodore." Her grin widened. "For some reason, I got the feeling that the mere idea of forming an alliance with you terrified the lady."

"Well, of course that notion would terrify Miss Murdock," Louise said. "She's very shy, and Theodore is known to be a gregarious sort." She reached out and patted his cheek. "I do believe I might have been mistaken when I told you she'd make you a suitable wife." She lowered her voice. "From what Katherine has insinuated, your interest lies elsewhere. Miss Murdock will be very relieved to discover she doesn't need to worry about you courting her."

Theodore turned to his sister. "What insinuations have you been insinuating?"

Katherine sent him a cheeky grin, grabbed his hand, and pulled him into the house. "Now, don't start brooding, Theodore," she said as she shrugged out of her coat in the foyer and hung it on a hook by the door. "You must have realized I'd put two and two together and figure out why you'd been asking me so many questions about Arabella, and oh . . ." She gestured out the open door. "Speaking of Arabella, we brought two trunks stuffed with her clothing. Mrs. Beckett told me you'd absconded with her daughter after you dumped her clothing on the floor *and* stuffed her into her own traveling trunk." She laughed. "I'm fairly certain Arabella couldn't have been too thrilled about that, darling brother. You might want to reconsider your wooing efforts."

Theodore swallowed a laugh, but then sobered when the ramifications of what she'd said sunk in. "You're aware of the fact Arabella's here?"

"Of course. Gloria told me. I went to check on Arabella once the roads cleared, and imagine my surprise when I found out you'd spirited her out of the city."

"So much for my undercover operation."

"I didn't tell anyone, and Gloria only told me because I mentioned I wanted to take a few days and visit my grandparents. Once she understood I was coming here, she thought Arabella just might appreciate having some of her clothes." Katherine suddenly punched him in the arm, causing him to wince. "Speaking of your undercover operation, you should have sent us a note regarding the fact that you sent some of your men to watch over me. I almost shot one unfortunate gentleman in the middle of Broadway yesterday." She gave a delicate shudder. "I was certain he was up to no good as he dogged my every step. Luckily for him, Eliza was with me and recognized him as one of the men who'd helped with her little situation a few months back. If she hadn't stepped in, I'm afraid the man might now be sporting a rather large hole in his body."

Theodore frowned. "What was his name?"

"I don't know. I didn't ask. Once Eliza realized he was one of yours, I let him go about his business."

"He must not have been doing a very good job of staying unnoticed if he drew your attention."

"He was quite stealthy, but you're forgetting, I learned all about subterfuge under your tutelage. Of course I'm able to detect if someone's following me. If I weren't, you'd be a fairly horrible private investigator."

"She does have a point," George said, stepping around Theodore to pull Katherine into an enthusiastic hug. He squeezed her tightly and then stepped back, his eyes twinkling. "I heard tell you've run into a little difficulty with that husband of yours, dear."

"Harold and I are currently not seeing eye to eye on matters, Grandfather. I've been staying with Mother and Father this past week, and to tell you the truth, I doubt Harold even cares that I left him." Her cheeks turned red. "He certainly hasn't made an attempt to get me back."

"That's not true," Louise said as she breezed through the door with Ethel at her side and stopped beside Katherine. "He did try to get your attention by throwing that rather large rock at the window. It was unfortunate he ended up breaking the glass. It was clear to me the desperate man had no idea what to do after that fiasco. I think he tried to flee so we wouldn't know it was him, but what with the deep snow and all, he simply sort of trudged away."

Katherine laughed. "It was not one of his finer moments, and we haven't heard anything from him since, which is fine with me." She turned to Ethel. "I hope you don't mind we've descended on you with no notice, Grandmother. I've always enjoyed helping you decorate for Christmas. I realize the holiday is still a few weeks away, but I'm hopeful you'll indulge me and decorate early." She bit her lip. "I was also hoping, as we decorate, that you might be convinced to part with some of your invaluable advice. I've probably never mentioned it before, but I do cherish your counsel."

Ethel looked positively delighted. "That is quite the nicest thing you've said to me in years, Katherine, and I would love to help you sort out your troubles." She leaned closer and dropped her voice to a whisper. "I have to imagine Arabella will enjoy having you in the house as well. She's been stuck with your grandfather and Theodore for a week now, and they've taken to having rousing debates, which I've refused to enter."

Katherine grinned. "Where is Arabella?"

"I'm here," Arabella called, walking down the hallway. She stopped to give Katherine a hug. "I thought I'd give you an opportunity to greet your grandparents before I interrupted." She tilted her head. "I'm surprised you were willing to risk traversing the roads. Did it take you long to get here?"

"It did take us longer than usual, but there were very few other travelers on the road, which made it easier for our driver."

"You didn't encounter anyone on your way here, did you?" Theodore asked.

"Just your men," Samuel answered. "I think they're probably riding up the lane as we speak."

Theodore excused himself from everyone and walked back outside. He squinted in the bright sunlight, and saw that, riding toward him, just as his father had said, were four of his men. He walked down the steps and waited as the men brought their horses to a stop in front of him. "Nice journey?"

Robert Moore, a big, burly man with long brown hair straggling out from underneath his battered hat, shook his head. "Not particularly. The roads are a mess, and I have no idea why your sister would decide to travel here in these conditions. I tried to tell your father we should wait at least another day or two, but he said your sister wanted to see her grandmother, so here we are. Not quite what I thought we were signing up for, Mr. Wilder."

Theodore choked back a laugh. His men were known for their toughness, but it was clear they were less than pleased to have been forced out of the city to traverse the snowy country roads on the whim of Katherine. He cleared his throat. "Any signs you were followed?"

"The only other conveyances on the roads were a few delivery wagons, and I don't think we have anything to fear from them."

"Wonderful." Theodore waved toward the barn. "There are grooms who can tend to your horses, and comfortable quarters above the barn, unless you'd prefer the house." He grinned. "I will warn you that we now have eight ladies in residence, so it's up to you."

"We'll take the barn."

He couldn't say he was surprised. He watched the men spin their horses around and make for the barn before he headed back into the house. The foyer had emptied, and he followed the sound of laughter, his pace increasing with every laugh.

There was something heartwarming about a house filled with laughter.

He stopped in the doorway of the library and allowed himself just a moment to watch everyone. His mother and father were sitting on a chaise, chatting with Ethel and George, and Katherine was sitting on the settee with Arabella. Their heads were together, and they were whispering as thick as thieves, the sight causing him to smile.

His sister, it seemed, had found a new friend.

He found the idea rather appealing.

If his sister approved of Arabella, as it appeared she did, and Katherine, as his sister, wanted only the best for him, well, she could join forces with him, and . . .

He frowned.

And what? Convince Arabella he was a capital fellow, and that she should . . . like him?

That sounded somewhat childish, and the feelings he'd been starting to feel for the lady were certainly stronger than *like*, but it was entirely too soon to proclaim his intentions.

Arabella would probably think he'd lost his mind if he blurted out that he no longer loathed her, but instead—

"Theodore, come join us by the fire," Louise suddenly called.

He strode forward, frowning when Arabella and Katherine suddenly stopped speaking when he passed them, and they looked rather guilty.

Had they been discussing him?

Maybe his sister was, of her own accord, laying the groundwork for him.

He sent them a grin that caused them both to blink, continued over to his mother, and took a seat by her side, pretending not to notice that she took it as an opportunity to scoot even closer to Samuel.

It was rather odd to see his parents acting as if they cared about each other.

"Tell me, darling," Louise said, "what have you been doing this past week?"

"I've mostly been shoveling snow and helping Grandfather with the animals."

"And Miss Beckett?"

"What about Arabella?"

Louise rolled her eyes. "Must I always have to drag everything out of you, Theodore? Couldn't you just once tell me what is transpiring in your personal life? Have you developed an affection for Miss Beckett?"

He dropped his voice, even though a glance to Arabella and Katherine showed them still to be deep in their own conversation. "You didn't used to like Arabella. You thought she was too independent."

"Your father and I have decided she's perfect for you."

Samuel leaned over Louise and winked. "Miss Beckett reminds me of your grandmother, and everyone has always known you favor your grandfather. With that said, your mother and I could no longer ignore the idea that Miss Beckett would suit you admirably." He leaned closer, practically smashing Louise into the settee as he did so. "It would be best if you didn't take too long to make your move, son. I have it on good authority that Grayson Sumner has professed an interest in Miss Beckett." He resumed his original place on the settee, patted Louise's knee, and shook his head. "I'm sorry to say that he's a distinct threat given the fact he's possessed of a title, a fortune, and stellar good looks, according to your sister."

Theodore opened his mouth . . . to say what, he had no idea, but then Katherine suddenly stood and walked across the room, drawing everyone's attention.

"As I said to Grandmother when I first arrived, Christmas is still a few weeks away, but Arabella and I thought it would be delightful to spend the afternoon doing a bit of decorating. Would any of you care to join us?" She sent Theodore a pointed look, and he couldn't help but grin.

"Do you need someone to bring down the decorations from the attic?" he asked.

Katherine returned his grin. "That would be lovely."

Arabella rose from her seat. "Would anyone mind if I invited Violet and the rest of the ladies to help us? I have the feeling they've never really had a proper Christmas, and I know I, for one, would enjoy sharing this tradition with them."

"I think that's a wonderful idea," Theodore said, and the room seemed to disappear of everyone except Arabella when she smiled at him.

She had such an enchanting smile, and when she smiled the

way she was now, a dimple popped out on her cheek, making him long to touch her face.

He blinked when Katherine appeared by his side, took his arm, and dragged him out of the room, muttering something about "embarrassing her" under her breath.

Her teasing didn't bother him in the least because he knew she just might have a point.

He was not acting like his usual self.

Katherine steered him to the kitchens, where she made a big fuss over Violet and Lottie, and after getting their agreement to help, they went in search of Sarah and Hannah, finding those two ladies in the barn petting the cows. By the time they returned to the house, Arabella and Ethel were sporting aprons over their dresses, and Louise, Samuel, and George were rearranging the furniture as Violet and Lottie set out a platter of iced cookies they proudly claimed to have made themselves.

He moved out of the room and began climbing the stairs, pausing when Arabella called to him from below.

"Wait for me. I'll help bring down some boxes."

She caught up with him and took his arm, her touch scorching through the fabric of his jacket.

"It was very thoughtful of you to include Violet and the ladies," he said as they began to climb the stairs.

For a second, her hand tensed on his arm, but then relaxed. "I'm afraid I've neglected to consider the plight of those less fortunate than I. I've taken some time while I've been here to examine my life, and although I've tried to assist women, I haven't tried to really care."

He paused and brought her to a stop. "I think you're being a little hard on yourself."

"That's sweet, but I'm not. Dot was right, Theodore. I've been judgmental and bossy."

"I think you're special."

Her face turned pink, she looked at him for a long minute,

and then she smiled. "I think you're losing your mind because we've been stuck in the snow for so long." Without giving him a chance to reply to that bit of nonsense, she dropped his arm and hurried up the steps, leaving him staring after her for a moment until he shook his head and realized she probably had no idea where to find the attic.

He caught up with her on the third floor, and they spent the next hour carting boxes down to the library, until Ethel finally demanded everyone take a break.

Violet and Lottie brought out more treats, and Ethel made a production of showing Sarah and Hannah how to pour a proper tea. Everyone finally found a seat, and conversation and laughter filled the room as the afternoon sun streamed through the windows.

"What we need is the scent of pine," Ethel said as she set down her cup. "It's far too early to think about cutting a tree, but a few wreaths spread about the house would be nice."

"I wouldn't mind getting some fresh air," Katherine said, dusting sugar off her fingers from the cookie she'd just consumed. She stood and turned to Arabella. "Would you care to join me?"

"Don't mind if I do," Arabella said. She handed Theodore the cookie she'd been about to eat, got to her feet, and stretched. "I'll just run and grab a coat."

Theodore watched her leave and then stood up, letting out a grunt when Katherine pushed him back into his seat.

"You're not coming with us."

"Why not?"

Katherine's eyes darkened right before she rolled them. "Honestly, Theodore, it's clear the two of you are moving in some strange sort of direction toward one another, but I don't think either one of you knows what to do next." She released a dramatic sigh. "That is why I'm going to take over."

Alarm shot through him.

"I don't think there's any need for that."

"I'll be discreet."

"You've never been discreet in your life."

"Do you want to find out if she returns the affection you're trying to hide from her?"

Theodore was about to tell his sister he wasn't hiding anything, but the knowing look in Katherine's eyes had him swallowing his words.

"Let Katherine do a little snooping," Ethel said, causing him to blink when she appeared right in front of him, as if she'd materialized out of thin air.

It was unbelievable, now that he thought about it, that he'd never suspected she'd been a spy.

"Since it appears I've been overruled, I'll stay inside," he finally muttered.

"Overruled about what?" Arabella asked as she stepped back into the room, looking adorable in a coat of dusty rose.

"Katherine wants me to stay inside and finish unpacking those boxes instead of escorting the two of you to fetch pine for wreaths."

For a second, Arabella looked somewhat disappointed, but then she smiled and lowered her voice. "You can spend your time trying to see if Violet and the ladies might consider accepting your grandmother's offer of employment. She brought it up to them earlier today, but they might need a little convincing, especially about actually being wanted."

"I didn't know my grandmother offered them employment."

"She's very stealthy," Arabella said before she walked over to Katherine and the two ladies left the room.

One hour later, he swallowed one of the cookies his mother had pressed on him and wondered if it was possible for a body

273

to explode from an excessive amount of sweets. He reached down and pulled a nativity set from the box Violet had just scooted his way, but paused as he glanced at the window and noticed the sun seemed to be setting.

A wave of unease swept over him, even as the hair on the back of his neck stirred.

"What's the matter?" George asked, pausing in his task of polishing a glass Christmas tree.

"Don't you think Arabella and Katherine should be back by now?"

George tossed aside the Christmas tree, ignoring the sound of breaking glass, and shot up from his seat the exact same moment Theodore did.

They raced to the door, and Theodore didn't even take the time to pull on his boots. He bolted down the steps and began frantically surveying the snow. A few moments later, he found Katherine's and Arabella's tracks.

He shouted their names as he ran and stumbled through the snow, his shouts becoming more desperate when they didn't reply. Before long, his men joined him, and the search continued with everyone spreading out and yelling the two ladies' names, over and over again, but to no avail.

Much to Theodore's horror, it soon became clear to him that Katherine and Arabella were not coming back.

19

The air in the small space she and Katherine were confined in reeked of something foul. Arabella squinted and looked around, trying to decipher in the dim light what was causing the smell that seeped through the wooden planks of the wagon. An overturned canister met her gaze.

They were in a milk wagon, one that had probably been stolen by the two men who'd abducted them.

She began breathing through her mouth, but even that wasn't enough to stop her from gagging. She heard Katherine making the same sound and reached out to grab her hand.

"Are you all right?" she asked.

"I'm really wishing I hadn't eaten quite so many cookies," Katherine muttered. "I have the sneaking suspicion they're about to come back up."

"We need something to distract us."

"A gun would certainly do the trick. We could shoot our way out of here, if only to breathe some fresh air."

"Unfortunately, that man pocketed my gun right after he hit me over the head with it." Arabella reached up and rubbed the lump that was forming on her temple. "I cannot believe we were taken by surprise like that. How did we not hear them approach?"

"It might have been because we were singing carols at the top of our lungs," Katherine said. "At least you had the foresight to carry your gun in your pocket. There was no way I could have reached mine, not with the heavy coat I had on over my gown. From now on I'm going to stuff it down my bodice."

"That'll look nice with the current fashion of fitted gowns."

Katherine laughed and then sobered. "It was rotten luck that you slipped in the snow. Otherwise, I'm sure you'd have gotten a good shot off and we wouldn't have been taken."

"We're lucky I didn't shoot you by accident. I slipped right as I pulled the trigger."

"Someone must have been watching out for us."

"If you're referring to God, I have to tell you, I'd have preferred He not allow us to get into this situation in the first place."

"Honestly, Arabella, this is hardly the time for you, of all people, to be put out with God. I readily admit I'm not always diligent in my relationship with Him, so we need someone—you, of course—to remain steady and tell us that God will show us a way out of this."

Arabella felt her lips twitch. "I didn't say I didn't believe in Him anymore, Katherine. Just that I'm a little bewildered as to why He let those men snatch us right from your grandfather's property."

"Well, everyone always says God works in mysterious ways."

Arabella's lips twitched again. "We should concentrate our efforts on figuring out how to get out of this mess and how these men found us in the first place."

"You still believe that one man is the man you shot back in Gilman?"

"I'm fairly certain he is, but . . . how did he know where to find me?"

"Maybe I led him to you. I should never have insisted on visiting my grandparents."

"Nonsense," Arabella said. "There was no reason for you to believe anyone would follow *you*. We've only recently become friends, whereas I've been seen more often about town with Agatha and Eliza. Besides, who would have thought anyone would travel into the country through the remnants of a blizzard?"

"I did."

"True."

Katherine heaved a sigh. "That man you shot must have a serious hankering for revenge."

"Or a hankering for selling us off to the highest bidder."

Katherine began to sputter. "We have to get out of here."

"I agree, but it's going to be tricky. Those men were somehow able to get past Theodore's guards, and I'm fairly certain Theodore only hires the best."

"That certainly seems to suggest we're dealing with rather cunning men," Katherine said. "Perhaps our first order of business should be to say a small prayer." She peered expectantly at Arabella.

"And I assume you want me to do it?"

"I did mention that I'm probably not as proficient at it."

"It's prayer, Katherine, and not that difficult. You simply have a conversation with God."

"You have conversations with God?"

"Yes, and even though I'm a little annoyed by this latest turn of events, I know He *will* see us through in the end. When I was in jail back in Gilman, I asked God for help, and the next thing you know, Theodore was standing outside my door."

"That fits."

"Fits with what?"

"Well, don't get upset, but I, and quite a few other people I've spoken with, have come to the conclusion that you and Theodore would make a perfect match. From what you just said, maybe God planned it."

"I think the smell is beginning to affect your thinking."

"He likes you, and you like him."

"I'm going to pray now," Arabella said, closing her eyes because this was certainly not the best time to delve into her feelings for Theodore.

They'd been abducted by unscrupulous men, and Katherine was right. She needed to talk to God.

Lord, as I'm sure you're aware, I'm in another mess. I could use some assistance in this matter, and I could use some strength. Please watch over Katherine, and please, keep her safe.

She opened her eyes and found Katherine staring back at her.

"Did you ask Him for help?"

"I did, and you could ask Him too. Again, it's not that hard, and we can use all the help we can get."

Katherine nodded, closed her eyes, and then a second later opened them.

"That was fast."

"I just said 'help' and thought God would understand and—"

The wagon suddenly tilted to the right, and Arabella grabbed hold of Katherine as they tumbled around on the floor, coming to a stop when they hit the rough sides of the wagon. She pushed up to a sitting position, shoved aside a lock of hair that had slipped into her eyes, and smiled. "I think God might just have answered our prayers. Unless I'm mistaken, we're stuck, and that's certain to slow those men down."

Seconds later, the door to the delivery wagon swung open.

Arabella leaned forward, trying to make out the man's features, but the setting sun was at his back, casting his face in shadow.

"You're going to have to push this wagon out of the snow."

Arabella crossed her arms over her chest. "I think not."

The man shoved a hand into his pocket, pulled out Arabella's pistol, and pointed it directly at her. "Don't tempt me to use this on you. You've caused me far too much trouble as it is, and even though I have a buyer for you, my patience is beginning to wane."

"You found a buyer for Arabella?" Katherine asked.

"He'll pay a pretty penny for you too, miss," the man said as he leaned closer, his face coming into view.

He was the man who'd given her directions to the farmhouse.

"You're almost as beautiful as that one there, even though you're not as young as we normally like. Wallace and I are thinking about telling our contact the two of you are sisters. Sisters always fetch a good fee."

"Wallace is the man I shot?" Arabella asked.

"I shouldn't have told you that," the man muttered before he brightened. "It doesn't really matter, though. Where you're going, it's not likely you'll find anyone to tell."

Katherine stiffened. "Out of curiosity, where are you taking us?"

"You're going across the ocean, my dear," the man said. "Our contact has a man in India who pays well for light-skinned women." He gestured to Arabella with the gun. "I knew as soon as I saw you get off that train in Gilman that our fortunes were about to increase. That's why we followed you here. Took us a bit of time to find you, and Wallace and I were run ragged trying to keep track of your friends, but when we saw trunks being taken out of the Beckett house, we knew we'd finally found a way to get to you." He rubbed his hands together. "The money we'll get from this venture will let us go on a nice little holiday until things settle down and we can set up shop again."

"Carter, what's the holdup? We need to get moving, because the nosy gent who brought that Beckett chit out here doesn't seem the type who'll just sit back and do nothing."

Carter turned and spit on the ground just as Wallace appeared beside him. Arabella couldn't help but feel a sliver of satisfaction when she noticed Wallace rubbing the arm she'd lodged a bullet in. She flinched when he set his sights on her and narrowed his eyes.

"It's unfortunate you're worth so much money to us, Miss Beckett, or I swear, I'd extract retribution for my arm right here and now."

Arabella lifted her chin. "It's unfortunate I only aimed to wound you."

"That's a mistake you'll never be able to rectify," Wallace said. He took Arabella's gun from Carter, stuffed it in his boot, and sent her a mocking smile. "Now, get out of the wagon and help us get it unstuck."

Knowing she had no choice, Arabella climbed out of the wagon and turned to help Katherine down. Katherine pushed down her skirt and set her sights on Wallace.

"For your information, that 'nosy gent' is not only a private investigator, he's also my brother. Add in the pesky little fact that he's a special agent for the government, and you must realize he'll never rest until he tracks you down."

Wallace exchanged a look with Carter and then turned back to Katherine. "You're just trying to rattle us." He gestured to the wagon. "Get digging."

Arabella slid through the snow to the stuck wheel and began digging with her hands, making certain not to scoop up too much snow. She needed to waste as much time as possible in case Theodore was already looking for them. Her hands quickly became numb, but she didn't stop, and a glance to Katherine showed her that her friend apparently had the same idea because Katherine was only throwing tiny bits of snow over her head.

She jumped in surprise when Wallace suddenly let out a grunt.

"This is no good. It's taking too long." He nodded to Carter. "We're going to have to free the horses. We can ride on them back to the city."

"Why didn't you think of that before?" Carter snapped. "We've been wasting time."

Wallace didn't bother to reply but moved to the horses and released them. He turned to Arabella and waved her forward.

Arabella stood there for a moment, her mind whirling. If she got on that horse, well, it would not be good. She lifted her chin, dropped the snow she was holding, and shook her head.

Stars suddenly erupted behind her eyes as pain washed over her. She stumbled forward and then fell, turning to squint up at Carter, who'd just punched her squarely in the face. She blinked as tears flooded her eyes from the pain, but held up a hand when she saw Katherine trying to get to her. "I'm fine," she said. She struggled to get out of the snow, rising on shaky legs to a standing position, lifting her chin again as she stared at Carter.

"You're despicable," she hissed before she made her way to where Wallace was now sitting on a horse. She took the hand he offered her and let him pull her up, fighting back revulsion when she was forced to wrap her arms around his waist when the horse started moving. She glanced over her shoulder to check on Katherine, rage coursing through her when she saw a trickle of tears running down Katherine's face as she sat behind Carter on his horse. Arabella tried to send her an encouraging smile, but found that her mouth was already swollen and stiff. The horse moved into a gallop, and she tightened her grip, her rage quickly being replaced with fear as the direness of their predicament set in.

No one spoke as the horses galloped the best they could down the snow-packed road. Time passed by in a blur, until Arabella looked up and discovered they were on the edge of the city. Panic began sweeping over her as she realized they were almost certainly close to their destination.

She needed a plan.

Nothing came to her except distracting Wallace until she could think of something helpful.

She cleared her throat and then pitched her voice to be heard over the pounding hooves of the horse. "Are you taking us where you've stashed the other women?"

"What?" Wallace asked.

"You know, the women you've been snatching off the streets. The prostitutes."

"I don't deal with prostitutes. Be quiet until I figure out where the building we're supposed to meet our contact is."

She ignored his request. "Surely we're not going to be sold tonight?"

"Surely you don't think I want to suffer one more minute than I have to in your company?" Wallace countered. "Carter and I had a sweet thing going in Gilman until you showed up. We were making a fortune, but then you brought the law down on us and we had no choice but to move on. You have only yourself to blame for your predicament. If you'd left well enough alone, we might not have felt the urge to come after you. You left us with a nasty mess when you stole that young girl from under our noses. Carter had already taken the money, you see, and we didn't want to give it back. Not that we could've, mind you. We spent almost every cent that man gave us, and then you stole our prize."

"You should have been more frugal."

"We'll pay the man after we collect the fee for you, and then we'll find him another sweet young thing."

"Do you ever consider the life you're forcing women into?"

"The ladies shouldn't have too many complaints. It's not like I'm selling them to poor, desperate beasts. I'm doing women a service, setting them up with a better lot in life. You'll be pampered and adored in India. I hardly see why you feel you have room to complain."

"Oh yes, I don't understand why I'm not falling at your feet in gratitude over the idea I'm to become some man's slave."

"Is that really any different from becoming some man's wife?"

Before Arabella could respond to that piece of insanity, Carter let out a whistle from behind them.

"It's up there, Wallace, just past that light."

Arabella peered through the darkness and saw the outline of a large building loom into her sight. From what she could discern, there was no one around to lend them assistance. She closed her eyes.

Please be with me, Lord.

She opened her eyes, took a deep breath, and launched herself from the horse, rolling over in the slush and jumping to her feet before Wallace realized what she'd done. She ran to his side and pulled her pistol out of his boot, but before she had a chance to pull the trigger, she was knocked to the ground by a blow to the back of her head. She kept her grip on the pistol even as a heavy boot planted itself on her back.

"You'll not be shooting anyone again," Carter said, grabbing her by the back of her dress and hauling her to her feet. Stars exploded once again as Carter backhanded her across the face.

A menacing growl sounded from behind her. "That was a mistake."

Arabella found herself flying through the air to land in

another pile of slush as Theodore's body plowed into Carter's, the sound of his fists pummeling the man loud in the eerie fog surrounding her. She watched in horror as Wallace jumped from his horse and entered the fight.

Her fingers tightened on her pistol.

She jumped to her feet, shook her head to clear it, and raised her hand.

"Don't shoot," Katherine screamed. "You might hit Theodore."

Before Arabella could even nod in agreement, another figure hurtled out of the darkness.

It was George, and it was immediately clear he'd spent his life in dangerous situations, because although he was almost eighty years old, he didn't hesitate to grab Wallace by the back of his shirt and swing him around, planting a fist in the man's face.

"Good one, Father," Samuel yelled, who seemed to appear out of thin air, jumping into the fray.

Less than two minutes later, it was over.

Wallace and Carter lay on the ground, both men unconscious as Theodore, Samuel, and George made short shrift of tying them up.

Arabella turned and found Katherine by her side. She reached out and put a shaking arm around Katherine's shoulders, pulling her in for a good squeeze. "That was a close call."

Katherine let out a watery snort. "Indeed it was, but at least we're safe."

Arabella frowned. "Not quite yet." She dropped her arm from around Katherine and slid her way over the slushy ground, stopping by Theodore, who was just finishing tying a knot around Wallace's wrists. "Wallace told me there's another man waiting around here somewhere." She shivered. "He was waiting to buy us."

Theodore glanced at the pistol she was still gripping in her hand before he lifted his gaze. "Is that loaded?"

"Of course."

He nodded to Samuel. "I need you to take Arabella's pistol and make certain you keep it trained on these two. Grandfather and I will go and see if anyone else is around, but if we're not back in five minutes, get Arabella and Katherine out of here."

Arabella shook her head. "We're not leaving without you."

"This is hardly the moment to argue, Arabella. I'm concerned for your safety."

"I'm not arguing, but we're not leaving without you."

"Fine, stay here then. Maybe someone else will come along who wants to do you in."

Arabella felt her temper flare ever so slightly as Theodore and George strode away. She turned to Katherine. "Did you just get the impression Theodore blames me for this whole abduction business?"

A trace of a smile teased Katherine's lips. "I'm sure that's not true. He's probably just worried about us because danger is still nipping at our heels, and he only has Father here to protect us."

"I do believe I've just been insulted," Samuel muttered.

"I certainly didn't mean to insult you, Father, but I have a feeling Arabella is better equipped to handle that pistol of hers. We'll let her keep it until Theodore and Grandfather come back."

Samuel looked as if he wanted to argue the point, but the sound of muffled carriage wheels drifted to their ears on the brisk breeze. Everyone froze for a second, but then Arabella spun around and leveled her pistol toward the sound. Her arm lowered when Samuel let out a sigh just as the carriage came into view.

"I should have known," Samuel said.

Katherine took one step forward and stopped. "Good heavens, what is Harold doing here?"

"He arrived just about the time we discovered you were missing," Samuel answered.

The carriage slowed, but Harold was out of it before it came to a complete stop. He charged up to Katherine, looked at her for a brief second, then pulled her into his arms, burying his head into her hair. "Don't ever, ever, ever scare me like this again."

Katherine pushed her way out of his embrace and tilted her head. "What are you doing here, Harold?"

"You didn't think I'd remain at your grandparents' after I found out you were missing, did you? I was preparing to unhitch the horses in order to join the rescue team, but realized Samuel, Theodore, and George had already left. Then Ethel and Louise descended on me, and I had no choice but to offer them a ride in the carriage. Good thing some of Theodore's men were in front of us or we would have never found the trail."

"Theodore's men are here?" Samuel asked.

"They rode up ahead when they saw Theodore and George heading for that building." Harold looked down and frowned. "Are those the men who abducted you?"

Katherine nodded.

Harold walked up to them and prodded Wallace with his boot. "Did they hurt you?"

"They didn't hurt me, but the one to your right hit Arabella."

Harold sent Arabella an odd look, moved to stand by Carter, and then calmly kicked him in the stomach. "Would you like a go at him?" he asked, turning his attention back to Arabella.

Arabella realized her mouth was gaping open, but before she had the presence of mind to snap it shut, two bodies barreled out of the carriage, and she was soon enveloped in a strong hug.

"My dear, you and Katherine have given us such a fright," Ethel said in a shaky voice as she released her and stepped back.

"Where did Theodore and George go?" Louise asked, giving Katherine a hug before looking around.

"They went to see if they could find the gentleman those two men on the ground were going to sell our daughter and Miss Beckett to this evening," Samuel said, moving to Louise's side.

Harold blinked. "Did you say *sell*?"

"They said we would fetch top price," Katherine explained. "Although that man you just kicked insinuated I wouldn't fetch as much as Arabella. He seemed to think I was quite a bit older than she is, and I know we're of the same age."

"Give or take a year or two," Arabella said with a grin.

Harold pointed to Carter. "He insulted you?"

"He did, and he divested me of my gun. But instead of keeping it, he threw it into the snow. It was my favorite pistol, and now it's lost to me forever."

"I'll buy you a new pistol, darling," Harold said. He then walked over to Carter and gave him another kick, earning a smile from Katherine. "What's happened to you?"

"What do you mean?"

"For one, you're here, and forgive me, but you're hardly your normal mild-mannered self. I've never seen you lash out at someone before, and I must admit I find it somewhat perplexing."

Harold crossed his arms over his chest. "Would you like me to apologize to the unconscious men?"

"Certainly not. They deserve a sound thrashing for what they attempted to do to Arabella and me."

Harold nodded and delivered another swift kick to both men, causing Katherine to laugh nervously. "I think that will be quite enough, Harold, although I do sincerely appreciate your unexpected support."

"You say that as though my support has taken you by surprise."

"It has."

"You sounded surprised by the mere fact I came after you."

"And you sound annoyed by my surprise," Katherine returned.

"I came for you three days ago."

"I know. I *was* there when you broke the window."

"You allowed me to leave."

"I didn't know you expected me to call you back."

"Of course I expected you to call me back. I thought that, just perhaps, you'd come to realize you missed me as much as I missed you," Harold muttered.

"You missed me?"

Harold rolled his eyes. "There's that tone of surprise."

"I'm afraid I'm confused."

Arabella stepped forward. "I think Harold's trying to tell you that he wants you to come home because he's discovered, while you were away, that he enjoys your company."

"That's exactly what I'm trying to say," Harold said with a nod. "Thank you, Miss Beckett, for summing it up so nicely for me."

"You're welcome, and . . ." Arabella's voice trailed off when a shot rang out in the distance. "Theodore!" she yelled, spinning on her heel and dashing off in the direction the shot had come from, ignoring the shouts of protests that sounded behind her. She got no more than a few yards before strong arms caught her.

"And just where do you think you're going?" Theodore asked.

"I heard a shot."

"And you thought you were going to do what? Come to my rescue?"

"It would make for a nice change of pace."

"Grandfather found the coward hiding behind some timber. He thought it would be fun to flush him out."

"But where is your grandfather?"

"He's still back there with my men. Grandfather wanted to question the criminal before we hand him over to the police."

"Why aren't you questioning him?"

"I wanted to check on you and Katherine, and my grandfather is perfectly capable of proceeding without me around."

"Will there be torture involved?"

"Of course not," Theodore said with a laugh, keeping his arm around Arabella as he steered her back where everyone was still waiting. "What odd ideas you come up with at times."

Arabella ignored the fact that his touch was causing her knees to wobble and tried to stay focused on the conversation. "It's not such an odd idea, given that your grandfather was a spy, and everyone knows spies use diabolical methods to get their targets to talk. And speaking of spies"—her eyes narrowed as she met his gaze—"your grandmother mentioned something about you and spying, and your sister told Wallace you worked for the government. Why didn't you tell me you were following in your grandfather's footsteps?"

Theodore stopped in his tracks and sent her an exasperated look, but then his eyes sharpened on her face and he lifted a finger to her cheek. "Did you suffer all that damage to your face from the blow I saw that man give you, or did he hit you more than once?"

Arabella couldn't help but notice the barely suppressed rage visible in Theodore's eyes. He'd been so affable while they'd spent time at the farm that she'd somehow forgotten that the heart of a warrior beat underneath his charming exterior.

"Umm, well . . ."

"I'll just ask Katherine."

"Carter hit me once before because I refused to get on the horse."

"Is Carter wearing the blue or the red coat?"

"Ah, red."

Theodore walked her over to Ethel before he stalked back to Carter, who was stirring on the ground. He knelt down and shook the man, causing Carter's eyes to flash open.

"I understand you hit Arabella."

Carter didn't respond.

"That's going to cost you," Theodore said in a quiet yet lethal voice. He leaned further over the man until he was almost nose to nose with him. "I'm going to make certain you land in front of the toughest judge in New York, and unless you tell me what you did with those prostitutes, you're never going to get out of jail."

"I didn't do anything to any prostitutes," Carter bit out. "The only harlot I was dealing with was your lady love."

Theodore smiled, drew back his arm, and then Carter quickly descended into unconsciousness. Theodore straightened, got to his feet, and set his sights on Arabella even as he shook his head.

"I think the only way I'm going to be able to keep you safe is to marry you."

20

Theodore eyed the festive bunch of mistletoe dangling over his head and quickly strode to a different spot, glancing up first before coming to a stop. It was just like Mrs. Murdock to use that particular plant for decoration at her Christmas ball. Granted, it was a Christmas custom, but really, did it have to be strung so thoroughly about, almost as if it were just waiting to take some poor, unsuspecting gentleman by surprise?

He'd always been more than happy to embrace the charming tradition of a kiss on the cheek under the mistletoe. Now, however, he only wanted to give his kisses—even those just reserved for a cheek—to Arabella.

"Ah, Theodore, there you are," Zayne exclaimed as he strolled over to Theodore's side, glanced at the ceiling, and grinned. "I don't think I've ever known Mrs. Murdock to be quite this diligent in her hanging of that delightful plant."

"I'm not moving from this spot."

"Now, that's no way to think," Zayne said before he turned, snatched two glasses of bubbling liquid from a passing servant, and thrust one of them into Theodore's hand. He took a sip of his own and tilted his head. "Sulking, are you?"

"I'm hardly sulking at an explosion of mistletoe."

"Arabella speaking to you yet?"

Perhaps he *was* sulking just a bit.

"Your sister is avoiding me." He took a gulp of his drink and caught Zayne's eye. "I've tried to see her, numerous times every day these past ten days, and yet the exasperating lady is making herself remarkably scarce." He shook his head. "I hate to admit this, given my reputation with the fairer sex, but it would seem as if I have no understanding of the female mind. None of the women in my family are currently speaking to me much, and when they do, it's not in a pleasant manner. Even *your* mother has taken to rolling her eyes every time she sees me. Granted, I was a little abrupt with your sister when I stated my intentions, but I thought Arabella would welcome the idea of marriage, as I'd come to the conclusion she liked me."

Zayne snorted into his glass. "I don't think Arabella is opposed to marriage in general, only marriage to you." He shook his head. "Truth be told, I think she *did* like you, up until you told her you *had* to marry her."

"My grandmother claims I made a complete muck of the entire situation."

"I would have to agree with her."

"I'd be more than willing to make amends if only Arabella would afford me a few minutes of her time."

"How would you make amends?"

Theodore shrugged. "I'm not certain. As I said before, it's clear I have little understanding of women." He eyed Zayne for a moment. "You could help me. Women seem to adore you, and I've never seen any woman, except Agatha, give you a difficult time."

"Women fail to give me a difficult time because I don't hurt their delicate feelings."

Theodore narrowed his eyes. "Arabella's tougher than most

gentlemen I know. She didn't even cry when I found her at the mercy of those men, which proves she's hardly delicate."

Zayne narrowed his eyes right back at him. "That's where you're mistaken. Arabella is a romantic at heart. She devours romance novels, dresses in pink whenever possible, and cries whenever she goes to the opera."

"She can cry on cue."

"True, but she can also cry for real." Zayne shook his head. "Honestly, Theodore, what were you thinking? Your grandmother told me you punched a man and then casually told Arabella you'd have to marry her in order to keep her safe. That's almost as bad as telling her she needs to marry you for her own good."

"I *did* punch that man on her behalf," Theodore muttered before he took another gulp of his drink, swallowed, and then grimaced. "You'd think I'd get a bit of credit for that."

"I'm sure you would have if you hadn't followed up your chivalrous act by behaving like an idiot."

"I suppose my attempt at proposing was a bit clumsy, but I've never asked a woman to marry me before, and it just burst out of my mouth."

"Perhaps if you had asked Arabella to marry you instead of blurting out the first thing that came to mind, you wouldn't be in this situation."

"I suppose you planned your proposal to Helena down to the last detail?"

Zayne looked down and began to study the cut of his sleeve. "I never actually asked Helena to marry me."

"What?"

Zayne looked up. "It's always been assumed we would marry."

Theodore threw up his hands. "Why am I wasting my time asking you about women? You know even less than I do."

"I know Helena would never resort to the dramatics you're

experiencing with Arabella. We enjoy a stable relationship and understand each other completely."

Theodore arched a brow. "How can you enjoy a stable relationship when she's traveling out west and you're still in New York?"

"I really don't think we need to delve into my relationship at the moment, Theodore. Your problems are entirely more daunting than anything I might be experiencing with Helena."

"I wouldn't consider my problems 'daunting.'"

Zayne blinked. "Did you not know that Arabella came here with Grayson, as in the debonair and charming and, let us not forget, wealthy Grayson?"

"Yes, thank you for that."

"So you did know?"

"Mrs. Murdock made mention of it the moment I stepped through the door."

Zayne laughed. "*That* explains her extremely happy demeanor. She believes you're back on the market."

"No wonder Felicia saw me and bolted from the room. Mrs. Murdock is probably encouraging her to entertain me this evening."

"Felicia's a lovely lady."

"This coming from a man who takes an almost fiancée out of his pocket anytime an earnest mother comes sniffing around."

"Again, not talking about me at the moment," Zayne said. "We were discussing you and my sister."

Theodore blew out a breath. "I have no idea how to proceed."

"You could always try groveling,"

"I've never groveled in my life."

"Maybe now would be a good time to try."

"Your sister would hardly think well of me if I suddenly threw myself at her feet."

"She might find it a lovely gesture."

"Or she might decide I've taken leave of my senses."

Zayne grinned. "True." He tapped his finger on his chin. "You could donate a large sum of money to her cause, or better yet, find reputable employment for Violet and all her friends."

"Didn't Arabella tell you? She and my grandmother have already settled Violet and her friends into positions. They are now working permanently on the farm."

"Doing what?"

"Well, Violet and Lottie have a great liking for cooking, so they're in the kitchen. My grandfather has taken it upon himself to convince Hannah and Sarah that farming is a reputable and fulfilling profession. I heard him mention something about helping them set up a small shop to sell herbs."

"That's unfortunate," Zayne muttered.

"It's unfortunate the women have gotten off the streets?"

"No, it's unfortunate your grandparents and Arabella came to their rescue. It leaves you with one less option to try to impress my sister."

"They might decide they're ill-suited to a respectable lifestyle," Theodore said slowly. "If that happens, I could swoop in and save them."

"They won't," Agatha said, stealing up beside them. "God is watching over them, and He helps those who seek to live a better life."

"A very poignant point, Agatha, but tell me, how do you think God feels about eavesdropping?" Zayne asked.

"Oh, I highly doubt God would judge me too harshly for that. Besides, it was not as if you were even attempting to lower your voices."

"Did you hear anything of importance?" Theodore asked.

Agatha let out a dramatic sigh. "Alas, no, nothing I was hoping to hear, such as what your plans are concerning Arabella."

"Zayne thinks I should grovel."

"Groveling might be called for, but may I suggest prayer?"

"It couldn't hurt," Theodore muttered.

"If you're not comfortable saying a prayer on your own, Theodore, I'd be more than happy to intercede on your behalf," Agatha said.

"I don't know why everyone has this propensity of questioning my faith," Theodore said. "I'm completely willing and able to say my own prayers, and I can assure you, my relationship with God is growing. If it makes you feel any better, my time at the farm has strengthened my faith."

"Hmm, well, fine then, but I'll still say a little prayer for you even if you're capable of doing it yourself. You've made such a mess of things that you're going to need a lot of assistance."

"I keep hoping that you'll someday become less annoying."

Agatha sent him a cheeky grin. "I wouldn't hold my breath, but enough about my annoying tendencies. *I've* come up with a plan to help you win Arabella."

"This should be good," Zayne mumbled.

"Your only suggestion was for Theodore to grovel," Agatha said with a sniff. "Mine will win him the love of his life."

"I never claimed Arabella was the love of my life," Theodore said.

"And that's why you're not currently engaged to her," Agatha returned. "You must make the grand gesture."

"I told him that," Zayne said.

"Actually, Zayne, you didn't suggest a *grand* gesture," Theodore corrected. "You simply said that if I did throw myself at Arabella's feet, she'd see it as a *lovely* gesture."

Agatha made a *tsk*ing sound under her breath. "Arabella deserves more than you groveling at her feet, Theodore. You must give her romance and love."

"I'm not really adept at proclaiming my affection."

"Hamilton wasn't either at first," Agatha said, "and look how well his relationship with Eliza turned out."

"Agatha's right. Hamilton did make a complete disaster of

his first proposal to Eliza, and if you will recall, it happened in this very same house," Zayne said before he winced. "It's almost as if I'm experiencing his pain all over again, but with you instead as the bumbling suitor." He blatantly ignored the fact that Theodore had taken to sputtering. "It was not well done of my brother to infer he only wanted to marry Eliza because she'd make a wonderful mother for Piper and Ben. Luckily for Hamilton, she gave him another chance."

Agatha grinned. "And now we get the supreme pleasure of watching them exchange lovey-dovey eyes on an annoyingly frequent basis."

"I don't think I'm prepared for lovey-dovey eyes," Theodore said.

"You might want to give it a try," Agatha suggested. "You are a very handsome man with intriguing eyes you could use to your advantage. I doubt Arabella could resist you if you turned on the charm and groveled a bit at the same time."

"Was that supposed to be a compliment?"

"Maybe a small one," Agatha said. Her eyes suddenly widened. "Good heavens, here comes Mrs. Murdock, and it looks to me as if she's actually dragging Felicia behind her, and . . . oh dear. I wonder why Felicia is wearing a gown with red and green bows attached to it. She looks like a Christmas tree."

"It must be her way of getting in the holiday spirit," Zayne said weakly.

Theodore turned his head and swallowed a laugh. Poor Felicia really did look like a Christmas tree. Her gown was bedecked with flounces and bows, and they weren't simply red and green. They were bright, almost blinding red and green. Her expression was entertaining. Appalled certainly, but resigned too, and a little amused.

He realized then and there that Felicia Murdock was more than she appeared. It was unfortunate his heart was settled so firmly on Arabella because Felicia was a woman of whom any man could be proud, even in a hideous gown and possessed of a mother with high social ambitions.

"Mr. Wilder," Mrs. Murdock exclaimed as she pulled Felicia up beside herself and came to a stop. "Mr. Beckett, Miss Watson, I do hope you're enjoying the ball."

"It's lovely," Agatha replied before she winked. "I have high expectations that something of a dramatic nature will occur, given what happened at your last ball."

Mrs. Murdock beamed. "That was something, was it not? Who knew I would throw a ball in which Eliza would disclose a fraud being perpetuated on society?" Her eyes twinkled. "I'll never forget when she ripped that necklace from around that imposter's neck. People are still talking about it to this day." Her smile dimmed. "I do hope no one will be too disappointed if something equally dramatic doesn't happen this evening."

Theodore let out a chuckle. "I, for one, am perfectly content to endure a normal evening for once. It has been entirely too chaotic of late."

"I did hear tell of your latest escapade, Mr. Wilder," Mrs. Murdock said. "It was very gallant and heroic of you to save Miss Beckett and your sister from those dastardly criminals."

"I'm sure anyone would have done the same," Theodore said. "In fact, I'm fairly certain Katherine and Arabella would have found the means to escape if I hadn't come to their aid. They're fairly resourceful young ladies."

"As is my Felicia," Mrs. Murdock said with a not-so-subtle prodding of her daughter that brought her front and center. "You should tell Mr. Wilder about your latest charitable efforts with the orphanage. Why, Felicia has put her life at risk numerous times in order to scour the streets looking for homeless orphans."

"I don't think visiting foundling homes is on quite the same level as being abducted by scoundrels and threatened with being sold to a man in India," Felicia said.

Mrs. Murdock abruptly changed the subject. "It is so lovely your grandparents decided to stay in the city for the holiday season, Mr. Wilder. I've always enjoyed your grandmother's odd sense of humor. I've noticed Mrs. Wilder spending a good deal of time with Gloria and Cora. I've been wondering if they're contemplating a new charitable venture together."

"I think the only venture they're contemplating is one of a personal nature," Zayne said.

"Oh?"

"Mother, Mr. Beckett said it was of a personal nature," Felicia said. "I hardly believe that requires an explanation, as we are not personally attached to their family."

"I am very good friends with Gloria," Mrs. Murdock said.

"Then may I suggest you question her on the matter?" Felicia asked before she set her sights on Zayne. "Eliza mentioned that you're intending to join Miss Collins out west soon. Will you stay in New York until after the holidays?"

For a moment, Zayne looked slightly uncomfortable, but then he smiled. "I've actually had a change of plans, Miss Murdock. I don't believe I'll be leaving until spring."

"Why not?" Agatha asked before Felicia had an opportunity to respond.

"Helena is in the process of moving to California," Zayne said. "We've decided that since the weather has turned somewhat unpredictable, it would be best if I didn't follow her until the snow stops."

Mrs. Murdock's smile brightened as she looked between Zayne and Theodore and then back to Zayne again before looking up and pointing. "My goodness, would you look at that? There's a single strand of mistletoe."

Theodore looked up, squinted, and couldn't help himself. He laughed. A small speck of green was attached to the very high ceiling. How someone had actually been able to place it in such a high spot was a matter to ponder at a later date, but he couldn't help but admire Mrs. Murdock's tenacity. He caught her gaze, saw she was fairly bursting with delight, and was about to congratulate her on her ingenuity when Felicia's mutters caught his attention.

He turned to her, found her bright red and bristling with embarrassment, and immediately held out his arm. "Miss Murdock, would you do me the extreme honor of taking a turn around the dance floor?"

Felicia blinked, her color increased, and she shook her head. "That truly isn't necessary."

He leaned in and lowered his voice. "It's either that or kisses."

Felicia grabbed his arm. "I would adore nothing more than to take the floor with you."

Theodore grinned, patted the hand with which she was now clutching his arm, and escorted her rapidly into the ballroom, his amusement swelling when he realized Felicia was actually setting the pace. "Trying to get out of your mother's sight?"

"I love her dearly, but she's enough to drive a girl mad." Felicia stopped in the middle of the dance floor and held out her arms.

"Are you going to lead?" Theodore asked.

"Don't be silly. Unless you don't like to lead, then I will. I've had plenty of practice with my brothers."

"They don't like to lead?"

"Mother believes a gentleman should learn both ways. That way, he's more apt to be considerate of his partner."

"That's quite clever of your mother."

"She is certainly clever. Now, if she'd just learn the art of discretion."

Theodore laughed and swept Felicia around the room when the music began. She was a proficient dancer, and she entertained him with her keen observations and sense of humor as they glided about the room. He suddenly stumbled when she changed directions mid-step. He recovered his balance and frowned. "Is something the matter?"

"I thought you'd prefer distancing yourself from Arabella. She just took to the floor with Mr. Sumner."

Theodore narrowed his eyes as he searched the crowd. Sure enough, Arabella was in Grayson's arms, laughing at something the man was whispering in her ear.

No one except him should be whispering in her ear.

He took a breath and twirled Felicia around in circles, trying to get closer to Arabella.

"What are you doing?" Felicia hissed.

"I need to speak to Arabella."

"From what I've heard, she doesn't want to speak to you. Eliza told me she's beyond annoyed with you."

"Yes, well, I'm a bit annoyed with her at the moment, so we're fairly even. When we get closer to them, I'm going to hand you off to Grayson and take Arabella."

"I don't think that's a good idea."

"Why not?"

"Umm . . ."

"You don't care for Grayson?"

"I'm sure he's perfectly delightful."

Theodore smiled. "You don't like him."

"It's not that I dislike him, but . . . he makes me nervous."

"Ah, your mother has set her sights on him."

"My mother has her sights on every eligible bachelor."

Theodore slowed his steps. "You don't seem to be nervous around me."

"I'm not nervous around you because you're not a threat anymore."

"I can be threatening."

Felicia laughed. "I wasn't insulting you. Of course you can be threatening and dangerous and all that goes with being a man, but you're clearly in love with Arabella, which makes you no threat to me."

"How do you know I'm in love with Arabella?"

"You watch her."

"I'm watching you right now."

"No, you're not. Your eyes keep darting away to settle on Arabella." Felicia smiled. "She's a good match for you. She won't let you run all over her, and that's what you'd try to do with someone like me. You need a strong woman to keep your interest."

"You're a strong woman."

Felicia shook her head. "I would never be able to stand up to you the way Arabella does. She watches you just as much as you watch her. If you ask me, that's telling. Don't you think?"

"What's 'telling' about that?"

"She loves you, albeit reluctantly. It's all in her eyes, but she's stubborn, as are you."

"Why did you say 'reluctantly'?"

"Because the two of you shouldn't suit," Felicia said. "You're opposites in almost every sense of the word, but for some peculiar reason I think you're meant for each other."

"I have no idea how to make amends with her."

"You need to tell her what's in your heart."

"I'm not very good at that."

"You'll never get better unless you try." Felicia took a deep breath and nodded. "They're approaching us, so if you're intent on switching partners, we should do it soon. Any suggestions on how we can make this transition smooth?"

"Could you act as if you long to dance with Grayson?"

Felicia arched a brow. "That might be stretching the truth, but . . ."

Before Theodore had a chance to even blink, Felicia stepped out of his arms, moved up to Arabella and Grayson, and tapped Grayson on the shoulder. She smiled brightly when the couple came to a clumsy stop. "I hope you don't mind, Mr. Sumner, but I find I just can't wait another minute to dance with you. Theodore, be a dear and take Arabella around the room."

For a minute, all Theodore could do was stand in the middle of the floor with his mouth gaping open as he watched Grayson consider Felicia with confusion in his eyes. To give the gentleman credit, Grayson blinked and a charming grin spread over his face when Felicia suddenly grabbed him by the arm and danced him away.

"I cannot believe you would stoop to such tactics," Arabella said, drawing his attention.

Theodore stepped forward and pulled Arabella into his arms, bracing himself for her reaction to his unorthodox manner of getting her attention. He didn't have long to wait.

Pain shot through his foot. "I cannot believe you just stomped on my toe," he muttered as he swung her around and into the midst of the other dancers.

"You're lucky I didn't bring my pistol or you'd be nursing more than a sore toe," Arabella replied sweetly.

"I needed to talk to you."

"So you coerced Felicia into aiding your cause?"

"I certainly owe her."

"She's probably mortified. I don't think she even knows Grayson very well."

Theodore lifted his head. He spotted Felicia's bright gown and couldn't help but laugh. "She's still leading, but she's at least smiling." He returned his gaze to Arabella. "I'm sure Grayson probably isn't used to a lady leading on the dance floor, seeing as he's an aristocrat."

"Grayson Sumner is a very nice man, aristocrat or not."

"I'm a very nice man."

Arabella stopped dancing. "No, you're not."

"Well, all right, perhaps I'm not always nice, but I can

change." He smiled down at her. "I'd like to take you to the opera."

"I beg your pardon?"

Theodore watched as Arabella began to nibble on her lip, the action drawing his attention to her lips' rosy hue. Out of nowhere it hit him, and a jolt of something wonderful took root in his very soul.

While he'd been trying to convince himself—and everyone else, for that matter—that he and Arabella were not suited for each other, he'd neglected to realize the obvious.

She fascinated him.

She was annoying and opinionated and bossy at times, but she was also . . . perfect for him.

He wanted to know everything about her, wanted to sit beside her at the opera and watch her cry. He wanted to grow old with this exasperating woman and argue with her as they sipped tea on the porch.

She would never bore him, and every day he spent in her company would be an adventure.

"Why do you want to take me to the opera?"

He drew in a deep breath and slowly released it. "I suppose because I've grown incredibly fond of you."

He winced when she narrowed her eyes.

"You've grown fond of me, and that's why you want to take me to the opera, and why you told me you had to marry me to keep me safe?"

"I think you neglected to hear the 'incredibly' part of that statement. To repeat myself, I said I was *incredibly fond* of you."

For some odd reason, her eyes narrowed to mere slits now.

He drew in another breath. "Arabella, forgive me. I don't seem to know how to go about proclaiming my feelings very well. May I make the suggestion we seek out a more private place to talk? Once we get out of this crowd, I will attempt to collect my scattered thoughts and strive to explain myself better."

Theodore wasn't certain, but he thought Arabella muttered something that sounded very much like "idiot" under her breath before she dropped her arm from his sleeve and stomped off the dance floor. He followed her through the throng of guests, past the dining room, and down a hallway until they reached a pair of glass doors. Arabella opened them and stepped out into the blustery night.

"Don't you think the library might have been a better choice?" he asked, even as he shrugged out of his jacket and placed it around her shoulders.

"Someone might overhear you talking about your feelings."

He felt his lips twitch at her tone, stifled the urge to laugh, and opened his mouth, but closed it when a rustling sound off to his right drew his attention. He reached for his gun as a man suddenly materialized in front of him. Before he could get his gun out of its holster, the man lifted his arm, a shot reverberated through the cold air, and pain exploded in his shoulder.

He heard Arabella scream, and he tried to fight the darkness gathering in front of his eyes. He struggled to remain on his feet as he stumbled toward Arabella, but lost his footing and crumpled to the ground. A howl of rage erupted from his mouth when he saw the man strike Arabella with the butt of a gun and then pick her up. He started to crawl toward them, his hand once again fumbling for his gun, but the darkness increased and his body slumped back to the ground. The last image he saw before black completely claimed him was Arabella being thrown over a wall. A feeble cry escaped his lips, and then everything went black.

21

$\mathcal{T}$ime was getting away from her, and Arabella had taken to using the arrival of the dinner tray to mark the days that passed. According to the scratch marks she'd made on the wall, six full days had come and gone since she'd been abducted. Six full days of being locked up in a dark and musty room with terror as her constant companion.

She was afraid to admit, even to herself, that she'd almost given up hope.

She was dealing with a madman, a man who seemed to derive pleasure from her fear.

Deputy Jud Hansen, the too-charming deputy who'd held Miss James's hand through the bars of the cell in Gilman, was the man responsible for her abduction, and he was anything but charming.

He was insane. There was no other way to describe him, as he'd been the one responsible for stealing all the ladies off the streets.

Those ladies were being housed in the rooms beside her, all of them still alive, although Deputy Hansen had alluded to the fact that this was only a temporary situation.

He enjoyed toying with the ladies, herself included, by giving them a small measure of hope that everything would be set to rights come Christmas Eve.

Unfortunately, Arabella had soon determined that his idea of setting matters right and hers were completely opposite.

She was fairly certain he intended to kill them. She was also fairly certain that, given the marks on her wall and the fact Mrs. Murdock had held the ball a week before Christmas, today was Christmas Eve.

She shifted on the rotting mattress and pushed herself to a sitting position, straightening her spine and taking a deep breath.

She couldn't give up.

She couldn't allow this deranged man to win.

"I'm home, my little lovelies. Time to come out and play."

The fine hair on the nape of her neck stood to attention. Jud was back, and he seemed to be in an unusually pleasant frame of mind.

That didn't bode well for anyone.

"Miss Beckett, I'm coming in now."

Arabella jumped to her feet and plastered herself against the far wall, desperately wishing she could melt into the cement blocks. She watched as the door swung open and the feeble light of a candle flickered into the room, illuminating the face of the man who held her captive.

His face did nothing to reassure her.

He was evil, plain and simple. His eyes gleamed with an unholy light, and his hair was slicked back with some type of grease. He was wearing a pristine white shirt with dark trousers, and she could smell the scent of sandalwood emitting from his person.

For some odd reason, it reminded her of brimstone.

"I desire your company at dinner," Jud said, throwing a

bag at her she didn't bother to catch. It landed on the floor with a soft *thump*.

"Now, we can't have that, can we?" Jud said, taking a step into the room. "Pick it up."

Arabella pressed herself further against the wall and shook her head.

Jud's smile caused her blood to freeze in her veins.

He really was insane.

She braced herself when he tilted his head and considered her for a moment, but then turned on his heel and strode from the room. She blew out a pent-up breath of air.

Perhaps he'd decided she wasn't worth his trouble.

Her relief turned to fresh horror a mere minute later when he walked through the door again, panting as he tugged one of the ladies of the night in beside him. The poor lady was white as a sheet and trembling from head to foot.

"You will pick that up or I'll harm her."

Arabella pushed off from the wall and rushed to the bag, scooping it up in her arms. "See, I got it, Mr. Hansen," she whispered. "You can let her go now."

"You'll agree to dine with me, be pleasant, and entertain me with lively conversation?"

Arabella gave a jerk of her head. "Yes, I agree. Please . . . just let her go."

Jud pulled the woman from the room, and Arabella steeled herself when he ambled back through the door and smiled at her. "We will dine in less than an hour. Your hair's a mess. Fix it. I expect you to look beautiful for me. You won't care for what will happen if you disappoint me."

"I'll fix it, and I promise you won't be disappointed with my appearance."

"Good, because there are ten other women here, and I would hate to have to hurt them because of you. It would not be good for your digestion."

Arabella swallowed. "Why don't you let them go? From what you've said over the past few days, it's me you've been after all this time. They've done nothing to deserve this."

"Now, that's not true, is it, darling?" he purred, his tone causing sweat to bead on her forehead. "Those ladies aren't exactly innocent, and they should be punished, just as I punished some of the women I kept in Gilman."

"You killed women back in Gilman?"

"No, I never killed them," Jud said slowly. "I only kept them for a spell, until they learned the errors of their ways and they began to bore me. Once I was certain they were changed women, I released them into the woods."

"You left them in the woods to die?"

"I never found a body, so I have to believe they made their way out alive." He let out a chuckle. "I kept expecting someone to come and question me, but apparently I intimidated the women so much that they never told anyone about me. That diminished the excitement tremendously."

Arabella closed her eyes for a brief second and then opened them. "Is that why you've decided to kill this time? You need more excitement?"

Jud shrugged. "I never actually said I was going to kill any of you, but I have been considering it. Those other women—not you of course, my dear—are exceptionally bad. God will be disappointed in me if I don't punish them most severely."

Arabella frowned as his words settled in her mind. "Forgive me, but I was under the impression you lured the women to Gilman in order to sell them, not keep them around for a while as if they were some type of a collection."

"My dear, dear, child, I was not part of that mess you landed yourself into, although it did give me a wonderful way to cover up my activities. Sheriff Dawson was so occupied with figuring out why beautiful women were flocking in droves to his little town, only to disappear, that he kindly overlooked what I was up to."

Arabella considered him for a moment, wondering how in the world she was going to reason with him. "You mentioned that God will expect you to punish these women for their sins, but don't you believe God expects His children to show each other mercy?"

"There will be relatively little pain involved if I decide to kill anyone. That will be my mercy."

"God commands His people not to kill."

He waved her statement away with a flick of his hand. "He also commands us to honor our fathers and our mothers, and my mother loathed women who were sinners. She brought me up to expect nothing less than perfection in a woman, and I truly did believe I'd finally found that perfection in you, until you went away with that Mr. Wilder."

A drop of sweat ran down Arabella's face as Jud's expression turned crazed and a line of spittle dribbled out of his mouth.

"When I saw you out at that farmhouse, I considered stealing you away right there and then, but Sheriff Dawson got in my way and I was forced to watch as he shoved you in that wagon and carted you back to jail. I changed my plan and decided I'd spirit you away once you were in jail, but then Mr. Wilder showed up and . . ." He paused and then let out a laugh that caused shivers to run over her body. "I was not sorry at all to put a bullet into that annoying man. I do hope you weren't too distressed that I killed him, but he deserved to die. He disrespected you when he took you out of town without a proper chaperone, and you should thank me for getting him out of your life for good. A lady can never be too careful in guarding her reputation."

"I'm hardly going to thank you for killing the man I love."

Jud's eyes began to burn. "You're a fool, and not perfect

in the least, but you can find contentment in knowing you'll shortly be joining Mr. Wilder in the hereafter." Jud looked her over from head to toe, let out an insane laugh, then turned and walked through the door, pausing for a moment to look over his shoulder. "Get dressed. I'll be back soon."

Arabella waited until the sound of retreating feet disappeared before she opened the bag and dumped the contents out on the bed. A single tear rolled down her cheek, but she brushed it away, not allowing herself the luxury of a good cry.

Theodore was dead.

She'd spent the last days of his life avoiding him.

She'd never told him she loved him.

Another tear plopped from her eye and landed on the silk material on the bed. She fell to her knees and folded her hands.

Forgive me, Father, for not seeing the gift you so clearly sent me in Theodore. I was a fool for turning my back on him, and I can only hope he's safe in your presence now. Please watch over him for me, and let him know that I do love him, even if I never took the opportunity to tell him that. I know the chances of my getting out of this alive are slim, but I ask you once again for your assistance. It seems I've been asking for it a lot lately, but if it is my time to leave this place, please give me courage, and please be with the other women here as we face the horror of this man. If there is some other plan, Lord, show me the way, and I'll try to see it through to the end. I leave my fate in your hands. Amen.

A sense of peace settled over Arabella as she sat on the floor. God had never forsaken her before, and He was hardly likely to do so now. If it was her time to leave the world, well, all she could do at this point was meet her destiny with courage and grace. She rose to her feet, slipped out of her soiled gown, and quickly dressed, taking a few moments to pry the tangles out of her hair with her fingers.

The sound of church bells came to her ears and she stilled. It *was* Christmas Eve.

She allowed the sounds of the bells to wash over her, giving her an added feeling of peace as she waited for Jud to return.

"What's he going to do to us?" a voice whispered through her wall.

Arabella walked to the wall, her fingers reaching out to touch the cold surface. "I'm not certain."

"I think he's going to kill us. He's crazy."

"I know," Arabella agreed. "What's your name?"

"Betsy."

"I'm Arabella."

"I know who you are," Betsy said. "I went to one of your speeches. You spoke after that Stanton lady."

"You were at a rally?"

"You sound surprised. I wasn't always a harlot, you know. Circumstances beyond my control caused me to take to the streets, but I still felt the need to support the cause. If women could vote on the laws that are passed in this country, maybe we'd discover a way to better our lot in life. It is women like you, Miss Beckett, who've made a difference already."

Arabella took a deep breath and slowly released it. Here she'd been questioning everything she'd done of late, and yet she had made a difference. She'd been on the right path.

She squared her shoulders and lifted her chin. It was not right that she and the other women were being made to wait for their deaths. There was still much to live for, and she wasn't the type of woman to simply give up.

She wasn't going to die until she knew her efforts meant something. She needed to live to see the day women would get the right to vote, which meant she wasn't going to be able to die for quite some time.

"Betsy, listen to me," she called through the wall. "When Jud comes back to get me, and after you hear us depart, I want you to search your room for anything you can use as a weapon. Spread the word through the walls and have the other women do the same."

"I don't think there's anything we can use."

Arabella's gaze settled on the bed. "Try to break the bed frame and hide the pieces in your dress, but wait until you're certain I'm gone. We can't allow Jud to hear the noise."

"Shh, someone's coming."

Arabella moved away from the wall and braced herself as her door swung open. Jud stood, framed in the doorway, his expression pleased as he looked her up and down. She fought hard to suppress a shiver, knowing it would only delight him to see her fear.

"Lovely," he breathed. He stepped into the room and offered her his arm. "Shall we dine?"

Arabella forced herself to accept his arm and allowed him to escort her out of the room. The hallway was completely silent as they marched down it, and she could only hope Betsy would be successful in arming herself and spreading the word to the other women.

"We'll be dining in the parlor this evening," Jud said.

"There's a parlor?"

"Of course there's a parlor. I've rented a grand mansion for my holiday festivities. You've been spending all your time in the basement, and for that you have my deepest apologies. I couldn't very well take the chance you or any of the other ladies would get it into your heads to pound on the windows to seek assistance, could I?"

"Where in the world did you obtain the money to rent a mansion?"

"My mother left me quite a tidy sum. I'm sure she would be pleased with how I've spent her fortune."

Arabella tripped on the hem of her gown as they climbed the stairs, but Jud simply hauled her back to her feet and pulled her the rest of the way up. She blinked when they came to the main floor and then blinked again as her eyes adjusted to the bright light coming from the massive chandelier hanging above her head. He'd not been lying; they were in a mansion.

The sound of passing carriages met her ears, and hope flowed through her. There were people right outside the house, people who would lend her assistance if she could just get out the front door.

As if reading her mind, Jud laughed and pulled her down a long hallway and into the parlor. He shoved her into a chair and wagged a finger at her. "Don't even think about moving or I swear you'll regret it. Brandy?"

"No, thank you."

"I insist," Jud hissed.

"I would *love* a brandy."

Jud strode over to a small table, poured brandy into a glass, and moved to her side, handing her the glass before returning to the table and pouring another, larger glass.

She decided then and there she'd do her best to get him drunk.

She pretended to take a sip as he took a seat beside her and watched as he gulped down half the contents of his glass.

It might not take long if he continued to guzzle his drink in such a fashion.

"No need to fear I'll get sloppy, my dear. I have an unusually high tolerance for alcohol."

Was the man capable of reading her mind?

"You promised to entertain me with stimulating conversation," he said. "I'm waiting."

"Would you care to hear about the latest lecture I attended? It was very stimulating, and the speakers were well-versed on the Constitution."

"I don't understand why you waste your time on that nonsense," Jud snapped. "Women have no business using their brains. That's why God made you so attractive."

"I don't think you really find women attractive," Arabella said slowly.

"I love women. I love collecting them."

Even though Arabella didn't want to hear more, she couldn't seem to stop the questions that began to pour out of her mouth.

"When did you start collecting women?"

"After my mother died."

"Why did you wait until after her death?"

"She would never allow me to have ladies in her house."

"But . . . why didn't you simply try courting a lady?"

Jud's eyes began to burn. "None of the good ladies of Gilman seemed to be receptive to me."

It would not serve her well to comment on that particular statement. Arabella cleared her throat. "How did your mother die?"

"I don't care to discuss that."

Jud stood and gestured around the room. "I hope you don't mind, but I thought we'd dine in here before having the other girls join us in the dining room for the rest of the festivities I have planned."

"That's fine," Arabella said, wondering how she was going to be able to get a single bite down her throat while Jud leered at her throughout the dinner.

"You're very agreeable. It's a shame we couldn't get to know each other better, but I've decided I simply can't allow you to live."

"You could always change your mind."

"No, I couldn't do that. It's Christmas Eve, you see, and this night is very, very special to me."

Arabella frowned. "Does Christmas Eve have something to do with your mother?"

Pure evil spilled out of Jud's eyes. "I don't discuss my mother."

Arabella's breath hitched in her throat when Jud suddenly moved to her side. She winced as he drew back his hand, but before he could strike her, a man burst into the room.

"We've got a bit of a situation, boss."

Arabella narrowed her eyes as Deputy Cunningham, a man she'd seen but hadn't spoken to back in Gilman, stepped farther into the room, his eyes wide and his clothing disheveled.

"What is it?"

"Sheriff Dawson spotted me."

Jud lowered his arm. "That complicates matters." He smiled. "I guess we'll need to speed up our festivities."

22

"Theodore, I hate to disturb you, but there's a man waiting in the foyer who wants to speak with you," Ethel said quietly. "Shall I send him in?"

Theodore rubbed a hand over his face and shook his head. "I'm afraid I have no time to spare at the moment, Grandmother. I'll be heading out as soon as Zayne arrives, and I'm not up to accepting anyone's sympathy at the moment."

"He didn't claim to be here to offer sympathy."

"Then he's most likely just another curious soul come to see if anything's been discovered."

"Shall I have him leave his card?"

"That would be for the best."

Before Ethel could leave, Agatha slid into the room, her features almost completely disguised by the wig and heavy makeup covering her face. She was dressed in a gown that was vulgar at best, and her eyes held a glint of what could only be described as determination.

He blew out a breath even as he rose to his feet. "We've been over this a million times, Agatha. You can't come with us."

Agatha planted her hands on her hips. "I'm going, and there's nothing you can do to stop me."

To his relief, his grandmother stepped forward and put her arm around Agatha's shoulders. "Dear, I know you want to help and that this has been incredibly hard on you, but you must think about your parents and about Arabella's parents. Poor Gloria is beside herself at the moment, and the last thing she needs is to have something else to worry about. You'll stay here with me while Theodore and Zayne hit the streets again."

Agatha shook her head. "It's my choice to help, Mrs. Wilder, and my choice alone. I can't sit by and watch everyone suffer without doing something. If nothing else, I can offer myself up as bait and hope the man who took Arabella comes after me."

"Dot said no other women have been taken," Ethel argued. "You're putting yourself at risk when there's no guarantee the man is even still roaming the streets. What if some other man approaches you and everyone is distracted from the situation at hand?"

Agatha opened her mouth, but time was running away from Theodore, and he didn't want to waste it arguing with her, even though his heart was near to breaking from her obvious distress. "Agatha, forgive me, but I can't allow you to come. The only reason Zayne and I are taking to the streets tonight is to search for Arabella's body. She deserves a proper funeral from me if nothing else, and the last thing I want you to see is her—"

"Don't say that," Agatha interrupted, her voice trembling and her lashes wet with unshed tears. "We don't know for certain Arabella's dead."

"It's pointless to think otherwise at this stage, Agatha," Theodore said. "From what I've learned through numerous investigations, if a victim isn't found within a day or two, it's rare to discover them alive. Arabella's been missing for a week."

Ethel drew herself up. "I have not given up hope just yet, young man. Arabella is a resourceful young woman. She wouldn't like the fact that you've given up on her."

"I didn't say I've completely given up hope, Grandmother, but you know, given the life you've led, that what I'm saying is nothing less than the truth. I would love to find Arabella alive. I would love to be able to see her beautiful face again and tell her how much I adore her, how much I love her. I dream about her every time I close my eyes, but then reality returns the moment I awake, and I know it's my fault she's gone. The thought that we were dealing with two separate evils never even entered my head. I thought Wallace and Carter were lying when they claimed to have no knowledge of the missing women. I didn't even bother to question them again after I handed them over to the police. If I would have been more diligent, I would have realized danger was alive and well in the city. I would never have allowed Arabella to remain in town."

"It does no one any good if you blame yourself for this, Theodore," Ethel said. "The odds of having two horrific crimes being perpetrated at the same time are slim to none. You're taking too much responsibility for what happened."

"I didn't protect her," Theodore said. "While I was lying in some hospital, Arabella was suffering."

"You'd been shot, Theodore. You lost a lot of blood," Agatha said. "You were in no condition to search for her."

"It was only a flesh wound, and I wouldn't have been shot if I'd been aware of the danger."

"Arabella would never think you were to blame," Ethel said quietly. "She'd tell you to quit being an idiot, and she'd also tell you to seek solace from God."

Theodore's eyes turned hard. "I have no use for God at

the moment, Grandmother. He allowed this to happen to Arabella, a woman who was filled with faith. He should have watched over her."

"Perhaps He still is watching over her," Ethel returned. "God didn't allow this to happen to Arabella, dear. A man was responsible, and it's your job to go out, find him, and bring him to justice. You have to put your anger aside and try to help Arabella."

"I think she's beyond help now."

"Don't you dare give up on her," Agatha said as tears dribbled down her face, leaving trails through her makeup. "You're the strong one, and I can't handle it if you let go of all hope."

The sight of Agatha's tears had Theodore's rage diminishing as he pulled her into his arms and placed a kiss on her head. "Forgive me, Agatha. You're right. All we have left is hope, and I'll try to keep that thought alive. I didn't mean to upset you."

"Agatha? Are you all right?" Zayne asked as he strode into the room and stopped by Theodore's side. Agatha let out a sniff and stepped out of Theodore's embrace and directly into Zayne's arms.

"I'm afraid I upset her," Theodore said.

"Perfectly understandable," Zayne said, his eyes blinking rather rapidly, obviously in an attempt to keep his tears in check.

"Theodore thinks it's his fault she's disappeared," Agatha said.

"It's not his fault. It's mine."

Theodore spun around, his hand immediately reaching for his pistol. He pulled it out and leveled it on Sheriff Dawson, who was standing in the doorway.

"Where is she?" Theodore growled.

Sheriff Dawson took one step into the room, but paused

when Theodore cocked the pistol. "As to that, I'm not certain, but I do know *who* has her." He gestured to the gun. "Would it be possible for you to point that in the other direction?"

"Not until you explain everything to my satisfaction."

Ethel moved up to stand by Theodore's side. "Dear, this is the man I told you had come to call. Am I to understand he's somehow involved in all this?"

Theodore arched a brow. "Well, are you involved in this, Sheriff Dawson?"

"Isn't Sheriff Dawson that shifty law officer who disappeared from Gilman?" George asked as he stepped into the room, his own pistol clutched in his hand.

"Indeed he is, Grandfather," Theodore answered. "Which should make the story he's about to tell us regarding what he's doing in New York particularly fascinating."

Sheriff Dawson shook his head. "We don't have much time."

Theodore didn't lower his gun. "Who killed Arabella?"

"I don't think she's dead, not yet at least."

A thread of hope spread through his veins. "Where is she?"

"I told you, I don't know, but Jud Hansen and another one of my deputies, Peter Cunningham, are behind her disappearance."

"You don't know where they are?" George pressed.

"I wasn't even sure Peter was involved until I saw him on the street just a short time ago. I tried to trail him, but Peter's one of the best trackers I've ever known, and he lost me."

Theodore's arm slowly lowered. He gestured to a chair. "I understand that time is of the essence, but we need to understand what we're going up against before we leave this house."

Sheriff Dawson looked as if he wanted to argue, but hurried to the chair and sat down. He took a moment, as if he needed to collect his thoughts, and then nodded. "I knew something was wrong months ago. Women kept showing up in Gilman, and then they'd just disappear, never to be seen in town again. I started investigating Wallace and Carter, and it took me a while to understand they were selling the women. I was going to move in for an arrest the day you showed up, Mr. Wilder, but everything fell apart after that. Wallace and Carter disappeared, and I readily admit I had doubts regarding my own men. I thought at least one of them was in on it, but I couldn't prove anything, and I didn't trust anyone."

"You should have come to me the moment you stepped foot into New York," Theodore said.

"They are *my* men. I thought it was *my* problem. I realize that was foolish, but again, I didn't know whom to trust. When Jud and Peter disappeared from town, followed by Deputy Black, I hoped they were simply pursuing Wallace and Carter. After I found that shed, well, I knew something beyond selling women was in play. I followed my men to New York, and I've spent the past few weeks trying to find Jud, but he's gone to ground. He's highly trained, has a fortune at his disposal, and I fear, from what I found in back of his house, he's insane."

"What did you find?"

"He found garments and trinkets belonging to ladies, all of them giving testimony to the fact Jud Hansen has been a busy man." Theodore glanced over his shoulder and settled his sights on the door, where a large gentleman who looked slightly familiar stood. "He also found silk ties, some of them sporting a bit of blood, which we've come to believe were used to keep those women tied up in Jud's house."

"Who are you?" George demanded.

The man moved into the room. "I'm William Black, the only trustworthy deputy Sheriff Dawson has at his disposal. I felt it prudent to join your meeting."

"Did you find any bodies with those trinkets?" Theodore asked as he strode over to stand beside William.

"Fortunately no, but that doesn't mean bodies aren't buried somewhere in the woods," William said. "My concern at the moment is the date."

Theodore frowned. "The date?"

"Jud Hansen was unnaturally attached to his mother. She died on Christmas Eve a few years back, and I don't know why—call it intuition, if you will—but I have a feeling he's planning something to commemorate her passing."

"Do you really think there's a chance the women are still alive?" Theodore asked.

William glanced at the clock before he nodded. "I would have to say yes, at least for now. I've hunted with Jud before, and he enjoys the hunt. If Jud has targeted this date as a warped way of honoring his mother, he'll want to draw the women's fear out. I think he'll wait until right around midnight to make his move."

"That means we don't have much time, and we don't know where he is. Every warehouse and deserted building has been searched and searched again. We don't even know if he's in the city," Theodore said.

"He's in the city," Sheriff Dawson said. "I told you, I saw Peter Cunningham out on the streets. They'll be together. Peter always idolized Jud."

"Would he kill for him?" Ethel asked, suddenly speaking up.

"I imagine he would," William replied.

What sounded like a nervous cough caught Theodore's attention, and he turned and discovered Violet standing in the doorway. He gestured her into the room.

"I do beg everyone's pardon for eavesdropping," Violet said, "but me and the girls couldn't seem to help ourselves."

Theodore glanced up and saw Hannah, Lottie, and Sarah peering through the side of the door. He waved them in and watched as they inched over beside Violet.

"You said that Jud fellow had money," Sarah said, looking at Sheriff Dawson.

Sheriff Dawson nodded. "He does."

"Then he'll be in one of the big houses, won't he?" Lottie asked. "He's planning this out like a celebration. He won't want it to be done in the stews."

Theodore's breath caught in his throat as Lottie's words settled in his mind. He strode over to her, bent down and kissed her soundly on the cheek, then straightened. "You, my dear ladies, are geniuses. That's exactly where Jud will be, and I'm ever so thankful all of you insisted on returning to town to keep a vigil for Arabella. You might have just saved her life. All we have to do now is figure out which house he's rented."

"Dot would know," Violet said. "She keeps good track of all the rich men who move into town."

"We need to find Dot."

"She'll be down at the docks this time of night," Violet said.

Sheriff Dawson got to his feet. "I know you have no reason to trust me, but this has been my fault. I'd like to come with you to help set matters right."

Theodore considered him for a brief moment. "You can come, but if you do anything to jeopardize this mission, or if I discover you've lied to me, I won't hesitate to hurt you."

"Fair enough."

Theodore walked to his desk and scribbled a note, turning to hand it to Ethel. "Have this delivered to my office. A few of my men have been staying there, and they'll get the word out."

"I'm coming with you," Agatha said.

"No," Theodore and Zayne said together.

"I can't just sit here and wait," Agatha said, fresh tears pouring down her face.

"You'll be doing me a service by staying with my grand-mother," Theodore said. He lowered his voice. "I can't concentrate on finding Arabella if I'm worried about you, and Katherine is due to arrive any minute. I know she would appreciate your company."

Agatha bit her lip, wiped the tears from her face, and nodded before she stood on tiptoe and placed a kiss on Theodore's cheek. She turned to Zayne. "Be careful."

Zayne looked at her, took a step forward, and then stopped.

Agatha rolled her eyes, moved in front of him, and kissed him on the cheek. "I don't think Helena would mind, not given the circumstances."

Zayne nodded, bowed to Ethel, and quit the room.

"Coming, Grandfather?" Theodore asked.

"Let me kiss my girl, and I'll be right behind you."

Theodore nodded and strode out of the room with Zayne, Sheriff Dawson, and William Black walking by his side down the hallway. "How long did you suspect something was going on with Jud?" he asked as they made their way outside and waited for the horses to be brought around.

"I think I always knew," Sheriff Dawson said. "I just chose to ignore the little voice that kept telling me there was something wrong with him. I felt sorry for him; it's one of the reasons I hired him. I'd heard the rumors regarding that mother of his. She kept him close to her, too close, and I always thought he must have been relieved when she died."

"How did she die?"

"Jud told me she passed away in her sleep."

"No one examined the body?"

"He held a funeral for her. There were no signs of foul play."

"Given the man's questionable sanity, do you think he might have done away with her?"

"That is something I shall certainly ask him if we find him," Sheriff Dawson said.

The arrival of the horses cut the conversation short. Theodore pulled himself into the saddle, turned, and watched as his grandfather, Zayne, William Black, and Sheriff Dawson did the same, and then urged his horse forward.

They had a plan now. It wasn't much of a plan, but it gave him a purpose and a sense of renewed hope, and that was all he could ask for at this point.

Time sped by quickly as he steered his horse toward the docks, and before he knew it, ships were coming into sight, as well as a group of ladies who were obviously working the streets. He pulled his horse to a stop and jumped off, relief flowing through him when he recognized one of the ladies as Dot. She saw him and waved, hurrying over to him.

"What's wrong?" she asked.

"We've gotten a lead on the missing women, but we're running out of time. I need to know if you're aware of any wealthy gentlemen who might have recently moved into one of the big houses in the city."

Dot tilted her head, her eyes vacant for a moment, before she smiled. "Two men moved into that empty mansion in Irving Place right next to Gramercy Park."

"When did they move in?"

"Less than a month ago, and they weren't friendly."

"Could be them," Zayne said, coming to stand beside Theodore.

"Would you ask the girls if they remember any other wealthy men moving into the city?"

Dot nodded, strode back to the women, and returned less than two minutes later. "There have been a couple others who've moved in, but we think they had families with them."

A church bell rang eight times.

"It's getting late," Theodore said. "We should scout out that house by Gramercy Park." He turned to Dot. "Would you be willing to travel with us and show us which house it is?"

Dot nodded and waited for Theodore to climb back on his horse before taking his hand and swinging up behind him. No one spoke as they galloped through the streets, and Theodore was thankful to have the time to get his thoughts in order.

Arabella might still be alive.

He could not let her down again if she was.

"It's up there," Dot said some fifteen minutes later, pointing to an impressive house that seemed to be completely dark.

Theodore pulled his horse to a stop, jumped off, and helped Dot down. He handed her the reins and pointed down the street. "You need to stay under the gas lamps, Dot. I don't want you to take any chances. Do not even think about coming in after us, no matter what you might hear."

Dot looked as if she might argue, but Theodore tilted her chin up with one finger and glared at her. "I mean it."

"Fine, I'll stay put."

Theodore nodded and turned, gesturing to the other men to join him. "We'll go around back. Keep your pistols at the ready, gentlemen. I think you're going to need them."

They filed silently across the street, keeping to the shadows, and then slid in between the houses to reach the back of the house. Theodore stopped and held up his hand. "Do you hear that?"

"Someone's yelling, and it sounds like a lady," George rasped.

Theodore's blood ran cold. "We have to get in there. Now."

He edged up to the house, thinking that someone was in for a nasty surprise if this was the wrong house. He moved to a window and tried to open it, biting back a groan when he realized it was locked. He moved on, trying window after window to no avail. They were all locked.

He paused underneath a bay window, rising slightly to peer through a sliver of glass where a faint glow of light slid out between curtains. What he saw caused rage to course through him.

Arabella was standing beside a man he thought might be

Deputy Cunningham, and that man was holding Arabella's arm, almost as if he were trying to hold her back. Her mouth was moving rapidly, and then his heart stopped beating for just a second when she raised her free hand, shook it at someone he couldn't see, and then spat on the floor.

Jud Hansen suddenly came into view, and Theodore's gaze went immediately to the knife the man was gripping in his hand. Jud gestured to where Arabella had just spat, then turned and disappeared from sight for a second, and then reappeared with a woman he grabbed around the neck right before pressing the knife to the woman's throat.

Theodore didn't give himself a moment to think as he took a few steps back and then ran as hard as he could toward the window, leaping at it and covering his face with his hands as his body hit the glass.

Chaos descended the moment he hurtled into the room. He jumped to his feet and ran straight at Jud, stopping abruptly when the man shoved the woman away and grabbed Arabella, pulling her up against him as the knife moved closer to the delicate skin of her throat.

Jud sent him a look that had evil stamped all over it, but then the man glanced to his right even as obscenities began to spill from his lips.

Theodore's gaze shot behind Jud, and he could barely believe the sight that met his eyes.

Countless women, clothed in barely-there dresses, were rushing toward Jud, gripping what appeared to be homemade weapons in their hands.

"Stop," Jud screamed, "or I swear upon my mother's grave that I'll kill this woman right before your eyes."

"Do as he says," Theodore yelled, and to his relief the women stopped in their tracks.

"Mr. Wilder, how good of you to join us," Jud spat, his breathing ragged. He pulled Arabella closer. "I was going to save this delicious little piece for last, but it seems she'll have to go first." He moved the knife almost lovingly down Arabella's face. "Look, love, your knight in shining armor seems to have survived that nasty bullet I put in him."

Theodore caught Arabella's gaze and shook his head slightly when it appeared she was about to say something. He couldn't risk Jud reacting out of anger. He needed to figure out a way to distract the man until the other men—more specifically, his grandfather—could come to their aid.

"Now, Jud, there's no need for you to kill anyone," Theodore said. "At this point, no real harm has been done, so I'm sure you and I could work something out."

"Save your breath," Jud snapped. "You and I both know that if I was to let this little filly go, you'd kill me without a blink of an eye."

It truly was unfortunate that he was dealing with a member of the law.

He needed to buy some time.

"Why did you take them, Jud?"

Jud shrugged. "I like women."

"And you like to keep mementos of them, don't you?"

"How do you know about my mementos?"

Theodore summoned up a laugh. "Why, Jud, I know quite a bit about you at this point. I know your mother abused you, and that you probably killed her, making it appear like a natural death." He nodded to Deputy Cunningham. "I also know that you somehow convinced that idiot over there to do some of your dirty work for you. Is he aware you planned on making him your dupe?"

"I'm no dupe. Jud and I have been hunting ladies together for a while now, and he told me my skills have begun to rival his," Peter Cunningham snarled, but before he could say more, Jud interrupted.

"Tell me, Mr. Wilder, how did you find out about my little

mementos? I thought I kept them well-hidden in my shed. I know you learned nothing about me when you scurried back to Gilman with all your little questions, or else you'd have come searching for me long before now."

"It's true that I never figured out the part you played in this madness . . . until now. And while I don't appreciate the fact that you've put the woman I love in harm's way, I just might let you live if you let Arabella go."

"Oh, how sweet," Jud growled, "you're declaring your feelings. I would have never taken you for an emotional sap." His eyes began to gleam. "I won't let her go."

"Then I'll have to kill you."

"Yes, I imagine you will, or at least you'll try," Jud said, and then he laughed, the sound causing Theodore to tense.

"Peter said something about the two of you hunting," Theodore said slowly. "If you enjoy the hunt, I imagine you must also enjoy pitting yourself against worthy adversaries."

Jud tilted his head, even as the knife he was holding moved closer to Arabella's throat. "What are you suggesting?"

"You know I'm considered a dangerous man. Why don't you and I have a go at each other?"

"I prefer delicate flesh these days," Jud said, sliding the knife up to caress Arabella's cheek.

Theodore saw red, and his hands clenched into fists. Swallowing his anger, he forced a laugh. "Come now, Jud, I'm more of a challenge. Arabella's just a little thing, hardly a worthy opponent for someone of your skill. Let her go, and then if you do best me, she'll still be here."

Jud's expression turned to considering. He nodded at Theodore's pistol. "You're armed. It would hardly be a fair fight."

"I'll fight you without weapons. You know I've recently been shot, so the advantage will lie with you."

"Theodore, he won't fight fair," Arabella yelled as she

began to struggle, the motion causing Jud's knife to nick her cheek.

Rage took over Theodore's every pore as he watched a trickle of blood run down Arabella's face. Every muscle in his body tensed, and he was just about to attack when Jud laughed and gestured with his head to Peter.

"Come, get the girl, Peter. It's time I showed this fool what a real man is." He thrust Arabella at Peter, handed the man his knife, and smiled at Theodore. "You didn't think I was going to completely let her go, did you? Now, drop your pistol like a good boy, and let's get on with this."

Theodore drew in a breath, forced his thoughts to calm, dropped his pistol, and waved Jud forward.

Jud dropped his head and rushed forward, plowing into Theodore with bone-crunching force. Punches began to fly, blood splattered the floor, and Theodore could hear screams echoing throughout the room. He didn't, and couldn't, take his attention away from Jud. The man was fueled by insanity, and he was strong, one of the strongest men Theodore had ever fought. A fresh bout of fury flowed over Theodore when out of the corner of his eye he glimpsed Peter holding the knife on Arabella, the man's expression filled with anticipation. He drew back his arm and let it fly, the impact causing Jud to stumble backward, blink, and then run straight toward Arabella, his eyes wild. Theodore heard a whistle, looked to the window, and caught the pistol George threw to him.

He didn't hesitate but pulled the trigger. He watched as Jud hovered a few feet in front of Arabella and then crumpled to the ground. Theodore charged forward, his attention settled on Peter, but the women standing around the room suddenly rushed into action, knocking Arabella out of the way as they jumped on Peter, wrestling the knife away from him while beating him with their weapons.

"I've got him, boy. Get Arabella," George shouted, racing past and jumping into the pile of thrashing bodies.

Theodore rushed toward Arabella and snatched her up into his arms. He buried his head in her hair and breathed in the scent of her, sending up a silent prayer of thanks to God for allowing him to find her alive and asking God to forgive him for doubting.

"You found me," Arabella said as she burrowed deeper into his arms.

"Of course I found you." Theodore allowed himself the luxury of a shudder. "I thought you were dead."

"I thought *you* were dead," Arabella said, her voice muffled as she hiccupped into his shirt.

He gave her a hard squeeze and set her back from him in order to meet her gaze. "I'm sorry I'm not very romantic."

Arabella blinked. "What?"

"I said I'm sorry I'm not very romantic. I made a complete mess of things before, and I swear I'll make it up to you."

A half laugh, half sob escaped Arabella's lips. "Good heavens, Theodore, you just did the most romantic thing a man could ever do for a woman."

"I did?"

"You offered up yourself in order to save my life. *That* was truly romantic."

"It was?"

Arabella smiled. "You know, it's suddenly clear to me what has to be done."

Theodore felt his lips twitch at the sight of Arabella looking up at him with what could only be described as mischief in her incredible eyes. "What has to be done?"

"You seem to get yourself in a lot of trouble, especially when you're rescuing me." She released a dramatic sigh. "I think the only solution available to us is marriage. It's the only way I can keep you safe."

He grinned. "You're going to marry me in order to keep me safe?"

"No, I'm going to marry you because I love you, and I never want to be parted from you again."

Theodore felt all the breath leave his body. He leaned his head closer to her. "I love you more than I have ever loved another person in my entire life."

Arabella tilted her head, and Theodore couldn't help himself. Her lips were right in front of him, and he needed to claim them. He settled his lips over hers and the world melted away.

"This is all very touching," George said with a snort, "but I'm almost eighty years old, and I could use a bit of assistance here. If you haven't noticed, we have a bunch of weeping women on our hands, one unconscious criminal, and a dead man. Kissing will have to wait until after the wedding."

Epilogue

I cannot believe there's another blizzard outside," Gloria muttered, moving to Arabella's side as she peered out the window of the church. "What a way to start the New Year."

"Weddings are the perfect way to start the New Year," Eliza said as she bustled into the room. "I cannot believe you and Cora were able to pull this off on such short notice, Gloria. Why, I just peeked in the church, and I think all of New York has braved the weather to come watch Arabella and Theodore get married."

"They've come to see what can only be described as a most peculiar circumstance," Agatha said, strolling into the room. "Who would have thought that one of the leaders in the suffrage movement and one of the most chauvinistic gentlemen we know would discover a real and binding love together?"

Eliza grinned. "It is a bit odd."

Arabella found she couldn't quite disagree.

She'd been so adamant in rebuking any and all suggestions that she and Theodore suited each other, but . . . she had certainly turned out to be wrong, and for once in her life, being wrong didn't bother her in the slightest.

"Auntie Arabella, Ben took my flowers," Piper yelled as she ran into the room, skidded to a halt, and smiled. She looked Arabella up and down. "You look beautiful."

"Thank you, Piper. You look very pretty as well."

Piper giggled. "Mr. Theodore told me he'd marry me if I was older, but I don't think you have anything to worry about. He was just kidding." Her eyes widened. "Oh, and I forgot, Miss Violet and her friends are waiting outside. They wanted me to ask you if they could come in for a moment to see you."

"Of course they can come in," Arabella said.

Piper spun on her heel and rushed back through the door, reappearing with Violet and her friends a moment later.

Violet moved across the room and pulled Arabella into a hug. "Oh, I'm going to cry. You look absolutely stunning." She stepped back and dabbed a handkerchief over her eyes.

"You do look lovely," Lottie said, and Hannah and Sarah nodded in agreement.

Violet swallowed what sounded like a sob and then smiled a rather wobbly smile. "Lottie and I wanted you to know that we've made you a special treat for after the wedding. We just *had* to do something to show you how much you and Theodore mean to us."

"They made your cake," Ethel said, beaming at everyone as she glided into the room. "Just so you know, they've promised to remain in my employ after everyone samples their baking. Why, I don't think George could live another day if he didn't have the wonderful cakes and breads they've been creating for us."

Violet grabbed hold of Arabella's hand and gave it a good squeeze. "We won't keep you much longer, seeing as this is your special day and all, but Lottie, Hannah, Sarah, and I wanted to thank you personally for everything you've done for us. You've given us a chance at a new life, and without your support we'd still be out on the streets. You're a special person, and we wish you only the best."

"I think you're getting that by marrying Theodore," Lottie said with a grin. "He is an uncommonly fine specimen of a man."

"Yes, thank you for that, Lottie," Gloria said with a returning grin as she turned from her position at the window. "Now, everyone out. We do have a wedding in a few minutes."

The room cleared as Eliza and Agatha went to stand in line beside Katherine who had been waiting there, the three women looking beautiful in their gowns of pink, all seemingly delighted that everything had turned out so well and they could stand as bridesmaids for Arabella.

Ethel gave her a quick kiss and went to join the bridesmaids, and Arabella couldn't help the tears that stung her eyes as she watched Theodore's grandmother take her place as matron of honor.

Cora Watson suddenly breezed into the room, escorted by Zayne. She dropped her hold on him, stepped up to Arabella, and hugged her, hard. "I wish you a very happy and amusing life." She nodded, just once, stepped back, and then turned to Zayne. "You would do well to emulate your sister and marry someone who amuses you." She turned and winked at Agatha, who was watching the exchange with clear horror on her face, and then quickly left the room after sending Gloria a wave, the telltale sounds of sniffing trailing after her, explaining the speedy exit.

Zayne cleared his throat. "Father's waiting to escort you down the aisle, but I wanted to wish you luck before I join Theodore in the front of the church."

"That is very sweet of you."

"I also needed to let you know that Theodore's responsible for the church."

"What do you mean?"

"You'll see," Zayne said, kissing her on the cheek before he turned to his mother. "I'll be escorting you down the aisle, so don't be too long. Theodore's anxious to make Arabella his wife, and I don't think he's willing to wait much longer."

Gloria rolled her eyes. "While I certainly have no intention of holding up the wedding, especially since I've been dreaming of this moment for years, I do need to speak with my one and only daughter."

Zayne rolled his eyes right back at her. "Fine, but again, Theodore's anxious, and he has been known to pull out that pistol of his when his nerves get the best of him. I'd hate for him to shoot his soon-to-be mother-in-law because she tried his patience."

After Zayne disappeared through the door, Gloria turned back to Arabella. "I truly have been waiting for this day for a very long time."

"You probably never thought you'd see this day."

Gloria reached out and stroked her finger down Arabella's cheek. "I always knew there was someone very special out there for you, darling. In fact, I knew Theodore was right for you the moment I met him. Why do you think I sent him to fetch you home?"

"I knew you planned this from the start."

"Someone had to get your life in order for you, dear. Who better to do that than your own mother?"

Gloria smiled, kissed Arabella's cheek, and without another word she marched from the room.

For a moment, Arabella was all alone. She moved to the window, gazed out at the falling snow, and then closed her eyes.

Thank you, Lord. You've given me more than I could ever imagine. I thank you for my family, for my friends, for my Theodore, and for my very life. You've filled me with your love, and I will be forever grateful.

"Are you ready, darling?" Douglas asked, causing her to open her eyes.

She walked over to her father's side, straightened his jacket, and nodded.

Douglas extended his arm to her, she took it, and on legs that trembled not even the slightest bit, she walked out of the room, down a small hallway after her bridesmaids, listened to the music begin to swell, and froze the second her gaze took in the sight before her.

The church was draped in pink satin. Pink ties adorned every pew, and there was even a pink runner down the aisle. The sun took that moment to break through the snow, and the effect was dazzling as the light streamed through the stained-glass windows.

Theodore had given her a romantic gesture.

Her eyes filled with tears, and she could barely see as her father escorted her down the aisle, but when she reached the end, her vision cleared and Theodore stood in front of her. Douglas passed her over to him, and the instant her hand touched his, she knew her life was complete.

"Do you like the pink?" Theodore whispered.

"I love it."

"I love you."

Arabella smiled and turned with Theodore to face Reverend Fraser, who was beaming back at them. As she recited her vows and listened to Theodore recite his, happiness flowed through her.

Theodore's lips lowered over hers after they were pronounced man and wife, and Arabella knew as she stood in the house of the Lord that God had brought Theodore to her, and that He would be with them for the rest of their days—days that were certain to be filled with love, laughter, a little compromise, and joy.

Acknowledgments

I'm constantly amazed by the efforts of so many people who help me get my books published. Those efforts deserve a rousing thank-you, and I truly hope everyone knows how much I appreciate all the help I've been given.

To my editor, Raela Schoenherr, for reading my work and knowing exactly how to make my story better. Your advice is fabulous and has helped me become a stronger writer.

To the marketing and sales department at Bethany House—Steve Oates, Noelle Buss, Debra Larsen, Anna Henke, Brittany Higdon, Stacey Theesfield, Chris Dykstra, Jennifer Parker, and Eric Walljasper. All of you are incredibly talented, and I couldn't do this without you.

To copy editor Luke Hinrichs, thank you for catching all those pesky little commas I can't seem to control.

To John Hamilton and Paul Higdon for yet another gorgeous cover.

To my agent, Mary Sue Seymour, for being my calm when I get a little neurotic.

To my brilliant friend Carla Laureano. Your support means

the world to me, and I love our daily chats. I can't wait to see your books in print.

To Rick Gustafson, a dear writer friend who seems to have acquired the daunting task of talking me down from that proverbial ledge, sometimes daily. Thanks for making me laugh.

To my brother, Dr. Robert Turner, for being an inspiration to the entire family, even if you did set the standards rather high for those of us who had to follow you.

To my sister, Tricia Gibas, for . . . everything.

To my brother, Jeb Turner, for being a wonderful big brother, and for always having my back, no matter what. You're a little bossy, but I still love you, and it makes me grin when you get so upset when anyone posts a less-than-positive review of my books. I appreciate your willingness to want to contact those reviewers, but, you know, that really isn't a great idea.

To my sister, Gretchen Humiston. I guess you've finally proven you're more than just a gorgeous face. Congratulations on passing the bar exam. Mom would have been thrilled that someone in the family is following in her father's footsteps.

To my little brother, David Turner. Even though Gretchen and I tormented you endlessly when you were younger, you've turned out remarkably well. Thank you for being so excited about my books.

To my mother-in-law, Dolores Turano Cousino, thank you for all the love and support.

As always, a huge thank-you to my guys, Al and Dominic. Love you both!

And, of course, to God, for making this mind-boggling journey possible in the first place. All I had to do was believe it could happen. . . .

Discussion Questions

1. Miss James, unwilling to achieve the horrible status of spinster, was willing to marry a gentleman she'd never met. What do you think it would have been like to live in a time when being unmarried was considered a disturbing state of affairs?

2. Mr. Theodore Wilder always assumed that, because his mother and sister married affluent gentlemen, they were living a perfect life. Do you believe most gentlemen of that time thought the same way as Theodore?

3. Arabella and Theodore are complete opposites. Why were they attracted to each other? Is it better to be similar or opposite? Why or why not?

4. Was Arabella responsible for Katherine's rebellion against her husband, Harold? How could Katherine have responded differently? And how could Harold have behaved differently?

5. Much to everyone's surprise, Arabella enjoys the color pink and reading romance novels. Why do we assume

things about others? What are some things about you that might surprise others?

6. Arabella comes to the unpleasant conclusion that she's been rather judgmental. Do you think her conclusion had merit? Have you ever been in a similar situation?

7. When Theodore and Katherine are discussing matters of faith, Theodore realizes the conversation is somewhat uncomfortable. Do you believe discussions of faith are uncomfortable for most people, and if so, why? How can they become more comfortable?

8. Dot, a prostitute, seems to be happy with her lot in life. Does that surprise or bother you? What would you say to her?

9. Do you think it was a common occurrence for the police to disregard crimes against prostitutes back then, and do you think that happens today? What can average citizens do in this type of situation?

10. When Sarah, one of the prostitutes, mentions she doesn't like crowds, Theodore finally sees her as a real person. Are people today guilty of forgetting to view others as real people? When does this happen and how can we avoid it?

Jen Turano, author of *A Change of Fortune*, is a graduate of the University of Akron with a degree in clothing and textiles. When she's not writing, Jen can be found watching her teenage son participate in various activities, taking long walks with her husband and dog, socializing with friends, or delving into a good book. She is a member of ACFW and lives in a suburb of Denver, Colorado. Visit her website at JenTurano.com.

If you enjoyed *A Most Peculiar Circumstance*, you may also like...

Masquerading as a governess, Lady Sumner is on a mission to find the man who ran off with her fortune and reclaim what's rightfully hers. But does God have something—or someone—better in mind?

A Change of Fortune by Jen Turano
jenturano.com

Forced off a train and delivered to an outlaw's daughter for her birthday, is it possible this stolen preacher ended up right where he belongs?

Stealing the Preacher by Karen Witemeyer
karenwitemeyer.com

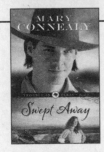

Ruthy nearly drowned before being rescued by Luke Stone. Now, he's left her little choice but to travel with him until they reach the nearest town. But is Ruthy any safer with this handsome cowboy than she would've been had she stayed on her own?

Swept Away by Mary Connealy, TROUBLE IN TEXAS #1
maryconnealy.com